MW00964293

The Yardstick

©Copyright 2007 Marie Warder
ISBN: 0-9733625-1-0
ISBN-13: 978-0973362510
Dromedaris Books
Box 82 Stn Main, Delta, B.C. V4K 1V0, **CANADA**
P.O. Box 938, Point Roberts, WA 98281, <u>USA</u>
P O Box 4964, Rivonia, 2128, **SOUTH AFRICA**

Tel: Canada (604) 948-0866   Fax: (604) 948-0867
<u>www.dromedarisbooks.com</u>   <u>www.writing.co.za</u>

email: <u>info@dromedarisbooks.com</u>   <u>mick@writing.co.za</u>

Printed in the USA

Library and Archives Canada Cataloguing in Publication

Warder, Marie
The yardstick / Marie Warder.

(Stories from South Africa)
Includes bibliographical references.

ISBN 978-0-9733625-1-0

I. Title. II. Series.

PS8645.A74Y37 2007   C813'.6   C2006-905010-4

"Our Lord knows perfectly that when once His word is heard, it will bear fruit sooner or later. The terrible thing is that some of us prevent it bearing fruit in actual life."
Oswald Chambers: My Utmost For His Highest
<u>Taken from My Utmost for His Highest by Oswald Chambers, © 1935 by Dodd Mead & Co., renewed © 1963 by the Oswald Chambers Publications Assn., Ltd. Used by permission of Discovery House Publishers, Grand Rapids MI 49501. All rights reserved.</u>
All quotations from Scripture are from the King James Version of the Bible (KJV)

MARIE
WARDER

THE
YARDSTICK

"Our Lord knows perfectly that when once His word is heard, it will bear fruit sooner or later. The terrible thing is that some of us prevent it bearing fruit in actual life."
Oswald Chambers: My Utmost For His Highest

A DROMEDARIS BOOK

2007

ANGOLA

NAMIBIA

BOTSWANA

MOZAMBIQUE

GAUTENG

◆Blouspruit

• Mafikeng

NORTH
WEST

•Pretoria
•Johannesburg

◆Nelspruit

Spoors-einde

FREE
STATE

Bethlehem
◆

KWAZULU
NATAL

•Upington

•Kimberley

•Bloemfontein

LESOTHO

•Pietermaritzburg

•Durban

NORTHERN
CAPE

EASTERN
CAPE

Cape Town•

WESTERN
CAPE

ACKNOWLEDGEMENTS

Cover art:

'Tracks and Prints' A painting by Leigh van der Schyff, *www.igoligallery.com*

(Photographed by Bruce van der Schyff)

The author gratefully acknowledges the contribution of Bruce van der Schyff and Luis Wiechers

The book:

Inside photographs: Clay Otto.

Map of South Africa: Belinda Kishimoto.

Sincere thanks also to David Willers, for access to a chapter on Angola, from a forthcoming book on diplomatic memories, and to Keith Bridgefoot, Josie Cooper, Mary Otto, Clay Otto, and Alta Alberts, without whose help and encouragement this book could not have been completed. I owe an enormous debt of thanks to Henry Abbott http://abbott-infotech.co.za/index-kalahari.html for introducing me to the splendour of the Kalahari, and for permission to make use of some of his references.

In addition, I wish to pay tribute to Canadian Senator, Lieutenant-General the Hon. Roméo A. Dallaire, O.C., C.M.M., G.O.Q., M.S.C., C.D., (Ret'd), author of the book *'Shake hands with the devil'*, who—as a result of an operational stress injury in Rwanda in 1994, developed a condition identified as post traumatic stress disorder (PTSD), and was subsequently medically released from the Canadian Forces in

April 2002—has used his experience to make the world aware of PTSD. He is currently deeply engaged in a project aimed at the elimination of the use of children as soldiers.

<u>AUTHOR'S NOTE</u>: Several incidents in this story are based on fact. In regard to his views on the conscription of his students during the Angolan war, I was the school principal, depicted here, as Biddy's husband, Mark Williams, and references to 'inner healing and deliverance' are not fictional either. I have been blessed to have been involved in Inner Healing Prayer Ministry, myself, for several years, and have twice witnessed actual instances of deliverance; one of them in a British Columbia Hospital.

The excerpted segment, also based on fact and ascribed in the book to Lucia, the teenage daughter of Matt Marais, was taken from an essay on Angola, with the kind permission of its writer, Lauren Camp.

THE DROMEDARIS CONCEPT

Dromedary: *Camelus Dromedarius*: a one-humped camel. Camels are commonly regarded as carriers—of both people and merchandise. Dromedaris was also the name of a ship which took our ancestors to South Africa in 1652. Our mandate, in the 'Dromedaris concept', is to bring a different kind of merchandise from South Africa to the rest of the world....Our books, written by acclaimed expatriate authors.

ABOUT THE AUTHOR

Before immigrating to Canada, Marie Warder was listed among South Africa's top seven "favourite novelists" by a South African Book Club. She was certainly one of the most prolific. Mary Morrison Webster, book critic of the prestigious Sunday Times, once recorded among her recommendations, two books written "in time for Christmas— in two different languages." Mrs. Warder's biography is included in the Archives of the National Council of Women among "Notable Women of Johannesburg."

Locally, where she lives in Tsawwassen, British Columbia, she was familiar for many years as a chaplain at the Delta Hospital while, to most people in the rest of the world, she is known chiefly as the Founder and President Emeritus of both the Canadian and South African Hemochromatosis Societies, and the Founder and former President of the International Association of Haemochromatosis Societies. Few know that, before embarking on her two ground-breaking books on Hemochromatosis—made available, together, in 2000, in the 'new edition' of *The Bronze Killer*, the 'internationally acclaimed best-seller' (Delta Optimist), which contributed to her being awarded a medal of honour and certificate of honour in Canada—she was already the author of 13 very successful novels; three of them used in South African schools. Not surprisingly, many of her stories take place in and around newspaper offices for, according to 'The Journalist', she became, at the age of seventeen, the youngest chief reporter in the world, having sold her first newspaper article at the age of 11 and her first short story at 17. During her career as a journalist she interviewed some the world's most famous people.

All in all, it seemed that she had a good career ahead of her in her native South Africa, but when—just before her 17th birthday—Frederick Abinger (Tom) Warder, a handsome, tanned young man in an Air Force uniform walked into the newspaper office one day, her life changed radically. It was a clear case of 'love at first sight' and, after that meeting, her life would revolve about him. She played the piano in Tom's very popular dance band; he was wholeheartedly supportive of her writing. And whenever there was a sword fight to be fought in a novel, or a chess game to be played, it would be her husband who worked out the moves for her.

When he was 42, he suddenly became ill and, as she tells in the book, *The Bronze Killer*, they had come to the end of the good times. For more than 28 years after that, except for a series of travel articles for a magazine she devoted her literary efforts entirely to the writing of more than 200 articles on the subject of Hemochromatosis, and to the production of patient literature for individuals, hospitals and other medical facilities. Her newsletters and brochures have gone out to more than 16 countries. Now she believes that she has done all in her power to promote awareness of the world's most common genetic disorder. Late in 2003, motivated by the discovery of the tattered scraps of the only carbon copy of the long-lost manuscript of a book, she decided that she was ready to move on. *Storm Water* and *With no remorse…*were released simultaneously less than a year later.

When you know that you know that you know! or The redemption of Benjamin Ashton (April 2005) caused a sensation. The response has been phenomenal. One reader describes it as "The best novel I have ever read!" Another reports that she read it "four times in less than a month", and wished that it were "twice as long!" This about a book that contains 576 pages! The setting of that book is a citrus farm called *'Beauclaire'*, situated in the district of Nelspruit in South Africa, and, responding to the clamour for more about Benjamin (Ash) Ashton and his friends, 'Dominic Verwey: Samaritan of the Sahara'—although of a different genre—continued the 'Beauclaire saga' in 2006.

About this book one reviewer wrote, "After the success of her South African novel, *Tarnished Idols*, Marie Warder has gone to the other end of Africa for the setting of her new one, *Samaritan of the Sahara*. Mrs. Warder's romantic imagination and facile pen provide plenty of local colour, and she captures the reader's attention from start to finish. The very unusual theme concerns the adventures of a doctor in the Sahara who, besides being skilled with the scalpel, is also a dashing figure of the Robin Hood type. Well worth reading and highly recommended."

Now, about to be released in 2007 comes *'The Yardstick'* this author's 21ˢᵗ book, *Volume three* of the gripping *Beauclaire Saga,* and her seventh book to be written in Canada. Although so much of the story is played out among the dunes of the Kalahari Desert of the Northern Cape Province of South Africa, we are also taken back to Nelspruit, Johannesburg and Louisiana, and recognize some of the well-loved characters from *When you know that you know that you know*, as the Beauclaire saga continues.

OTHER NOVELS BY MARIE WARDER

Storm Water—ISBN 0-921966-05-9

In exchange for giving him a son, the proud and fascinating Count Louis de Maupassant offers wealth and an elevated position in society.

This historical novel about South Africa, set in the very early days of the Cape of Good Hope, transports the reader to a distant, romantic past—to the adventurous days of the Dutch East India Company, when the Colony was young.

With no remorse... ISBN 0-921966-03-2

An extraordinary narrative of daring and courage, of sacrificial love and rock-solid loyalty is, at the same time, a tale of suspicion and jealousy; of devilish cunning and despicable treachery.

During World War 11, Joshua Naudé, a young South African agronomist, is sent on a clearly defined mission to the strategic island of Malta. His gentle, plucky but frail wife, Anna, accompanies him. Not long after their arrival on the island, they are joined by Joshua's devastatingly good-looking airman brother and, through him, they become acquainted with beautiful and captivating Stephanie Velez; a ruthless charmer of volatile Latin temperament.

Tarnished Idols—0 921966-07-5

"No mortal is perfect enough to be idolized." Around this proven adage, Marie Warder has woven a gripping

tale—a story in which pure love and flaming passion are interchanged with venomous envy and bitter hatred.

In convincing manner, the writer relates the story from the point of view of Paul Jansen, the man who sincerely loves the beautiful Jeanne, but can never be more than a brother to her. The reason? Jeanne already worships another man—an idol with 'feet of clay'. Her initial adoration and later struggle against this 'idol' make for an intensely moving story, sensitively recorded

<u>*The Beauclaire Saga #1*</u>
When you know that you know that you know! ISBN 0-921966-09-1

> *or*

The redemption of Benjamin Ashton
Under the Southern Cross, an awesome awakening amid the orange blossom on a South African Citrus Farm.

Set amid orange groves in the lovely town of Nelspruit, South Africa—among 'Bougainvilleas, Flame trees, Jacarandas and Poinsettias; Scarlet Flamboyant and Bottle Brush, yellow Bird of Paradise, crimson Erythrina, salmon, rose pink and white Oleander, interspersed by a riot of the sky blue, Duranta'—the air is heavy with the perfume of orange blossom in this well-written novel with an unusual plot, unusual complications and an unusual conclusion. It is the story of a successful young American, one of the wealthiest men in the world, who travels to South Africa where, going in search of his brother, he finds God—and, in so doing, finds himself! To say more would be to spoil for our readers what should prove to be a captivating read.

In the stockade of an outlaw band in the Sahara desert, Doctor Dominic Verwey is introduced to the Bedouin chief as '*Sahbena el-Hakim*'—my friend, the doctor. But he would very shortly thereafter earn a second name; that of '*Hamid Pasha*'—protector and leader of his people, 'refuge of the refugee and sanctuary of the oppressed'. His main purpose is to settle a score with the unprincipled Arab, Abdel Sharia, who incarcerates innocent men in his labour camps and enslaves beautiful women in his harem...

NON-FICTION

THE BRONZE KILLER:NEW EDITION ISBN 0968735800

Original Edition... Autographed Collectors' Item— ISBN 0889258856*The Bronze Killer: New Edition*— **DROMEDARIS BOOKS**

The story of a family's fight against Hemochromatosis—the most common Genetic disorder—including the first-ever 'layman's' reference: "Iron...the other side of the story!"

THE BOOK THAT GAVE A DISEASE A NEW NAME, *evolved from 'Iron...the other side of the story!' (1984) which was the first book ever to be devoted entirely to the subject of Hemochromatosis—iron overload. (Please note alternative spelling, outside of North America, where the disorder is known as 'Haemochromatosis'.)*

Since this book was first published in 1989, thousands of families around the world have found it to be a valuable resource. More than just the personal account of a family who have suffered through the ravages of this terrible disease, it has been a source of information, encouragement and enlightenment to many. Included is *'IRON...the other side of the story*!' which provided the world with first 'layperson's reference to the genetic disorder that, if untreated, can lead to a destructive overload of iron in the body; far too often with fatal results. Recommended by physicians and clinics in Canada and further afield, *'The Bronze Killer'* earned high praise for the author in her 1991 citation for the Canada Volunteer Medal of Honour and Certificate of Honour, which read in part: *"Through Marie's research and most noted book, 'The Bronze Killer', she has educated doctors and the general public about the disease. As a result, Hemochromatosis is now recognised as Canada's most common genetic disorder and routine blood tests for the disease may soon become standard diagnostic procedure."*

This from the former South African Director General of Genetic Services who wrote:

"We are highly impressed by the evidence you have collected and summarised, regarding the importance of Haemochromatosis as a genetic disease in South Africa and on the potential for preventing its consequences.

"Your efforts, as outlined, fully coincide with our objectives, i.e. to promote the prevention of inherited diseases and/or their consequences by the means at our disposal."

Hemochromatosis.—There was a time when nine out of ten people had never heard of it, and physicians considered it to be 'too rare to be of concern'. It is now known to be the most common genetic disorder of all, and Marie Warder has played no small part in, as she puts is 'bringing into the light of day the research that was mouldering on the shelves or in the filing cabinets.' In *The Bronze Killer*, she provides much needed information about this common enemy, from recognizing its symptoms to stressing the importance of early detection and treatment.

PEOPLE WHO FEATURE IN THE BEAUCLAIRE SAGA:

IN THE UNITED STATES:
The Ashton family of Bentleigh:

Benjamin (Ash), Amy-Lee and their children—James ('James Ashton the Fourth'), Eugenie (Zhaynie) and Albert Jordan. (Now a physician in Johannesburg).

Ferguson, the chauffeur.

Deceased: James (Jamie)—'James Ashton the Third'. Founder of a centre for black children and their mothers near in Bethlehem, South Africa, where he died after falling from a windmill he was repairing.

The Crawfords: Formerly from South Africa. Now, except for Tony, living at Bentleigh with the Ashtons.

The Rev. Doctor Peter ('Fallah'), Marina, and their children: Antoinette (Tony) Gregory, Isobel (Izzie) and Benjamin.

IN SOUTH AFRICA
The Verwey family:
(Living in Nelspruit)

Dr. Paul and Stella Verwey and their son, Dominic (now married to Eugenie Ashton)—who run the citrus farm, Beauclaire, established by Benjamin Ashton near Nelspruit.

(*Living in Kwazulu Natal*)

Dr. Dominic Verwey—El-Hakim (Uncle Dominic) and his wife, Princess Thérèse.

Dr. Stephen Verwey (his grandson) married to the former Antoinette (Tony) Crawford.

Dr. Philip Verwey—brother of El-Hakim.

(Also in Nelspruit)

The Mostert family:

Albert (Bert) and Isobel—Marina Crawford's parents, and grandparents of Antoinette (Tony), Gregory and Isobel (Izzie).

The Connaughts
(*Formerly from Bethlehem, SA—now in Louisiana*)

The Rev. Clifford, and his wife, Thora. Their sons Timothy and Tristan (a physician).

(Living in Spoors-einde, in the Kalahari)

Doctor Hugo Connaught, Clifford's uncle.

The Hilliards
(*Living on the farm, Blouspruit, in the Kalahari Desert*)

Professor Jasper Hilliard and his daughters, Meredith and Susan.

Other prominent South African characters: Felicity Seymour (who loved the late Jamie Ashton) and her adopted son, Reginald.

Phyllis (the former telephone operator), Mrs. Nolte, her daughter, Mercia, and Mercia's husband, Nico.

In loving memory of Tom…

One cannot measure anything without some scale of measurement, whether it be visible, tangible, audible, or even experiential. One needs a yardstick—and you remain mine!

PART ONE

CHAPTER ONE

My name is Biddy. I once saw a woman, much like me, described in a magazine as 'fair, fat, and on the wrong side of forty'; but, if the truth be told, I prefer to think of myself as plumpish and not bad looking. On the other hand—well let's be honest—I did turn forty-eight last February, so I suppose I'm more like on the right side of fifty.

Be that as it may, and although it may not be too modest of me to claim this for myself, I honestly feel that I am the only person competent to tell this story. I knew everyone involved, personally, and have thus been in a position to view the entire saga as it unfolded, from more than one angle. Furthermore, before this new doctor and his wife came to take over, I was old Doctor Hugo's receptionist, cum housekeeper, and Tristan is his great-nephew. In addition, I was *very* friendly with Meredith Hilliard's mother, and so I can claim to be acquainted with every detail of that singular, tragic history, too.

Perhaps I should start at the beginning, which is probably the best place to commence a story, and I shall have to beg your indulgence when I go off at tangents. I've never written a book before, but hopefully I might improve as I go along, because I honestly believe that this is a tale worth telling.

Now where was I? Oh, yes, at the beginning!

Well, as I recall, the part in which I was most personally involved, really began on the day Tristan Connaught came from Johannesburg in response to Doctor Hugo's request. I could, of course, guess at what was afoot, because Doc had asked me to send the message to Tristan, and I knew that the old man had been toying with the thought of retiring for some time. (Here I must admit that my heart grew heavy at the mere thought!) A finer man and a better doctor had yet to be born—and that was not just my opinion. Any of the sick in our arid, isolated little village, had only to see that, now slightly stooped, figure come through the door, to feel instantly better. After the Creator had finished making Hugo Connaught He must have thrown away the formula....There has never been, and probably won't ever be, anyone quite like Doc. Unfortunately, blood-relative or not, great-nephew Tristan was a coin of a different denomination! Clever, charming, and good-looking as all get-out, he really got under my skin at times...the pompous, conceited young upstart!

In his defence, he had at least had the decency to come in obedience to the summons—a long, arduous journey, I must say!— And while he and Doc Hugo were closeted in the study, discussing the situation, I made it my business to remain in the vicinity so that I did not miss anything. The potted plants on the windowsills had never been given so much water. In due course, most of them gave up the ghost, keeled over and died. (Most probably drowned...!)

"Well, Tristan, my dear boy," was Doc Hugo's patient, affectionate reaction to something his brother's grandson must have said, as he faced him across the solid old mahogany desk, for, just as I came in carrying a tray, I heard him add: "I am disappointed that you won't reconsider your decision."

"My decision should never have been in question, Uncle Hugo. It should have been a foregone conclusion," Tristan came back at him, in his customary arrogant manner. "You knew—

or should have known that—from the moment I returned from the States to settle permanently in South Africa. And now that I have succeeded in carving out such a comfortable niche for myself in Johannesburg, the mere suggestion that I should comply with what you want of me, is preposterous!" He took his teacup from me, with a laconic, "Thanks!" And, helping himself to one of the biscuits Doc Hugo had asked me to bake especially for the 'crown prince', he went on: "I realize that it has always been your heart's desire that I should someday choose medicine as a career, and then come and take over from you.—I am only too well aware that it has long been a cherished dream of yours, to have the Connaught name remain on the brass plate at your front gate—which is the only reason I have come at all...*But Tristan Connaught, in Spoors-einde*! You are asking me to bury myself alive!"

"I don't agree," Doc Hugo said gently. "On the contrary. You would rather be making your life worthwhile. You have had excellent medical training, Tris, and could perform miracles... practise real medicine...in a place where, precisely because it is so remote, people really need you...But, instead"—the old man's voice suddenly rose, to sound almost contemptuous— "you choose to devote your God-given gifts and talents and, from all accounts, your considerable medical skills, in order to squander your life on trivialities—like injecting a bunch of spoiled, wealthy, society women with Botox, or pandering to their boredom-induced hypochondria! Your indulgence is almost tantamount to encouraging them to take on whatever complaint happens to be in fashion! And because you are sought-after and earning a colossal income, you have left yourself nothing for which to strive!...You almost make me wish that I were able to choose a successor from a wider field!"

"I don't *want* to strive! But if I had more incentive to specialize, I'd like to be able to dig into people's minds. I enjoy figuring out what makes people tick!"

As I carried the tea things back to the kitchen, I reflected on what had just transpired, and, while my heart ached for the disappointment in the old doctor's voice, I was not one bit surprised. I had known Tristan since he was seven years old, ever since the first time his parents had sent him to South Africa from Louisiana—where they oversaw an admirable facility for children made homeless by war or other disastrous circumstances—to spend a part of that school year with his maternal grandparents in Bethlehem. That is the town in the Free State, where, until he had been obliged to seek voluntary exile during the apartheid era, Tristan's father, Clifford Connaught, had been the greatly loved rector of a small church with a mainly black congregation. While ministering as the incumbent at St. Jude's, he had met, and married, a local girl, and had come to know a remarkable American called James Ashton.

Theirs had become what could truly be defined as a 'David and Jonathan' relationship. Few people have even seen an officiating cleric weep while conducting a funeral. And surely no one (including me) who was at Jamie Ashton's, will ever be able to forget how Clifford Connaught—clearly not your average 'stiff-upper-lip' Englishman—had broken down twice; once while offering the eulogy, and again when concluding his homily with lines from verses 25 and 26 of Second Samuel Chapter One, quoting from David's Lament for Saul and Jonathan: "...*Jonathan lies slain on Your heights!...I grieve for you, my brother; you were very dear to me...!*"

But I digress. There came a time, when having been imprisoned without trial, Clifford—together with his wife and two small children, of whom Tristan was the younger—was fortunate to escape to England, with the aid of Jamie Ashton's brother, Benjamin. Upon arriving in London, he, Clifford, and his wife, Thora, were offered positions, in a Children's Home established in Louisiana, by Amy-Lee Ashton—the sister-in-law of his tragically deceased friend, James.

The Connaughts' other son, Timothy, had settled down, loved being in Louisiana, and related admirably to the 'displaced' kids in his parents' care. Tristan, however, had become more rebellious and less manageable with each succeeding year. He openly despised the children whom his parents sheltered, and only when the Ashton family came on their periodic visits to *Beauclaire*, the adjoining estate, did he briefly emerge from his shell of truculence to become comparatively sociable.

When his parents decided to send him back to South Africa, he was enrolled in the Bethlehem school at which my husband was a teacher, and proved to be one of the most difficult pupils with whom Mark had ever had to work. Not that Tristan was headed for a life of crime, drug addiction, or anything like the sort of thing one would read about in the newspapers. Far from it! He was arrogant, and contemptuous of everything and everybody, both in the town and at the school, but who knows, perhaps it was that very contempt which led him to strive and to become such a brilliant scholar, just to prove his superiority!

There was no reason for me to linger in the study, but I confess that the conversation then began to take such an interesting turn that I shamelessly eavesdropped from the passage. Because I had always found it difficult to take to

Tristan, I wholeheartedly supported Hugo Connaught in all that followed. *'If only Tristan could have been like Jordan Ashton',* was the thought that involuntarily came to me. *'"That admirable young man who came to help out during the diphtheria epidemic two years ago, and again, more recently, when Doc Hugo suffered that heart attack!'* And, although I don't believe in this telepathy business, I can't account for how it came about that, while I was still thinking about the likeable young American, I heard Doc Hugo ask: "By the way, is Jordan still with you?"

"He is," Tristan replied. "Now there's a guy who would appreciate a sermon such as you have just preached! Jordie's a good sort, and a really fine doctor." Initially giving the impression that he was in no way put out by the senior Connaught's criticism, he had to go and negate that by adding: "But I find his intensity extremely tiresome, and not a little boring!...He's so darned narrow-minded," he went on fiercely, "that he won't even buy a lottery ticket—insisting that God provides for him, which is simply ridiculous! If anyone does provide for him, it's more likely to be his father, because, as we all know, the Ashtons are loaded!"

To Doc's distress, Tristan, unexpectedly revealing long-suppressed resentment, suddenly grew perceptibly heated. "Believe me, there are times when he can be a regular thorn in the flesh! It's not enough, as far as he is concerned, to put a weird guy, a former patient of mine—whom I'd say is clearly bi-polar—on a mood stabilizer and an anti-depressant, and be done with it....No! He has to go on delving, until he comes up with the far-out theory that the man is suffering from some long-neglected, post-traumatic stress syndrome—just because he happened to have been in the Angolan war!...And now our friend, Jordan Ashton—*my partner*—is passionately, and vociferously involved in some sort of campaign on behalf of every Angolan vet whom he deems to be in the same boat!"

There was no stemming the tide of bitterness. "Another thing that embarrasses me acutely, is that he prays for his patients—which I consider to be undignified and most unprofessional!"

"You *would*!" I thought. Like the rest of his family, Jordie was altruistic and compassionate to a marked degree. Moreover, of all Benjamin and Amy-Lee's children, he was, by nature, the one most like his uncle Jamie—'James Ashton the third'—who had renounced a fortune, and had devoted his life to the care of black children at a centre he had established in Bethlehem. There he had unfortunately been killed while repairing a windmill, from which he had fallen and been mortally injured.

Everyone in Bethlehem was familiar with the story of how, before establishing the centre—now bearing the name of his grandmother, Eugenie Beauclaire—Jamie, the former heir to the massive Ashton consortium, had been provided with accommodation by the charitable De Beer couple, known far and wide, simply as Aunt Minnie and Uncle Charlie, who had grown to love him like a son. The river that runs by what used to be their farm, is called the *Jordaan*, the Afrikaans name for the Biblical Jordan, and Aunt Minnie had indicated to Jamie that it would please her if he would someday name his first-born, 'Jordan'. Sadly, there was, of course, to be no 'first-born' for Jamie, but before Aunt Minnie's death, his brother and sister-in-law, who had grown to know and love the old people, had, in part, fulfilled Aunt Minnie's wish by bestowing the chosen name upon one of their own children. Although he was baptized 'Albert Jordan', he was always, unfailingly, referred to as 'Jordan.'

The Ashtons, whose permanent home was now in the United States, had retained their interests in South Africa, as directors of the international consortium which still owned a factory in Isando, near Kempton Park, and another facility, close to a citrus farm—originally also called *Beauclaire*—which was established by Benjamin Ashton near Nelspruit, in the mid-seventies. As their daughter, Eugenie, and son-in-law now lived there, and helped to run the plantation, the senior Ashtons made *Beauclaire Estates* their headquarters whenever they happened to be in the country, but also returned frequently to Bethlehem, in the Orange Free State; never failing to spend as much time as possible with the people who had so loved Ben's brother, James.

As the years went by, young Jordan, fast developing into a man more and more like his late uncle, chose, as he grew older, to devote most of his vacations to helping the De Beers on their farm—which he eventually inherited. Sadly Uncle Charlie, like so many other white farmers, was brutally murdered, and, before long, Aunt Minnie, who had survived the attack but was never quite the same again, went, in death, to join the man without whom she did not wish to live. For some years after that, even as a physician with a growing practice in an upscale area near Johannesburg, Jordan tried valiantly to keep the farm going, and only the ever-increasing squatter problem could finally have driven him off that land.—Squatters enjoyed prior rights, it seemed, and very soon, despite the proximity to the river, there was simply just not enough water for everyone.

It boggled my mind that he would tolerate Tristan Connaught as a partner in his Bryanston medical practice; much less invite him to share his home! Tristan was older by six years, but young Ashton always struck me as the more mature of the two. Strangely, and despite Tristan's bitter resentment of the fact that his family lived on a property owned and made available to them by the Ashtons, their relationship—which had sprouted during periods spent together on the adjoining estates in Louisiana—had grown closer over the years. He and Jordan had been drawn together, further, by the strange happenstance that both also had ties to Bethlehem, where they were often together. Jordan, tall and well built like his father and brother, was enormously protective of his older and less robust colleague, and it infuriated me that he should repeatedly allow himself to be put upon to such a degree. Naturally it was he, rather than Tristan, who came to our rescue when Doc Hugo was indisposed or we had a crisis on our hands.

As I said, I don't hold much with telepathy, and Benjamin Ashton had convinced us years before that there is no such thing as 'coincidence'. *"It is a simply a 'God' incident in which He chooses to remain inaudible and invisible,"* Ben always used to say. So now I won't say that this happened by chance, but it was weird how, while Tristan was still going on about how boring he found Jordan's 'intensity', the telephone rang. "To tell the truth..." he had begun, but I never found out what he was about to tell us, because it was at precisely that moment that Jasper Hilliard phoned. Tristan was interrupted by that long, urgent ring which, in small country towns, indicates a long-distance call.

Then the oddest thing happened!

Through a crack in the door, I could see that Tristan's eyebrows were arched inquiringly, and I almost fell through the doorway from curiosity when I heard Doc Hugo ask incredulously: "You mean that you actually want me to come out there?...Truly, Jasper, this is the most extraordinary request! Your daughter must be very sick indeed....Right! I'll leave immediately!…Yes, I understand!…Of course! Good-bye!" With a muffled exclamation, he replaced the receiver, shaking his head in disbelief. "Well I never!"

"Really, Uncle Hugo," Tristan mocked him, an infuriating smirk on that handsome mug of his. "You seem surprised! Is it such a rare event for someone in this *dorp*[1] to call the doctor?" He chuckled cynically. "Seems as though you find this call quite sensational!"

"It is," Hugo Connaught replied seriously, and evidently, in view of this new development, not permitting himself to dwell on his young relative's recent outburst. "But not for the reason you so sarcastically suggest. What you don't know"—there was a dramatic, thoughtful pause—"is that this will be the first time in nearly twelve years that Professor Hilliard is willing to allow any stranger—let alone a white man—onto his property. And now only because his younger daughter appears to be seriously ill!"

"But why this antipathy towards strangers, and with such particular emphasis on the Caucasian stronger sex?" Tristan's voice sounded sardonically amused, and I—determined not to miss any part of this astounding development—knocked loudly, and marched purposefully into the room, ostensibly to see if I had cleared all the tea things away.

"Actually, there is a tragic history behind all this, if you want to hear some of it while I get my things together." Doctor Hugo passed me the sugar bowl, which I had fortuitously overlooked, favouring me with a smile and a friendly nod of that noble silver head, before turning to Tristan once more.

I knew the story all too well. As I have said, I had known the mother of the patient for whom the doctor had now been summoned, very well indeed—but, as I sensed that something momentous was about to happen, I nonetheless pricked up my ears. This was proving to be a far from boring day!

Picking up his familiar and well-used medical bag, Doctor Hugo confided, while checking to make sure that he had all that he might possibly need: "Professor Hilliard's elder daughter must have been eleven or twelve years old when her mother, an exceptionally beautiful woman, some years younger that her husband—a brilliant man, but perhaps too pre-occupied for Rosalie's liking—ran off with his assistant, who later ditched her for another woman. Because he adored her, Jasper forgave her unconditionally, but, tragically, only two weeks after he had found her, she died. It is possibly for this reason that he has never been able to forgive the bounder who ruined her life."

And neither could I! I mourned the Rosalie Hilliard who had been my friend and confidante, before, and after I had come to be Doc Hugo's housekeeper....My husband, who, until his untimely death, had been the principal of the small local school (which was the reason we had left Bethlehem to come to *Spoors-einde*), missed the sweet face of Rosalie's daughter, a promising young student who lived with us during the school week, as much as he missed the long, stimulating discussions he had formerly enjoyed with her father, the professor, when he brought her back from *Blouspruit* on Sundays.

Since the day after Rosalie's demise, no one in the village had ever again set eyes on Jasper Hilliard, his daughter Meredith, or her sister, Susan!

"It is difficult to believe that such a clever, ostensibly sane man could resort to such drastic measures," Doc Hugo went on pensively, shaking his head, "but, for a while he was beside himself; like a man possessed. He made a vow that he would protect his daughters, at all costs, from the slightest possibility of their suffering a similar fate, and, in order to fulfill that vow, the professor has kept them completely isolated from the outside world, for close on twelve years! He has never revisited the University to which he remains attached—working strictly from the seclusion of his farm, *Blouspruit*, about forty miles from here—and neither Meredith, who must be about twenty-three, nor Susan, who should be nearly sixteen, has ever again been away from there. In all these years they have never set eyes on any white man other than their father and, from time to time, Father Cruickshank, an elderly, retired priest appointed by the government to invigilate examinations!"

"Good Lord! How absolutely archaic!" Tristan cried incredulously. "Perhaps this professor of yours had read too much Dickens, and had become hooked on the story of Miss Havisham and Estella in 'Great Expectations'!…Then again— how positively Gothic! This sounds like some, dark, far-fetched tale from the middle ages!"

"It is true, nevertheless," said the elder Doctor Connaught. "And I shall be able to tell you more when I return…"

'What a stir this could cause in the village!' is what I, Biddy, could not help thinking.

"But I don't want to wait until you get back!" protested Tristan, now vastly intrigued. "You have to tell me *now*, before you go…what language do these poor creatures speak? Are they civilized? What do they wear?"

Apart from retorting that, if Jasper Hilliard had anything to do with it they probably spoke more than one language, and could not be anything but civilized, Doc Hugo was, of course, not in a position to enlighten him further. With the exception of the admirably discreet, priestly invigilator from Upington, no one beyond the environs of *Blouspruit* was. It was small wonder that the inhabitants of *Spoors-einde* invariably referred to the place as *'Verlate Vlakte'* (which means something like 'forsaken', or 'deserted plain') rather than by its real name, which one could translate as 'Blue Stream.' However, after the tragedy, Mark, my husband, used to refer to it as *'Rooi Verdriet'* (Red Sorrow), which I considered more appropriate, on account of the sorrow inside, and the red sand outside of it; and, in any case the word, 'vlakte' was hardly appropriate, because *Blouspruit* lies among the dunes. Those red, red dunes!

For some months after my husband's death I had seemed to cope until, one day in the late autumn of that year, the reaction came, and I fled back to Bethlehem—thinking that, perhaps if I returned to nursing, the intensity of the ache could be lessened. This did not prove to be the case, however. The 'outback' was in my blood forever, and those dunes of the remote, far reaches of the Northern Cape, with all its memories, beckoned. I returned to *Spoors-einde* where Doctor Hugo offered me a job but, before taking him up on it, I allowed myself three days and two nights to think, in one of Mark's favourite places....Deep in the *Kgalagadi, 'The land of thirst'*, where we had spent many a memorable weekend in the past, among the red sand dunes, the sparse vegetation, and the dry riverbeds of the Nossob and Auob. Nothing compares with the experience of being there, alone—except for someone you love...

Before returning to advise Doctor Connaught of my decision, I did not cross the border into Botswana at the frontier, as I had contemplated doing at some stage. Instead, upon finally leaving the frontier park, through the southern gate of the *Twee Revieren* (Two Rivers) camp, I turned right, as my dear Mark would have chosen to do; but, whereas his intention, while in the vicinity, was always a visit with the Hilliards, my detour was prompted, in part, by base curiosity—and the more compelling need to prolong my absence from *Spoors-einde* for just a little longer.

In recent years, I had only been able to see *Blouspruit* from the road, and with its high, electrified fence, the place would have looked to me more like a concentration camp, were it not for the Camel Thorn trees, (correctly known as *Acacia Giraffe...* now *Acacia Erioloba*), and, especially, a few fine specimens of the striking *Boscia albitrunca*—the Shepherd's tree—of which I managed to catch a glimpse through the railings. At least something Rosalie had loved was still there as a reminder, making the place somehow seem less forbidding. When the white, gnarled stem of the Shepherd's tree with its dark green foliage, is seen against the vivid orange-red of the dunes, under a blue, blue sky, and—rarely—white clouds, that must be one of the most glorious sights and colour combinations anyone can ever imagine.

It had not surprised me to see a guard at the gate. In itself, the original property, although not very large, had already seemed depressingly remote when last I had visited there, situated as it is, deep in the 'Southern Kalahari', in one of the loneliest parts of the Northern Cape—north of the Orange river, and even further Northwest than *Spoors-einde*. Virtually an impenetrable compound, *Blouspruit* appeared to be more isolated than before, by virtue of the fact that Jasper Hilliard had purchased, and added to it, much of the land surrounding it.

While it was known that servants, long-time Bushman employees, had, on occasion, been known to go by Landrover to Upington, it was also rumoured in *Spoors-einde* that supplies were sometimes dropped off by the helicopter which (landing in the veld, outside of the enclosure) came to pick up whatever it was that the professor periodically sent to Pretoria, or some place in the United Kingdom. And maybe once in two or three months—or whenever an urgent order was phoned in—a truck from Van der Merwe's store made deliveries, collecting a COD cheque in payment. I was told by Betsy van Rooyen, the postmistress, that an agent in Johannesburg paid all bills other than Van der Merwe's, but how she would know this, is a mystery to me!

"What do they farm there?...How do the girls pass their time?" Tristan demanded to know. "Do they have a radio, or television?...They obviously have a telephone!"

Doc Hugo's answer rather discomfited me.

"I advise you rather to ask Biddy," he suggested, with no sign of rancour or disapproval in his tone. Typically all lingering thoughts of Tristan's recent behaviour had been set aside! "I know just about all there is to know about my patients and their affairs, but when it comes to matters like this it's always better to ask a woman.—Not because I want to suggest, for one moment, that they gossip," he added hastily, glancing in my direction. "It's just that they are more interested, perhaps have more time to concentrate upon such details, and are also better able to ferret out secrets than we males are.—Now I really must go."

My thoughts had suddenly gone off at a tangent and, once again I was abruptly brought back to my immediate surroundings by the sound of Tristan's voice, this time employing Jordie Ashton's pet name for me. (If this was done as a means of eliciting my cooperation, he succeeded!)

"Well, Auntie Bid?"

"I doubt if farming is the professor's main source of income, but I have often wondered that, myself," I said thoughtfully. "Ostriches perhaps, or goats? One can't see much from the outside, but rumour has it that the house is as comfortable as before, with its own electric plant and, of course, the telephone."

"There *must* be more to tell! Surely..."

It did not surprise me that Tristan was riveted by the story—it never failed to grip the imagination of anyone hearing it for the first time—but I don't think he should have done what he did. He was bored stiff with *Spoors-einde*, after the lights and the sights of the Golden City, and ever since he was a lad he had been able to wind his great-uncle around his little finger. Once he got an idea in his head...!

Ever since the first time the boy had come to us (because, I suspected, his maternal grandmother Burkett, in Bethlehem, who would frequently declare that the boy had 'the devil in him', needed a break during the school holidays), Hugo Connaught had had this soft spot for the great-grandson whom his elder brother, a Battle of Britain hero, had not lived to see. Perhaps also because, of Clifford and Thora Connaught's two children, Tristan most closely resembled the lamented WW2 pilot.

"Think of the kid's background," the doctor had once protested, rising to his defence when I seemed unduly displeased. "A father summarily and unjustly imprisoned before his son's birth, and a distraught mother, about to deliver, perpetually stressed, and having to seek shelter on the De Beers' farm, instead of being in her own home. Not too long after that, they all have to flee, first to Britain, and then to the States, where, finally the bewildered boy ends up in Louisiana. There his parents are soon so busy sharing both their time and their love, with so many needy children, that it is a relief to Tris to be able to go next door, be temporarily absorbed into an amazing, exceptionally close family, and be surrounded with luxury....Finally, because his parents can"t cope with him, he is sent away to another country—ours—where even the accents are different. No wonder he immediately latches onto the one and only familiar being—Jordan! Fortuitously about the most altruistic and understanding of all the 'genetically' loving Ashtons!"

It would be many years before I would understand Tristan.—And not before he had done many things far worse than toadying to the rich.

Just as he had reacted when he was a child, he cajoled, pleaded and sulked. He ranted, raged, and bargained—even trying a rueful, "I know you think I'm incapable. Haven't you just been telling me so?"—until finally, ruthlessly resorting as a last resort, to allusions concerning Doc Hugo's indifferent health—you've guessed it!—he managed to persuade the old doctor to let him go in his place!

Oddly, the moment the matter had been settled, I was privileged to see, briefly, another side to the man. Tristan, the doctor.... Tristan, the professional; his entire demeanour and attitude changed. And I must say he asked some pretty erudite questions, as though consulting with an equal, a respected colleague, rather than just 'Old Uncle Hugo'.

After a crisp and laconic, "Please put me in the picture, as concisely as possible. I'd appreciate your giving me every salient detail the professor passed on to you!" and—after much pursing of his lips, or frowning with concentration—he nodded.

"Just one final thing, Uncle. This couldn't be some insect-borne virus, or the after-effects of a scorpion sting, could it? I don't know enough about the risks from any of the other critters you have here, but I have never forgotten your warning about the *Parabuthus*, and how I should always shake my shoes out before putting them on. I also remember that, when I was a kid, you were strict about my wearing the tall, calf-high boots you bought me for added protection, if I should venture out into the veld."

"I doubt that Hilliard would have required a physician, if that were the case," Doc assured him. "He would have been able to deal with such a problem himself. A sting such as you suggest, Tristan, can kill very quickly, but, he knows how to make his own anti-venom, and he clearly has knowledge of numerous Bushman remedies. Considering that he has been able to cope for so long, without ever needing me, he must, as well, have had adequate experience with a fair number of other emergency situations!"

Actually, in my opinion, Tristan's had been a fair question, all the same. Although I was inclined to think that the professor would doubtless have imposed the same strict guideline on his girls that Doc did on us, the boy was right to take all possibilities into consideration...A *Parabuthus* scorpion can easily grow to a size of 150mm (6 inches) from pinchers to stretched-out tail. To sting, the scorpion faces the enemy straight on, and, by arching its whole body, including the tail, it can easily reach the ankle above an ordinary shoe. And, thinking of Jasper Hilliard and his family, I also couldn't help reflecting that catching a live scorpion to make anti-venom, without getting stung, was a tricky undertaking. You have to use a large box, somewhat reminiscent of an over-sized matchbox, slide it open partially, drop it over the scorpion, and shut it tightly. Sounds easy enough, but not when you are dealing with a lightning-fast, deadly predator with a lethal sting in its tail!

"*Malaria?*" Tristan, who must have been pondering what lay ahead, halted momentarily to call out as he was backing Doc's dependable old Jeep into the street. "Do they ever get mosquitoes round there?"

"Unlikely—although they have had an unusual amount of rain in that area!" Doc shouted back.

"Mark's mother," I put in, also yelling so that he could hear me, "once told me that, when she was about seven, the first Game Warden up at *Witdraai*, and his sidekick, both died of Malaria....Be sure you don't take the first turn-off—and check your petrol whenever you come to a pump!"

"Don't worry," Tristan yelled back, "I have my cell phone and my laptop if I run into trouble.—May I assume that they will work?"

At that, something else suddenly occurred to me, and, just as he was about to drive off, I ran towards the Jeep, calling after him: "There's a satellite dish. I saw it!" For this I was rewarded with such a disarming grin of approval that, encouraged by that rare expression on his face, I added, still at the top of my voice, "Professor Hilliard would no doubt have to be well-equipped in order to keep up his long-distance work for the university, and I'm sure you won't have to wander around all over the show in order to pick up a signal. There are some quite high places where he lives…"

"Great! Thank you, Auntie Bid. In that case, if I'm at all unsure, I can call Jordan to contact a specialist for me!"

Spoors-einde no longer lies at the end of the track or spoor, as the name suggests. However, although, the 'Red Dune Route' from Upington is tarred now, after leaving *"Twee Revieren'* to drive in our direction, it is not; and the turnoff to *Blouspruit* is particularly difficult to find. He kept an eye open for a Camel Thorn bearing the enormous 'sociable weaver' nest which, his uncle had told him, would indicate that he was approaching the Hilliard property, but, as he encountered several such trees, and even poles festooned with similarly enormous 'bird hotels', he still managed to go too far, and had to reverse. He was then to discover that, as so little traffic passes that way, the road ahead, where the veld grass had been flattened over the years, was hardly more than a faint, rutted, bumpy path, and he could not have been in a good mood by the time he arrived at the Hilliards'.

His natty, tailored suit was certainly not as immaculate as it had been when he had waved to us from the garage door, and he must have been very grateful for the fact that he had not had to drive there in his own, posh, city car. (By the way, he had the grace to admit to me, in years to come, that, despite the offhand manner in which he had appeared to wave aside my admonition to take a heavy sweater with him—even though it was so hot that, at times, mirages along the way almost totally obscured what lay ahead—he did find it cold once the sun had set!) As it was, Doc's Jeep was literally covered in the dust that made his eyes sting, and seemed even to have got in between his teeth.

He was made to realize only too well how far he was from what he regarded as 'civilization' when, along the road, he saw a couple of ostriches, a mongoose, several black maned Kalahari lions, meerkats, a Black-backed jackal, and, judging by the distinctive black and white markings of the face and body, the black stripe from mane to tail, and the 'V' positioning of the formidable, spear like horns, what could only be a *Gemsbok Gazella*. Having at last seen one, he remembered that it was said to be the largest of its species. He had also heard people refer to it as an *Oryx*, from a Greek word meaning a 'pickaxe'— a name which he now considered to be most appropriate.

It had been a long day, and, in due course—after having had to be at the Johannesburg airport long before seven that morning, and then, after the flight from Johannesburg to Upington, enduring the long ride from there to *Spoors-einde* in Hennie Vercueil's 4x4 that doubled as a taxi—he found it difficult to stay awake. Not many miles from his destination he thus stopped, briefly, to watch a group of Springbok perform their graceful, prancing ballet, and, although it was probably against the law to do so, he succumbed to the temptation to take a chance, get out of the Jeep, and stretch his legs.

Fortunately, because the heat hit him in the face with such intensity as he opened the door, he had hardly set one foot on the ground before changing his mind. He reached out quickly to close the door again, and, as he did so, he was horrified to see a yellow snake, hardly discernible against the sand, and at least a metre long, slither away, out of the shadow of the vehicle and into the bright sunlight, to where it became clearly visible. While he did not know enough to recognize this as an Egyptian Cobra, common sense told him that it had to be of an extremely poisonous variety, and suddenly all thoughts of the niggling situation in Johannesburg, and Jordan Ashton's disproval of it, were banished from his mind, leaving him more alert than he had been for days.

He could recall numerous hair-raising stories about how snakes could wind themselves around under-parts of automobiles, only to appear later, and, reflecting on this, he realized that, until now, his mind had not fully been on his surroundings or the mission on which he was bent; nor had he been able to give his full attention to the verbal exchange with his uncle, earlier that day.

No matter what he did, or where he went, the situation with Adéle, and the question of what he was going to do about it, obtruded, and he sat, deep in thought for a moment or two longer, before turning on the ignition once more. It was still of the snake that he was thinking when, his throat burning from the dust, and his legs stiff from the long journey, he finally climbed out of the Jeep, and he made very sure that nothing threatening was to be seen before he did so. His knees were still shaking slightly when, minutes later, he found himself in front of some pretty imposing metal gates. He pressed a button to set a bell clanging, at the same time straining his neck to see through the fence. Presently the guard, about whom I had told him, appeared in response to his summons, and peered suspiciously at him through the iron railings.

"Askies, baas. Die baas moet samblief die baas se naam sê, baas!" ("Excuse me, baas. The baas must say the baas's name, please, baas!"), the Bushman instructed politely, most likely repeating the professor's instruction, verbatim. *"Baas Jasper hy verwag iemand..."* ("Baas Jasper he is expecting someone.")

"I am Doctor Connaught," Tristan was able to reply truthfully and with impressive confidence. "*Ek is die dokter.* Professor Hilliard put through a call to *Spoors-einde...*" And in response to this evidently satisfactory information, the heavy gates swung open.

Driving slowly, he followed yet another sandy track to the house, where he climbed out of the Jeep, lifting the bag he had brought, from the back seat. Then he took a moment to survey his surroundings, with renewed interest and eager anticipation. Nothing was as he had expected....The low, whitewashed house with its thatched roof was surprisingly attractive, and although of no definable style, had a certain charm; appearing to be cool, inviting, and somehow friendly.

He mounted the wide steps and walked across a well-swept stoep, hammered loudly on the massive front door, where he waited expectantly, and, still looking around him, he was astonished to spot a scarlet, climbing rose; a bright splash of colour against the stark whiteness of one of the pillars which supported the roof. Temporarily lost in thought as he pondered the incongruity of this, he has, since then, shared with me the degree to which he was startled out of his reverie by the deep, booming voice behind him.

"*What the devil are you doing here*? Who the hell let you in?" the man thundered

Swinging around smartly in response, Tristan knew right away that the tall, powerful man on the steps behind him could only be Jasper Hilliard. He made a valiant attempt to suppress the excitement he felt, in order to give as calm a response as possible. "I am Doctor Tristan Connaught," he stated levelly. "Doctor Hugo's great-nephew. My uncle could not come personally, as he is not very well these days, and, in addition, he already has a number of urgent cases to attend to!"

"This is a despicable, *damnable* trick!" the professor exclaimed, as he came closer. His attitude was almost threatening, and he towered over Tristan, who, though not exactly short, had to look up to the man who muttered bitterly, his teeth clenched: "Hugo is perfectly aware of my sentiments concerning men—young men, in particular—yet he permitted you to manoeuvre your way in here, with unmitigated deceit!"

I may have neglected to say that, despite his other shortcomings, Tristan is never at a loss for words. He has a good head on his shoulders, and can be exceedingly sly if a situation warrants it. He now stretched himself to his full length, which—while not to be compared with that of Jasper Hilliard, as I have said—was not inconsiderable, and snapped: "Excuse me, Professor, but I have neither the time nor the inclination to stand here arguing with you. I came to *Spoorseinde* for a well-earned break from a very busy practice, but because I was led to understand that your daughter is perhaps critically ill, and as my uncle is weighed down with work, I agreed to undertake this long and most unpleasant journey in his place. As you are clearly not in need of my services, after all, I bid you 'good afternoon'!" And with this he began to descend the steps, rapidly, but with all the dignity he could muster.

Before he could reach the Jeep, however, the professor's anxiety about his child was enough to override all prejudice, compelling him to cast aside any semblance of pride—precisely as Tristan had calculated upon his doing. With an expression of mingled frustration and resignation on his tired, though unexpectedly still young-looking face, the near frantic father was obliged to go after the doctor and implore him to return. Seconds later he led Tristan into the house.

They walked together through the spacious hallway, and then Hilliard went ahead of the visitor; down the long passage that led to where the patient lay. Following him, Tristan, who was surreptitiously looking around him, decided that this family had to be very comfortably off. Some of the furniture was among the finest he had ever seen. How Jordan's father, Benjamin Ashton, would have admired it! The antique, Cape Dutch 'stinkwood' cabinets—probably priceless—with high, gabled, 'linen fold' doors and traditional, skilfully carved ball-and-claw feet, gleamed with a lustre that only many years of faithful polishing could achieve; and from what he, Tristan, was able to see, this house, emanating an almost tangible atmosphere of elegance and comfort, was perceptibly well-run. A profusion of yellow Mimosa—unexpected in this part of the world—and autumn-hued flowers, spilled over from a gigantic, well polished brass urn, onto the mirror-like surface of a small table in an alcove, and it was opposite this that the professor stopped to push open the door of the sick girl's bedroom.

The patient was lying on a bed next to an open window, and the light fell full upon her sister, who sat beside the bed, engaged in sponging young Susan's hands and face. When Meredith Hilliard, setting the basin of water down on the floor, rose to her feet to be introduced to him, Tristan Connaught was obliged to take a *very* deep breath, for, in spite of the fact that she wore what was just about the most hideous, ill-fitting dress she could possibly have chosen to wear, he realized that—if Zhaynie Ashton were left out of the equation—he was looking at the loveliest girl he had ever seen!

CHAPTER TWO

When Tristan phoned to say that he was staying on the farm overnight, I was livid, and did not hesitate to let Doctor Hugo know that.

"Mark my words," I fumed, "it won't be for only one night! He took a whole suitcase of clothing with him, and that means that, for reasons known only to him, he will be able to offer Jasper some plausible explanation, like having not yet had time to unpack since his arrival!...I tell you, Doc, he intended making an extended stay of it, all along, and I am far from easy in my mind about this!

"I'm terrified," I carried on, "that he may see it as a challenge or a lark, to try and turn that poor, innocent, Hilliard girl's head. And mark my words, he will think nothing of trying to combine business with pleasure!" was my additional, cynical observation. "No matter how sick a patient may be, a doctor does not, as a rule, take up residence in the house!"

Doc had sometimes—but very rarely—reprimanded Tristan, himself, but it never did any good to carry *my* concerns about Tristan to him. "Boys will be boys!"—or something like that—was all I ever got out of the benevolent old physician. He would only laugh when I clicked my tongue disapprovingly.

But Tristan was not a 'boy' any longer.—Far from it! Nearly thirty, he was a hard, calculating, experienced man of the world, and, as already said, he was devastatingly attractive...if one liked the cunning, sophisticated kind! A thin, beguiling, 'naughty boy' veneer masked a shrewdness that I deemed 'calculating'.

I knew Tristan too well not to guess what he had on *his* mind. As I have said, he had spent a great deal of time here with us over the years. Every term, as soon as the schools closed, he would be sent to *Spoors-einde*, and, no matter how hard I tried to be like a mother to him, and despite all my good intentions *before* he arrived, it was inevitable that I would soon be counting the days until he left. Possibly because he would never regard me as anything but 'hired help'....Believe me, it was always good news to learn that his parents wanted him in Louisiana for a spell.

With the passing of the years, he had become physically more and more attractive.—As far as I was concerned, far too handsome for his own good!—In addition, he excelled—both at sport and in his studies—and was, from all accounts, idolized to the same extent by the local girls as he was in Bethlehem. How many hearts had he broken? Was it only obvious to me that he was selfish through and through, and irresistible to women, just because he could be so charming when he wanted to be? I could only speculate upon the degree of devastation he must have wrought among the female students at the university, and it had been a relief when he finally decided to settle permanently in Johannesburg.

To a large extent, it could only have been the fact that Jordan Ashton was uncommonly selfless, and independently wealthy, to boot, that must have precipitated our young Doctor Connaught's ardent desire to go into partnership with him; for, while of a different calibre, Jordan is, if anything, perhaps even better looking than Tristan, himself. Tristan, persisted, however, finally persuading Jordan of the advantages attached to taking him into partnership; cleverly using, as a lever, young Ashton's heavy involvement in a clinic he, Jordan, had established in a slum area. He worked too hard, our Tristan contended, and deserved to enjoy a little more leisure.

If I was furious about Tristan's prolonged stay at *Blouspruit*, his uncle was not; nor, in due course, was Jasper Hilliard (until all the trouble started!) And, no matter what was to follow, even I have to admit that, without him, the Hilliards might have found it difficult to cope. Apparently, upon questioning her father—before his initial inspection of Susan Hilliard, and while he dried his hands and face on a freshly laundered, sweet-smelling towel—Tristan was at first led to suspect tick-bite fever, which is common in South Africa, but he soon changed his mind. Before lapsing into a coma, Jasper Hilliard told him, she had indeed displayed some of the symptoms—a severe headache, flu-like symptoms, muscle aches and fever—but Tristan had not seen a patient quite this ill from a tick-transmitted *Rickettsia* bacterium. This seldom led to serious complications or death, he thought, unless—and this was his immediate, underlying concern—it was Lyme disease, which he had encountered back in the States.

But the young girl had no sign of a rash, he noticed, when he took the precaution of giving her a thorough examination, checking for a black mark, or *eschar*, which has the appearance of something like a spider bite, and could indicate the site of a possible bite from a tick. Moreover, as her father continued to dispute the likelihood of that as the root cause of what ailed Susan, insisting that it was impossible because his girls never went wandering into long grass, Tristan conceded. It was when the professor went on to say, further, that he had never come across a tick, in all his years at Blouspruit, that Tristan, for no explicable reason, was suddenly made to remember what, not too many hours previously, I had told him about the Game Ranger at *Witdraai*...

He took the girl's temperature again, and observed, thinking aloud: "It's the coma that concerns me. In addition to the other signs, there is the intensity of the headache of which she complained before lapsing into it, as you have described to me. Some of her symptoms seem to suggest a form of inflammation of the brain, probably caused by a virus, and thus, even if you were able to assure me—as positively as you have done with regard to ticks—that there is no likelihood of a Culicine mosquito ever being found in these parts, I would be reluctant to rule out West Nile Encephalitis as an acceptable diagnosis."

"I think I'd recognize the signs of Malaria, and would probably know a *Culex* if I were to come across it," the professor said thoughtfully, "although I can't say that I have seen the latter since my student days—in a Biology lab, hundreds of miles from here...And though I might be inclined to advise you to rule out all mosquito-borne viruses, I can't.—That's because of the unusually heavy rains we have enjoyed this year. For the first time in years, though short-lived and hardly blue, there really was a '*spruit*' running on this property again, after it had long been just a dry *donga*, or what I once heard people in New Mexico refer to as an *arroyo*.—But what would have brought such a menace to these parts, in the first place?"

Listening to Hilliard's cultured voice, and wondering what had brought *him* to these parts, Tristan suddenly discerned, all at once, that this learned man, who had, voluntarily if perhaps foolishly, sequestered himself from those of his own kind out of love for his children...the very one who was so notoriously antagonistic towards all men...was, by now according him a marked degree of deference, beginning to exhibit signs of trust and confidence in him. Somehow this infused the physician in him with a hitherto unknown glow of gratification, with the result that he involuntarily began to thaw in return. Meanwhile, the elder daughter, who was exquisite enough to be favourably compared with the only girl he had ever loved and desired with every fibre of his being, was staring at him bemusedly; open-mouthed and with the most incomprehensible, expression on her face. She was positively wide-eyed, and those eyes were quite touchingly innocent. Not since Jordan's sister, Eugenie Ashton, had married Dominic Verwey, and gone off to Nelspruit to help him run a citrus farm, had he been led to look at any woman without inevitably comparing her, to her detriment, with 'Zhaynie', as her family and friends usually referred to her.

He pulled himself together with something of an effort, in order to respond to the professor's question, less curtly than he had previously done.—"Who knows? Could have been brought in somehow....In North America it is suspected that, in some cases they have arrived by aircraft, perhaps in someone's luggage.... Have you noticed any dead birds around here, Professor? They are quick to die, once they have been bitten by a virus-bearing mosquito!"

"No. If there were any, I'm sure that the vultures would have dealt with them, and even if they did not like them, the carcasses would rapidly have decomposed and soon have been absorbed into the ground. Dead things are quickly disposed of by the heat, in this climate," Jasper Hilliard informed him. "Are there any precautions I should have taken, or can still take, in order to protect Meredith?"

"So far there is no recorded evidence of any such a risk, by contact," Tristan replied reassuringly, and smiled, glancing in her direction. "She would have had to have been bitten, herself. However, I don't blame you for any concern you might have. When one is confronted with someone who exhibits such an alarmingly high temperature, it is natural to think in terms of possible infection or contagion.—My partner once introduced me to a friend of his family, a brilliant physician who...!" he began, but stopped short...

It was then that, out of the blue, and again for no explicable reason, Tristan had a strange, momentary flashback to Doc's office in *Spoors-einde*. He heard again the disappointment in that gentle voice. *'You could...practise real medicine...in a place where, precisely because it is so remote, people really need you...'* and suddenly he cared about helping this girl in a way he had never cared about any patient before. He wanted desperately for her to recover, and speaking rapidly, he turned to her father. "I need to make a phone call, if you don't mind, sir!"

"Unfortunately our telephone exchange has already closed..." The professor seemed startled, both by the physician's announcement, and the noticeably abrupt change in his manner. "I'm sorry..."

"Then I'll have to use my cell phone."

"You'll need to go outside, sir," Meredith Hilliard observed respectfully, making herself heard for the first time, while abstractedly smoothing the damp hair away from her young sibling's forehead. "The signal is not good indoors!"

"Thank you," he said. "Is one spot better for reception than any other?"

"Go with the doctor and show him, sweetheart," her father instructed. "I'll stay with Susie."

"Thank you," Tristan said again, and, turning to follow her, he explained, talking over his shoulder: "I brought my laptop in case I need to look up something obscure, but it would be quicker to speak to my partner. He will know how to contact the best consultant I know of.—A specialist in tropical diseases. A man internationally recognized as the authority on what might possibly turn out to be this disease, among others. He has published papers on the subject, and while I'm sure they must be accessible on the Net, there are one or two things I'd like to have someone ask him, personally."

His first call was thus to Jordan Ashton, and he was fortunate to find him at home. But when he requested him to contact the expert in Pietermaritzburg, on his behalf, Jordan apologetically had to tell him: "I'd phone him myself, but I'd prefer to stay off the line because I am awaiting a really important call from my parents. They are back in South Africa and should have arrived, or just be arriving, at *Beauclaire.*"

"I thought they were only expected there later this year, in time for the birth of Zhaynie's baby..."

"So did I," Jordan admitted, "but evidently something's come up, that needs my dad's urgent attention. Why don't you call Stephen Verwey, yourself? He's always more than ready to help, and I recall that Antoinette[2] Verwey gave you their phone number. You entered it into your cell, remember?... You met him at Zhaynie and Dominic's wedding, so Stephen already knows you, but, even if he didn't, I assure you, he wouldn't mind at all.—By the way," he added quickly, before Tristan could ring off, "please give Stephen a message for his grandfather....My dad wants him, Stephen's grandfather, to know that Ruth Morgan, Aunt Stella's mother, has passed away, and he—*El-Hakim*—might want to attend her funeral. She used to be Ruth Talbot, and her husband was the *aide-de camp* to Sir Humphrey Talbot....Stephen's wife, Antoinette, wrote about her in the book about *El-Hakim*, remember?"

"I do remember. And I'll do that," Tristan said, thanking him for the suggestion.

With Meredith Hilliard standing quietly by, openly hanging onto his every word, and with her expressive eyes following his every movement, he entered the number he had been given. The phone rang only twice, and his heart sank when a man's voice responded with: *"You have reached the home of Doctors Stephen and Antoinette Verwey. Neither of them is available at the moment!"* His disappointment quickly gave way to elation, however, when it transpired that this was not an automated message. "Is there any way I can be of assistance?" the speaker continued. "I am Stephen's grandfather, Doctor Dominic Verwey!"

The girl's face reflected the undisguised surprise on his own, and her eyes widened at the eagerness with which he, Tristan Connaught, the so-called, hard-boiled sophisticate— reacting like some callow youth, or schoolboy fan—cried: *"El-Hakim?* Can that really be you, sir—*in person?"*

He could hardly believe his ears or his good fortune. The world-renowned *'Samaritan of the Sahara'* answering the telephone, *in person!*

" Forgive me if I sound overwhelmed, Doctor. My name is Tristan Connaught. I am one of your greatest admirers, and while I was calling Doctor Stephen Verwey for advice on a case, I had actually hoped that he would consult with you, too.—What a bonus, to get *you,* at first go! It did not occur to me that you might be there, or that you might answer the phone! I was given Stephen's number by my partner."

"And who is your partner, Doctor?... A friend of Stephen's?"

"His name is Jordan Ashton. His sister, Zhaynie, is married to yet another member of your family—Dominic Verwey, Dr.

Paul's son—and your grandson knows his whole family. In fact, Stephen told me in Nelspruit, at the wedding of Dominic and Zhaynie, that he and Antoinette had become engaged on the same day as those two, in the Ashtons' home on Long Island!" Tristan realized only too well that he was gushing, but could not restrain himself.

"Well Stephen and Antoinette are actually on their way to Nelspruit, as we speak," *El-Hakim* explained. "Apparently there is some sort of crisis involving Tony's grandfather, Bert Mostert, as well as the Ashtons. And, until her parents are able join them in some crucial decision-making, they, Stephen and Antoinette, have gone to give Bert their moral support."

"I came to know Tony well, while she was living with the Ashtons, and I have read her book about your adventures in the Sahara," Tristan put in, somewhat irrelevantly.

The great man chuckled. "Don't ever believe that I was half the hero she makes me out to be....Well, well. So you're in partnership with young Jordan, Benjamin Ashton's son? How amazing! Your name is familiar to me, too. Your father must be the priest who runs Amy-Lee Ashton's child sanctuary in Louisiana so efficiently. He is a man for whom I have the greatest respect and admiration.—But let us not waste time.... Your patient's problem must be an urgent one, or you would not be calling long-distance....Where are you and what can I do for you?"

"I'm in the Kalahari, on an isolated farm belonging to a Professor Hilliard, whose daughter may be infected with the same virus with which your brother, Philip, was afflicted in the Sahara. Fortunately I recently re-read the paper you published in the sixties, as well as the one you co-authored recently, with Stephen, and I am ninety-nine percent sure that my patient has something very much like West Nile.—But not quite!"

"Do you mean to tell me that you are at *Blouspruit*? Jasper Hilliard's place? This is indeed a night for surprises! I haven't heard from him in years? Please pass on my *salaams*!...His girls must be quite grown up. Which one is sick—Susan or Meredith?"

"Susan....Although I am almost sure that my diagnosis is correct, what surprises me is that she could have contracted this *here*!—Could this be the same thing?"

Tristan then went on to describe what had led him to his conclusion, also answering a few probing questions put to him by *El-Hakim*, who listened attentively to all that the younger physician had to tell him; kindly reminding the latter of the patient's youth, because studies had shown people over fifty to be at greater risk. When he had heard Tristan out, the eminent researcher then gave him the benefit of his own experience, concluding with: "While it does sound as if what you are dealing with *might* be related to the St. Louis encephalitis virus found in the United States, I would surmise that what you have there is more likely to be a *flavivirus*, which is more commonly found in Africa.

"As you must also have read, I now know, of course, that it wasn't really necessary to take such stringent precautions against contagion when Philip was ill. Neither my brother nor anyone else could have 'caught' it. They had to have been bitten....Some of my people actually claimed, at that time, to have had experience of it, so it could not have been new to that part of the Sahara, either. It was just unfortunate that he and my friend, Raschid, happened to be the ones on duty when the already sick refugees from Abdel Sharia's encampment were brought in, and probably the only mozzie hiding in someone's *burnous*, was the one that escaped to alight on them.

"Here's what I suggest you do...First try to establish whether your patient does indeed have something viral, and see to it that she is provided with the best possible nursing care, such as my wife was able to provide for my brother. That is what she needs most. In case it does prove to be West Nile, be on the alert for signs of secondary infections like pneumonia, problems in the urinary tract, and so on. Should the situation appear to be worsening into something more severe than anticipated, you'll have to arrange, somehow, for her to be flown to a hospital in Upington or Kuruman, for intravenous intervention with fluids and nutrition—and, God forbid, airway management. In that case, she might need to be put on a ventilator...but why don't we just pray, and hope for the best?—If Benjamin Ashton were here, he'd tell you that 'prayer' is the operative word.—And doesn't he have good cause to know this?"

"Thank you, sir," Tristan said, preferring to ignore Verwey's question. With a priest for a father, he'd had enough of God at home, and he wondered how Antoinette, Stephen Verwey's wife, had stuck it with yet another priest, for hers. As far as he was concerned, any credit for Amy-Lee Ashton's healing should be laid squarely at the feet of her surgeon, and prayer had nothing to do with it, but he refrained from saying so. He chose, instead, to seize the opportunity to refer again to the recently published writings of the two Verweys—*El-Hakim* and his grandson, Stephen.

"Talking about West Nile and Malaria, Jordan and I discussed your theories on iron overload recently, and I was quite fascinated by what you and Stephen had to say on the subject."

"They're hardly theories, my boy," said Verwey, the renowned authority. "As you know, iron is an essential growth factor for the multiplication of most bacteria. Research over many years has shown that fungi, parasites and viruses also feed on iron—as do many cancers. Right here in South Africa, as in the States, we have men like Bothwell and Finch, respectively, who have been writing about this for years!...But how many physicians know about this, or take into consideration this when making a diagnosis, even if they do?...I have enjoyed talking to you, Doctor Connaught—but now I think I must let you get back to your patient! I can come on pretty strong when it comes to this sort of thing"

"I have been privileged, and have enjoyed talking to you, too, sir. Thank you for all you have told me! I hope to meet you in person some day. You have confirmed everything I thought I should be on the lookout for. But, if I may ask you one more question before you ring off...Supposing this is West Nile, why here? I still can't get over the possibility of my encountering this virus—here, of all places!"

"Somehow I don't believe that what you are dealing with where you are, is precisely the same; but, even if it is, it may not have cropped up there for the first time. In the early seventies there was a fairly serious epidemic in the Karoo, after almost record rainfall in that usually very dry region, and it was during the following summer that so many infections of both humans and birds were recorded.

"If this is indeed an insect-borne problem, which we must not take for granted now, we cannot rely on the mosquito responsible for Susan Hilliard's sickness being the only one; nor that the virus is identical to the one that laid my brother low....In time I had to come to the conclusion that the culprit must have been brought from the filthy environs of Sharia's prisons, because those that carry West Nile breed in dirty, stagnant water with organic matter in it—which we did not have in our stockade. And somehow I can't picture Hilliard tolerating anything like that around his place, either—which means it would have had to have been brought there from somewhere else."

"I agree," Tristan said. "I have been told that supplies are dropped off occasionally by helicopter, and perhaps that is how whatever it is, was brought here. Nevertheless, that does not make the diagnosis any easier, and I have assumed the awful responsibility for the well being of these people. It is odd that Susan seems to be the only one who is sick..."

"Well just try to bear in mind, and remind Meredith and her father, too, that, in the end, both Philip and Raschid made a full recovery. Before you settle on any virus as the cause, however, I'd like to suggest that you do a Gram stain, to rule out a possible *bacterial* infection. I wasted a great deal of the Penicillin that was so precious to us in the Sahara, that time, because I had no way of carrying out a stain." Unexpectedly, Tristan heard a delighted chuckle bubble up in *El-Hakim's* voice. "As it turned out, it was worth it, though!—Just think...if I hadn't thought that Philip needed a nurse to administer his injections, I might not have been married to a princess!

"Anyway," he went on, serious once more, " until you are certain that Susan has not contracted a mosquito-borne disease, do get everyone else at *Blouspruit* to take precautions. Instruct those who will listen, not to go out at dawn, dusk, or in the early evening, and not to risk wearing shorts outdoors. Persuade them rather to wear protective clothing, like long-sleeved shirts and long trousers, whenever they are outside. And because the little pests can sting right through clothing, perhaps outerwear should be sprayed with a deterrent...

"What you're going to have to do about the Hilliards' Bushmen, in such a situation, I don't know—because they'll go around half naked, whatever you say—but do your best. One good thing is that they have such wonderful medicines— preventives and cures of their own—that some of the big pharmaceutical companies, having finally woken up to that fact are negotiating for patents!"

"I was not aware of that," Tristan confessed. "It would be a shame if the *San* were to be exploited....Anyway, as you say I must get back to my patient. Thank you again for your time, sir, and, before I forget, Jordan has asked me to pass on a message from his father, to the effect that Mrs. Morgan has died.... Mrs. *Ruth* Morgan..."

There was silence at the other end for a moment, and then El Hakim said, in a low voice: "My wife will be as shocked as I am to hear the news! Ruth Talbot, as she was then, probably saved my life in Egypt, many years ago, and were it not for her, my wife might very well have faced a fate worse than death!"

Throughout this conversation, Tristan kept his gaze fixed on Jasper Hilliard's daughter, and, led by *El-Hakim's* remarks concerning the need for protective clothing, to imagine her in shorts, he had to smile. He tried to give his full attention to the specialist, but, at the same time, could not help wondering whether the body she was hiding under that ghastly, ankle-length monstrosity, was anything as beautiful as the face above it. He had never come across anyone like her before. She was certainly the least sophisticated, but, at the same time, one of the most intriguing females he had ever encountered. Her long, blonde hair hung in a single braid over her shoulder, her tiny feet were clad in *velskoens,* probably handcrafted from the skin of some sort of deer, and her hands, equally tiny, though shapely, bore evidence of hard work.

Abruptly becoming aware that Jordan's father's friend, the man they called *El-Hakim*, was still speaking, he was forced to tear his gaze away from her. "And for heaven's sake, Doctor Connaught," Verwey was saying, "don't be in too much of a hurry to leave there. That family will need your help, at least until the girlie regains consciousness!"

"I don't intend to leave until Susan does regain consciousness and appears to be out of danger," he promised, inwardly exulting..... *He had just been given the perfect excuse for remaining at Blouspruit—and for as long as he liked! Difficult personal decisions could safely be shelved, for the present!* "My name is Tristan, sir," he said.

Meanwhile the girl—listening intently to some of his observations, her attention captured by some of his own words, as well as whatever was merely being repeated—had been drawing some of her own conclusions. Having heard Tristan protest, "You must know that there isn't a lab within easy reach!...*Microscope?...Gram stain?...Here?*...Doctor, I'm miles from *anywhere...*!" she was already conscious of an urgent need to reassure him, and even more so when he admitted: "I'll just have to wing it, I'm afraid. Thank you for both your time and advice, for which I am extremely grateful.... No, it's *not* a case of your not having told me anything that I did not know already. Even just getting your slant on what I suspect, has taken a vast load off my mind!"

By that time she had fought and overcome her awe of this magnificent person to a degree sufficient to enable her to find her voice, she offered shyly, "*I* have a microscope, Doctor, and I know how to do a Gram stain.— Would you like me to do it for you?"

***

The next ten days were a revelation to Tristan Connaught. The first surprise was the visit to a lab, which, he only later discovered, much later, was Meredith Hilliard's own, and where he witnessed a dramatic change in this enigmatic girl. On her own turf she was transformed; her own mistress, and entirely devoid of shyness or self-consciousness. There was nothing obsequious or timid about her as she set to work, competently and with quiet confidence, examining the smear he had obtained from her sister, while he looked around him, fascinated by all he saw.

Having changed into an overall made of some cool, filmy material, and rid of the bulky garment, she seemed smaller than before, and he noticed that she had to use a step to climb up onto the high stool on which she sat hunched over her microscope. He could hardly believe the quiet confidence with which she booted up her computer, and then, before proceeding with the Gram stain, searched for the relevant references needed to compare the negative and positive images of a possible bacterium.

What he found most astonishing was the fact that everything she required was right there at her fingertips— which led him to wonder in which field of research her father was involved. Opening a glass-fronted cabinet mounted against one wall of the room, she ran a practised eye over the contents for minute, humming to herself until she found what she was looking for. She then soaked the sample, which had been smeared onto a slide, with violet dye, before treating it with iodine; after which she rinsed it with alcohol, prior to counterstaining it with pink safranine dye.

Waiting for her to complete her analysis, he was given an opportunity to wander around what, to him, was quite the most peculiar laboratory he had even been in. Plants under domed bell-jars, all painstakingly labelled, were crowded on tables and shelves, surrounded by a bizarre assortment of paraphernalia, among which he saw a juicer, secateurs, rack after rack of test-tubes under florescent lights, and, in front of each rack, a chart with some remarkably well-drawn biological illustrations. He saw, lying on a sheet of glass, under another microscope, a sharp knife, and beside it, some thin, slimy fibre, not unlike the skin of a fruit, under another microscope. Some of the transparent containers were filled with roots, others with bulbs of various sizes, shapes, and colours, and all were sealed with colour-coded lids—also carefully labelled, and bearing scientific names that conveyed little to him.

Finally, having established the diagnosis, she slid down off the stool and turned to him, smiling with satisfaction, and what she said next, temporarily robbed him of speech.

"It's not a virus, sir! As you know, viruses, lacking the cell wall to take up the stain, cannot be seen, but here bacteria are visible. What shows up is purple, so Susie must have a Gram-positive *bacterial* infection, and not a virus. It is unfortunate that I am neither able to do a blood test for bacteria, nor screen for parasites to help you make an exact diagnosis of her sickness, but at least, when a specimen is first obtained, a Gram-stained smear can often yield valuable dividends that cannot be obtained from culture of the specimen alone. Nevertheless, whatever the case, it seems that, whatever she has, I can't do much for her!... On the other hand, now I come to think of it, I could take a shot in the dark and try an extract of Helichrysum, which has been brought for me, from Angola...!"

She cocked her head and held her hand to her cheek, considering the problem for a moment. "But, reminded of mosquitoes, there are appropriate steps I should, in any case, take for the rest of us.—How remiss of me not to have taken precautions long ago. Anyway, for now I can at least do something to make you and the rest of us a little safer....I constantly lament the fact that we do not have Baobabs growing here, as the juice has a vitamin C content nearly six-times that of an orange, and elsewhere the *Khomani San* use it to ward off malaria. However, I still have some of the juice of the fruit Platjie, one of the numerous relatives of Malgas and Mieta, brought me last night. It's in the refrigerator."

He was confounded to the extent that he could only walk behind her wordlessly, to be amused at her incredible naiveté one moment, and taken aback, the very next, by unexpected flashes of self-assurance displayed by this child of the desert. Now, having followed her into the kitchen, he could hardly believe his ears when, unsuspectingly, he seemed to have been catapulted straight into a scene from *'The Gods Must Be Crazy!'* For the first time in his life he heard a white girl clicking away in the *San* language of the Kalahari, as she chatted away animatedly to a small, wizened Bushman who was wearing nothing but a leather thong!—Obviously the 'Platjie', bearer of the Baobab fruit, and who, in introducing him, she was quick to explain quite protectively, called himself a Bushman, and yet preferred to have his people referred to as the *'Saasi'*, and their language as *'!Kabee'*! Written with an exclamation mark preceding it to denote the 'click'.

Tristan remained almost mesmerized as she poured the juice into a glass, and then held it out to him, temporarily seeming relaxed in his presence, and, surprisingly, becoming quite conversational. "As a precaution, I'm giving you some, too, Doctor, and then I'll take a dose of it to my father ...If only my supply were unlimited, and if I had had the slightest inkling of the threat hanging over my sister," she went on regretfully, "I would have made her drink it by the gallon!...

"Blessedly the fruit Platjie has so fortuitously brought me now, as a gift from Botswana, is at least a foot long and I can use every scrap of it, but I wish I had more—and I wish that he would sometimes also be able to bring bark and flowers. The leaves can be boiled and eaten, and one can make excellent glue from the pollen..." She stopped short. " Come on!" she instructed firmly, handing him his glass, "Drink up, Doctor! I'm having some, too, and then I'll take Daddy his!"

She spoke so authoritatively that he instinctively obeyed, feeling more bewildered with every passing moment. The fleeting, 'big sister' self-assurance in the tone of her voice, reminded him, at times, more of a little girl playing the cajoling, indulgent 'mother' at a doll's at tea party, than of a grown woman; and mistakenly regarding this as condescension, it irritated him. "Look here, Meredith," he said firmly, "I don't know how old you are, but I am sure that I am not too much older than you are.—If I'm to remain here much longer, we'll have to treat one another as equals. That also means that this 'sir' and 'doctor' stuff will have to stop! My name is Tristan!"

For a moment she seemed confounded, as though trying to process the rebuke. Then she frowned with mingled embarrassment and remorse. "I'm sorry if I have offended you. You are...well...it is not easy for me to decide quite what... who...! It's just that...!"

She responded awkwardly, her apologetic demeanour now, if anything, more childlike. And, perceiving that she was struggling, he hastened to restore her confidence. "Well, never mind that now. Within a few more days you'll be used to me. Meanwhile, I quite understand," he reassured her—although he knew this to be far from the truth. And being as ill-equipped to deal with unsophisticated females as she was with strangers, he was forced to acknowledge to himself that he found her every bit as difficult to assess as she so clearly did him!

Following her as she took the juice to her father, he was reluctantly obliged to inform the professor that it had not yet been possible to make even a tentative diagnosis of Susan's malaise. He repeated parts of his conversation with Dominic Verwey, explaining in detail why this was the case, and taking care to mention Verwey's request that he not leave there too soon.

"So that was the 'expert' you wished to consult," Jasper Hilliard exclaimed, after obediently knocking back the liquid his daughter had brought him. "Well I never! I've known him for ages! He is originally a Free Stater, and I came to know him in my young days when, after I had delivered my very first lecture—which happened to be at the University in Bloemfontein—I was persuaded to go to Ficksburg, with some of his students, and watch him play polo somewhere near there. After we chanced to meet up again, years later, in Britain, we became good friends, despite the disparity in our ages.

"He must be getting on now, but he seems to be one of those people who just don't age. The last time I saw him, was just after he had returned to South Africa from his second stint in the Sahara, and I would since have contacted him, myself, had I known where to reach him.—How did you manage that?" And no sooner had Tristan put him in the picture, mentioning Jordan in the process, than there was a detectable, new warmth in the professor's voice. Clearly the fact that they had knowledge of both the Verweys and the Ashtons, in common, was a plus.

"You're in partnership with young Jordan Ashton, did you say?—Now I am even more acutely aware of how the years have flown!...Jordie, a doctor? I can hardly believe it!"

"I remember him!" Meredith cried, excited at the recollection. "He was always so nice to Susie and to me! I remember the day she dropped and broke something that Jordan's father had brought for mother.—Remember, Daddy, when Mr. Ashton and Jordie came here with two men, one of whom had taken them to places they called *Rietfontein* and *Witdraai?*—And, when Jordan tried, but couldn't fix it for her, his father promised to send her another?"

"I do remember, sweetheart. And he didn't forget. I don't know how he found it, but he sent your mother another figurine, just like it. It's that little shepherdess on the piano....The one man you're talking about, the one who had taken them to where he used to be stationed, was a retired police sergeant; one of the South African policemen associated with those areas, years ago, when the border was patrolled on camels. Mr. Ashton had evidently expressed a desire to see those places for himself...

"The other one was a Mr. Marais, whose son had been in the Angolan war. The reason why he came here with the other two gentlemen, was to try and find some of the *KhoiSan* who had been of so much help to his son, somewhere on the border of Angola and what is now called Namibia—and, having heard from Mr. Ashton about the Bushman family that have been coming and going, to and from *Blouspruit* for generations, he hoped that they might help him in his search."

"Nico Olivier, the former police sergeant you are talking about, is about to retire," Tristan interjected, having recorded Susan's pulse, and now engaged in taking her temperature. Deciding to press the advantage while the going was good, he added: "After being in charge, for many years, of security for the whole area encompassing the *Beauclaire Estates* citrus groves near Nelspruit, as well as the adjoining properties belonging to the Ashton conglomerate."

"Indeed?" the professor, watching Tristan, commented distractedly, now far more concerned about the patient than the former policeman. "I'm trying to read your face, Doctor," he confessed, laying his hand on his daughter's burning forehead. . "Is there any improvement?"

Tristan shook his head. "Not really, I'm sorry to say. However, as I am now sure that this is a bacterial malady, I'm going to start her on antibiotics. I'll give her a shot, and it's a good idea to keep sponging her down—but I do wish there was something more I could do to bring down this temp!"

"I know of something you should try!" Meredith put in diffidently. "There is no better antipyretic treatment or febrifuge that I know of, than Baobab leaves which, unfortunately, we do not have; however the pulp of the fruit is almost as effective!" She appealed to him. "But how to get it into her while she's unconscious?"

When he did not reply, she remained thoughtfully silent for a moment, head cocked to one side, as he had seen her do before, and holding a finger to her cheek as she weighed the pros and cons. Then, nodding as though having decided, she said, addressing her father this time, "I think it is better we should try just the pulp. I have other remedies, but we don't want her sweating too vigorously!…Umm…No…Pulp it will have to be!—Why didn't I think of that sooner? I suppose I've just been too worried, too tired, and too confused, to think straight." Then turning to Tristan again, she informed him, "I can prepare something very quickly for you to administer to her!"

"Certainly not while she's unconscious," he stated emphatically; wondering if, by 'sooner', she meant to imply 'before' summoning him. "As I know nothing of this concoction, I'd be most reluctant to inject it, if that is what you are hinting at, Miss Hilliard—whether it be into a vein or muscle. In fact, I flatly refuse. I will do no such thing! "

"Well then," Meredith insisted, not put off in the least, and revealing unexpected determination, "Why not try giving it to her as a enema?"

There was silence, until Tristan, almost snorting with derision as he strove to suppress his scornful mirth, decided to put an end to this nonsense once and for all. "Don't be ridiculous!" he sputtered. "This is ludicrous! You must be joking!" Watching her face he realized, however, that she was in earnest, and, unprepared for yet another facet of her personality, he had to register an emphatic protest. "*Certainly not*! Surely you can't be serious! How can I, a reputable physician, be expected to instil into a patient some weird extract—unknown to me, and unheard of until this moment—and that as an *enema*, for heaven's sake?"

"You've just ingested a 'weird, unknown' substance by mouth, haven't you?" she flashed back at him, defensively and with uncharacteristic fervour, clearly forgetting for a moment who and what he was. "I don't see you keeling over or having convulsions because of it! We have a rectal bulb syringe and, rather than waste another moment unnecessarily, I'm going to fetch it and prepare the pulp—and then, if needs be, I can give her the enema myself!" And with that, she swung on her heel and went out quickly, moving soundlessly in her homemade *velskoens*.

For a moment the doctor was at a loss for words, until, collecting himself, he appealed to the sick girl's father. "I've never heard of anything so absolutely insane, and I will *not* take the responsibility for such an unorthodox procedure!—You're not going to sanction this, Professor, are you?"

Contrary to his expectations, and to his astonishment, the older man seemed serious in his response.

"Why not? There's no harm in this that I can see. Besides, I have complete confidence in Merry.—Her research into the 'curative and nutritional' properties of Kalahari plants and trees was the basis of the thesis for her Master's!"

CHAPTER THREE

Of course Susan Hilliard recovered, and of course it rankled that some home-schooled, more or less primitive female, could have known something that he, Tristan Connaught, darling of the Gauteng fast set—with years of university and hospital training behind him—did not; but, upon reconsideration, he decided that, so far, nothing had been quite as infuriating as the manner in which everyone, including Meredith's father and *El-Hakim*, had kept dragging Jordan's name into the conversation....And that, at the slightest provocation! It would not be long, however, before he tumbled to the fact that reference to the Ashton name lent him credibility, providing an assured passport to acceptance by Jasper Hilliard, and allowing him to make capital out of his friendship with that family. Although it continued to annoy him that this should be the case, there would soon come a day when the fact that Jordan was his partner, would clinch a difficult deal for him. Meanwhile he took his time about returning to *Spoors-einde*. He magnanimously elected, at frequent intervals, to watch over the patient, giving the other two a chance to rest, and cunningly creating the impression that it was at some sacrifice to himself that he prolonged his visit,

It soon became evident that Meredith Hilliard's outburst had been a rare occurrence, and that, away from any situation in which she felt totally safe and in complete control, she was insecure and vulnerable to a marked degree. She was remarkably beautiful, amazingly intelligent and well read; and, at the same time so unfathomable that she fascinated him. She bewildered him—to the extent that he was temporarily able to put the Adéle situation on the back burner.

It was gratifying that, after the first time she, Meredith, could bring herself to address him as 'Tristan', she gradually began to reveal a delightful, child-like trust, which was very appealing. Paradoxically, however, she continued to bother him; especially when he allowed himself to face up to the fact that the strong aspiration to heal her sister, which had overcome him at the girl's bedside, had subconsciously been evoked by nothing more noble than the need to impress the Hilliards with his brilliance. And then—recalling the incident—he almost cringed. Meredith, the strange, unpredictable child-woman, had minimized the desired triumph in one fell swoop, with something as preposterous as an enema!

There was something surreal about his entire stay at *Blouspruit*. Even taking his turn at keeping Susan company while she began her recuperation, was very different for him. At sixteen she was hardly a baby any more, but he was not comfortable with her. He hated children, and had little experience of teenagers. If the truth were known, when he had been one himself, he had considered his contemporaries (with the exception of Jordan Ashton) too boisterous, too ignorant, and far too uncouth for his liking.

These days, although she was extremely bright, having to deal with a young adult like Susan Hilliard still made him feel awkward. Most of the patients who comprised his city practice were over thirty, very sophisticated, and very wealthy, and he *never* made house calls! If he went to their homes, it was for cocktails or some other social event. He was not like Jordan, either. Not for him, the senseless trekking into the slums, tending deprived, snotty-nosed kids, as seemed to be his partner's idea of fun. He, Tristan, had seen enough of such intolerable small people during visits to his parents in Louisiana; although, in all fairness, he had to concede that those children did not remain deprived or malnourished for long...

It was galling that, considering he and Meredith spent twenty-four hours a day under the same roof, he was granted comparatively little of that time alone with her. Having the entire responsibility for running the household, she was constantly busy. When she wasn't attending to her sister, she seemed to spend a great deal of time in the kitchen, her garden, or supervising the servants. If he wanted to be with her, he had to spend a fair part of his own day, following her around, and gradually it began to sink in that this extraordinary girl had been carrying the responsibility for the well-being of everyone in that place, since she was hardly twelve years old!

What he found most incredible was that she appeared to do this with few of the commodities that other 'housewives' took for granted. Sitting at the kitchen table, talking to her one morning, he was astonished to learn that what she was stirring with a large plastic spoon, while standing on her stool—with all the windows open, and a large fan blowing more air through the kitchen—was soap; the lye for which she and Platjie had obtained by burning a large quantity of some indigenous hardwood at a high enough temperature to make 'white ash', and then mixing it with the last of the precious rain water she had stored in a tank. She evidently also made the starch for stiffening the brims of the sunbonnets which she and her sister wore outdoors, made dessert from minute wild bulbs, boiled in goats' milk and sweetened with honey, and even the aspirin in the medicine chest was 'home-made', derived from the ashes of Willow roots.

She gave him gum to chew from the same tree that had provided her with whatever she had utilized to make the starch and, to his surprise, it was not bad at all! If the supply of commercial coffee seemed to be running low, she augmented it with her own—again made from roasted roots of some tree or another—or she served a coffee-like beverage, not unlike Postum, brewed from those of the tree to which she referred as 'my mother's. He should inspect the Shepherd's tree, the magnificent specimen of which grew at the front of the house, she told him, chatting away as she worked, and went on to list the numerous attributes of the *Boscia albitrunca*....

He found the berries delicious, and it was it hard to believe that it was from the boiled roots that she had derived the sweet syrup she had had him pour over pancakes and porridge—made with flour from the same source. "Every part of it has medicinal, or food uses," she explained, "and I have also used the roots to flavour some of the dishes you have been eating. In the olden days, before refrigerators, my grandmother would have used them to preserve butter and milk!"

When she baked a honey cake—with the rest of the Ostrich egg, left over from a remarkably good omelette—she was plainly astonished to learn that city women bought baking powder from a store. Why would they want to do that, she wondered, when it was so easy to make? After all, all you needed was tartaric acid and potassium hydroxide, in the right proportions!

Unlike Upington and the surrounding areas—where, she had been told, there were numerous vineyards—here at *Blouspruit* they did not have any vines at all. For this reason, she explained, she did not have 'real' Cream of Tartar, a natural, pure ingredient left behind after grape juice has fermented, but she managed very well with what she derived from the fruit of the Baobab, the essential 'Cream of Tartar' tree—and, when she happened to be there, Mieta's daughter, Saartjie, could also clean the brass with it!

He had to grin when she puckered her brow, wondering aloud whether the folks at Van der Merwe's shop in *Spoors-einde* knew about such things, and he, in turn wondered, secretly, what his fellow-members at the country club would say, when he told them how much time he had spent in a kitchen where the before-mentioned Saartjie, one of the personal assistants to the lady of the house, was bare-breasted, just about bare everywhere else, and almost constantly feeding the infant she carried on her hip! At least, while passing the time in the captivating company of the beautiful, but peculiar little Miss Hilliard, in these unfamiliar surroundings—and certainly bizarre circumstances—the longing for Zhaynie Ashton, from which even Adéle was powerless to distract him, could be temporarily assuaged!

Later, reflecting on Meredith's remark about the General Dealership in *Spoors-einde*, it amazed him that a girl with a science degree should be so completely ignorant about so many, everyday things, which other women took for granted; and, with so much time on his hands, he was able to devote a great deal of thought to this. Before long he began to wonder how she would react to her first kiss. Her forthright admiration for him, as well the openly displayed enjoyment of his company— innocent, artless little thing that, in so many ways, and despite her mental brilliance, she undoubtedly was—both amused and fascinated him. Unprepared though he had been, to encounter such rare intelligence and so much wide general knowledge of other, loftier matters, in someone he had pictured as either 'untamed' or, at best, a curiosity, he had nonetheless anticipated that a visit to a place like *Blouspruit* would prove to be anything but boring....Well, he could never have dreamt how very far from boring the reality would turn out to be!

It was an experience to walk through her garden with her. In her sunbonnet, she reminded him of an illustration from a Victorian nursery rhyme book, but there was nothing make-believe about the knowledgeable manner in which she spoke about what she grew. She knew perhaps more than some of the horticulturists Jordan had consulted when he was laying out the garden of the home they now shared in Bryanston, and it astonished him to find—among her many treasures that were indigenous to that area—a few from other parts of South Africa, which she had managed to cultivate. This explained the rose that somehow survived the climate, at the front door, and it was upon his remarking on it, that he heard her mention her mother for the first time. It immediately became clear, when she did so, that Jasper Hilliard had never revealed the true story of his wife's desertion, to his children.

"She grew the first rose on the front stoep, in a tub," Meredith reflected "and, after she got so sick that Mr. Brady had to take her away to Springbok for treatment, I began to look after it. I was about nine at the time, and I did *exactly* what she used to do. I got Platjie, who happened to be here at the time, and Mieta's husband, Malgas—he's the guard at the gate—to carry it into the house in the winter, but, a few years later, when my father had to go away and fetch her, because she was not getting better, it was already beginning to look very sick, too—perhaps because I was not doing a very good job. Then my dad took Susie and me to stay with Aunt Biddy and Uncle Mark in *Spoors-einde*, while he went to get Mother, and my sister and I came home to find that both had died, at the same time!" Her voice broke. *"My mother, **and** her rose*!—Did you know that her name was Rosalie?"

There was audible pain in her voice as she went on passionately: "I should never have gone away! And now it is my responsibility to look after my dad, my sister—and the new red rose, which I have planted in memory of my mother!— And this time I *have* to do a better job! Fortunately it seems to like spending the winter in my lab..."

While perforce remaining within the environs of the enclosure, they went some distance beyond the cultivated garden—she in her bonnet and he, at her insistence, wearing an ancient Tilley hat, belonging to the professor—and finally reached the ruins of another, smaller, and considerably older dwelling. This, she explained, had been built by her great-great-grandfather, when, at the turn of the nineteenth century, he had brought his bride to this inhospitable place in a covered wagon. One of his children had been killed by wild dogs, and he had been mauled by a lion when hunting up on the banks of the Orange River, or what was then known as the 'Gariep', leaving his widow to provide for a young family. A few years later, she had been murdered by marauding Korannas, and, by the sound of it, when Meredith's great-grandmother was no older than she was when her own mother, Rosalie, had gone away, she—the great-grandmother—had led a life very similar to that of her dainty, present-day descendant....The only difference was that Meredith did not have to fend off Korannas and wild animals; and what she was obliged to endure in this, the twenty-first century, had been decreed for her by her father!

Her ancestors, she made very clear, had hunted for food, not trophies, and Tristan, heard numerous stories about how they had made their clothing from animal hide—using as thread, the sinews drawn from the dried meat—and how they had learnt to live on what the Kalahari provided for them. Somehow, although he found much of this rather tedious, he schooled himself to endure it, for he guessed that, perhaps because she had not talked with anyone other than her family for so long, telling someone about the past gave her pleasure.... And he did like the way she spoke—when she wasn't trying to guilt people into doing things they did not want to do!

Whatever had possessed those people of whom she told, to want to leave the relative civilization of the South-Western Cape, in the first place, he would wonder cynically. The dark, untamed parts of Africa were not for him. Thank God, if there was one, that he had been born into another century! He'd take Neon lights and paved roads, any day, and fortuitously he was in a position to set high standards for himself...which luckily included his choice of female companions. He liked his women in real mink and genuine De Beer's diamonds, and he detested this new 'faux fur' and 'costume' jewellery craze. He preferred an emancipated city dweller; however, as the stories unfolded, he began, by degrees, to comprehend what had equipped a girl with the ability to earn a Master's degree by correspondence, to lead the kind of life she did—and with such good grace and equanimity.

In spite of his long friendship with the Ashtons, and his unrequited love for Zhaynie, he had never before had the opportunity to spend almost twenty-four hours a day in the company of any one woman, and, as he grew to know Meredith better, he found her an engrossing study. One day it occurred to him that the 'coaxing little mother at a doll's tea party', manner in which she had spoken to him earlier—and which he had found so intensely irritating—might have been acquired over the years during which she had indeed had to play 'mother' to Susan; perhaps having had to entice a bewildered little girl to eat, or persuading her to do whatever else was best for her.

He could appreciate her affection for her servants, Mieta and Malgas, relics from her grandmother's day, and how she had come to speak their language, and he ceased to be surprised at how their relatives from across the border came and went, slipping in and out of the country at will. How they accomplished this remained a mystery, until she explained that, for them, there were no boundaries, and Malgas would certainly not refuse them entry at the gate.

"Do not make the mistake that so many others do, of thinking that all Bushmen are the same, Tristan," she cautioned. " There are many clans and some are even very tall. Some have become relatively urbanized, because, sadly, very few *KhoiSan* are able live in the traditional way; however, although their relationship with the people of our household may give you a false impression, in many ways the lifestyle of those you see here is very little changed from the way it was long ago. They are part of a small number of so-called 'wild' *Khomani San* Bushmen who continue to maintain their ancestral ways as hunters-gatherers.—A truly stone-age way of life, to which they have clung for at least twenty thousand years. Like the Springbok they still roam the plains, but I doubt if they are able to hunt Gemsbok so freely anymore—and I've never known them to turn up here with dogs and spears!

"You are very fortunate to observe them at such close quarters, because nowadays one doesn't see many of them. They are becoming scarcer by the day, and I find this tragic when I think of how the *Khomani San* have battled to maintain their way of life against all odds, and against many dedicated extermination campaigns! For many years they were actually hunted as wild animals or 'vermin'! Possibly by your forefathers or mine. White, Black and Coloured people, both together and separately, were involved in these exterminations, and there is ample historical evidence of this."

In view of what she had said, and her passionate concern for these people, he could find no explanation for something that puzzled him. The fact that, from what he could see, there was nothing in the way of accommodation for these diminutive visitors with the peppercorn hair and protruding buttocks. And, upon mentioning this to Meredith, he was taken aback at the unexpected nonchalance of her response.

"They sleep outside in the open, of course—as their people have been doing since time immemorial. As I have said...for at least twenty thousand years. They don't like to be indoors! If you went far enough from this house, you might, however, find that Platjie has built a small hut somewhere, as they continue to come here quite often, just as their parents and grandparents did, before them. We still follow the precedent set by my own great-grandparents, and allow them to slaughter a goat or whatever they may need while they are here.

That was when it came to him that none of his friends had ever met anyone like Meredith, and probably wouldn't believe the half of what he had to tell them; and there arose a growing speculation, soon to be uppermost in his thoughts. An ignoble but utterly fascinating prospect..... What a sensation she would cause at a cocktail party!

Thus far the professor had, at no stage exhibited any degree of excessive warmth. He could hardly have been said to encourage intimate friendship; however, as Susan's condition improved, he began to unbend perceptibly, and finally reached a stage where he hesitantly inquired whether Tristan would care to join him for a beer. In due course, for the remainder of the doctor's stay, that became almost a ritual before dinner each evening—sometimes on the stoep, where they reeked of the Citronella oil with which Meredith had to insist they smother themselves, to ward off mosquitoes—and he found the house brew better than anticipated. After so many years of self-imposed exile, Jasper Hilliard must, no matter how reluctantly, have found himself enjoying the company of another man, and they would sit there chatting and nursing their glasses, in typical male fashion, until again it was Meredith who had to remind them gently that the dinner would be spoilt if they did not come to the table.

Before too long it became evident that Jasper Hilliard was gradually warming towards him, and further surprises awaited him. After breakfast one morning, the professor, albeit a little awkwardly, showed him through his outstanding library, inviting him to make use of it whenever he felt inclined, and then took him on a tour of his own 'laboratory', which turned out to be a far cry from anything Tristan could ever have imagined. Somehow Doc Hugo's allusion to an 'assistant' with whom Hilliard's wife had run off, had led him to picture a large room, equipped with Bunsen Burners and test tubes, where specimens were dissected, and evil-smelling gases and solutions created. The reality was nothing like that. If it had not been for electricity, it could have reminded him of scenes from movies he had seen, in which mediaeval monks, and other literary scholars, pored over manuscripts, or sat on hard, wooden chairs in ill-lit cells, meticulously penning translations of impressive, priceless, antique tomes!

For a few days after that, inexplicably, and to Tristan's chagrin, Hilliard suddenly reverted to his former, stiffly guarded self, remaining aloof, as though fearing that he risked revealing too much of himself—until one evening he again astonished the visitor by agreeing to accompany Meredith on the cello when, at her sister's request, she played the piano after dinner. This was to celebrate the first time Susan was well enough to join them in the living room, where she lay down on the couch, and it happened to follow a very recent experience which their visitor had found extremely uncomfortable.... When passing Susan's bedroom, on his way to the stoep for the customary, before-dinner sundowner, and hearing singing, he had stopped in his tracks for moment, and had seen Meredith and her father on their knees beside the girl's bed. What he heard was, *'Praise God from whom all blessings flow!'*—a doxology his parents and brother used to sing, back in Louisiana. Not long after that, Hilliard's deep, rich voice reached him out on the stoep, through the open window...

"*I will sing of the mercies of the Lord for ever: with my mouth I will make known His faithfulness to all generations,* " Tristan heard the professor reading to his daughters, and, although he did not recognize the source, the reading from Psalm 89 exacerbated his discomfort, reminding him too acutely of his own father, the priest.

That night, as usual, the evening meal was a pleasant affair, with the elder daughter of the house playing the role of gracious hostess with quaint, old-fashioned charm. By the light of her homemade, beeswax candles, which were always lit even though it was still fairly light outside, her hair, once released from the tight braid, and brushed until it shone, was spun gold; but this time he secretly wished that the 'sundowner' he had previously downed could rather have been a stiff Scotch or a Martini—to fortify him against the ordeal of having to sit through another interminable thanksgiving during Grace!

Later, when Susan had been helped back to bed, and made comfortable for the night, Meredith, sat on the stoep with the men, watching the awe-inspiring Kalahari sunset, before going back indoors to attend to the hundred-and-one tasks which were her contribution to the smooth running of the household. As quiet and introverted as such a long period of isolation had made her—except when provoked!—Tristan was strangely aware of her absence as soon as she was not in the immediate proximity; and, as usual whenever he found himself alone, his thoughts inevitably dwelt on the singular background and circumstances of this family....Above all, on how he could contrive to take Meredith back with him, and put her on show!

He had already, very soon after his arrival, begun to speculate on the possibility of a light flirtation with the lovely Miss Hilliard, but he had sufficient common sense to realize that he would have to proceed slowly—despite the dawning adoration he read in those beautiful eyes. Although it was exciting to witness that awakening, she somehow reminded him of a young gazelle, and could very likely take off just as swiftly if startled....What did she know of sex, he wondered?

**

When Tristan had been gone five days, I succeeded in persuading Doctor Hugo, that it was his duty to drive out to *Blouspruit* and make peace with his friend. Naturally I was a little embarrassed when he laughed at me and said knowingly: "Alright, Biddy. You might as well admit it! You're dying of curiosity!" And, even if my vigorous denials did not persuade him otherwise, he finally said, "Very well. I'll go—and, as I know you'll never let me hear the end of it if I don't take you along, you may come, too. I'll phone and ask if we will be admitted."

If that had been an eventful week for us, it had been nothing short of a mighty upheaval in the lives of Jasper Hilliard and his household. The saucer-eyes of the Bushman gatekeeper evidenced that he was of the same opinion....*Blouspruit* had not seen that many strangers go through its gates in nearly twelve years!

Of course I fell in love with the grown-up Meredith, at once. She was precisely the sort of daughter I would have loved to have had, myself. Despite the fact that this was the first time the little family had received visitors in a very long time, and her very first experience at playing hostess in such a situation, her manner was admirable. Grace and decorum personified, she must have been dreadfully nervous; but, outwardly, she betrayed no sign that the reception of guests was not an everyday occurrence, and she did her best to shield her still fragile sister from unnecessary stress.

I had taken the precaution of baking a cake (which, in truth, was actually not as light as the one she had made), and packing a few other goodies in a cool box, to help with the lunch, but after one look at Rosalie's daughters I wished I had brought them clothes, instead! Where or how they had acquired those dresses, I did not know, but if Meredith had made them, she had proved that dressmaking was *not* one of her many skills!

What I did approve of, however, was that she turned out to be to be such a capable hostess. Although she was modest and did not talk too much, I detected no sign of awkwardness—and I was watching her like a hawk, I can tell you! I know that Doctor Hugo was also impressed, and took to her immediately, because later, on the way home he told me that he was glad that all she had inherited from her fickle mother was her marvellous beauty! He harboured a great affection for Jasper Hilliard—I can only appreciate now, how moving that reunion must have been for him—and when he remarked that Meredith was her 'father's own child', he meant it as the ultimate in compliments.

Very soon after our arrival, he and his great-nephew went off to Susan's room in order to take a look at her, while

Meredith, politely refusing my offer of help, went to make tea. This left her father and me to sit alone, in rather uncomfortable silence on the stoep at the back of the house, until she came back with a tray, accompanied by the San woman, Mieta—hardly changed at all since Rosalie's day—carrying another. I was thus given the opportunity to scrutinize Jasper's stern, hawk-like features, closely, cudgelling my brain for something to say, while he concentrated on the antics of a Secretary bird marching across the veld as though his life depended on it. I still liked what I saw, as much as I had in days gone by.

This was the man Rosalie Hilliard had considered too staid, but he had never come across like that, to me. He had perhaps aged a little—but hadn't we all?—And his expression was a bit stern (perhaps he frowned with uneasiness, or tension), but I felt sorry for him because of the uncertainty and confusion I read in his clear blue eyes, when he did look directly at me. He feared the outcome of these new developments, and I could not help but pity him. Hoping to break the prolonged silence, I said, and really meant it: "Meredith has turned out to be a lovely, charming girl, Jasper, and she does you credit!"

I was happy to see his face light up. The taught lines of his jaw relaxed, and, as though by magic, the closed look disappeared from beneath those fierce eyebrows. Unexpectedly he smiled, revealing even, white teeth that were still remarkably good.

"Yes, she is lovely, isn't she?" he agreed affectionately, and with undisguised pride.—"And Susie is equally so. When she is well, she's the ball of fire in the house, while Merry, belying that nickname, has, through circumstances, become the responsible one. She is habitually quieter—until she fears that anything might be threatening her little family.—Then she's a force to be reckoned with!" He chuckled indulgently. "Now that Tristan Connaught is under our roof, he seems to be regarded as part of her responsibility. Heaven help him if he goes outside without a hat—or dares to come out in the evenings without mosquito repellent....She has even had him drinking Baobab juice, and I think he finds it amusing to be disciplined, along with the rest of us!...At least I haven't heard him offer any resistance!"

Later, dwelling on that conversation and thinking about Meredith, I believed I knew and could understand what motivated that sweet young soul. To me, it was tragically obvious that the loss of her mother had left such deep scars, that her entire life was dedicated to protecting the few precious people that were left to her. Everything she did was geared towards preventing further losses, and warding off any possible hurts of a similar nature, in the future.

I realized that that was probably the longest conversation Jasper Hilliard had had with a woman of his own age, in years. And it seemed as though, once started, he could barely stop. Meanwhile alarm bells had begun to ring in my suspicious old brain.

"You people will miss him when he goes away, won't you?...Tristan, I mean," I remarked, baiting the hook.

"We shall, indeed," he admitted unexpectedly. "Nice young fellow. Friend of the Ashtons, you know. Well, perhaps he'll come out and visit us sometimes, when he is permanently installed in Hugo's practice. Forty miles is not that far, so I'm looking forward to a another game of chess, from time to time!"

For a moment I felt as though I could hardly breathe. "Did Tristan actually tell you that he had accepted Doc Hugo's invitation?" was all I could manage—seeing Meredith and Mieta approaching—and I had to cough, to hide the crack in my voice as I choked!

"No," he said. "But he told my daughter he was seriously considering it!"

The two doctors Connaught were just returning from their examination of Susan as Meredith began to serve the tea, presiding over the teapot with quaint, old-world grace, like someone out of a Jane Austen novel, and the rosy flush that stained her cheeks as Tristan hurried forward to help her, was not lost on me. I watched him suspiciously and—excuse my coarse language—I felt like throwing up! He positively exuded charm, and his humility and affability would have been amusing if they hadn't been so infuriating! None of his blasé, city patients would have recognized their slick, city medical practitioner, in this modest, accommodating young fellow, who was evidently only out to please; ready to concede to our slightest whims, and positively radiating helpfulness and well-being. Good heavens, he even offered to refill Jasper's cup!

And something else made me even more furious...

Dear old Doctor Connaught had idolized this young man for far too long. In his eyes Tristan could rarely do wrong, and I could appreciate that he saw him as the son he had never had; but, fond as I am of Doc, there were really times when I could cheerfully have driven that indulgent beam of pride from his face, with a hearty shake! This was one of those times.—I could not miss his hopefully raised eyebrow when, upon returning to the stoep, he overheard our conversation concerning Tristan's plans. Regrettably, right at that moment I was unable to interpret the full significance of this.

Was Tristan simply involved in an impressive charade, or had his association with the Hilliard family suddenly wrought a miracle in him? As it would have taken too much to convince me of the latter, I gritted my teeth and asked outright: "How long do you still intend to remain here, Tristan?"

There was a pregnant silence during which he regarded me fixedly, while a slow, provocative smile began to spread across his face, revealing the dimples that the ladies seemed to find so devastating, and then he replied, meaningfully, and very deliberately: "That all depends!"

I knew that he had caught my drift!...And I had most certainly caught his!

Before we left, I helped to carry the cups to the kitchen, and, finding myself alone with old Mieta—who had known the children before they were born—I, shamelessly fishing, asked her in a roundabout way, what it was like to have a visitor staying in the house.

"Daai ene issie goetie, Missies. Ekke vertrou hom net niks.... Nessie baas wat vir Nôi Rosalie hie kom wegvat het!" she said, in her peculiar Afrikaans. ("That one is not good, Missus. I don't trust him....Just like the baas that came and took Miss Rosalie away!")

As it had already been a long day for Doc, and he had patients to see after six, we were on our way back to *Spoorseinde* very soon after that, but I could not get *Blouspruit* and its people out of my mind. For all his brusqueness, Jasper Hilliard was as guileless as a newborn baby, and his daughter's face bore a telltale radiance....The sort of glow that only emanates from people in love. How could I help being worried?

Another three days passed. Jordan Ashton phoned, anxious for news of his partner.

"I didn't realize that he intended to be away for quite so long," he explained, and I thought again what a nice voice he had. Gentle, but clearly audible, without being too loud.—I detest it when people who call long distance, think they have to shout to make themselves heard over the phone, which would have been particularly annoying in Doc's house because, as he was getting to be a trifle hard at hearing, the volume on ours was already turned up as high as it could go!—Anyway, although Jordan certainly had every reason to be displeased with Tristan's lack of communication, there was not a vestige of reproach or criticism in his tone. Not a word about his yearning to be at *Beauclaire* with his family at this time. He did not expect Tristan to be gone so long, and he was concerned that the patient might not be responding to treatment. That was all.—A simple, businesslike explanation. No complaints about having been saddled with twice as much work as normal!

We were old friends. I had taken a liking to him in Bethlehem, when he was just a thoroughly nice young American boy eager to help our friends, the De Beers, for his late uncle's sake, and I had grown to know him better as an adult and a caring doctor. He had come to help out, the first time, when Doc had a heart attack, and then had spent three weeks with us the following summer, when we experienced that outbreak of meningitis, suspected to have been brought to our village and the surrounding area by a member of what Doc contemptuously referred to as a *'loose cannon safari group!'* Although eleven months had passed since then, Jordan now conscientiously inquired after his patients, remembering them by name, and even recalling that, while he was with us, I had suffered a migraine. What a nice young fellow!

After he had rung off, I put through a call to *Blouspruit*, and requested Jasper to ask Tristan—who, I was told, was with Meredith, some distance away from the house—to get back to me when he returned. Then I had to listen, tongue-in-cheek to some of the other information..... Susan was well enough now to get about, and could thus be of more help to her sister, giving Meredith a little more leisure time....The previous evening, she had been able to go for a walk with Tristan and Meredith, in the garden started many years ago by their mother and her mother, before her, and which Meredith now tended conscientiously, managing to cultivate many plants that would not normally not have survived the climate....Today had, however, really been a red-letter one for both girls, because he, Jasper, had given permission—after much arm-twisting—for them to go through the gates, for the first time in all these years, and to take a short drive with Tristan in the Jeep. ('Aha!' I thought.)...Now there seemed to be little point in restricting Meredith's movements any longer..... And it might be possible for young Doctor Connaught to be back in *Spoors-einde* by the end of the week...

Two days later, while I was outside feeding my chickens, I heard the telephone ring in the house, and moved quickly to go and answer it. However, when the ringing stopped, I concluded, correctly, that Doc Hugo had taken the call himself. A few moments later he came rushing out of the house, calling out to me, and wearing the most indecipherable expression on his kind, weathered countenance.

"Biddy," he panted, sounding bewildered when he caught up with me near the fowl run, "the most incredible thing has happened!"

I was immediately alarmed because of the way he kept shaking his silver head, as though what he had learned was too much to process, and I knew that the news had to be close to earth-shattering. "What is it, Doc?" I cried concernedly. "Tell me quickly! Are you alright?"

Then, all at once, the full significance of what he had learnt must have begun to penetrate, for, as a smile of gratification slowly spread across his face, completely transforming it, he grabbed me jubilantly by the arm.

"Biddy, my dear, Tristan tells me that he and Meredith Hilliard are to be married before he returns to Johannesburg!"

"What!" I gasped rudely, and had to lean against the henhouse for support. "**WHAT**?"

CHAPTER FOUR

With what colossal arrogance and characteristic self-confidence Tristan had made his intentions known! What he had said was, in effect, that he had decided that this was to be; therefore what he desired was a foregone conclusion, a *fait accompli*! But I, for one, was not so sure that Professor Jasper Hilliard would too easily be persuaded that there was any wisdom to be found in such a step. I could imagine the mental agony he must be going through, and, if he was anything like the man Mark and I had known in days gone by, he would be spending a great deal of time on his knees. Well, as it turned out, my presuppositions in all directions were not groundless...

Very early the next morning the professor turned up at our house.—His first venture into the outside world in many years! Of course Doc invited him to have breakfast with us, and I regarded it as a particular compliment that he was prepared to discuss such a weighty matter in my presence.

I agreed wholeheartedly with every obstacle Jasper raised. Conversely, the benevolent Doctor Hugo was enveloped in such a rosy glow of bliss that he cast each and every one of Jasper's objections aside with an optimistic, almost flippant, wave of his hand. Forgotten was any criticism he had ever levelled at his nephew. I firmly believe that all my beloved old friend and employer could see in this new development, was the prospect of Tristan's settling in *Spoors-einde*!

How absolutely right the professor was to protest that Tristan was the first young man Meredith had seen since she had outgrown her childhood...."As engaging as he—or any other personable, eligible young man might be—she has no one with whom to compare him!" he protested. "One cannot measure anything without some scale of measurement, whether it be visible, tangible, audible, or even experiential.—*One needs a yardstick, Hugo!*" he insisted passionately. "She is *incapable* of knowing whether what she feels for Tristan Connaught is really love!"

His breakfast untouched, Jasper buried his face in his hands at one stage, speaking in a broken, muffled voice as he pointed out how young, and how particularly unversed in the ways of the world she was. In vain! Hugo Connaught would only argue that Meredith seemed a very sensible girl, and was, to his knowledge, the first girl in whom Tristan—with all his experience of women and the world—had ever shown enough interest to want to marry her. Most important of all was the fact and that 'the boy' was more than able to support her in a very comfortable lifestyle. She would want for nothing! If they were to settle in *Spoors-einde*, everyone in the village would rally around them and make her transition into the outside world as easy as possible.

What a pity it was that, even while Jasper felt free to unburden himself to this degree, he could not bring himself to tell us, that day, why he felt pressured to an extent that might well move him to give his consent in the end—no matter what it cost him, or how much it hurt. He did not share with me, until some days later, the reason why Rosalie had been unhappy enough to run away. Nor did he tell us that, when Tristan had come to *inform* him that he was taking Meredith away with him, he, Jasper—ever mindful of what had happened to her mother, in the end—had retorted: "My daughter goes nowhere with any man to whom she is not married!"

All the poor man could come up with, in response to Doc's remarks about how the *Spoors-einde* folk would rally around Meredith when she and Tristan returned from the Golden City to make their home back here, was to point out, with a deep sigh: "You know how people are, Hugo! Wherever she goes, their curiosity will be overwhelming in the beginning! She will be regarded as some sort of oddity....I don't, for one moment, mean to suggest that your great-nephew won't be an eminently suitable life's companion for my daughter, but, to me, marriage is no estate into which anyone should enter lightly! Women—all women—inevitably find it difficult to adapt, in the beginning, and Meredith is not like any other woman you can name. Right from the outset she will have tremendous, daunting readjustments to make....The opposite sex is a completely unknown quantity to her.... To be the doctor's wife will be difficult enough in itself!...I am supposed to be a wordsmith by profession, and yet I do not know how to express myself in this instance. For the first time in my life I cannot find the right words!" He shrugged his shoulders hopelessly.

Both men remained silent for some time after that, until I asked gently, "And what does Meredith, herself, have to say about this?"

The professor again sighed, deeply, and when I met his eyes I read naked suffering in them. How well I could understand how he felt!—And, sadly, how well I knew how unworthy Tristan was. ...The last person to whom I would entrust a daughter of mine, if I had one, no matter how worldly-wise she might be; but I could not utter those thoughts aloud.

"My daughter is so illogically in love with this man that she is willing to risk *anything* for his sake!" he said simply. He lowered his head and covered his face with his hands. "It's my own fault!...No one else's! How unwise and how cowardly it was of me when I resolved to isolate my children to this extent.—How unwise...and how selfish!" His whispered words were barely audible.

"But have you spoken to her in the way you have done with us, Jasper" I asked him. "Does she know exactly how you feel?"

"She knows *exactly*! I laid it all out for her, just as I have to you, Biddy, but she has an excellent answer for everything I say. Not even the reminder that she will be abandoning her work just when she is well on her way to obtaining her doctorate carries any weight. In her heart she might be a little apprehensive, but outwardly she betrays no sign of that!"

While we still sat around the breakfast table, wordlessly contemplating the situation, I heard the Jeep stop in front of the house, and, presently, Tristan's footsteps coming down the passage. He put his head around the door, an ingratiating grin on his face. "Oh! I see the senate is already in session!" he observed, with a mocking chuckle.

Doctor Hugo jumped up so quickly that his chair nearly fell over backwards as he rushed forward eagerly to meet his brother's grandson. He took Tristan's hand in both of his, and the joy he felt was audible in his voice when he addressed him. "Tris, my boy, I cannot tell you how ecstatic I am to learn the news! That little girl has already stolen my own heart, and if I had had to pick a wife for you, myself, I could not have done better than to choose the daughter of my dear and trusted friend!" He drew up a chair for the newcomer, and sat down again, himself, positively radiating happiness. "You've reconsidered my proposal concerning the practice, haven't you?"

Tristan stared at him in amazement. "Now Uncle Hugo, please don't go making me feel bad! You know how hard it is for me to disappoint you, but how in the world can the fact that I am to be married, possibly change my plans in that direction?"

This outburst was met with a most uncomfortable silence. Doc Hugo could obviously not believe his own ears. His astonishment and disappointment were plain to see. I suddenly realized that the professor had not said a word since Tristan had arrived, but he probably could not ignore Doc's pleading glance in his direction, for he instantly stepped into the breach.

"Surely it can't be difficult for you to recognize what has precipitated this expectation on your uncle's part, Tristan," he said very quietly. "Of your own accord you have decided to marry a girl who is totally unfamiliar with the outside world. It would exact a tremendous effort on Merry's part to adapt to living even in as small a community as *Spoors-einde*. Surely you are not planning to thrust her straight into the hustle and bustle of city life?

"When you asked if you could take her with you, I took it that you only intended that to be a brief sojourn. Just a short holiday! I must honestly say that your declaration, now, has disconcerted me to an even greater extent than it has your uncle—especially in view of the fact that you mentioned to me that he had invited you here specifically to discuss your taking over his practice. Having been given an impression which now turns out to have been incorrect, I took it for granted that you were willing to make that move!"

There was another uncomfortable silence. Tristan fixed his gaze on the toes of his shoes while Doc stared with unseeing eyes at the grapevine immediately outside of the window. I sat, with my hands folded on my lap, staring at Tristan, and Jasper clasped and unclasped his, periodically holding them to his mouth. We were all painfully aware of the drama unfolding before us. The future happiness of more than one person hung in the balance...

"And what is your response to that, Tristan?" Meredith's father asked, at last.

Tristan reluctantly raised his head. He had suddenly again become the surly child I had more than once felt like slapping when he was a kid.

"What is there for me to say?" he demanded truculently. "I wish to marry Meredith, but, at the same time, I am not willing to accept any condition my uncle chooses to hold over my head, simply in order to sway your decision in my favour! I think you are all being most unfair, trying to drive me into a corner by using Merry as a lever to force me into doing something I am not prepared even to consider! I am sure that she would be the first to assure you that she does not expect this of me. She would never be happy, knowing that she had been the cause of my making a sacrifice that I might regret for the rest of my life!—Would she be happy to discover, some day, that I had harboured a hidden resentment for which she was responsible?...Are you and my uncle not perhaps being a little selfish in your condemnation, Professor?"

The underlying intensity in the young man's voice struck a chord with his uncle, who turned his head to look Tristan straight in the eye. "Perhaps we are being selfish, Tris, but it is a selfishness that springs from our love for the two of you. What personal benefit is there for either Professor Hilliard or me?...It won't prolong my life by a single day, or make me a single cent richer, whether you, or a complete stranger, take over my practice. The professor, on the other hand, has to entrust his beloved child to you, and whether she lives here in *Spoors-einde*, or in Johannesburg with you, will not change the fact that he will no longer have her at home with him...No, my dear boy, if we are behaving selfishly, it is purely because we are selfish about guarding your best interests! I want you to come here, because, with my heart and soul I want to see you make your life worthwhile. On his part, Professor Hilliard plainly supports me, because, in you, the Lord may be providing him with the solution to a tremendous burden he has unquestionably brought upon himself.—Unfortunately that solution would only be easier, for all concerned, if the transition were not going to be so overwhelming for Meredith!"

"But, Uncle Hugo," Tristan muttered furiously, his teeth clenched as though he restrained himself with difficulty, "is that not precisely where you are making your biggest mistake? Here in *Spoors-einde*, where everyone knows her history, she would find it even more difficult to adapt! She'd be too scared to go out into the street in case people stared at her and pointed her out to one another. In the city, where everyone is far too taken up with his or her own affairs, to take much notice of her, she'll be in a far better position, from the outset, to begin on an even footing with everyone else!"

Albeit reluctantly, I had to admire the blighter. He would have made an outstanding advocate. Did I not say, long ago, in precisely the same way, that despite his other shortcomings, Tristan was never at a loss for words? That he had a good head on his shoulders and could be quite sly if a situation warranted it? He was no fool. Until that moment I had wondered where Rosalie's poor child had found the courage to consent to such a formidable step, and then I suddenly remembered how clever Tristan was!...He must have played on Merry's sympathy! He must long ago have summed her up....Meredith, the devoted little policewoman, trustee and keeper of her family; the one dedicated to guarding the happiness of those she loved.

Then, the moment he had become convinced of how besotted she was with him, it could not have been difficult to tell a pathetic, heartrending story of how no one had ever put *him* first. How no one had ever really loved him. In contrast, her father and her sister had each other, and the Bushmen who worshipped the ground they walked on. Susan had been well trained, and if she, Meredith had managed to oversee the housekeeping from the time she was twelve, Susie, at sixteen-going-on-seventeen, should cope even better.... But he?...Poor Tristan, who loved her with his whole heart, had to go back—all alone—to that place where no one cared whether he lived or died—and that after he had become so gloriously dependant on someone who even told him when to wear a hat!

What I did not know, at that stage, was that, to Tristan, the most reassuring factor, and one that finally seemed to have worked in his favour, was probably the recollection of that spirited little flash of determination he had witnessed at Susan's beside. Recalling Meredith's response to his derogatory remark about the Baobab preparation, he must have smirked at the recollection of her spurt of anger, when, clearly setting aside her habitual diffidence, she had come back at him with that sharp retort about his not 'keeling over or having convulsions because of it!'

If the occasion justified it, she would become defensive, and he had counted on the same sort of reaction to anything her father might say in objecting to their marriage. Though it was clearly not a habit with her, unless severely provoked, that might well have happened in this case.

Because Meredith was of age, she did not need her father's consent, but Jasper Hilliard knew she would never go through with this marriage, without it. When he had left *Blouspruit* so early that morning, it had been to seek our advice as to whether or not he should give this monumental step his blessing. However, by now, the conversation had begun to take off in such a different direction that the original bone of contention had faded into the background. I could not help wondering if Tristan were not gloating at this.

Jasper sighed deeply. He pushed his hair back from his forehead with a tired hand, and then did something that really put me on the spot. He looked at me beseechingly, and, at the end of his tether, appealed to me. "Biddy, Meredith does not have a mother of her own. If it were your own child who was concerned in this matter, what would you do?—Please advise me, I beg of you!"

Poor man! In what an unenviable situation he found himself! And how very unkindly life had dealt already with him! For the first time I could fully appreciate what bitter suffering this proud, scholarly person must have endured when his wife had dealt him such a shocking humiliation. There were people who criticized him, who maintained that it was sheer cowardice that had driven him to withdraw himself from the world, as it were, but I had seen his farm and his children for myself that week, and I knew that, however misguided, whatever he had done, was for them. I knew what had prompted him to put his own life on hold, and to care for those children to the very best of his ability, while imposing upon himself something very close to the ascetic life of a monk!

Opposite me sat Tristan; arrogance personified! What I would not have given to be able to express my thoughts bluntly! How I longed to be able to say outright how unworthy I considered him. The problem of Meredith's return to the world at large was huge enough, but, if Tristan really loved her, he would be able to do much towards removing troublesome obstacles from her path....But then, how deep was that love?

Unfortunately there was no way in which one could establish whether it was not just because a girl like her, while exquisitely lovely, was also unquestionably something of a novelty; that for the very reason that she was in so many ways unique, he didn't simply regard her as some sort of trophy to be exhibited to his friends.—And then, of course, there was the additional, heady stimulation, the particular challenge of the hunt in these extraordinary circumstances, that had to be taken into consideration.... And Meredith? It was possible that she was genuinely in love with him—but how had her father expressed it? What was her *'yardstick'*? What would future encounters with members of the opposite sex not perhaps engender?

I knew that all three men waited anxiously upon my response, but I had to choose my words very carefully...

Under my breath I prayed for guidance!

Years ago, after completing my training at the National Hospital in Bloemfontein, and soon after arriving in Bethlehem, to begin nursing there, I asked the Lord, in a little 'black' church on the outskirts of the town, for the *'Gift of Discernment'*, and I know, unshakeably, that He heard me. Ever since then I have frequently been able to discern whether people are sincere or not, whether they are telling the truth or not, and whether something is not as it seems on the surface to be. Often the knowledge has come to me in the form of 'pictures' or mental images, and I was convinced that I was right about how Tristan had approached Meredith with his proposal. Only the Lord knows how earnestly I prayed at that moment for the discernment to understand why he wanted her...but nothing came to me.—Perhaps because Tristan did not know the real reason for that, himself.

Now please forgive me if I go off at another tangent here. I did warn you that I might do so, and I feel justified in doing that, right now!...Isn't it marvellous how, in thought one can travel millions of miles in a split second? Go back instantly, in memory, to events of long ago?

In recalling that the name of the little church was Saint Jude's, I could also remember that the rector happened to be none other than Clifford Connaught, Tristan's father, and that I had been taken to the service by our librarian, Felicity Seymour, who was the one who had bestowed upon me the nickname of 'Biddy'. Because I was lonely, I haunted the library, and because she was still trying to get over the death of her sweetheart, Jamie Ashton—Jordie's uncle—she befriended me, and very soon shortened my name, Bridget Dewey, to that of just plain 'Biddy'.

Borne further on the wings of reminiscence, I could remember, clearly, when and where Tristan was born and who else was there...and, because I was on duty at the hospital that night, I could also recall details of his difficult birth. By then his father had already escaped to Britain; and his mother, Thora Connaught, her firstborn, Timothy, and her best friend, Felicity, were temporarily living on the De Beer's farm when she, Thora, had gone into labour. If memory serves me correctly, the other three—Felicity, Aunt Minnie and Uncle Charlie de Beer—all came with her from the farm to the hospital, to give her moral support, but Uncle Charlie remained in the car, because little Tim was asleep on the back seat, and children were not allowed in the maternity section.

As I also remembered a man called Edgar Finch, and Reggie—the lad who had worked in his *Seed and Feed* store, until Felicity in her loneliness had adopted him—I realized what an important rôle she had actually played in all our lives. It was she who had introduced me to the newly arrived young schoolteacher, Mark Williams—a fellow bookworm, who was to become my husband.—She who had taught me to read Oswald Chambers, daily, (as Jamie had taught her), and she was one of those who had given evidence in support of Benjamin Ashton at his benchmark trial in Nelspruit, in the seventies. It was a credit to her that, with some financial assistance from Benjamin Ashton, Reggie—like Jordan, Ben's son, and Tristan, the Connaught boy—had become a physician, only Reggie was not in private practice; choosing, instead, to work in field hospitals in some of the most dangerous places on earth.

One would have expected nothing less of the adopted son of someone as devout as Felicity. It was together with her and Mark that I attended that memorable three-day 'Mission' conducted by the Rev. Peter Crawford of Nelspruit, at Saint Jude's (Clifford Connaught's church), the subject on the first day being *'The Gifts of the Holy Spirit'*, as outlined by St. Paul in 1 Corinthians: 12; *'Inner Healing Prayer'*, on the second, and the teaching on the last day was on *'Healing of Memories'*....And as I relived that weekend, I was suddenly most agonizingly convicted. I felt so ashamed that I could have hung my head and sobbed...

I thought of Tristan's parents and had to blink to hold back my own tears, as I had a sudden mental picture of Thora Connaught, back on the De Beers farm, feeding her tiny, new baby boy, looking into his eyes as tears dripped from hers onto his little face. I can still hear her singing to him, *'When Irish eyes are Smiling'*. Thora wept, Felicity told me, because she missed Clifford so intensely, and little Tristan resembled his father so strongly that it made her heart ache to look at him.

He had the Connaught eyes, she would say of him, and as I also relived that particular incident, I looked up at Doc, to notice, with a start, that although his hair was silver, and his face lined with the evidence of years of self-sacrifice, there was no mistaking those same Irish genes that he and his great-nephew had in common..."

How often had I not fumed at Doc's defence of Tristan! And how wrong I had been to do so! How dared I to have condemned any fellow human being, as unconditionally as I had fallen into the habit of doing with Tris—this outwardly successful physician, but hurt and immature man, inside—without keeping in mind what else Saint Paul had taught?... That we are not given the *Gift of Discernment* in order to judge—but to *pray*! That day I resolved that I would; but, oh dear, I did not foresee then how difficult that was going to be...!

Still permitting my thoughts free rein to traverse that particular path of memory, what struck me most profoundly was the unique relationship that existed between the Ashtons and the Connaughts, who seemed to take turns at rescuing each other.... First there had been the bewildered and distraught Benjamin, whom the Rev. Father Clifford had taken under his wing, upon his, Ben's, arrival in Bethlehem to look for his brother, Jamie—James Ashton the third.—And then, when that association had, in time to come, led to Clifford's arrest and voluntary exile from South Africa, during the Apartheid era, it was the Ashtons' turn. It was Ben and Amy-Lee who had helped, first him, and later the rest of his little family, to get to London, and from there to Louisiana, where Clifford, Thora, and their family had lived ever since—until Tristan had found that living in South Africa best suited his needs.

This led me to think of the children....Two of the Ashtons, Eugenie (Zhaynie) and Jordan, were born in South Africa, in Nelspruit to be exact, during periods spent by their parents on their citrus farm. Tristan Connaught—as I have already said—was born in Bethlehem, and now there was yet another generation to carry on the tradition. Now it was young Jordan's turn, it seemed, for another Ashton to take a Connaught, namely Tristan, under his wing....I would have given a great deal to be able to discuss the present situation with Jordie, and, better still, with his parents!

At that stage I did not yet know that Tristan was so deeply in love with Eugenie Ashton (now Eugenie Verwey), who, having almost giving up hope after years of disappointment, was expecting her first child within months, or that her parents, who were planning a trip to South Africa to be near her when the time came, had arrived sooner than expected.

"There is an old saying," I began slowly, "that love conquers all, and if that is true, and if Tristan and Meredith sincerely love one another, love must surely conquer all in their case, too. But now is the time to be practical; not the time for sentimentality. It is also the time to be practical and not theoretical. If Meredith truly feels that she is prepared to take on the responsibility of a being a doctor's wife in a suburb of Johannesburg, of all places, that is her business. And if that is what she chooses to do, I must say that, as far as I am concerned, one very big blessing will be the fact that Jordie Ashton will also be there to look out for her.

"However, reality sometimes differs drastically from our dreams or what we like to imagine.... How difficult it often is to reconcile the finished dwelling with the architect's plan originally chosen for a house!...If Meredith and Tristan marry—and if you decide to give your blessing to the marriage, Jasper—it is probably meant to be; but I honestly feel that, in this case, unnecessary haste is both unnecessary and unwise. I know that it is Tristan's desire to have the marriage take place before he returns to Gauteng, or whatever the Witwatersrand is called these days. In my opinion, however, that would be a mistake. If Merry were indeed my daughter, and if this were my home and not Doc's, I would suggest that she spend at least a month here in *Spoors-einde*, with us, to begin the process of what I can only describe as her 'acclimatization!'

"I would gradually ease her into meeting people again, and have her comfortable about conversing with all and sundry. I would take her to the cinema—as old-fashioned as our set-up here in the church hall might be, to the city-dweller—and I would take her to our one and only café for tea on a Saturday morning, when the entire population of *Spoors-einde* and the outlying areas seem to gather there at some time or another. In other words, I would gradually help her to get used to everyday living, as I know it. Even so, the city will be a shock when she gets there, but that's the best I can offer!"

There was more I still wanted to say, but Doc Hugo forestalled me.

"An excellent proposal!" He rubbed his hands together enthusiastically. "Of course she must come here!" he proclaimed—as I knew he would. My hinting had had the desired effect. "And where would she find a better opportunity to experience, first-hand, what goes on in a doctor's house! Witness what housekeeping in such an environment entails!" He chuckled. "Especially the irregularity of mealtimes!"

Jasper rose to his feet, a crooked smile on his still very attractive face. "I know when to acknowledge defeat!...Biddy, you have taken a great load off my shoulders. I know that my child will be safe with you!" He turned to Tristan. "I am prepared to give my consent, young man, provided you are willing to wait a month. Let Merry visit here with my friends, Biddy and your Uncle Hugo, while she prepares for the wedding, and you go back to your own environment where—without Meredith's presence to influence you—you can review this matter very thoroughly. Then at least the two of you will be able to say that you did not act on impulse." Doc was the next to be addressed. "And Hugo, if you will be so kind as to permit Biddy to take my daughter under her wing, she can perhaps take her to such shops as you have here, so that Merry can choose a few dresses that are more suited to the city. Possibly also visit a hairdresser for the first time in her life!"

The vehemence of Tristan's reaction was totally unexpected. "But then you will be spoiling her!" he burst out in protest *"You will change her*! And I want her just as she is! Not some ridiculous carbon copy of a hundred other females!"

And at that moment I reluctantly liked him better than I had ever done before. I found it most touching that he could be so madly in love that, in his eyes, the beloved was perfect!—It wasn't until after Jasper had left, Doc was busy in his surgery, and the phone rang, that I was so dreadfully disillusioned…

"Don't worry, Tris," I tried to reassure him. "We shan't spoil or change her, I promise you! She will still be your own, sweet little Meredith, when you come for her!" I smiled encouragingly at him.—Right then I felt ashamed that I had misjudged him in suspecting that, for him, Meredith's only attraction lay in that peculiar 'difference'!

Remember how I said I hated people to shout over the phone? Doc had gone through to open the waiting room, and I was rushing to clear the table before the first patients of the day arrived, when a call came through, and Trix Hoffman, the operator, asked: "Do you still have Doctor Connaught—the young one—staying there with you Biddy? I have a Mrs. Adéle Bradshaw on the line for him." And, having replied in the affirmative, I handed the receiver over to Tristan, and continued brushing the crumbs off the tablecloth.

"Hi, Sweetie!" I clearly heard that distinctive, abrasive sound of a voice at the other end of the line, the way it comes across in films, or when one is not right up against the instrument, oneself. "What *have* you been up to? Your mobile phone seems to have been turned off for more than a week! And I only I managed to worm this number out of your elusive hunk of a partner, by telling him some garbled story about the club manager wanting to let you know about a change in your play-off time...

"How *are* you, and when are you coming back?...I can't wait, and the whole gang is anxious to know. You mustn't miss the tournament at the country club next Saturday....And you still haven't put your name down for next month!"

"I'm fine, thanks," Tristan told her. "I'll be back in time to participate this weekend, but I'm skipping the next one. I have to get back here. I'm coming back to fetch someone...She's coming to stay permanently."

"You are? That sounds interesting! Does she play golf?"

"No!" he began, and then, all at once, could obviously hardly speak coherently for trying to restrain himself. "She's never seen a golf course in her life! She...she..." he spluttered. "Wait till you see her! You're not going to believe this, Adéle!" At this he began to laugh out loud, but there was derision in that laughter, and not mirth! "She doesn't play golf.—*She makes soap!*"

I don't know that I have ever been so disgusted with anyone in my life. I marched over to him, snatched the phone out of his hand, and banged it back on the cradle! "Tristan Connaught," I all but hissed. "You are despicable! I can hardly credit it that anyone could be so low!" Then I stalked towards the door that led to Doc's waiting room but hesitated, as I was about to turn the handle, to say over my shoulder: "You are not expected to believe this, but not twenty minutes ago, I had what my dear Mark used to call a 'love-bubble', for you....Now I could cheerfully strangle you!"

How could any of us older folk have guessed how amusing Tristan found it to reflect on the sensation he was about to cause when he launched his little oddity among the deathly bored, 'smart' circles among whom he moved? No wonder he had been in such a hurry to get the marriage ceremony behind him as quickly as possible. I wonder whether, if he had not been accountable to Jasper, and if he, Merry's father, had not been there to look out for her, Doc Hugo's precious 'boy' would ever have made Meredith Hilliard his wife.

Although Tristan might have been fuming at my interference, he must nonetheless have realized that, firstly, there was no point in trying to raise objections, and, secondly, he had no alternative but to accept Jasper's conditions. If, during the short time he remained with us in *Spoors-einde*, I thought I read venom in his eyes, I'm sure I was not mistaken.

First thing next morning, he borrowed the Jeep and made a quick trip to *Blouspruit* and back, obliged to make the visit a brief one because Doc was expecting to be called out to a confinement, and would need transport. Upon Tristan's return he did not remain with us for very long, either, before taking the antiquated taxi from Hennie Vercueil's garage to Upington, electing to spend the night there, in order to be in time to catch the plane back to Johannesburg next morning.

He had already reached there when, that afternoon, Jasper Hilliard brought his daughter to me.

CHAPTER FIVE

I had really taken to the 'grown-up' Meredith ten days before, and now that she had arrived to stay with us, closer association did not disappoint. She was a credit to her father's upbringing. I found the 'child' to have a most delightful disposition; gentle without being dull. (Somehow, perhaps on account of her vulnerability, I could not get out of the habit of referring to her thus!) Another point in her favour was that her table manners were excellent. No pointing with the knife or fork, or talking with her mouth full, and cutlery was always replaced on her plate while chewing. (No waving about in the air!) When she set the table, she did so with the full complement of utensils, including a fish knife and fork on Fridays; she broke a bread roll, and did not hack through it with her knife, and, in addition, she waited for Doc to say grace before commencing her meal. She also waited until everyone had been served before starting on dessert.

It was as much of a surprise to Katryntjie, Doc's faithful, long-time maid, as it was to the rest of us, that Meredith was able to speak to her in the ancient *Khoekhoegowap* language—because it is believed that, today, few can converse in it, and only about five to ten thousand people even understand it!—But, to me, best of all was the delightful discovery that Rosalie's child possessed a fine sense of humour. It has long been my experience that anyone who can dispel tension with a good laugh is capable of facing life head-on..... How wonderful it would have been if she were my very own daughter! Pretending that really she was, I made two 'Princess-line' dresses for her, and I'm happy to record that she really liked them.

Understandably she was a little subdued for a day or two. This was a tremendous transition for her, and no doubt she missed her family. Furthermore she quite justifiably felt bad about leaving her father so precipitously to take care of Susan on his own; and it was very evident that, although she had known him for such a short time, she missed Tristan intensely. But it must also be said, in her favour, that she was not one of those objectionable people who allow their own state of mind to blight the lives of those around them. What further endeared her to me was that she was so willing to help around the house. She kept her bedroom in immaculate shape, and hastened to perform all manner of small jobs for me, which I had certainly not expected of her. Doc was happy to make use of her in his consulting room, where she had the opportunity to come into contact with strangers, and got on surprisingly well with the patients. It so happened that Doctor Hugo Connaught was one of the very few physicians left who still dispensed many of his own prescriptions—his cough syrup and ointments were excellent, and should have been patented!—And, as she was a quick learner, it was immediately clear that her experience in her own lab back at *Blouspruit* was a great asset to him in the small pharmacy attached to the house. We were, of course, very careful not to reveal who she was, having agreed that life could be made unnecessarily difficult for her if people became too inquisitive; but, at the same time, we had to face up to the fact that, due to our being on a party line, it was unavoidable that the news would leak out sooner or later. Meanwhile we hoped for the best because Doc feared that his waiting room might soon be filled to overflowing with people who were not sick, and would come solely out of a compulsion to have a look at 'the Hilliard girl'!...

She wrote to Tristan every day, in the fine, scholarly script, undoubtedly taught her by her father, and when the post brought an envelope bearing Tristan's surprisingly good handwriting (for a doctor, that is!), I could not help but share in her joy...I was still praying for him, but I must confess that, at the same time, I could not help mourning the fact that he had to be the one sent by the Almighty to be the object of such pure, girlish idealism and dreams.

After a week had passed without any untoward occurrences, I decided that the time had come, to take her on her first excursion into the village, and, despite the fact that the few *Spoors-einde* store windows that displayed anything at all (except fly spots!), would hardly have warranted a second look in a place larger than ours, Meredith could hardly tear herself away from them. For this very special expedition I especially chose a Saturday morning, when many of the farm folk came to town; and at times she was quite overwhelmed by the number of people on the streets. Somehow I could not help thinking of Tristan; playing golf, while this lovely, sensitive girl—whom he no doubt planned to exhibit to his fellow club members, at some stage—more than once stood riveted to the spot on our dusty excuse for sidewalks, looking around her in silent amazement, and completely bemused. I wondered how she would react to one of the large shopping malls in the 'Golden City'!

As her father had promised, she had been provided with a generous amount of pocket money, and because I appreciated what an exciting experience it was going to be for her to shop for the first time since before she became a teenager, and to make her own purchases, I saved Van der Merwe's Department store for last. This was the one with whose name she was familiar and which—despite the uneven wooden floorboards and the hideous counters (topped with black and white chequered linoleum, and fronted by dark green, oil painted 'tongue and groove wood-panels)—was the only comparatively worthwhile venue for my purpose. Here, too, the selection would scarcely have been considered exciting by a more sophisticated shopper, but Meredith seemed to find it extremely so; and contrary to what I had predicted before taking leave of Doctor Hugo that morning, it was not to face powder or lipstick that she headed first.

It was quite fascinating to watch how clothes and household goods seemed particularly to capture her attention, although whoever stocked the shelves most certainly had no flair for that sort of thing. Merchandise was arranged with complete absence of artistic taste, and with no view whatsoever to attracting the prospective buyer's attention. 'Soft' goods were crammed in with no regard for display, and dresses, on wire coat hangers, hung haphazardly from rods, which, with the chrome plating peeling off in places, had seen better days.

But none of this mattered to Meredith. She revelled in just being there, and ecstatically left with a selection of teacloths, a new-fangled can opener, and a wide, flower-patterned skirt that would stand her in good stead—if she ever went to Hawaii!... Oh, yes, I nearly forgot! She also bought an embroidered 'Magyar' blouse with a red silk drawstring tie to gather in the neckline, as well as a pretty pair of red sandals to go with it.

On reflection, she was such a charming mixture of an over-developed sense of responsibility and childlike innocence, that it was not difficult to conclude that the former character trait had undoubtedly developed as a result of her having for so long taken care of all that the management of the *Blouspruit* ménage entailed, while simultaneously having to play the combined roles of older sister and mother to Susan.

This was made very obvious to me when finally we went to the café, where we sat at the 'Milk Bar', on high, chromium barstools with red, padded plastic seats. While she sipped a ginger beer float through a straw, and I, a bright pink strawberry milkshake, the only cloud to which she confessed to having marred her 'perfect day', thus far, was the absence of her sister. After she had repeatedly remarked that she felt bad about having such a good time, when Susie was not there to share it with us, I had to console her with the promise that I would ask their father to bring her to town on the following Saturday. Meanwhile we chose some material, together, and when I called Jasper I also spoke to Susan, asking her to phone back and provide us with her measurements, as her sister and I were in a sewing mood.

Words would fail me if I tried to describe the day I took the complete Hilliard family to town with me. It was more fun than when the circus used to come to Bethlehem! I loved being there with Jasper and his daughters—who were delightedly wearing their new dresses—and enjoyed the privilege of helping him over the hurdle of his own reintroduction to *Spoors-einde* 'society'! He clearly found it as touching as I did, that Meredith wanted to repeat exactly what she and I had done the previous week, and in precisely the same order, so that her father and sister would not feel that they had been left out of anything. We even had the strawberry milkshake and the ginger beer float, but one extra activity was added to the routine. While we were in Van der Merwe's store she took her father's big hand in her small one, and, like a child, she led him to the grocery section, where she made him stop at a particular area, of which she had made a mental note on our previous visit to the store.

"See, Daddy," she said, pointing to a tin of baking powder, "Tristan was right!—One *can* buy it—ready to go!...That takes a great load off my mind. I know it's a long way, but now that you and Susie have come to town, once, you can easily come again. Instead of always having supplies delivered, you can sometimes fetch them....And having seen how many things you can buy here, and which Susie won't have to make—as *Ouma* showed me, and I have been doing—I'll feel far happier about leaving her to look after you!"

The Thursday after that memorable day happened to be a public holiday, which meant no 'surgery' for Doc, and we had hardly risen from the breakfast table when, to our pleasant surprise, Jasper turned up again, unexpectedly, bringing Susan with him. Something else I did not expect, also occurred. Whereas Meredith and her father were clearly taking all these new developments in their stride, it appeared that young Susan was, metaphorically speaking, losing her sense of balance. She was completely, what I think is these days described as 'hyper'! She seemed to be in such a daze of nervous excitement that it threatened to overwhelm her.

It was five days since the shopping expedition, but if anyone as much as referred to it, she carried on like an hysterical child who had seen a Christmas tree for the first time. I could see at once that, while to start off with, Jasper had only exhibited signs of slight embarrassment, his consternation seemed to mount as, more than anything else, her behaviour brought home to him very pertinently the degree to which the isolation of his children had deprived them of normalcy. I could sympathize with the child's reaction, for, setting aside her long separation from the outside world, and even though it would be stretching it a bit to describe the settlement of *Spoors-einde* as a 'town', would not I have reacted in like manner if, at her age I had, for instance, suddenly been taken to shop on Fifth Avenue in New York?

The professor laughed, far too heartily in my opinion, and probably with relief, when, offering this point of view to excuse Susan's behaviour, I put it to him like that, making it seem normal, considering the circumstances, and I think that, in making light of the situation, I at least succeeded in putting him at ease. Presently Doc was called out to see the De Bruyn's baby, and Meredith took her sister off, ostensibly to catch up on the time that had elapsed since they had last had a girl-to-girl talk; but mainly, I suspected, to show off all the interesting things she had accumulated since she had left the farm. To obviate any likely awkwardness in their absence, I made more tea, and brought out some *soetkoekies* (sugar cakes) I had baked earlier, while I chatted with Jasper.

It had struck me before, but not as forcibly as it did then, that, just as Tristan had been the first young man Meredith had seen since she had grown up, I was the first woman, discounting his daughters, with whom the professor had talked in a long, long time. Little did I know then that—just as alarmed as I had been, from the start, and just as much as, in these singular circumstances, I still worried about Meredith—I would some day find myself worrying about her father. Both were too inexperienced and therefore, in my estimation, incapable of making a rational judgment concerning the choice of a suitable life's companion!

That evening, after her family had returned to the farm, and Meredith was tidying up her room, I sat at the foot of her bed, and talked more directly to her than I had done thus far.

I asked her outright whether she had ever chafed at having to be cooped up like that on the farm, and if she had ever borne a grudge against her father because of it. Being Meredith, she considered my questions very seriously for a while, before she replied.

"Although I did sometimes feel that I was possibly missing out on life, I cannot say that I was remotely rebellious.— Never!...And it also never occurred to me to feel any resentment towards my father." She looked at me directly as she added, with unreserved warmth: "It must be obvious to you, Aunt Biddy, that my father is a man in a million. Although Susan and I were perhaps deprived of much that other children might have taken for granted, my father was such a wonderful companion to us, and such an understanding, comforting presence, that, over and over, he amply compensated for all that we might be considered to have missed. I guess that, in the beginning, I was probably just very proud of the fact that I was able to fill such a great void in his life, and it also delighted me to know that the full control of the house rested on my shoulders.

"Then, gradually, as I grew older, and the novelty of it all began to wear a little thin, I was content in the knowledge that I was also responsible for Susan; and it was almost as though, with the passage of time, I forgot that I was a young girl, and that there was possibly a different future ahead of me. I began to accept the state of affairs as normal.—Sometimes, paging through the National Geographic magazines that my father orders to be periodically dropped off for us, and perhaps briefly longing to see some of the attractions of the outside world, I very quickly succeeded in suppressing those urges. I set store by the knowledge that my family depended on me, and I supported my father's point of view in all that he said and did, to the extent that I accepted his restrictions without reservations. Later I became so used to the status quo that it almost seemed to me as if no other world existed."

"And now?" I asked gently. "Now that the habits of many years must give way to a new way of life, how do you feel about that? Won't you perhaps think back longingly to the days when the problems of everyday life in the city were not only unknown to you, but, in your extraordinary circumstance, never threatened to touch you?"

"That is a difficult question to answer, right now," she admitted with disarming candour. "I have just confessed to you that I was never actually, or knowingly, dissatisfied with my lot, but now—and I'm a trifle ashamed to have to say this— Tristan has irrevocably changed things for me! Even if he had never given me a second look, and even if, at the end of the day, he had left there without leaving me any hope that he would ever return, I could never again have been completely happy on the farm. If anyone had tried to tell me a month ago that I would be talking to you like this today, I would vehemently have protested the mere suggestion. Now I must confess that even my work would no longer have been fulfilling enough.

"I also told you, just now, how gratifying it was, and how proud I was, to think that I was such an important part of the lives of my father and sister, but I know now that I only really grew up during the short time that Tristan was there with us....Will I ever be homesick and long for those sheltered, carefree days?...That I cannot say now, because I have given no thought to the matter. My mind has been filled entirely with dreams of the future.—Nevertheless, no matter what happens in that future, I am convinced that what has happened is for the best.

"You saw Susie and how she carried on here today, for yourself, Aunt Biddy, and I knew that the same thoughts that came to me, must have occurred to you. That is not a healthy or a natural life for that child. Whereas I was completely satisfied to live that way—possibly because I had my work and my studies, and I had seen something of the outside world before our father closed the gates of *Blouspruit* to it. Susie, on the other hand, would inevitably have become rebellious. Our natures are very different. I am more like my father, I think, whereas she?...Well, let's just leave it at that! Anyhow, I am happy and grateful that God used such inexplicable circumstances to send Tristan to us, and to help us shake off our shackles; and now that I have done so, it will be much easier for my dad and Susie to do likewise.

"At the same time, I realize all too well how very difficult it is going to be for Dad to carve out a new way life for himself, but blessedly he is a man of great faith, and I look forward to the day when he brings Susan to visit me in the city. It will mean a great deal to her, and to me!"

Despite her reassurance, something that she had said, disturbed me, and I knew I would have to clear it up if I hoped to sleep that night; so I took her hand in mine and said outright: "Meredith, my darling girl, you must be wondering why I dared to interrogate you like this, so I'll tell you. It is because I have been so terribly afraid that all you might have found in Tristan was a way of escape. Your assurance that you are not desperate to get away from *Blouspruit* has made me a great deal happier, but please answer only one more question for me, if you will, and then I'll leave you in peace....Are you sure that you have not chosen to do this, impulsively, because you saw no other way out for Susie?"

Her unfeigned surprise comforted me more than anything else could have done.

She stared at me incredulously. "Aunt Biddy, you are really making me feel guilty! You oblige me to have to admit that I have been so selfish in this so new, overwhelming love for Tristan, that, until this afternoon, I have given little or no thought at all to my father, my sister, or my work! You don't know how ashamed I am of that! Have I not just had to admit that it was only when I saw Susan so out of control here today, that I realized, for the first time, how she and my father could actually benefit from my marriage?"

I actually believed that, in taking that particular weight from my shoulders, she had assured me of good night's sleep, but it was not to be. I sat down on my bed and turned off the light, but, just as I was about to lie down, I had a flashback; an image of Meredith as, during our shopping expedition, she had stood 'bemused', as I had thought, on the sidewalks, taking in everything she saw in the stores. And I suddenly knew that everything she did notice, was seen through the eyes of 'Meredith the little mother', ever mindful of her sister and how the outside world would affect her....She was just being Meredith, the surrogate!...Meredith, the little substitute caretaker of her family. Then thinking also of Jasper and his other child, I suddenly saw them—all three Hilliards—as bruised, broken, and in desperate need of healing.—And in the darkness I cried out aloud to my dead friend: *"Rosalie, how could you?...How could you do this to them?"*...And then I cried out to the Lord, *"Please God, don't let Tristan hurt Meredith! I beseech you; don't let any of them be hurt any more than they already are!"*

CHAPTER SIX

The days flew by. All in all, it was a happy time, although there were a few incidents, which could have upset Meredith if it were not for her fine sense of humour. Every time I related one of these incidents to Doc Hugo, he would declare that the admirable manner in which she rose above these situations was further evidence that my fears concerning her ability to adapt to Tristan's life in Johannesburg were groundless. What neither he nor I realized, was that Meredith simply did not allow herself to be troubled by these incidents. Only matters concerning Tristan were close enough to her heart to touch her. Unless he was involved, she was able to console herself with the thought that she would not be in *Spoors-einde* for very much longer, and she had consequently made up her mind that, while she was still there, she was not going to be upset by anyone. As Tristan had insisted would be the case, when we had first discussed the pros and cons of village versus metropolis—and as he had probably impressed upon her—she was secure in the fact that people in the Golden City would be totally unfamiliar with her history, and that was all that mattered.

This proved to be a blessing when Mrs. van der Vuywer, probably the number-one gossip in *Spoors-einde*, came to see Doc one day, on the pretext that she had run out of the medication he had given her. Hardly had she seated herself in the waiting room, than she began to inquire among the other patients if it were true that the pretty young girl who had been seen coming and going from the doctor's house, was, in fact, the elder daughter of the notorious Professor Hilliard of *Blouspruit*. And naturally she had no difficulty in capturing the attention of everyone else who was waiting to see the doctor.

Thus encouraged, she confided that Trix Hoffman, the telephone operator at the Post Office, had told her (off the cuff, of course) that, about ten days previously, Jasper Hilliard had put through an emergency call to the doctor, during the recent illness of one of his daughters. Then another waiting patient conveniently recalled that he had noticed a man closely resembling the professor—whom he had not seen for years, of course—alighting from a car at our front door, so it was not long before two and two were put together! When Meredith happened to walk through the waiting room a few minutes later, on her way back from the pharmacy into the house, one patient significantly nudged another, and the whispering began. After that it was not very long before the news spread through the village like a veld fire!

One morning, Meredith was waiting for me in front of the butchery, when a woman hastened towards her, and quite brazenly began cross-examining her.... Did she not regret having missed so much schooling, and would it not be impossible to catch up? After all, education was so important!...Was she not afraid of cars when crossing the street?... Had *Spoors-einde* changed very much since she had last seen it?...Had she ever listened to a radio? And so on, and so on! Most of the people among whom we lived, were very nice; nevertheless, Merry had already learned to steel herself against all unnecessary provocation, for it was difficult for her to distinguish between those who inquired after her well-being out of the kindness of their hearts, and those who were just plain nosy. As a result the woman was dumbfounded to have this young person, whom she no doubt regarded as 'backward', chuckle, and reply politely, in her cultured, beautifully modulated voice: "We may well live on a farm, *Mevrou,* but not on another planet! Our electrical installation and electronic systems have been modified or upgraded by my father, to the extent that we probably enjoy far better reception at *Blouspruit,* than you do here!"

The interrogator first gaped at Meredith, incredulously, and then, at a loss for a suitable response, could only beat a hasty retreat.

I was so proud of Jasper's daughter! Proud of her nice manners, her presence of mind and her uncommon beauty. The encounter had left her visibly shaken, but what she had said was true. *Blouspruit* was not on another planet, and years of stimulating conversation with the kind of father with whom she was fortunate to have been blessed, had, in my humble opinion, indisputably elevated her above the lamentable small-mindedness of quite a few of *Spoors-einde's* inhabitants.

In spite of this, that particular encounter had made me realize that it was time she 'socialized', and, deciding that I had better begin with someone upon whom I could rely, I made an arrangement with Sally Vercueil, and took Meredith over to her house for tea. Sally, wife of the taxi operator, had been Doc's receptionist before me, and had, since Rosalie's death, been my true friend and confidante. I knew she could be trusted with the story that lay behind my seeking her help, and I had called Sally primarily because she was one person who could be depended upon to set Merry at ease, but before very long I would have reason to be grateful for having introduced the two of them. They took to one another immediately, and promoting that visit very soon proved to have been a wise decision on my part.

Late one afternoon, at the start of the third week, Tristan turned up unexpectedly, in a vehicle he had rented in Upington, and his explanation that he had been unable to hold out another day, made Meredith's expressive little face glow, and put a knowing smile on the face of Dr. Hugo. I gave Tristan supper, and then his uncle and I carried our after-dinner coffee out onto the stoep, where we sat in the brief African twilight, allowing the two young people to be alone; and, all the while we were out there, the dear old doctor could not repeat often enough how happy this relationship between his late brother's grandson and Jasper Hilliard's daughter had made him. Then, very early next morning, Tristan and Meredith set out for *Blouspruit*, and I hardly need to mention what that did to the tongues of those who saw the two of them driving through the village together.

Meredith took the opportunity to do a last check through her lab, tidying up what needed to be done, and taking leave of the servants, but the newly engaged pair could not have been on the farm for very long before we received a phone call from Jasper Hilliard. Doc Hugo, who happened to be at home, emerged from his study, beaming, to ask whether it would inconvenience me in any way if the professor and Susan returned with Tristan and Meredith, and had supper with us.

"There are a quite a few matters that we need to talk about together, now that the wedding day appears to be imminent," my exuberant employer explained, "and it is difficult to discuss all the details over the phone. It is not just that we have a limited time in which to do that, but, all the while Jasper and I were talking, I was very acutely aware, and I'm sure he must have been, too, that Trix Hoffman was eavesdropping. By tomorrow she will no doubt have repeated our conversation, verbatim, to our one-woman news service, Mrs. van der Vuywer—which means that the whole town will know every detail of whatever we are planning, in no time flat!"

This was the first time I had ever heard Doctor Hugo Connaught criticize anyone, but, where Tristan was concerned, he was like a broody hen. People were free to gossip as much as they liked, about him (as if he ever he gave them cause!), but Tristan was off limits. No one was permitted to make life difficult for him, or his bride-to-be!

"Of course it won't be inconvenient for me, Doc," I assured him. "But don't you think we should ask them if they would like to stay the night? Even if Susan and Professor Hilliard come in their own car, it's a long way for them to drive home again."

"That's just what I was thinking," he exclaimed happily. "In fact I have already told Jasper that you would not mind."

"What a good thing that I bought such a lovely roast this morning," I observed, expressing my thoughts aloud as I went out, immediately, to begin making preparations, and thinking with gratitude of how well stocked the linen cupboard in the doctor's house was. It was an unmitigated pleasure for me to be once again making ready for guests. I made a bed in the doctor's study for Tristan, prepared his (Tristan's) room for the professor, and had a divan put in Meredith's, for Susan. After that I quite ruthlessly robbed the garden—despite the fact that, in that part of the world you don't, without due consideration, pick such flowers as you've managed to grow—and fortunately I was still left with enough time to bath and to change into my favourite dress.

I was busy in the kitchen when the visitors arrived, and that was where Jasper, looking harrowed—for all the world as if he had not slept a wink the night before—found me. He set down a basket he had brought, laden with what my husband used to refer to as 'Kalahari bounty', and, after greeting me, he leant up against the kitchen counter, and said diffidently, in a low voice: "I remember how you and Mark used to like these in the old days, but maybe you should be warned, Biddy. I have an ulterior motive in bringing them for you today.

"There is a condition attached to this gesture, my dear, and being engaged in a new translation of Virgil's 'Aeneid', at this time, has made me think that perhaps I should caution you to be wary of 'Greeks bearing gifts', as the saying goes. I assure you, though, that this is not a parting gift, like the Trojan horse that was left at the gates of Troy! It is rather indicative of an urgent need for help! If there is an opportunity to do so while we are here, could you and I please have a confidential chat...some time...somehow...anywhere? I desperately need to ask a favour of you!"

I don't know why I had to go and get all flippant and skittish at that, but I was out of practice when it came to having good-looking, erudite men ask anything at all of me, and I suppose I was just a bit embarrassed. Whatever the case, I thanked him, but busied myself with carefully unpacking the basket, without looking at him. "I'd be pleased to oblige," was all I could think of to say after that, except for exclaiming how delighted I was with the gift of 'Kalahari truffles' or sand potatoes, which have a less pungent taste and smell than that of their French counterparts. They are used in small quantities to flavour other dishes, and their taste has been described as something between that of button mushrooms and avocadoes.

"I think I'm going to use these right, away," I told him, again thinking aloud. "They'll be excellent with what I am cooking...When would you like to talk, Jasper?"

"Well," he began hesitantly, "maybe we should just wait for an opportunity to present itself. Perhaps after dinner?"

"Very well. Let's do that," I said, and he went out to join Doc and the others, leaving me perplexed, and not a little apprehensive…

The compliments expressed that evening, concerning my dinner, were really flattering, and I could not help thinking how nice it would have been to be able to cook for a large family, always. Of course only for people who enjoyed their food, and—most important of all—could be relied upon to be there when dinner was ready! Poor Doctor Hugo! He was seldom if ever in time for any meal.

It was only after they had left the table and I had given Katryntjie instructions to take the coffee to the living room for them, that the family discussions began in earnest. I had tactfully decided to take my knitting to my bedroom, but Meredith would not hear of that. She came to fetch me and reprimanded me, frowning with mock disapproval. "Aunt Biddy, what are you doing, sitting here, when we need your counsel so badly? We can't begin until you are there!" Really these people were so good to me!

Apparently the problem with which they were wrestling at that stage, was the question of a suitable place for the wedding ceremony. Tristan refused point blank to be married in *Spoorseinde*, and Meredith—exhibiting surprising inflexibility—was equally determined that the ceremony would not take place in Johannesburg. She patiently explained that she would not be happy unless her 'family', which included her father, Susan, doctor Hugo and (very graciously) myself, were present. This, of course, suited Jasper, who had stipulated from the outset that he would not allow her to go away with Tristan, unless they were already married.

After having the matter thrashed out from every angle, it was Doctor Hugo who settled it by maintaining that the most suitable place would be Upington; bearing in mind that it was from there that the newly-weds would have to take their plane to Johannesburg, and also, the distance from there, back to *Spoors-einde,* was not so great that he would have to neglect his patients for more than a day. In addition, the professor and Susan would be able to return to *Blouspruit* immediately after a wedding luncheon at some nice place—preferably overlooking the Orange river—at which the bride and groom could also spend the night, making it possible for them to take the one and only flight back to Gauteng[3] next morning. This left us with only the details of the ceremony, itself, to sort out, and Tristan, having already obtained a special licence, undertook to begin making arrangements over the phone, as soon as the relevant places were open the next morning. He would then also make reservations for their flight to Johannesburg.

All the while these plans were being made, I kept a close watch on young Susan, whose face was as easy to read as litmus paper. Her expressions varied from despondency and stress—tight lips and eyes shining with unshed tears—to what might have been dread of the future, as the full impact of how her life was being changed, suddenly began to hit home, and I was vastly relieved when I saw her begin to lighten up. Concern about how she would cope without her big sister to mother her, gradually began to give way to the exciting, 'romantic' aspect of the situation.

"Merry told me about the lovely outfit she saw here in one of the shops," she cried, by this time blissfully swept up in the excitement. "Can't I also have a special dress for the occasion, Daddy?"

"Of course you shall have a new dress, my darling," the professor responded lovingly. "It's not every day one's sister is married...so, if Doctor Connaught would not mind putting up with us a little longer, and if Aunt Biddy does not feel that we are shamefully taking advantage of her kindness, perhaps she will go to town with you tomorrow, between consulting hours, and help both of you to choose something really, really special!"

We spent a happy rest of the evening together, until Doctor Hugo had to rush out to an emergency on a farm about twenty miles away. He flatly refused Jasper's offer to accompany him, and would probably have done the same if it had come from Tris—but I had to fight hard to repel the cynical thought that it would have been a nice gesture if the younger physician had at least tried! Susan then went off to her bedroom, so that the lovebirds could say goodnight to one another properly, and it was at this stage that Jasper gave me a knowing look, and a nod in the direction of the front door, indicating that we should go outside.

"Do you feel like taking a short walk before we turn in, too, Biddy?"

"I'd like that," I said, obligingly. "Just give me time to get myself a cardigan."

There were no streetlights in that part of town, but fortunately the moon provided just enough light to prevent my stumbling over any obstacles that might have impeded our progress. Nevertheless, Jasper gallantly offered me his arm, and we walked a short distance in silence, each busy with our own thoughts, until he suddenly stopped short and turned me around in the gloom, to face him.

"Biddy," he burst out, sounding desperate, as though the words were being wrung from him, "this is exceedingly difficult for me, but I need you to answer a question for me— and I beseech you to be completely candid, because I can't face any more hours of agonizing like I did last night! You were Rosalie's best friend and you knew her better than most....Do you think that, in reacting like this to Tristan's presence in our home, Meredith is manifesting the same weakness that caused her mother's downfall?...The thrill of the conquest?... The passionate need so easily triggered by the mere proximity of a stranger?— Do you think Meredith really loves Tristan, or is she simply fascinated by him? He choked as he uttered these words. "Scott Brady wasn't the first you know! I think that, for Rosalie, he was just the most compelling."

I swallowed hard, and my voice must have betrayed my consternation. "I can't believe that!" I exclaimed. "I'm stunned!...I would never have guessed! You poor man!...How awful for you, Jasper, and how well you have succeeded in hiding this...for all these years! But no! I don't believe for one moment that you need worry about Meredith. She is an extraordinarily level-headed girl with a remarkable sense of responsibility, and, inexperienced as she is in the ways of the world, there's no way she would be carried away to the extent that she would lose her head, or risk causing you even a single moment of unhappiness. Trust me. Even in taking this monumental step, she seeks to find some benefit to you and Susan in it!"

"Well, all I can say about that is that I like Tristan well enough," he admitted, "but I can't help wishing that, if my daughter had to become infatuated with the first young man she has known since she became a woman, it could rather have been Jordan Ashton! My one consolation is that they will be sharing his house!"

"Do you think that's all it is, Jasper? Infatuation?"

"What else can it be?" he demanded.

"Oh, I have no doubt that she loves him," I told him without hesitation. "I think she adores him! You only have to see the way her face lights up when he appears. At the same time, I also think she senses something 'lost' in him and feels a need to mother him the way she does Susie."

"But he's nearly seven years older that she is!"

"All the same...!" I hesitated, weighing my words. "That is not exactly to be taken as a black mark against him. Apparently she does not seem to think so, and he must have considered that!"

I could have said more. I was about to voice my concern about Tristan's motives, when I thought better of it. Jasper must, however, have guessed what I was thinking.

"An age difference can be very important. Things were never between Rosalie and me the way they were with you and Mark, Biddy. How I envied you the way you two were able to hug and kiss; to throw your arms around one another so spontaneously. Your freedom in displaying affection sometimes made me ache with envy..."

"Perhaps you were just a little too inhibited to try, Jasper," I suggested, as gently as I could.

He shook his head. "No. Everything about our marriage was so different!...Oh, my mind is in such turmoil! I keep asking myself whether it was my complying with her father's stipulation that, after our marriage, my wife and I remain at *Blouspruit*, and I carry on my work from there, that might have been at the root of our problems. She was like a caged bird! I had never been in love before, and would have promised anything in order to gain the old man's permission. Unfortunately I did not know then that, in the first place, Rosalie had persuaded him to let her go away to university, solely as a means of escape...

"I saw at once, of course, that she had absolutely no interest whatsoever in Classical Studies, but I never guessed that she had set her sights on me, the only single, available and comparatively eligible professor on campus, for the same reason.—To get away from *Blouspruit*! Even if I had known, I think I would still have married her. What lonely bachelor could have resisted that ethereal loveliness?... I was completely bowled over! Knocked sideways!...I deluded myself, Biddy!

"Now I am tormented by the realization that, precisely as my father-in-law did with us, I could well have inflicted a similar situation on my precious child. Because of what happened to Rosalie in the end, I insisted that Tristan marry her before I'd let her go away with him!—Was that not, in effect, imposing a similarly unfair restriction on them?"

How was I supposed to react? There was a long silence, during which I would willingly have given the poor man a hug to show him how sorry I was for him, but that might have startled him.

"Come," I said brightly, tugging at his arm instead. "What you need is a cup of hot chocolate. There's enough of a nip in the air to warrant that, and it might help you to sleep!"

But evidently he had not yet finished. He looked down at his feet, and cleared his throat before he found the courage to continue. "My dear friend," he said awkwardly, "I have tried to provide my girls with the best education it was in my power to give them. Academically I think I have equipped them— possibly better than most—but I have erred in leaving them unprepared for *life*!"

He cleared his throat again, nervously, and when he spoke again the words came haltingly. "They speak several languages fluently, are well versed in the classics, have unfailingly attained good marks in National and International examinations. Merry has become an above average musician; but...but...in one respect I have failed her miserably! She is to be married shortly, and she is still woefully ignorant of what that really entails...She knows nothing of the intimacy of the married state, because I have shrunk from the responsibility of discussing it with her!...I...I have never been able to talk to her about...about...well, about the facts of life!— Biddy, my girl does not have a mother to enlighten her, and you are after all, a nurse. Please, *please*, will you talk to her!"

I had to take a deep breath before I could answer him. "Jasper Hilliard," I asked then, with brutal directness, "What is it that you are trying to say to me?...Are you asking me to talk to your daughter about *sex?*"

We had reached the front of Doc's house by then, and, in the light streaming from the windows, I saw him nod.

"Biddy, why do you think I wanted to walk in the dark with you?...Do you have any idea of how difficult this is for me?"

"I do," I said. "And I will. But don't forget that her husband-to-be is a physician. I'm sure he will know how to approach the situation." I spoke as reassuringly as I could, while secretly I almost choked at the thought of how experienced that particular physician might actually be! Probably far too experienced for my liking...!

As planned, the girls and I went shopping next morning. Meredith chose a really nice blue 'two-piece' and a stylish little white hat, with white shoes and handbag to match, which, I thought, showed very good taste. Susan, as might be expected, went into raptures over everything she saw, and if Merry and I had not restrained her, she might have bought everything in sight!

Glowing from the heat, but blissfully happy, we arrived back at the house just after noon, and I quickly prepared lunch, as I knew that the professor was anxious to be on his way. The doctor had not yet returned from his rounds by the time they left, but I undertook to pass on their thanks to him.

It had already been arranged, in our absence, that, on the following Friday, we would all gather at Doc's house, from where we would go in convoy to Upington. Doc Hugo and Tristan would go ahead of us, in the latter's rented truck, and Jasper would follow in his, with Meredith, Susan and me. Later, returning home, via *Spoors-einde* after the wedding proceedings, there would be room in the professor's vehicle for Doctor Hugo, as well, seeing that Meredith would then be with Tristan at the hotel. And after all this had been sorted out, I was pleased to see that Jasper looked comparatively cheerful.

The next few days flew by in a flash. Almost too quickly. Katryntjie and I had secretly made a rich fruitcake, because I thought it would keep better than a sponge, and I had moments of panic while it still needed icing, but I did manage to get it done, and Meredith's delight when she saw it was a more than adequate reward.

"Aunt Biddy, you darling!" she cried excitedly. "A real wedding cake! And with these dear little silver horseshoes on it! Wherever did you get them?"

"*Ach*," I mumbled, embarrassed, "it's just a perfectly ordinary cake....Nothing special...I wanted a tiny bride and groom, too. In fact, I would have liked to have all sorts of lovely things on it, like, for instance, a red, icing sugar rose for you to take with you to Johannesburg as a memento, but I didn't know how to make one, and here in *Spoors-einde* one can seldom find anything worthwhile...!"

"It's perfect, just as it is!" she assured me. "I would not have wanted it any other way!"

On the Saturday evening before the wedding, Doc Hugo suggested that Tristan should take Meredith and me to the somewhat unpredictable film show in what passed for the 'Town Hall' on weekdays, the movie theatre, twice a month, and became the church for various denominations, in turn, on Sundays; but for some inexplicable reason, Merry's new fiancé went into a sulk, and refused point blank to go. I thought he could have had the decency to offer some sort of excuse, no matter how tame; however, when he remained obdurate, I began to wonder if it were not because he would have to drag me along with them. I went to my room and considered the situation for a moment or two, and then marched back into the living room to raise the subject once more.

"Tristan," I began, as innocently as possible, " I know that you said the matter was closed, and I don't want to nag, but if you or Doc would give me something for this nagging headache, I'd be willing to go with Meredith, in your place. I was unable to take her last time, too, and she has been dying to see a movie! She's been looking forward to it!

It was amazing to witness the change in his demeanour!

"You say she's never seen a film while she's been here with you?" was his unexpectedly eager response. "In that case, of course I'll take her! And if the magic *muti*[4] I'm about to give you, works, and you feel better, you must come with us!" With that, he went straight to Doc's pharmacy to fetch a painkiller for me, and I felt extremely guilty, as I did not have a vestige of pain!

We sat on the hard, wooden benches in the town hall, with Meredith between us, and I must say he could not have been nicer. This sudden, unpredictable change of attitude was completely beyond me. Clearly I had guessed wrong in concluding that he did not want me playing gooseberry. Only much later that night, as I lay on my bed staring at the ceiling, did an acceptable explanation come to me.

In dwelling on some of the events of the past weeks, I was able to recollect how morose he had become on the afternoon I suggested that Meredith stay with us for a month; how passionately he had protested that we would irrevocably change her. I believed, that, earlier that very evening I had found the key to a repeat performance of exactly the same kind of behaviour....Of course, I thought! How romantic and how sweet! He had wanted to be the first to introduce her to a new experience—even if it was only something as ropy as the *Spoorseinde* 'bioscope', which is how we referred to the cinema...

This discovery immediately saddened me. Instantly contrite, I was greatly moved by the thought that Meredith was able to engender such childlike sentiments in Tristan, and I promised myself never again to prejudge him so readily.

Then, on the Sunday, when I asked him to take us to church, the same thing happened. Only once he had determined that such an experience would be new to her, did he agree to accompany us. In the days before her family's life had been so tragically disrupted, her parents had usually fetched her home to the farm at weekends, which meant that she had never been able to attend a service before, and no sooner had Meredith mentioned that, than he seemed to perk up. When she added that, as a further consequence of spending most weekends at *Blouspruit*, she had only once or twice gone to Sunday school with friends he seemed instantly reassured, submitting the opinion that such memories could be discounted. They were not to be compared with the reality of 'church', as would be the case on this occasion. Actually, what surprised me the most, was that he was prepared to go at all!

Sitting on the same hard benches we had occupied the previous night, in order to watch 'Seeking Neverland', I could not succeed in restraining my wandering thoughts any better than I had during the film. It was a wonderful show, and I had loved the cast, but most of the time, like Tristan, I had been too busy watching the changing expressions on Meredith's face in the flickering light. On the Sunday my gaze was again riveted on the two beside me. What a singularly beautiful pair they were! I can find no other word to describe them, and somehow, for entirely different reasons, while feeling guilty that I was not following the sermon, I thought of their mothers. Then and there I made up my mind that I would insist that Tristan advise his parents of his impending nuptials.

Smiling to myself as I saw how attentively Meredith was listening to the sermon, I decided that she was equally as exquisite as Rosalie had been, but her face was free of the petulance and discontentment that had marred her mother's beauty. I got quite a lump in my throat when I saw that she had unselfconsciously taken Tristan's hand in hers, and it made me wonder whether, having somehow sensed his discomfort, she instinctively reacted as she would have done with her sister, in similar circumstances.

I suddenly felt a need to pray for Tristan as I found myself back in the maternity ward in Bethlehem, on the night he was born; and, recalling how joy at the birth of Thora's now so complex son, had been clouded that night by the absence of her exiled husband, I thought of all that Doc Hugo constantly repeated in defence of Tristan.—Tristan who was such an enigma!

Perhaps, in being secure in the adoration of this lovely, unspoilt girl, he now found balm for his wounded soul, I mused, briefly allowing my thoughts to wander.—But then, from all accounts, he had a multitude of women running after him in the City of Gold. How had it happened that it was to this arid place he would have to come to find a wife? Earlier mention of Jordan Ashton had made me think of Benjamin, his father, and of how vigorously Ben would have disputed the very possibility that coincidence could have had played a rôle in having Susan Hilliard take ill—precisely when Tristan happened to be in *Spoors-einde*!

I forced myself to listen again to what the preacher had to say about loving one's neighbour, and, for a very short while, permitted myself to return to that repentant, compassionate frame of mind, in which my heart went out to Thora's son— until, like a bolt of lighting, there came that awful moment of truth....*The definitive moment when all illusions were shattered...*

Tristan and I were again sitting with Meredith between us, as we had done the evening before, but this time I was at the end of the row, next to a wall against which I was able to lean comfortably, examining the two of them while trying to force myself to pay attention to the sermon. I had been acutely aware of all the eyes focused on us, earlier, as we had walked down the aisle. Until a proper engagement ring could be purchased, the signet ring with the Caduceus of Hippocrates, the symbol of medicine—a staff, with a serpent coiled around it—which Doc had given to Tristan upon his attaining his medical degree, was now on the middle finger of Merry's left hand (because it was much too large for her ring finger); and knowing that the young couple were the subject of a great deal of speculation, I involuntarily glanced across at Tristan.

His gaze was fixed on Meredith, and the expression in his eyes came as a shock.

As though he had also temporarily forgotten that we were supposed to be there specifically to heed the words from the pulpit, he was, as might be expected, intent only on watching her; but it was not with the affectionate examination of a lover that he was doing so. His attitude was rather akin to that of a researcher involved in a concentrated, scientific study. The cold, calculating manner in which he was examining the girl next to him, sent cold shivers down my spine...

She makes soap!

Somehow I was abruptly reminded of the remark made to that Mrs. Bradshaw who had called him from Johannesburg, and was made to recall the cruel derision hidden in his laughter.....In vain I tried to remind myself of my resolve never again to misjudge Tristan or harbour prejudice against him. At that moment I was suddenly enabled to see, with painful clarity and beyond any measure of doubt, what his plans for Jasper's precious daughter might encompass.....

When we came through the door of the church after the service, the return of the handsome physician from Johannesburg was hailed with some excitement. He was besieged by young women who had learnt to know him during his periodic visits with us; all clamouring for his attention! And, somehow, I did not find it strange that Merry, who was left standing alone until I could signal to her to join me, exhibited no sign of jealousy or animosity. This was simply because she had never learnt to resent anybody. It was rather as if she empathized with any woman who found her fiancé attractive, and was proud to have his presence acknowledged so enthusiastically.—And I could have wept for her as I saw that same fiancé taking careful stock of her reactions.

Tristan Connaught underestimated me. I think I have mentioned before, that I had not always been Doctor Connaught's receptionist or his housekeeper. In days gone by, I had, as the wife of the school principal, been regarded as a woman of some consequence in *Spoors-einde*. My husband had been an intelligent, learned man with whom both the literary scholar, Jasper Hilliard, and I had enjoyed many a discussion centred on the strengths and weaknesses of authors, and such works as had been assigned to his students as subjects for study. Although all three of us belonged to the generation to which the description of 'baby boomer' has now been attached, our tastes varied. I preferred narrative poetry, and, perhaps it was because I was younger, and had vivid memories of clinging to my pilot father as he went off to war, that I loved Ralph Nixon Currey's poetry so much. I could relate to the South African poet who was born here in the Northern Cape, in Mafeking (now renamed Mafikeng), nine years after Baden-Powell had founded the Boy Scout movement there, and, no matter how often I did so, I would become emotional every time I read Currey's 'Unseen Fire'.

"*The pilot sits among the clouds, quite sure,*
About the values he is fighting for...."

This was because I knew about '*the solid wall of heat*' that would come between those lines, and the conclusion...

"*We could not help them, six men burnt to death—*
I've had their flesh in my lungs all day!"

And I could also relate so well to the experience described in '*Ultimate Exile*'...

"*How wonderful to sit in the cinema*
And have the war brought to you..."

How often had I not done that? But, for me, the poet's words painted a picture more vivid than anyone can see on a movie screen, as he described where he was at the time, and the circumstances in which, he found himself—so very far from home!

"How lovely are the waters of Babylon (referring to the Euphrates river)

Removed these three thousand years, three thousand miles"...

There would follow the skirl of bagpipes, to stir me, and I could almost hear the beating drums, join in the search for booby traps, and hear the barrage of continuous shellfire...

"And all for two shillings, sit in your seat
And never feel the brazen heat of the sun,
And the daze, and the heat and the stun
Of the guns as they fire......"

But Mark and Jasper delved deeper into literature than sentiment, word pictures, or the attitude of the reader. They quoted Latin and Greek, paraphrased, and dissected, examined everything from Chaucer, to A.A. Milne and Doctor Seuss, and that Sunday, waiting outside for Tristan in the blazing sun after church, one of those thought-provoking conversations came back to me. My breath quickened as memory rekindled Mark's views on the subject of Bernard Shaw's *Pygmalion*, and Jasper's analysis of what had motivated Professor Higgins—as opposed to the character by the same name, in Greek mythology. And like a dash of icy water in my face, it hit me that Tristan might well be seeing himself, in the present situation, as some sort of modern-day Higgins.

Then, immediately moving from that memory to how Doc Hugo had reproached Tristan, more than once, for having left himself nothing for which to strive, an addendum to one of the younger man's favourite rejoinders came back to me.—"I don't need anything....I don't *want* to strive! But if I had more incentive to specialize, *I'd like to be able to dig into people's minds.*

I enjoy figuring out what makes people tick!"...And instantly my throat was constricted by fear. Had he found, in Meredith, a subject for some bizarre exercise? Did I dare suspect that he was prepared to marry Jasper's beautiful daughter for some cruel purpose known only to him?—And, if so, I was powerless to prevent this from happening!

CHAPTER SEVEN

For the next two days I was weighed down by depression and sick with anxiety. Small wonder that I developed a migraine. To approach Tristan was, of course, out of the question for, although I had played no small part in raising him, I was, nevertheless, only too conscious of the fact that I was, after all, merely the housekeeper—an employee in his great-uncle's house. As such, I hardly had the right to interfere in his, Tristan's, affairs, and when I could not get my suspicions out of my mind, I made several fruitless attempts at raising the subject with Doc. True to form, however, there was no way he was going to allow me to voice any dismal ideas or gloomy predictions.

"Oh, my dear Biddy," he said on one occasion, shaking his head reproachfully, "why do you always have to be such a pessimist? I believe that everyone has the right to be as happy as possible, but, to listen to you, life is nothing but a trap with hungry, eternally gaping jaws, lying in wait for the next unsuspecting victim!"

How hard I prayed for Jasper miraculously to make an appearance! Two days before the wedding I went as far as to put a call through to him *at Blouspruit*, but unfortunately, by the time I reached him, the others—namely Doc, Tristan and Meredith—were also in the room with me, and I could not voice the real reason for my eagerness to talk to him. I searched my mind almost frantically for an excuse to justify my forwardness in phoning, and, painfully aware of the questioning looks on the faces of those around me, I giggled like a fool, and came up with the most ridiculous reason. Stammering, I managed to mumble something about it being considered unlucky for a bride and groom to spend the night before their wedding, under the same roof.

"Yes, I know." I detected amusement in the deep, pleasant voice at the other end. "There are foolish people who believe in such nonsense, but, Biddy, as a Christian, surely you know that there is no such thing as 'luck!—Are you suggesting that I should fetch Meredith?—I can come and get her this afternoon if you like."

It distressed me to be displaying myself in such poor light and I took the coward's way out. "She is right here," I said hastily. "Why don't you ask her what she thinks?"

I handed the receiver to Meredith and, holding my breath, I was relieved to learn that she had been having similar misgivings, and had already said more or less the same thing to Tristan. However, contrary to expectation, it was Tristan whom she wanted to be sent off to *Blouspruit*. She, it turned out, wished to remain with us, and her reason for choosing to do this, was that she wanted to look fresh and immaculate when we left for Upington, which would not be the case if she already had one long trip behind her. To my further surprise I also heard her inform her father that Tristan was quite amenable. He had already announced his intention of leaving immediately after lunch, to spend the night with him and Susie, and wanted the professor to know how much he looked forward to a game of chess!

To my unspeakable relief, Tristan accordingly departed early that afternoon, but having been granted this golden opportunity for a frank talk with Meredith, I still could not bring myself to take advantage of it. My courage failed me once again, and I now depended on Jasper, hoping with all my heart that, in the short time that was left, he would somehow discern that Tristan's intentions were not what he would have us believe.

That evening I took the trouble to prepare a tasty cold supper, and it turned out to be quite a jolly meal because Doc Hugo, taking advantage of the fact that he had been blessed with a night free of calls, opened a bottle of champagne and gallantly proposed a toast to the young couple, having us drink to a long, happy, healthy and prosperous life for them. Not very long after that we went to our rooms, but, as it turned out, not to sleep! Or let me rephrase that. At least two of us were not destined to have too much rest that night.

I lay awake for the longest time after getting into bed. My heart was as heavy as lead, and I simply could not repel an overwhelming sense of impending tragedy. Eventually, at my wits end, I turned on the lamp beside my bed, hoping that if I read for a while, I would get drowsy. But I had no sooner taken up my book, than I became aware of another, unfamiliar sound. I listened intently. Yes, there it came again! Unmistakably a smothered sob, and it came from the bedroom next to mine. In the doctor's house, we were so often disturbed at night, that I had the drill off pat. Without hesitation, I reached for my robe, which was always conveniently left on a chair nearby, put on my slippers, felt for the flashlight I kept handy, and went on tiptoe to check on Meredith. Her room was in total darkness until I entered, and either becoming aware of my presence or roused by the beam of light I shone before me, she moved the pillow away from her face and raised a pair of tearstained blue eyes to mine. After turning on her light and carefully closing her door so that we would not disturb Doc, I moved forward quickly to sit down beside her on her bed, and put my arms around her.

"What is it my girlie?" I whispered concernedly. "It's a good thing your wedding isn't tomorrow. You wouldn't have made a very beautiful bride with those lovely eyes so red and swollen!" As that only made her weep all the more, I decided to let her have a good cry while I just held her and sympathetically stroked the damp hair away from her face. Finally she calmed down and we sat in silence for a time before I risked questioning her again. "Tell your Aunt Biddy all about it, sweetheart," I then said to her.

There was another long silence during which, surmising that she did not speak because she was finding it difficult to put the reason for her distress into words, I volunteered: "Are you nervous about Friday, my darling. Are you suddenly unsure of Tristan, or is it that you are no longer sure of your own feelings? Don't be afraid to tell Aunt Biddy, because I can easily arrange to have the wedding postponed..."

That was when she sat bolt upright. "No, no, Aunt Biddy! That is not the case at all! I am as sure of my love for Tristan as I am that the sun will rise tomorrow. Oh, no, no! Please don't talk about postponement! I can't wait to be his wife! It's just...just...!"

"It's just what? You don't have to be shy to tell me, lovey. Feel free to open you heart!...You can safely be quite candid," I said encouragingly.

She took my hand in hers and held it very tight. Still inhaling with deep, shuddering sighs, as a child will do after crying, she began shakily: "It's just that I am beginning to doubt that I am really worthy of him!—Shall I make him a good wife, Auntie?"

I, of course, wanted to respond instantaneously to this, but I could see that she was not done. "Ever since he left here this afternoon," she resumed, "I have been doing some serious thinking, and many things have become very clear to me. All the time I have been here with you and Uncle Hugo, I have felt safe and so very much at home that I had begun to congratulate myself on my 'adaptability'.—I put it like that because I can't think of a better expression at the moment.—I have been able to look forward to the new life that awaits me, with complete self-confidence, but dear Aunt Biddy, tonight I am suddenly *sooo* scared!

"At first I attributed my agitation to the fact that the venture into the great unknown is becoming so close, but now I know, that I only felt safe here because of *you*! You have been here to remove every possible thorn from my path, and my father and Susan—with the support and encouragement that they represent—have been just a phone call away. But soon I shall be leaving behind everything that is familiar to me! I am about to take an irrevocable step, and suddenly the colossal unfamiliarity of all that awaits me, has become absolutely terrifying!"

I could understand this so well. My heart bled for the child, and I thought it would make her feel better by my saying, "But you'll have Tristan at your side, sweetheart. Are you not convinced that you can depend on him?"

"Of course I can! I realize that. But that is not the consolation you would expect it to be. It is, in fact, precisely because the very thought that he will be there to observe any mistakes I make, and have to try not to flinch when I blunder, that I am so unhappy. Can't you see that, Aunt Biddy?...I did not mind that you were there when people tried to belittle and humiliate me, or went out of their way to make me feel like some kind of freak. I knew that my shame was not your shame, because you were not directly and personally involved. But how will Tris feel when he senses that his friends are laughing up their sleeves at his wife? Won't he blush with mortification? Won't he come to regret the very day he met me?"

No matter how hard she strove for self-control, her lower lip had again begun to quiver, and suddenly bursting into another storm of weeping, she threw her arms around my neck, and surrendering to sheer despair, she laid her head on my breast. "Oh, Aunt Biddy," she besought me, "come with me, I beg of you! Please come with me on Friday, and help me through the trials of the first few weeks! If I had a mother, she would do that for me—and you have become like a mother to me!"

I gasped with astonishment and was temporarily robbed of speech. Whatever could have possessed the child to ask such a thing of me? Not that I could not readily have gone with her! It was years since I had last taken leave, and Doc was forever going on about how it was high time that I had a holiday....But to accompany newlyweds on their honeymoon! To become an intruder in Tristan's home? The entire prospect was ridiculous!

"You know there is nothing I would not do for you, dear heart," I began slowly, uncertainly, "but now you are talking recklessly. Tristan would have an absolute fit!"

"He won't! He won't!" she cried, with the confidence of renewed hope in her voice. She sat up and regarded me with mounting excitement. "How can he refuse, once I convince him of how badly I want this? If he truly loves me—and I know he does—he will want only what is best for me, and he will surely have to concede that it will make things much easier for me, in the beginning, if I can have someone of my own to ease me into what could otherwise be an intimidating experience." The soft, rounded arms tightened lovingly around my neck, to weaken my resolve. One by one my objections faded into the background. All my life I had longed for a daughter, and Meredith was as close to being that daughter as I could ever find.

"You're being far too hasty, Merry-love," I cautioned, calling her, for the first time, by the pet name which was always accorded her in my thoughts. "You must give me time to think!...I...I..."

In vain I tried to sound cautious. She detected my weakening and grasped at it like a drowning person seeking a secure footing.

"I knew you would not let me down! First thing tomorrow morning I shall phone Tris, and don't be concerned about Uncle Hugo, either. I'll fix things with him, too, and I'll make him a promise not to keep you away from here for too long!

"Oh, I do feel so much better now," she sighed contentedly as she climbed back into bed. "I expect to sleep very well indeed!" She was already sounding drowsy as I pulled the blankets up over her shoulders, and she sighed blissfully as she snuggled down once more, this time clearly at peace.

I kissed her softly on the forehead and before I reached my own bedroom she was already sound asleep, of that I am convinced. But don't ask how I, Biddy, passed the rest of that night! One would need to have too vivid an imagination to get an idea of the frantic thoughts that kept churning around in my head! Not only did I dwell uncomfortably on the unfeasibility of what Meredith desired of me. I was tortured by the recognition of my own moral cowardice. I could have kicked myself! If my desire was to thwart Tristan, and prevent this marriage, I had not only procrastinated....Against my better judgment I had actually helped to promote it!

I was aware of the dark circles under my eyes when, limp and exhausted, I arose from my bed next morning. I felt as though the whole world rested on my shoulders. I felt like someone on the way to the gallows, dragging an innocent child along with me. It was my firm intention to go straight to Meredith, the moment she opened her eyes, and break it to her, very firmly, that I found it impossible to comply with her request; but I was already too late! She must have been sitting in the passage, waiting for me to emerge, because I had hardly opened my bedroom door, when she hastened towards me— with the news that she had apprised Tristan and her father of our decision, and that Doc had readily given his blessing! My friend, Sally Vercueil, who had been his receptionist before she retired, and I came on the scene, would temporarily return, and Doc had solemnly promised to arrange for meals at the lodging house nearby.

And, after all this, the present situation had been revised! No longer anxious about the future, and no longer apprehensive, it seemed that Meredith had relented, was missing Tristan too much, and now wanted him close to her. Superstition had evidently taken a back seat, the *Blouspruit* folks would return with him, after lunch, and I would have to spend every available moment packing! My only consolation when the ramifications began to sink in, was the knowledge that Jordie Ashton would also be in Johannesburg and, if the need arose, I could turn to him for guidance...

***

Friday came all too soon, and, before we knew where we were, Tristan, looking every bit the suave bridegroom in his immaculate (and no doubt very expensive) suit, and Doc, the dignified and impressive stand-in for the bridegroom's father, set off after a quick, very early breakfast, in advance of the rest of us. Jasper and Susan had also spent the previous night under Doc's roof, as arranged, for, to have embarked on their journey from *Blouspruit* would have made the day too arduous. It was a blessing, Jasper and I agreed, that both vehicles were air-conditioned, for we had a long journey ahead of us, and certainly did not want to be incapacitated by heatstroke before we reached our destination.

The departure of the Connaughts gave Merry a chance to change into the outfit that Tristan had not yet seen, and provided me with an opportunity to make sure that I had not overlooked any details that would bother me later. Meanwhile Jasper was able to say a last few, intimate words to his daughter (who looked stunning), before shepherding her, and her excited bridesmaid, to his 4x4, from where he called out to me to say that they were waiting for me; adding some rueful comment about wishing that he was in a position to drive the bridal party in a more glamorous vehicle than Kalahari travel demanded.

Finally, I, too, was dressed and ready to go, and having given Katryntjie some superfluous instructions for the care of Doc, I was already on the front steps, about to join the others, when the telephone rang, and running back, I was just in time to respond to a call from Jordan Ashton.

"My goodness you're up early, Jordie!" I exclaimed breathlessly. "The sun has only just risen.—I'm sorry you have missed Tristan," I told him, "but I can tell you that he's on his way, and should be home with you in Bryanston by lunch-time tomorrow. Unfortunately I have to rush, dear, so I can't talk too long now, but, as I'll be seeing him in an hour or two, I can give him a message, if you like."

"That would be great, thank you, Auntie Bid. It's a relief to know that. As early as it might seem, I already have a waiting room crowded with patients down at the clinic, because I'm going away for a few days, and I'd appreciate it if you would just let Tris know that I shan't be at home when he gets back... I have waited as long as I could, for him to return, but now I need to join my folks in Nelspruit. There are some urgent decisions to be made...

"Please also tell Tris that I have been blessed to find a locum. I explained my predicament to Tony, Antoinette Verwey, who is already there, and she happened to mention that Reggie Seymour, Aunt Felicity's adopted son—you must remember him from Bethlehem—is back from Indonesia, where he has been helping out since soon after the Tsunami, and he confesses that he is more than ready to get back to normal, general practice for a while! I hope to see all the most urgent cases in Sandton today, too, as I am obliged to leave him and Tristan to take care of my patients until I get back!

"My dad's jet is parked in his hangar at the Nelspruit airport, and he has been waiting for a phone call from me, to let him know when to come and get me; but, I've decided to go by car instead of flying, which is why I plan to make such an early start. An old friend of ours, Matthewis Marais, arrived unexpectedly from Canada last night, and because it is a long time since he has been back in South Africa, I thought he'd enjoy seeing something of the country again, so I'm picking him up in Kempton Park early tomorrow morning, and will drive him to Nelspruit.

"I recall hearing your father mention him, long ago." I said. "So he did emigrate to Canada?"

"Yes. He is the son of Uncle Willie Marais, who met my father on his arrival nearly thirty years ago, to become the very first friend Dad ever made when he came to this country, and they're still like brothers! Matt, as you might recall, Auntie, is the elder of the Marais sons, the one his family used to call 'Mannetjie' (little man) long ago—and he is the one who lost a leg during the Angolan war....Like me, he is going to the Lowveld to provide his father with some moral support, and perhaps to give them the benefit of another opinion. Now the two of us will have plenty of time to talk along the way."

I smiled affectionately to myself; amused at the way this American boy had so easily picked up the South African practice of referring respectfully to any adult older than himself, as 'uncle' or 'auntie'.

"Aside from the main topic to be discussed in Nelspruit, I hope to have an opportunity to question Matt on a project in which he is involved in Canada. There is much talk in North America about 'Post Traumatic Stress Disorder' resulting from the Gulf War, which for you, as a former nurse, should not be difficult to understand, Auntie Bid. In Aunt Minnie de Beer's day, it was probably called 'Shell shock", because it was believed that the noise of exploding shells caused it.

"Matt has become very interested in what a retired Canadian general, Roméo Dallaire, now the Honourable Senator Dallaire, himself a victim of the disorder, has had to say about this, since having been in Rwanda. General Dallaire has said openly that the impact of the trauma of Rwanda physically affected his brain, and put him in a state where there was no capability left of any desire for life, or any desire to even consider life....It is good to read that the general has improved with treatment, as I have a patient, a veteran of the Angolan/South-West African conflict, whom I believe might well be suffering from something similar. That might well be what lies at the root of his problems."

"But that was *years* ago, Jordie! Surely he can't still be affected by that?"

"I don't know so much, Auntie. Not since reading Lieutenant General Dallaire's book, '*Shake hands with the devil'*. He has become a hero to Matt, who campaigns on behalf of Canadians who might have been similarly affected by the fighting in Afghanistan, and he first made me suspect what might lie at the root of my patient's problems. Because of this, I have been emailing Matt for some weeks. I need to refer this man to exactly the right kind of specialist, and it would be great if I could also interest Tristan in him."

"Yes," I commented dryly. "Our friend, Tris, does talk a lot about being interested in 'what makes people tick', doesn't he?"

"He does," Jordan said, and I could hear the grin his voice. "However, he consistently maintains that I have a screw loose, myself!"

"See you drive carefully, Jordie," I cautioned, before he rang off...."And please, I don't want to be nosy, but you have me worried. What is wrong that your respective families need you so urgently? I hope they are all okay... Your mother and sister?"

"Everyone seems be fine, thank you," he responded, "although my father is worried sick about my mom's one eye, which is very bloodshot. We all know how absolutely fanatical he can be about her eyes.—They use a commercial airline between the USA and Britain, but one reason he keeps his own plane in England, and flies Mom out here, personally, is that he is terrified that the insecticide that has to be sprayed in commercial aircraft between Johannesburg and Heathrow on the return journey, will irritate them.

"Well, apparently there is some roadwork going on between the Nelspruit airport and *Beauclaire*, and unfortunately, in driving over it yesterday, some white, powdery stuff—which my dad thinks is lime—was sucked into the car when the window was briefly opened. Now he is almost beside himself with worry because the eye has been bothering her ever since.... He does concede, however, that her eyes are invariably irritated by the dry air on planes.

"That's another good reason for my driving to Nelspruit. I'll take a look at her and, if necessary, having the car, I can bring them both back with me to see Doctor Fisher. He's her eye specialist when she is in South Africa, and his rooms are in Sandton City, not too far from mine. Chadwick Fisher is an excellent guy! He, was recommended to my mom, after her cornea transplants, by Sir Colin Foxcroft in London.

"But, Auntie Bid, I digress. That's not the reason for the 'crisis' talks at *Beauclaire*. They have something to do with land reform, about which, in this country, the wrangling never seems to stop. If it's not about financial constraints, it's about the lack of human capacity on the ground, and the fierce resistance from white farmers as well as frustrated blacks. We, for example, need to make some formidable decisions, as a family, about what is to happen, not only to *Beauclaire Estates,* but also to the land next to it, on which the Ashton 'showroom' facility is situated, and that's where Mannetjie and his father come into the picture. Uncle Willie is the Managing Director of Ashtons' in South Africa, and Matt is attached to the Canadian plant. Both will be affected to some degree by our relinquishing our claims to the relevant properties."

"Is that also why Antoinette is there?"

"Yes. Her grandfather, Bert Mostert, has already signed over his assets, which has devastated my father, especially as it was Uncle Bert who gave Dad his first job there—which is why I have 'Albert' as a first name. Tony and her husband have come to help her grand-parents decide where they want to go from here!"

"What a difficult situation in which to find yourselves!" I exclaimed sympathetically. "I recall reading a report some time ago, in one of the newspapers we get here, that the government has vowed to transfer thirty percent of white-owned land to blacks, either through land redistribution, land restitution or land tenure, by 2015. Evidently they, the government, paid sixty-three million South African Rands to buy the Mataffin farm from the Halls, the former 'white owners', as the paper put it. That's a pretty significant step. Mataffin has been an institution in the Lowveld, for as long as I can remember—since before I was born, I'm sure!"

"I having been reading about that, too, and I also read that many farms owned by whites who have no intention of leaving them, are still under review. The transfer of Mataffin to the Mdluli clan is said to be an excellent example of how successfully white managers and the new black owners can work hand-in-hand, but many white farmers are terrified that South Africa will end up being a second Zimbabwe!"

"How can that happen, Jordie?"

"Perhaps because, so far, only three, of the thirty percent of that promised land, has been transferred from whites to blacks, and already there's not enough money in the land reform budget to buy out all the farmers on their list. A recent report has it that the budget will have to increase at least four-fold to reach that target. We can't overlook the 'Landless People's Movement' which carried out that 'No Land, No Vote' campaign in advance of the national elections, and, to add fuel to the fire, more and more whites are dying in violent attacks in rural areas!"

"That's true," I agreed. "And we can't overlook the squatter problem, either. No one should know that better than you, Jordie!"

Caught up in this discussion about matters which were constantly on the minds of so many people in our country, we had talked far longer than we had intended to, and, looking around to see Jasper patiently waiting in the doorway for me, I felt guilty and made a gesture of apology, but he waved it aside, shaking his head; and his smile as he did so, signalled that he was not impatient.

I nodded gratefully; however, as anxious as I now was, to get off the line, I could not let Jordie go until I had prepared him. "I suppose we must all be making tracks, but, before you ring off, I should tell you..." I began, but realized that he was still speaking...

"By the way, Auntie Bid, how's the little Hilliard girl?"

"Susan? Fine, thanks. As a matter of fact, she and her sister are also on their way to Upington, as are her father and I. Doctor Hugo and Tristan left earlier. I was about to tell you that you are about to be invaded....Tristan is getting married today—to Meredith, Susan's elder sister—and both the bride and I will be coming to Joh'burg with him after the wedding. I hope you don't mind!"

PART TWO

CHAPTER ONE

Benjamin Ashton had long been in wholehearted agreement with the Afrikaans poet, C. Louis Leipoldt, who had declared October to be the most beautiful month of the year. In Ben's opinion, here on *Beauclaire,* his South African citrus farm, it indisputably was. There was no month he loved more, and no other place on earth as dear to his heart as this home, set amid orange groves and surrounded by Bougainvilleas, Flame trees, Jacarandas and Poinsettias. He was grateful for his gracious mansion, *Bentleigh,* on Long Island, and for the other *Beauclaire,* a plantation left to him by his grandmother, in Louisiana, but this was where he was most content. This place where he had only to stand on his front stoep in order to look down, as far as the eye could see, upon the green and gold glory of his orange trees, the scarlet of Flamboyant and Bottle Brush, the yellow Bird of Paradise, crimson Erythrina, and the 'salmon', rose pink and white Oleander, interspersed by a riot of sky blue, Duranta.

It was a glorious Saturday afternoon, the air was heavy with the perfume of orange blossom, he was sitting under his much-loved Syringa tree—surrounded by most of the people he loved best in the world—and yet, notwithstanding his gratitude to the God who had given all this to him, his heart was heavy. His wife, Amy-Lee, the darling of his heart, must have sensed this, for she reached out to take his hand in hers. She, too, had precious memories of this place. Here, lying on a rug in the shade of the gigantic tree, she and Ben had often come to relax, side by side, in the afternoons. If she craned her neck, now, she could see the French doors leading into the bedroom that had been hers when she first arrived, and she recalled the day when, before she had regained her eyesight, she had misjudged the distance, and, to Ben's consternation, had fallen into the Poinsettia beside the step. That was the day that he had come very close to confessing that he was in love with her! The railings beside the steps were the same ones he had installed that very night before he would go to bed.

Not since the *braai*[5] to celebrate Ben's acquittal, nearly thirty years ago had so many people gathered here on the lawn. That barbeque had been organized by the first people he had come to know upon his arrival in Nelspruit: the motherly, once indefatigable and feisty, and now very frail Mrs. Nolte, and Mercia, her daughter...They had immediately taken to the likeable and very hungry American stranger when he walked into their establishment one day, in search of lunch, and they had grown to love 'Ash' Ashton as though he were a member of their family.

Glancing across at them, Ben realized that what had befallen them had contributed to his despondency. Nolte's Tearoom had become the regular meeting place for him and his friends, whenever he went into town from the farm. Working together as a team, the mother and daughter had, without a doubt, provided the people of the town—among them John Myburgh, the magistrate, whose wife did not much like to cook—with a warm and welcoming place to visit. There Mrs. Nolte, astonished to find that her 'Handsome Yank', as she referred to him, would even know what they were, had taught him, Ben, how to make *vetkoek*[6]!

Only once, since the death of Mr. Nolte, had the tearoom been known to close on any day other than Sunday, and that was because the owners wanted to be in court to support their *protégé*, Benjamin Ashton. Surely no one who was in court that day, would be able to forget how Mrs. Nolte, already incensed at the very thought that anyone would need to prove the integrity of her favourite customer, and no longer able to restrain herself, had called out to the Bench at one stage: "*That's true, Johnny! I can vouch for that!*"...And now Nolte's Tearoom was only a memory. A memory clouded by bitterness—exacerbated by the realization that that was because it was symbolic of so much else that distressed him.

He remembered a time when there were metal detectors at the entrances to public buildings and shopping malls on the Witwatersrand, which was now a part of '*Gauteng*'. A time when ladies had their purses checked, the banks first installed the plate-glass 'cages' which still existed, and through which only one client at a time could leave or enter. Small businesses began to keep their doors locked, and customers had to identify themselves before the doors would be opened to them. But, not since he had returned to South Africa in 1988, and, driving down a Kempton Park street, had seen gaping holes instead of store fronts, and bombed-out buildings without glass, had he been as shattered as he was when he saw what had become, not only of the building in which Nolte's Tearoom had been housed, but of the entire street!

This was not due to bomb damage, however. After the Nolte's, having been robbed twice at knifepoint, had moved out, the building had simply, systematically and wantonly, been vandalized. Broken bricks were strewn across the sidewalk, garbage littered the curb, and all around him he noticed similar signs of neglect and dereliction. Now he could understand why

Antoinette Verwey's father, the Rev. Doctor Peter Crawford, had been so disheartened when, after a service, he emerged from the beautiful church of Saint Boniface, in Germiston, and was confronted with what was left of the once highly-rated hotel across the street, and of what used to be regarded as a prestigious apartment building, opposite it. Ben was shocked to learn that the formerly excellent Carnegie Library in that city, was now only another fine building reduced to 'slum' status.

He could have taken this sort of thing in his stride in parts of New York, or even San Francisco, but evidence of such unjustifiable destruction, *here*—in this town that he had come to look upon as home—had stunned him!

Sitting opposite her parents, in the circle on the lawn, Zhaynie Verwey's eyes misted, and an affectionate, indulgent smile tugged at the corners of her lovely mouth. Studying the changing expressions on her father's face, it was not difficult to conclude that his thoughts, mirrored there, were not happy ones. She never ceased to marvel that this should be so. Inscrutability was essential in achieving success in business, one was told, and yet this awesome man—who from the time he was in his late teens, had writhed every time the admiring media referred to him as 'The Kid Tycoon'—was as transparent as a child. Perhaps, she reasoned with herself, that very transparency was his greatest asset. With Benjamin Ashton, people said, you got what you saw, and no matter how determined he was, or how high he set the odds, you knew that they would be fair, and that he would not lie to further his own ends.—How, she wondered for the umpteenth time, had he ever kept up the charade that was played out for so long, here in Nelspruit, before his true identity was revealed?

And seated next to Zhaynie, Phyllis de Klerk's thoughts were running in the same direction. Smiling mischievously to herself, she suddenly called out to Ben: "Hey, nutcase! Nobody died, you know! You've weathered worse than this before, Ash, and you're still around to tell the tale!"

Ben, who could not help smiling upon being addressed in the familiar, pert manner, brightened visibly, and an almost sheepish grin spread slowly across his face, as memory took him back to the first time he had heard her say this to him. "You're right, Phyl. I—we all—still have a great deal to be thankful for, and I thank you for reminding me!"

Zhaynie giggled. "Auntie Phyl, why do you always call Daddy 'nutcase'? He doesn't seem to mind, though?"

"That began, quite spontaneously, on the day he wanted so desperately to question Sir Colin Foxcroft about your mother's injuries, and, via the party line which existed then, I heard him complaining to our friend, Doctor Evans, that, if Foxcroft could not be available earlier, by the time he, Ash, was able to reach the great man in London, our local telephone exchange would be closed. I was the operator on duty that evening and..."

"Please let me tell her!" Ben, overhearing her, intervened. "I remember so clearly!...Word for word, what you said to me was: *"Hey, nutcase! What makes you think I wouldn't come back especially for you?'*...You've been a good friend to us all, Phyl, and I will never forget that!"

"*Ach!*" came the prompt rejoinder. "Kind as it is of you, to say that, my dear Mr. Ashton, you have omitted the best one. The day I called you a nutcase for a very different reason. Do you remember? I said I thought you were completely mad! That you—who actually wanted me to help you keep the secret that you were Nelspruit's Bill Gates, on the quiet—had probably chucked aside a Rolls Royce or two to go riding around Nelspruit in that *tjorrie*[7]! That old *bakkie*[8] that was falling to pieces!— And I was right, wasn't I?"

Ash nodded, smiling ruefully. How many good people he had come to know and love in this town! Memories came crowding back, and his spirits lifted as he was momentarily cheered, especially in remembering the verbal exchanges over the years, with the comically predictable Phyllis.... Phyllis, the telephone operator who had known everyone's business and did not mind their being aware of it. His smile widened as he thought of the night when, talking to his doctor and fellow golfer, Dick Evans, he had stayed on the farm line too long for her liking, and Phyllis had cut in with: *"Hey, you two...make it snappy! I've got a date!"*

"Do you still think my father is the best-looking man you've ever seen, Auntie Phyl? Zhaynie asked, a few minutes later, when she found an opportunity to whisper in Phyllis's ear. "Before last night, I hadn't seen him for six months, yet I still think so—even if I adore my Dominic—but then I'm biased!"

"Honey," came the conspiratorial murmur, in reply, "long ago your mother asked me to describe Ash Ashton to her and, without having to stop and think, I said, using one of your American expressions, 'He's just drop-dead gorgeous!' And thirty years later I have no reason to revise that!"

"They are a beautiful pair, aren't they?" Zhaynie observed affectionately. "In so many ways. I've heard them do it all my life, but I still love the way they murmur to one another in Louisiana French. A dear old man called Jenkins, who used to be our butler at Bentleigh, and who knew them both when they were little more than babies, told me that they had communicated that way from the time they first learnt to speak. That's why I am called Eugenie—Eu-*zhaynie*—and not Eu-*jeanie*. It was my French grandmother's name, and my great-grandmother's, before her.

"My father made a joke once, about sleeping with Mom before they were married, and the very prim Jenkins hastened to explain that, as toddlers, they had frequently been put down together, when being cared for, in turn, by their respective and equally adored maternal grandmothers."

"How sweet!" Phyllis remarked wistfully. "I wish the history of my parents could have been like that. But that only makes it harder to understand why yours had to be so unnecessarily separated later—when one only had to look at them to sense the mutual adoration."

"I know," Zhaynie responded. "I get quite weepy when I think about it. My mother is afraid of nothing when Dad is around, but it must have been terrifying for her to lose her eyesight when she was alone like that in London. We talked about that once and he agreed. 'I guess I knew her before she was born,' he said.... 'She frequently stayed with us in my grandmother's house, and one of my earliest memories is of this tiny, frightened little thing running into my room and climbing into bed beside me, during a very bad storm!'

"When he said that he had known her before she was born, that was more or less true. *Gran'mère* Beauclaire, my great-grandmother, must have been pretty enlightened for her day, for she did not hedge when he asked about the bulge in my Mom's mother's tummy. She explained that it was a baby, and he could not wait for it to come out.—He was three years old, and apparently asked every day, 'Has it come yet?' and, when 'it' did, he adored it!...I would like my own baby to look like Dominic, of course, but I would certainly not complain if he or she resembled either of my parents."

"Ash is concerned about your baby being born here, isn't he, Zhaynie?" Phyllis asked, suddenly very serious once more.

"Yes. I know he is. And now he has Dominic also worried about whether it wouldn't be advisable to travel, while the going is good, and for me to have the baby in the States. There would be plenty of room for us, and for as long as we like, at *Bentleigh,* or even down on the Louisiana plantation where—while we decide upon the future—we would have the entire place to ourselves, and still be surrounded by people whom we love. I guess that what my men folk are thinking is that, wherever we choose to go, over there, if ever the need arose, our child would someday be eligible for American citizenship.

"This thing with the Noltes has hit Dad hard. Personally, I suspect that, ever since he made the difficult decision to go back to the USA all those years ago, and to take control of Ashtons' once more, he has cherished a secret ambition to retire here. Now, with his complete—and well-placed—confidence in my big brother, James, who recently agreed to take over as the Chairman of the Ashton' Board, the realization of that dream seemed to be in sight; but, while that opportunity could well be open for my dad, he has been sadly disillusioned by what he has seen here...even in this short space of time! To make matters worse, even before he arrived back in South Africa, he had already been shocked to hear from my other brother, Jordan, that one of his, Jordie's, patients had been the victim of an armed robbery, right in front of a friend's house, and inside her 'secure' property. She had taken her friend shopping and was dropping her off when it happened.

"There was the usual heavy security—electric gates requiring a remote control for access—but even then, even within those massive gates, it was not safe. The moment the car doors were opened, the robbers were there, holding guns to the ladies' heads....All their keys were stolen—including those of their car- and house-alarms—plus their bags, all documentation, such as credit cards, as well as their mobile phones and jewellery. There were three robbers, all were young blacks, and I shudder to think what would have happened if the friend's little seven year-old grandson, who witnessed the whole thing, had not had the presence of mind to run into the house and find his mother, who then alerted the security company.

"The robbers must by then have realized that there were other people in the immediate vicinity, and, becoming hasty to leave, did not take Jordie's patient's car. However, the entire computer of the car, plus keys had to be replaced, costing thousands. Every lock in her house has had to be changed, because the stolen ID documents show the address of the residence to which the robbers would have been provided easy access. The battle to replace her documents, credit cards etc., has been a nightmare, she told my brother when she came to see him about a myriad of problems related to stress. He has since had to send her for counselling!"

Phyllis was unusually silent for quite some time after that. She had known Benjamin Ashton too long, and too well, to accept that what had happened to Jordan's patient was enough to drive him, Ash, out of South Africa. She did not believe, either, that it was entirely the fact of the Nolte's having been held up at knifepoint that could have had the effect on him that she was witnessing. He would be shocked, perhaps, or angry; sympathetic and solicitous, but not as desolate as he appeared to be. He would pray for them for healing of those frightful memories, and for their protection in the future; and he would do everything in his power to make as much as possible, right again for them—as well as for Mercia's husband, Nico.

All the while she was pondering this, something was stirring in her memory, and, all at once, she found that she could recall another, classic occasion on which Ash had been similarly crushed...

Ash Ashton had been in countries where even genocide was common. He had seen the most terrible violence in the rest of Africa, the Middle East, and even in his own country—but clearly, what he deplored most, even more than the violence and the bloodshed, was the evidence of man's basic 'inhumanity to man'!...Cold-bloodedness afflicted him as a personal hurt.... Letting the rest of mankind down was, in his estimation, an offence tantamount to doing the very same thing to him, personally. He would instinctively regard that as an insult to his Maker. A sword in the very heart of the One who had paid a terrible price for the privilege of being able to plead: *"Love one another, as I have loved you!"*

Somehow Phyllis found the words to convey these thoughts to Ben's daughter, using, as an illustration, an incident which had occurred about a week before her own marriage, and one which had involved the long-time retainer at *Beauclaire*, Phineas Mohubedu. It had been especially difficult for Ash because he had learnt to regard both Phineas, his *Bapedi* friend, who had recently been elevated to the status of a bishop in his church, and his wife, Sarah—both long-time employees—almost as surrogate parents, and the revelation of a hitherto unsuspected facet of the man's personality had shaken him to the core. It had depressed him immeasurably.

The first the Ashtons heard of the 'bishop's' assignment was on their return from a trip which had already taken a toll on each of them individually. Just as Ben was helping Amy-Lee out of the car, Phineas, sprouting the beginnings of a beard, came around the corner and hailed them eagerly. *"Dumela, Baas! Dumela kleinmiesies!"* ("Good day, baas! Good day little missus!"). Immediately after that, they were stopped in their tracks as this effusive salutation was followed by the decisive announcement: *"Ntshwarele* baas," ("Excuse me, baas") I go home now! I just wait for you to come." And, pointing to his 'church truck', "I go on the *chech lorry*...I go now!"

Only then was their attention drawn to the sight of the familiar vehicle parked near the servants' quarters, and judging by the smoke issuing from the back of it, the driver was indeed preparing for imminent departure.

"Just a minute!" Ben exclaimed. "What's this all about? How long will you be gone, and what's the hurry?"

"I go," Phineas stated calmly, "because much trouble in my village. Last week, and also this week, lightning strike many *kayas,* (huts) and now four people dead.....I go *pakisa* (fast) baas, to see which man he has the bad eye, before more trouble..."

And Ben was so tired and so bewildered, that he could only respond: *"O be le le bolokegilgo, Phineas!* ("Have a safe journey, Phineas!") I hope you are successful!"

"Before they had left on their trip," Phyllis related to Zhaynie, "Ash had suggested that Amy-Lee include Nico Olivier—the then police sergeant, who was about to act as the best man to my fiancé—and Nico's mother, in an invitation to dinner for Chris and me, and, immediately after our arrival, he began to question Nico on the subject of 'the bad eye'. He wanted to know what Phineas could possibly have been talking about, and Nico explained that it was what Ash might refer to as the 'evil' eye.

"In Nico's opinion they were undoubtedly blaming some member of the tribe for the lightning strikes and the deaths, which puzzled Ash, because he could not figure out what Phineas had to do with that, or how he was supposed to decide who the culprit was."

"That's what I would like to know, too," said Zhaynie.

"Well, as Nico explained, Phineas had acquired a certain prestige, and the authority that went with it. It had become his responsibility to pick out the 'guilty' one! Chris, who was the postmaster at that time, agreed," Phyllis went on, "and he warned Ash that, from what he, Chris, had learnt about that kind of thing, from some of the native postmen and other post-office staff, it would maybe take up to ten days before Phineas came back.....Preparations for the ceremony would probably have started off with the killing of a beast, followed by quite a prolonged time of feasting, and then the whole population of the village would form a circle, after which the person divining who the one with the evil eye was, would point him out!

"I remember that your mother shuddered. 'That gives me the creeps!' she exclaimed. 'It reminds me of the time, long ago, when Ash's brother took us to see that old black-and-white film, 'King Solomon's Mines'—I think it had Stewart Granger and Deborah Kerr in it—and some ghastly old crone called Gagula, or something like that, went around with a sort of fly-whisk with what looked like a putrid animal tail attached to it, and when she had circled the group a few times, she suddenly struck one of them on the shoulder—and that was it!'

"What happened after that?" I asked. I'm sure I was wide-eyed with fearful expectation, but I still have to smile when I think of what Amy-Lee's response was. 'I don't know!' she admitted. 'I was so darned scared by that time, that I had my head under Benjamin Ashton's armpit!' And we all had a good laugh at that.

"After some consideration, my fiancé observed that, whatever it was, it would have been dreadful. For Amy-Lee's benefit he went on to tell that he believed that Sir Henry Rider Haggard had based his novel, '*She*'—which in turn must have been the basis for the movie your mother saw, and also for the famous character, *She-Who-Must-Be-Obeyed*—on our famous Rain Queen, *Modjadji*, of the Lowveld.

"I naturally found that enthralling. Although I'd lived here for so long I had never known that!...But I still wanted to know what sort of punishment Ash's man, Phineas, could impose on the supposed miscreant who gave people the evil eye—'Can he have him killed?' I wanted to know.

"I spoke flippantly, but I remember that Chris's cousin, Sergeant Olivier, was quite serious. 'He'll probably impose the same kind of punishment as has been meted out in cases I have heard of before—and the wretched person will wish he or she had rather died! They will set the dogs on that individual, to chase him out of the village, after sending runners out before him to warn every other village for miles, to do the same. He will not find food or shelter anywhere, and in the end he will welcome death!'

"Ben was plainly horrified. 'That is despicable!' he cried, making himself heard for the first time since he had raised the subject with Nico. 'How positively inhuman!—These people are supposed to be committed Christians!'

" 'So they are, Mr. Ashton,' Mrs. Olivier, Nico's mother, said, 'but with much of the Old Testament *eye-for-an-eye* idea of judgment, and some of their inherent superstitions thrown in!'

"Amy-Lee was of course interested in what the criterion for the 'evil' eye would be, and was horrified when Chris explained that it could perhaps be nothing more than a common or garden squint! 'Possibly nothing more innocuous than a cast in one eye!' was his opinion.

"Ash simply could not get over it," Phyllis continued. "To make matters worse, this happened immediately upon his return from Bethlehem in the Free State, where he had gone to see what could be done about the Anglican priest, Clifford Connaught—the father of Jordan's partner, Tristan. Connaught had been apprehended on suspicion of conspiring against the Apartheid government, and had been given '180 days detention without trial'.

"Added to the shock of Father Connaught's arrest, and the surreal facts surrounding that, he wondered how he could ever look at Phineas again without shuddering, and something akin to the claustrophobic constriction he used to feel when going under the river in New York, long ago, tightened his chest and made him breathless. All of a sudden, your mother has since told me, he felt alien...foreign...and even the Southern Cross, and his beloved groves, had somehow lost their fascination!"

At that moment Ben's cell phone rang, and Amy-Lee, his wife, smiled at the alacrity with which he responded. His entire demeanour had changed, and, as he put the phone back into his pocket, he turned to the company at large, grinning broadly. "Okay. We can put the kettle on now!...He says he'll probably be here before we can pour the tea!"

It was unnecessary for anyone to be told who the caller was. Ash Ashton adored his family. If his wife was the light of his life, his son, James—'James the Fourth', who was married to Isobel, Antoinette Verwey's sister—was the pride of it, and a fitting successor to the former Ashtons who had borne that name.... His second child—Eugenie, the beautiful, sweet young mother-to-be—was his precious little girl, and Jordan? Well, he was just special, that's all, and the father's voice took on a special tone when he spoke to this boy who, had Benjamin Ashton believed in any such possibility—which he did not!— was to him like the incarnation of the brother for whom he still mourned.

He jumped to his feet, calling out, first to his son-in-law, "As you are technically the 'baas' of this house now, Dominic, perhaps you should be the one to go and give the necessary instructions for tea!" Then, addressing Antoinette Verwey and his friend, Willie Marais, he asked: "Would you two like to stretch your legs? I'm going to walk down and meet Jordie, and I'd really like it if you would stroll down to the tractor gate with me. I arranged with him, last night, to wait there for me, and he can give us a ride back."

As they went off together, Amy-Lee could not help wondering why he should have singled out these two, in particular, but confident in the knowledge that Ash always knew what he was doing, she got up and went over to the deck chair just vacated by Antoinette, where she sat down beside her daughter. "The two of you have been looking positively conspiratorial?" she remarked, joking with them while trying to pretend that she wasn't just as impatient as Ben was, to see her son. "You seemed to be very much engrossed in whatever you were discussing."

Phyllis laughed. "I was telling Zhaynie about the time Phineas had to go off to deal with the 'evil eye' and how shocked Ash was by what Nico and Chris had to say about that."

"Yes. Tell me please, Mother, how he managed to get over it so well," Zhaynie begged. "Phineas and his family are still so very much in evidence, and so much a part of our lives, that Daddy could not have held whatever had been so upsetting, against him, for too long."

"No, he didn't," her mother said. Then she added pensively: "He did finally get over it, and you have ample evidence of that. Being Ash, he spent a great deal of time up on the ridge, or down here, on his knees in his study. Although he was initially appalled, and he suffered keenly, he came to terms, in time, with what had thoroughly desolated him. He has a great affection for Phineas."

Just talking about it, Amy-Lee had already been taken back to that night, and she relived the effect the disillusionment had had on Ash. He had clung to her, putting it to her that all that was still as familiar to him as his own skin, was she. She had become infinitely more precious than ever before, and there was nothing carnal in his desperation to hold her as close to him as he possibly could, and never let her go.

"Amy-Lee," he had told her after their guests had gone, "I'm trying not to sound hysterical or melodramatic, but tonight I thank God more than ever, that you are here. You represent everything that is familiar, decent and normal, at this moment, and I'd be scared out of my wits if, as I sit here, I could not hold your hand as I'm doing now!...I miss my brother...and I miss Jenkins!...I want my father!...And I want my mother! Somehow, I feel very vulnerable tonight. I feel that a veritable sword of Damocles is hanging over me, and by a *very* flimsy thread!

"Please don't ask me to explain, now," he had pleaded, "but I am so shattered by the realization that someone as seemingly uncomplicated as Phineas can be a party to such bizarre, superstitious practices, that it is no longer quite so difficult to comprehend how some of those Basotho women in Bethlehem could actually have sworn that they had either seen my brother's ghost, or that someone they thought dead, was only pretending to be!"

"And yet you did not make such a big thing out of the *Tokoloshe*[9] business, when you were telling me how Phineas and Sarah had raised their bed, in case the hairy demon should decide to pay them a visit. You appeared to have taken that in your stride!"

"I know, but all these things have suddenly been magnified for me, and I am utterly bewildered!"

With every word his voice had sounded more strangled, and she, Amy-Lee, whose hearing had been sharpened at that time by the loss of her sight, was filled with compassion at the desolation she detected in it, when he admitted: "I really do feel lost tonight, Amy-Lee. It is as though I don't really belong anywhere! I thought this was my home, but I wonder whether I'll ever understand this place! Priests suffering for helping black people, and black people turning against the very ones who help them most!...Then you have the police hounding both! It's beyond me!...It's like Barrie's story—with the crocodile chasing Hook; Hook chasing Peter Pan; and Peter Pan chasing whomever...and so on, and so on...

"I'll tell you one thing I *do* know, however, and that is that anyone who comes here as a tourist, or has paid this country a fleeting visit, has got a darned nerve to go back home and pretend to be an authority on South African affairs. It takes generations for people to *begin* to know *any* part of Africa—and sometimes even that is not enough!"

"Are you trying to tell me that you want to leave, Ash? That you are ready to go home?"

"Not unless I'm forced to, dear heart. Despite everything I've said, this is my home now, and, with God's help, I can get through this!—What about you, Amy-Lee? Are you any closer to making up your mind?"

"Right now, if I were to listen to my heart. I'd say I want to stay, but the writing seems to be on the wall, doesn't it? I have responsibilities that will probably force me to go 'home'...even when I no longer feel any place but here to be my home!...But what will you do about Phineas when he comes back, Ash?" she asked, after Ben had read the nightly portion of Scripture to her, they had prayed together, and they were ready for bed. "Will you question him?...Condemn him?"

"No. I've decided I shall say nothing.—What good would it do? You must have heard Nico Olivier tonight, trying to convince me that Phineas was only doing what he believed to be his duty, and so, after deliberation, I'm going to try and cling to what our Lord instructed when he said, 'Judge not that ye be not judged!' "

"I did hear what Nico said," she assured him. "And what has also stuck in my mind, is what else the sergeant said to you. I mean about scrapping his advice concerning the burglar bars, and not sleeping with doors and windows open....He said he thought you would be safe as long you retained Phineas in your employ....Do you remember him saying, 'After this, no one would dare mess with him or his people?'—And I guess that includes us, Ash!"

Unexpectedly he had chuckled, and her heart had lifted at the sound. "Boy, oh boy, we must prepare ourselves!...If that beard is going to be permanent, we're going to have to like it! If Phineas now sees himself as a Nazarene, he'll never, ever, shave his face again!"

Next morning, hoping to keep his mind off the subject, she had suggested: "It seems to be so cool and fresh outside, this morning, and I was hoping that, if I was up and ready, early enough, this might finally be the day you'd take me for that promised ride on the tractor."

"Let's do that!" was Ben's eager response. "That's what Jenkins would have described as a 'capital' idea.—Wait on the stoep for a moment, and I'll also go and pull on some suitable clothes!"

"Please," she begged, "as it's so early, may I go without the hat and the sunglasses you always make me wear outside? I want to feel the breeze on my face and in my hair!"

"We're going on a tractor, dear heart. Not in a Ferrari!" Ben laughed. "Now off with you!"

He had done all he could to try and make her see what he saw as they proceeded down through the orange groves, as far as the stream, then west as far as the fence which divided his property from the one about which Paul Verwey the citrus inspector, who had since become his daughter's father-in-law, had expressed concern; and finally he took her up to the ridge behind the house, where he picked some of the wildflowers for her to hold; confessing almost bashfully how he had found himself unable to disturb the area in order to plant pineapples.

They had sat there for a long while, talking about many things, and she had heard both pride and paradoxical humility in his voice, as he described the view over the roof of his house, and the vista that stretched out before them.

He had looked over towards the *kaya*[10] he had built for Phineas and his family and that was when he told her: "Amy-Lee, I had some very profound thoughts in the night, about what I'd said about Phineas and his beard, and I am both convicted and ashamed. I had no right to make fun of him...to be tolerant, tongue-in-cheek or amused, in the supercilious, superior manner we are prone to adopt towards black people, and often also towards those from other countries...and I shall never do that again! Phineas and his family have taught me many things, and, whether some of their ways are foreign to me or not, I shall try and respect them."

"But you always have!" she protested. "As small as I was then, I can remember clearly what a wonderful relationship you had with the people on your grandmother's plantation in Louisiana. What a grand time we all shared when you made music!"

"Yes," she told her friend, Phyllis, and then kissed Zhaynie's soft cheek. "He got over it alright. That happened nearly thirty years ago, and I have since learned to appreciate that, at first sight, strangers too often mistake my darling husband for a superficial, rich playboy, because he is so incredibly good-looking. But Ash has vulnerable depths to his character that even I have not completely fathomed. He looks deeply into things that appal him, and tries to look in behind what others only see as violence and cruelty. He is tremendously perceptive, and he probes and suffers mightily when he has to try and comprehend what makes people do bad things! He is tortured by the very fact that anyone would come to do them in the first place!

"Jordie is so much like his father, in that respect, that I fear for him. Jordie does not expect evil in any one, and therefore he is not quick to see it. And consequently it hurts him when he finally does. Both of them suffer acutely when they are disillusioned by the behaviour of others—and most particularly if those 'others' are people they care about deeply!"

Zhaynie and Phyllis, who had been hanging onto her every word, were prevented from commenting, by the sound of car doors slamming, and all heads immediately turned expectantly in that direction. A few minutes later, a beaming Ben approached, leading the way with his arm around his son's shoulders, and, behind him, Willie Marais—all smiles—with Matt beside him. Following them, and talking so much that their progress was slower than that of the rest, came a man with flaming red hair and freckles, and, by the way in which an ecstatic Antoinette clung to him, that man could only be the one she called 'Fallah', the Reverend Doctor Peter Crawford, home from the United States of America...

CHAPTER TWO

I can't help wondering how it is that, while some details of Meredith's wedding day are still so deeply engraved on my memory that they could have occurred yesterday, there are many others that are hardly more than a dream. On reflection, I also wonder how Jasper Hilliard and I happened to get into such a deep discussion about Angola, especially in view of the conversation I'd had with Jordan Ashton just prior to our departure. How strange that Jordie should have made mention of Matt Marais' having had to have his leg amputated!

Among the vague recollections are those of how haphazardly I grabbed such clothes and toiletries as I thought I might need for my trip to Johannesburg; how lovely Meredith looked as we drove off in her father's 4x4 truck on the morning of the significant day; and how excited Susan was—about both her new dress, and her sister's romance. Impressions that are among the more vivid are Tristan's stiffness when he took leave of me earlier that morning, the joy in Doctor Hugo's voice as they went off, and the worried little frown that furrowed the professor's brow when I joined him in the truck. He appeared to be disappointed by the news that Jordan Ashton would not be at home when Meredith and Tristan arrived in Johannesburg.

Jasper insisted that I should sit in the front with him, with the two girls at the back, and I was touched by the sincerity in his manner when he thanked me for the solace I had provided him in being willing to accompany Meredith to the big city. It was a long trip, the girls chatted away like two budgies on the back seat, and, by the time we arrived in Upington, their father and I had become even firmer friends than before.

What suddenly led him to want to talk about my husband, I don't know, but he surprised me by suddenly asking: "Biddy, what made Mark want to give up the Vice-Principalship of a secondary school, to work with elementary schoolchildren? His knowledge and qualifications were such that he could have become a university lecturer, if he had chosen to do so. I can never put into words how precious those Sunday evening discussions or chess games were to me, when I used to bring Merry back to your home. It was a privilege to have him for a friend."

I did not have to stop and think. "To answer your question in one word, Jasper—Angola!"

"I beg your pardon?"

"*Angola*," I repeated. "Mark got to the stage where it just about broke his heart, when, year after every year, as a new group of his boys turned sixteen, he had to start handing out the forms for registration in the armed forces. He'd seen too many of them return, changed forever! South Africans had never been conscripted before. 'Our country has had a proud history of volunteering for active service—because our men and women believed in a cause!' he would say desperately. 'Now they're being pulled into a Vietnam-like conflict that has nothing to do with them, and which they cannot understand; and, when they return, some maimed and crippled—not only physically, but mentally and emotionally—it is to find that others are occupying the jobs they might have had!' "

"I can understand that someone as sensitive as he was, and who loved his students so dearly, would have hated that", said Jasper. "I, myself, was only called up periodically for three-month spells at a time, but that was bad enough. At times not as much because of what we endured, as from what we *saw*! Some of the fellows were quite excited to be going, but there were many like me.—Young, angry, and unable to understand why we were being made to go!"

"Mark did not use his sensitivity as a shield, Jasper," I felt compelled to explain. "Nor did he leave the Bethlehem school only because he shrank from playing a part in the conscription of his students. He organized some pretty heavy protests, and I don't think everyone in authority appreciated them! On the other hand, I have a strong feeling that many people who left the country at that time, must have done so precisely because they felt as Mark did, and they did not want their sons involved.

"I remember once meeting a lady called Marina Crawford who had strong views on the subject.—Her husband, Peter, an Anglican priest—who, together with his family, is now living in the home of Benjamin Ashton in America—came to conduct a mission at the church where the father of your son-in-law to be, had been the rector until he had to go into self-imposed exile in England. Marina's first husband had been killed in Angola, and the news had reached her only hours before the birth of her son. Apparently some years later she and Father Peter Crawford fell in love, but she refused to marry him unless he would agree to emigrate. She did not want to raise her young son only to become what she called 'cannon fodder', like his father.

"Mrs. Crawford's own father was greatly embarrassed when she went on about that one day, in the presence of their American friends. He was angry with her, she told me, and contended that the United States' support of the same factions as the South African regime, regardless of the fact that its involvement in Angola was drawing harsh criticism from the international community, should have belied her fears."

"How incredible it is that such controversy can still exist, about that part of it," Jasper reflected. "And it helps to remember that, while today, 'Islamic fundamentalism' is the chilling word in many countries, in those days it was 'Communism'! I can understand that, with Mozambique just across the border to the East of us—and, if you come to think of it, not too very far from Nelspruit—with the border of what was then South-West Africa, not too far to the west from, let's say, Upington, and with Angola above that, to the North, it must have given serious cause for alarm when, late in 1974, sizeable shipments of arms and ammunition were being ferried from the communist world to the Popular Movement for the Liberation of Angola. That had sprung from a Marxist party founded in1956, with a strong following in the Angolan capital of Luanda.

"I find myself less angry now after coming to believe that there was ample evidence of the extent of the military support flooding into Angola, to the MPLA, throughout the 1975 run-up to the elections. But what I still find inconceivable is that Cuba would protest that Castro only decided to send troops to Angola on November 4, 1975, *after* the South African invasion of that country, rather than vice versa, as America's Ford administration persistently claimed.

"By the time Angola achieved independence in November that year, and by the last day of February in 1976, which, as I recall, happened to be a Leap Year, all the Portuguese forces had withdrawn. Cuban forces had begun to move into Angola in April of the previous year, and South Africa then faced the prospect of a communist state bordering South-West Africa."

"Which at that time, in terms of the Peace of Versailles, was still a South African protectorate," I put in, nodding my head in comprehension of what that situation would portend...

"Precisely. One school of thought has it," Jasper continued, "that, after the reverses Henry Kissinger had recently experienced in Vietnam, and the paranoia about Communism at that time, he would naturally have wanted to support the pro-west 'National Union for a Total Independence of Angola', which as you must know, was a largely military force in the Angolan Civil War fighting Angola's Marxist regime. Experts describe the Angolan war as 'one of the most prominent Cold War conflicts, with one side being aided militarily by the United States, and the other, receiving similar support from the Soviet Union.

"My own, personal belief is that the insurgencies of Jonas Savimbi's UNITA rebel movement in Angola, the 'Mozambican National Resistance', as well as the CIA-backed advance of South African troops in Angola, were indeed supported by America. After all, Kissinger did make it clear that unless Cuba withdrew its forces from Angola and Mozambique, diplomatic relations would not be normalized."

"Mark would have agreed with you, wholeheartedly," I said. "And that entire Angola-South-West African thing went on interminably! You know, Jasper, I am ashamed to confess that, until this moment, I had forgotten how widespread the anti-Portuguese revolution was. My earliest recollection is of lying on my bed in the Nurses' Quarters, listening to the Lourenco Marques radio from Mozambique, because we did not yet have a commercial radio station of our own in South Africa at that time, and hearing what was probably the first sounds of impending trouble, shortly before the transmission was interrupted. Lourenco Marques used to be a favourite holiday resort, and it was sad to learn that friends who used to live there had had to flee to Portugal.

"As the years have gone by, it has been tragic to see pictures of people in Mozambique with limbs blown off by landmines—a situation later brought to the attention of the world by people like Princess Diana—and to learn of the desperate state of affairs in a neighbouring country, but somehow I never connected that war with what later happened in Angola. What made it all so confusing to someone like me, totally absorbed by that time, in my husband, my home and my work at the hospital, was that there were so many rebel 'factions', if I might refer to them like that—all referred to only by letters of the alphabet—that eventually I could not remember which was which. I certainly cannot, as I sit here, today!—Wasn't the liberation movement in Mozambique called FRELIMO? Short for "Free Mozambique, or something?"

"That's correct. And, apart from FRELIMO in Mozambique, and ZANLA and ZIPRA in Zimbabwe, there were the liberation movements of SWAPO in Namibia, the MPLA in Angola, and the ANC and PAC in South Africa. All were supported by the Marxist Eastern Block, and fighting to get rid of the colonial yoke in the subcontinent. Meanwhile, the irony of the situation for us, here, surrounded on the North, East, West, and troubled within, was the fact that, while we were banished from the international community for our government's infamous 'Apartheid' policy, we were still recognized as being 'pro-western', and consequently had the silent blessing of most Western Governments for fighting against the perceived threat of Communism."

"Well, as I said, although it bothered Mark that the South African involvement was spreading from Angola to the border of South-West Africa, I tried very hard not to worry too much about a situation which, for me, remained remote, until one day, in 1988, our librarian friend Felicity Seymour, happened to show Mark an article in the New York Times, written by Bernard E. Trainor, now Lieutenant General Trainor. He wrote about how starkly evident the high 'human cost of the 15-year conflict along the border between South-West Africa and Angola' was, and went on to comment that most of the wounded at the No. 1 Military Hospital in Voortrekkerhoogte[11] were teen-age soldiers serving in segregated units of the South African Army. He particularly mentioned one eighteen-year-old who had lost his right leg when rebel jet fighters attacked his unit. Like most of the white patients, the lad was doing his required two years' duty in the military. Someone to whom Trainor spoke, assured him that the army would fit the lad with a prosthesis, train him in a civilian skill, and give him a lifelong disability pension.—But that was enough for Mark! That was day he started becoming voluble in his opposition to South Africa's participation in the conflict."

"And yet," Jasper responded thoughtfully, "I still think that what made it all worse for us—even for me who, as I said, did only three-month stints at a time, myself—was the fact that, when we were so close to winning, the government suddenly withdrew our troops....That made it all so futile! What was it all for?"

"To this day I don't think that *any* of that was worth it!" was my impassioned view. "And in a 1997 interview with President Ford, he certainly didn't seem to think so either. When the interviewer asked him whether he thought that, if aid had been able to flow unimpeded to Angola, it would have made a great deal of difference in the long run, he replied: 'Probably not, because they're still fighting there!' He considered the net result to be that Angola was destined to have continued turbulence between the government on the one hand and rebel forces on the other.

"By the same token, didn't someone actually go as far as to say that President Ford had permitted Kissinger to 'design a disaster in Angola'? Again there are so many controversies. One explanation was that the United States could not ignore Soviet and Cuban attempts to gain an African foothold when Angola was about to receive independence. And then, when Congress decided that no more money was going to be poured into this conflict, the field was left clear for the introduction of far more Cuban troops and Soviet arms. I think it was John Stockwell, the chief of the CIA Angola task force, who said: 'Most serious of all, the United States was exposed, dishonoured and discredited in the eyes of the world.' They had lost, and fifteen thousand Cubans were installed in Angola 'with all the adulation accruing to a young David who has slain the American Goliath.'

"None of us harboured any resentment towards Ford, personally," Jasper commented. "The US Senate had withdrawn monetary support, and we just felt that America as a whole had let us down. I recently read somewhere, perhaps on the Internet, that South Africa was 'defeated'—but it was *not*! We just plain and simply had the carpet pulled out from under out feet!"

"And what Marina Crawford, the lady I told you about, had to say on that score was, 'Where were the Americans in the end? *They weren't there*! As for Angola, things had gone from bad to worse, and the plight of the people had become unspeakable.' "

"And so the question, 'What was it all for?' remains unanswered," Jasper commented ruefully. "And for Mark's boys who came home maimed—or the families of those who did not come home at all—was any of it worth it, in the end? The Cubans arrived in force, to be met by Operation Savannah counter-reinforcements sent in by Pretoria. The South African Defence Force Fox-Bat, X-Ray and Zulu columns were already within sight of the lights of Luanda *when they were recalled!* Once embroiled in this, the South Africans, having entered Angola during Operation Savannah, had within thirty-three days, covered more than three thousand kilometres. Within artillery range of Luanda, they were forced to withdraw when covert Western support was withdrawn!"

"And then," I put in, "within months after Angola had achieved independence, the Portuguese forces had withdrawn, leaving behind the Cuban forces, and South Africa—with Mozambique now a communist state, to the east—was faced with the prospect of another, bordering what is now Namibia."

We remained silent for some time after that, each busy with our thoughts, until Jasper, who must have been dwelling on what I had told him, suddenly expressed his own, aloud. "But why *Spoors-einde?* I mean it could hardly have been a young man's dream, and with a dickey heart like his, I would have thought that the climate would have put him off!"

"This part of the Kalahari fascinated Mark. It was his favourite place, and I suppose he was drawn to *Spoors-einde* because it was the closest he could get to where he wanted to be." I chuckled with fond reminiscence. "He loved to tease me by telling people that he married me because I was the only girl he could find, who was willing to spend her honeymoon in the *Kgalagadi!*"

***

Of Tristan and Meredith's marriage ceremony, I remember only that the heat and the dark, dusty stuffiness of the office in which it took place, made me feel quite faint. With almost cold-blooded swiftness it was over, and both the professor and I had little appetite for the luncheon that the bridegroom had arranged as a sort of celebration. It was comforting to observe, however, that, now that the immediate future no longer seemed so intimidating, Merry was absolutely scintillating. More than once I heard her happy laugh ring out. Meanwhile Susan, who had never been in a town larger than *Spoors-einde*, and had certainly never been present at any function like this (let alone in a hotel) finally settled down to give her full attention to the menu.

Very soon after the conclusion of the luncheon, we had to go our separate ways; the people from *Blouspruit* and *Spoors-einde*, to return to their individual responsibilities, and Tristan, his bride, and I, to embark on the first leg of our journey to Johannesburg. Upon taking leave of Jasper, he gave me a warm hug, and pressing a kiss on my cheek, he whispered in my ear, "Thank you, Biddy. God bless you!" Then he handed me a small bag, with an explanation that made tears sting my eyes: "There is a cell phone for each of you in here. Please call me if you ever need me—and don't worry about the cost. I shall be taking care of that..."

So far everything had gone without a hitch, but there was one, very tense moment, when Tristan's mask of affability temporarily slipped. This was occasioned by Meredith on our way towards the main highway, when she happened to read, aloud, a sign on a gate as we were passing.

"Look, Aunt Biddy!" she cried with delight. "If Jesus reigns over this place, our marriage can only be blessed!—Right?"

I leant over her shoulder and kissed her cheek, sending up an earnest prayer for guidance in responding. "Right! If that's what you believe, Merry-love, it will!"

She then consulted Tristan, who had made no comment thus far. "It will be, won't it, Tris?" And his reaction was a shock.

"For God's sake! Don't you two start now!" he snapped. "I get enough of that bloody nonsense from my parents!"

The three of us spent the night in a little town where the hotel made me think of some of the 'cowboy' films I had seen. Immediately after checking in I made myself scarce, and, as soon as we had been shown to our rooms, I closed my door behind me, and did not emerge until we were ready to depart next morning. I ordered room service, to the consternation of the proprietor who, although he was clearly not familiar with demands of this nature, fortunately had a wife who was kind-hearted, and, upon hearing my rather tame explanation for requiring this, finally complied.

Alone in that cheerless place, I spent a great deal of time praying for the two young people who were just starting out their lives as a married couple, and, at one stage, thinking of my beloved Mark and the *Kgalagadi* I burst into tears. That was what Meredith deserved. A special time to remember till the end of your days. A magic place to be alone together, where you could pretend that you were the only people in the world! She also deserved to have memories of a wedding day as glorious as mine was. She would, of course, have made a breathtaking bride, but then, even I, surrounded by friends and well-wishers, had the joy of feeling that I was beautiful, that day, for Mark repeatedly told me so.

When at last I lay down to sleep, I was greatly comforted by the memory of something Ben Ashton had said to me once... that, no matter how splendid the wedding, or how marvellous the bridal pair might look, the real happiness came when, with the passing years, the love deepened, and each of you considered the other to be growing more attractive by the minute!

Next day, I took little part in the conversation along the way, being careful not to intrude. Fortunately, Meredith kept the conversation going so animatedly that I doubt if either she or Tristan noticed my silence. I must admit that, after that initial truculence, he had begun to treat me with relative courtesy; perhaps realizing that Meredith would not have tolerated anything less.

At last, thirsty, tired and dishevelled, we reached the outer limits of the 'Golden City', and, from then on, both Merry and I kept looking around us, wide-eyed and involuntarily exclaiming with wonder from time to time. This then was the infamous Johannesburg; the City of Gold—'Sin City'—of which, long ago, the *Spoors-einde's* people used to speak with awe and trepidation. Nowadays people did so with fear. It had become known everywhere as the city of violence and terror.

At first I could see nothing except the towering skyscrapers and what I would learn to know as 'rush-hour' crowds, that looked menacing or particularly dangerous to me, but Meredith was dumbstruck!...Having been reared among the *San*, the *Nama* and the *Khoi*, she had never seen a black person before, and here, millions of people, of all colours, thronged the sidewalks. I noticed that, while surveying the inhabitants of Johannesburg for the first time, her sweet mouth was wide open!

My respect for Tristan mounted as I observed how adroitly he was able to thread his way in and out of the traffic, avoid pedestrians, and simultaneously dodge the reckless newspaper sellers and other vendors who would periodically dash in, right in front of his car. What I found incredible was the information, in response to our periodic nervous chorus of alarm, that we were bypassing the inner city; and I could not help wondering, if these were the outskirts, what that 'inner city' would have been like!

I became really afraid, for the first time when, as we were approaching a corner at which he had to slow down, Tristan ordered us peremptorily, to roll up our windows lock our doors, and place our purses on the floor, and there was such urgency in his tone that we obeyed instantly. Only as, merging with the oncoming traffic, we began to turn to the right, did I notice the number of uniformed policemen gathered there, and both Meredith and I were almost dumfounded to learn that that was not because of any recent 'police incident'. It only added to our consternation when Tristan explained quite calmly: "There are always police there. That's where motorists are often targeted and robbed at gunpoint as they wait to merge with the traffic on the main thoroughfare!"

After that it was an enormous relief when we could leave the hectic 'outer' environs of the city behind us, and enter a suburb with tall, shady trees, beautiful gardens and magnificent residences such as I had hitherto believed could only exist in Hollywood. Voicing my thoughts aloud, I actually made Tristan laugh as I wondered whether the dwellers in those mansions needed maps in order not to get lost inside!— Just think how great my astonishment was, when he pressed a button on some contraption he held in his hand, massive metal gates that would have put Jasper's *Blouspruit* ones to shame, moved apart, and he drove in through them, to come to a stop in front of one of these palaces!

He switched off the ignition and then turned to Meredith. "Well, sweetie, what do you think of it?" He spoke with pride and I truly could not blame him for that.

"Is this really our house, Tristan?" She sounded incredulous.

"Well actually mine and Jordan's..."

He walked around to her side of the car to open the door for her, and as he was helping her out, I was pleased to see Reggie Seymour, hands outstretched, come running down the steps to meet us. He put his head through my window and favoured me with a smacking kiss on the cheek.

"Hi, Aunt Biddy!" he cried, greeting me warmly. "How nice to see you again! The last time was in Bethlehem, and that was ages ago!"

"Welcome back, Tris!" He shook Tristan's hand. "And this must, of course, be Meredith....I am Reg, and I am delighted to meet you! Jordan told me you used to be a very pretty little girl, with the promise of great beauty, but he sure was not able to predict how beautiful you would really grow up to be!.... To tell the truth I am neglecting his patients shockingly, in order to come and see for myself, and now I know that he was guilty of understatement!"

"Thank you Reg," she replied, in her lovely gentle voice. "You're making me blush! How kind of you to come and welcome us! I knew who you were, the moment you came down the steps, because Tris has described you to me."

"I have also described good old Jord, as he is now," Tristan put in...."The guy who does most of my dirty work for me!"

Reggie's comeback was good-natured, but I detected a subtle change in his tone of voice. "Don't say that, Tristan! Just say 'work'.... Incidentally, Adéle is waiting for you in your study and she asked me to let you know that, the moment you arrived!"

"Is that so?" Tristan responded eagerly. "In that case I had better go and say 'Hi' to her right away. She has probably come to welcome me back into the fold.—Reg, old chap, if you are not too anxious to return to Jordan's deprived fans, I'm sure you won't mind showing Meredith and Aunt Biddy to their respective rooms, and then perhaps you can bring them back down again, with you!"

"Nothing would give me more pleasure," Reggie said gallantly, and I felt instinctively that Meredith would have a valuable ally in young Doctor Reginald Seymour.

To this day, I can hardly credit the fact that, as I was about to follow him up the broad staircase to the upper floor, I was already saying to myself, "*I don't think I am going to like this Mrs. Adéle Bradshaw very much! It should not only have been Tristan's duty to introduce his bride to her new home....It should have been a pleasure and a privilege!*" I also can't account for what possessed me to do this—and I know that I'm about to reveal that I can be underhanded at times—but I impulsively requested the other two to go ahead of me, suddenly swung around, and, offering an excuse about having dropped something, returned quickly to where, through the open door, I could see into Tristan's study.

"Adéle!" he was saying, hugging the woman who had risen to greet him. "How great to see you! Did you miss me so much that you couldn't wait for me to come to you? Have you heard that I'm married? I brought back a little barbarian for myself, as a souvenir of my sortie into the desert!"

"Oh, Tris, what have you been up to this time? You're incorrigible!" she laughed. "How could you do this to us? Fortunately Reg had prepared me, and I managed to catch a glimpse of her as she went by. She's actually quite good-looking—but those clothes! Did you say the 'desert' or the 'Ark'?"

Riveted to the spot in the hallway, I clenched my fists and gnashed my teeth. My face must have been as red as a beetroot from both fury and embarrassment. How dared Tristan talk about Meredith like that?—And the malice in the voice of the woman in the study!...That lovely outfit Meredith had so proudly worn especially for her arrival in her new home!...Too late I realized that what we considered stylish in *Spoors-einde* would make us look ridiculous here in Johannesburg. If everyone was wearing skirts above the knee, my own was at least four inches too long!—But the woman was speaking again.

"You didn't actually marry her, did you, darling?" (What she actually said was '*dahling*'!) "Reg wouldn't tell me any of the details. I think he feels sorry for her, and of course he doesn't like me! He probably doesn't want me criticizing your little trophy!"

"No, it's quite true!" Tristan laughed. "I am indeed a safely married man—but that shouldn't make any difference to us! Her father would have had me murdered if I had persuaded her to run away with me, and not married her—particularly after having devoted twelve years of his life to preventing precisely this sort of thing from happening! But she is indeed very beautiful, and I couldn't help thinking how amusing it could be to go to work on her. Recreate her. Tame her, sophisticate her, and teach her how to dress, and so on—and, in addition, her father is very wealthy!...But, careful, here they come now! I think I hear the voice of another of our perennial doers of good—old Reg!...Hell! Are he and Jordan ever a straight-laced pair!...Bloody pains in the neck!"

His words were a timely warning and I was just in time to set my foot on to the bottom step, giving Reg and Meredith the impression that I was on my way up the stairs, and about to join them.

"Who on earth is that woman?" I demanded brusquely of Reg, pointing over my shoulder, in the direction of Tristan's study.

"One of Tristan's patients" he replied evasively.

"Then why does she have to come here? Doesn't he have consulting rooms somewhere? This is not *Spoors-einde* where Doc's office is a part of his house!...I distinctly heard Jordan say something about a place called Sandton City when he talked about his practice!"

"Well," he said, sounding decidedly uncomfortable, "she's also a friend. A member of the same club." He lowered his voice. "She's a divorcee who, in my opinion, suffers more from her imagination than anything else!"

I had known from the start that Meredith's life was not going to be an easy one, and I had anticipated that there would be some thorns in her path. And how right I was to anticipate that Adéle Bradshaw was going to be the sharpest of those thorns! Less than ten days later, I found Merry face down on her bed, sobbing as if her heart would break, and I could only sit beside her, holding her hand; powerless to help.

From where I sat, I could clearly hear the dance music downstairs, the sound of many voices—all trying to talk above it—and periodically a woman screeching with laughter. Meredith was also listening, and as if the events of the past few days were marching in a hurtful parade through her mind, she had to give vent, aloud, to each memory in turn. I already knew all too well why she had fled from a party ostensibly arranged in her honour. As though unaware of my presence, she spoke aloud, to herself, in a voice that was both toneless and bleak.

She relived her sister's illness and Tristan's arrival at *Blouspruit*. How quick he had been to convey *El-hakim's* instruction about not leaving there too soon, to her father.

"But Meredith knows a great deal about nursing," Jasper had protested. "She has cared for her sister through many a childhood illness, and has, moreover, done intensive correspondence courses in First Aid and Home Nursing. I feel sure that she would be able to manage very well, if you would just be so good as to leave her explicit instructions."

"That's all very commendable," had been Tristan's observation. "Nevertheless, this is a case that demands practical experience such as I feel sure could not have been provided by a correspondence course. Even if it sticks in your throat to do so, Professor, can you bring yourself to put up with me for about a week? Your daughter's life might depend on it!"

To my extreme discomfort, Merry then had to go over her first intimate conversation with Tristan. "Has anyone ever told you how beautiful you are, Miss Hilliard? Especially in the moonlight, with the faint perfume of Mimosa in the air?"

"There has never been anyone to do so," had been her shy response.

"How wonderful to know one girl who finds everything I say, original. Incidentally, I have to return to *Spoors-einde* on Saturday. It has been sheer torture for your father to have me here, and I must not stay a moment longer than is absolutely necessary. In fact, I am surprised that he permits you to be alone out here with me."

"Perhaps he has realized by now that you are completely trustworthy."

"Am I?" Tristan evidently remarked wryly. "Then he has certainly forgotten how absolutely enchanting you are. I don't think that you can be considered safe with any man. Or let me rather put it like this...I don't think that any man is safe with *you*!"

How many times had I not gnashed my teeth during the past ten days! I did so again, right then. The reprehensible, unmitigated unprincipled, deceitful cad! (I couldn't come up with enough suitably critical adjectives!) Meredith's delightful sense of humour—the first of the many loveable characteristics I had discovered in her—was small defence against humiliation such as she had been obliged to endure on several occasions since coming to this house. It may be wonderful to be able to laugh at oneself, but some hurts go too deep for that.

I knew only too well why Tristan had not seen to it that his wife had a suitable dress for this occasion. It would have been his duty and responsibility to take her in hand. It should have been a joy to him, and I could have kicked myself for my own stupidity. I had, after all, known that his actions were suspect long before we left *Spoors-einde*, and I had overheard that awful woman's comments on the afternoon of our arrival. Furthermore, it was that very same, callous woman who was behind the planning of this disastrous party!

It had naturally been her idea that such a function should be organized at all, and, although she must have known that it would hurt Meredith, she had swept through that house like tornado, giving instructions and undertaking all the preparations. Adéle of course enjoyed Tristan's confidence, and I had no doubt that they had cooked up the whole thing together. Under the pretext of giving his wife an opportunity to meet his friends, they had, in truth, created a golden opportunity for displaying his little 'barbarian' before he went to work on her.

Have you ever seen those advertisements for cosmetic products, with photographs under the headings of 'Before' and 'After'? That must have been precisely Tristan's intention. Introduce her as she was then, to shallow people with a warped sense of what was funny, odd or ridiculous; so ensuring that the eventual transformation would be all the more striking.

How far they would have got with their cruel prank if Adéle had not spoken so loudly upon our arrival, I cannot say. And perhaps it was providential that Meredith had overheard her cruel remarks earlier that very evening....On the other hand, Adéle may well have intended that it should be so. Whatever the case, Meredith happened to be in the vicinity and was able to hear every cutting word.

"Gloria, old girl," was what Adéle said to a friend who was standing with her in the hallway, at the foot of the stairs, "have I got news for you! You have been away for so long that you can't be up to date on the latest goings-on! Have you heard that Tris is married? My deah it's absolutely sensational! She had spent almost her entire life on some remote farm in the *bundu* and had never seen a man—except for the ones in the household, of course—naturally fell head-over-heels for him, and somehow manoeuvred him into marrying her."

"Dahling," came the response from this Gloria person, "what are you telling me? Does the creature bath? Is she civilized? What language does she speak? "

"Don't laugh! She's actually frightfully well educated... knows all about nuclear fission and that sort of thing!... What?...Well, you see, her old man is a professor!"

"Oh, she's not completely primitive then! Anyway I bet old Tris soon gets sick of her!"

"Possibly already having regrets," was Adéle's meaningful rejoinder. "I'm sure I have already seen something very close to desperation in his eyes at times!"

Meredith, who was on the landing, halfway down the stairs, did not wait to hear more. She well nigh flew up the steps and, seconds later, burst unceremoniously into my bedroom, where I had gone to fetch a handkerchief. And supposing her to be unwell, I took her to her own room where I compelled her to lie down. It wasn't long before the tears began to flow. "Aunt Biddy, oh, Aunt Biddy," she sobbed, after I had listened to the sorry tale, "what must I do?"

I do not enjoy having to be devious, but I felt, somehow, that this was not the time for straight talk. Truthfully, the situation seemed completely hopeless to me, but, right at that moment, I did not want to give the impression that there was no possibility of improvement. I could only hope that the unpleasant day of reckoning could be postponed; perhaps to be averted altogether.

So I took her hand and said with conviction I was far from feeling: "Sweetheart, you mustn't allow two jealous women to ruin your marriage or rob you of happiness. If Tristan had wanted to marry either of them, he had plenty of opportunity to have done so. However he chose to remain single all this time, and it was not until he met you that he found a woman with whom he was prepared to share his life. Would he have proposed to you if he had not seen a chance to be happy with you? And what does it matter if they criticize you, as long as you remain beautiful and desirable to Tristan?"

Meanwhile I was wondering what Jasper would have said at this moment. Had he not feared the likelihood of her having to deal with precisely such situations as this? Wasn't this why he had wanted me to be with her?

"Yes, but Aunt Biddy...!"

"This is no time for any 'but Aunt Biddy', " I interrupted her sternly. "The price one pays for experience is often very high, but one should be prepared to learn from every setback. What do you think your Aunt Biddy looks like to them? They probably snigger every time they catch a glimpse of my straight hair and an unbecoming 'bun'.—Not that I blame them. I have come to realize that a 'bun' is a far cry from what the fashion writers call a *'chic chignon'*!

"I had already made up my mind before this happened that I'm not going back to *Spoors-einde* until I've done something about my appearance. In fact, I have made an appointment with a hairdresser; at quite a posh place I noticed when Reg took us to Sandton City yesterday. I'm going to have a perm, buy some lipstick—for the first time in nearly ten years—and get myself some pantyhose that's so sheer that the folks in *Spoors-einde* will be able to see the very freckles on my legs through them! And talk about high-heeled shoes! I'll learn to walk in them again, even if it kills me!"

As though the word picture I painted was too much for her, she burst out laughing. She laughed until tears rolled down her cheeks again, but this time those tears did not distress me, and when she had dried them she faced me with renewed courage. "You can count me in, too!" she declared.

Before long we were enthusiastically making plans. We'd show that malicious, self-satisfied bunch a thing or two! The more we talked, the more excited Meredith became. We could not wait to get going. We could already picture how Tristan and his friends would be rubbing their eyes in astonishment, when we showed up at the house after our venture into the world of the modern-day city socialite!

As soon as I saw fit, I persuaded her that it was essential for her to go back downstairs, and because she was no coward she saw the wisdom in this, and rose immediately to go and wash her face. Then, after releasing her glorious hair from the habitual braid, I brushed it, and without drawing it back too severely, I tied it into a ponytail, which suited the lovely little face admirably. Once we were ready, however, I found it puzzling that she should take so long about making the next move—until I realized that she still clung to the hope that Tristan might miss her and come to fetch her.

But it was not Tristan who came. She had taken a deep breath and indicated that she was ready to take the plunge, when there was a knock at the door, and, opening it with joyous anticipation, it was to find Reg standing there.

"Are you feeling any better, Meredith," he inquired anxiously. "I saw you darting up the stairs and wanted to follow you right away, but I thought it wiser to give you time to recover. Shall we go down together now and join the others?" Without waiting for her to respond, he tucked her arm under his, and, as though to bolster her confidence, he closed one hand gently around hers.

***

Later that night I was just about to get into bed when Reggie, having tapped gently on my door, asked if he might have a word with me, and I was surprised when, after I had invited him to come in, he carefully closed the door behind him.

"Aunt Biddy," he said in a low voice, without further ado, "there's something very troubling going on here, and I'd be grateful if you would enlighten me. I overheard a very odd conversation between Tristan's patient, Mrs. Bradshaw, and some other female this evening, and I saw that Meredith was greatly disturbed by it. And then there was Tristan's extraordinary behaviour on the day you arrived. If you feel free to enlighten me, I'd be grateful to know what was behind that.

"While I realize that he is hardly the type to carry a woman over the threshold, I would have thought that any husband would be besotted with a wife like Meredith—but from the moment I told him that he had someone waiting for him, he seemed to forget, completely, that he had just brought home his new bride, and that she was deserving of a special welcome in her new home!"

I pointed to a chair, indicating that he was welcome to sit, then sat down heavily on my bed, myself, and, taking a deep breath, closed my eyes for a moment as I contemplated how much to tell him, and where to begin. In the end, knowing and trusting him as I did, and omitting only the details of Meredith's long enforced isolation within the *Blouspruit* enclosure, I started right at the beginning…with the story of Rosalie's desertion, and how her daughter had tried for so many years to fill the void left by her mother. I told him how Merry had dedicated herself to raising Susan, and finally shared with him how I had been tormented by the possibility that Tristan's declared love for Jasper's child was less than sincere. It was a relief to put into words, to someone as understanding as Reggie, my enduring fear that she, having known little of the world beyond the desert, might be nothing but a cruel experiment to our arrogant young Doctor Connaught.

When I fell silent at last, he sat for some time, deep in thought and shaking his head. Then he said: "I have been in some dreadful places during the past few years, Aunt Biddy, and I have seen dreadful things, so perhaps I have been hardened to a certain extent, but what you have just told me is unspeakable. When Jordan told me about Meredith, he described her as an endearing, particularly sweet little girl, and, although he knows nothing about the circumstances of her life since he visited the Hilliards with his father, long ago, I can't help feeling that he is not quite at peace about her having married Tristan.

"While trying hard to 'love my brother as myself', I, personally, do not have any illusions about Tristan, and I have often wondered why Jordan puts up with him—but he is far more charitable that I am. He makes excuses for Tris because of his background. And yet there was something in Jordie's voice when, after having spoken to you before he left, he repeated your conversation to me, and I detected a note of concern. In fact he said that he would have to pray for them!—And heaven knows, after what I heard tonight, they're going to need those prayers!"

This was when I told him of my plan to take Merry on a jaunt next day, and he was so kind. "Just let me know when you want to go, and when you need to be picked up," he promptly offered, "and, if I happen to be with a patient when you call, I'll send Jordan's driver to get you."

"Jordie has a *chauffeur*?" I was quite taken aback. "He never struck me as the sort...!"

Trying not to laugh, Reg explained, grinning: "It's not as though he has suddenly become a sybarite or a playboy, or something, Auntie. If you were to see some of the places Jordie goes to visit, or if you went to his clinic—a far cry from his office in Sandton City—you'd realize why he can't go alone. And, while I'm okay in army trucks and ambulances in disaster areas, as long as I'm the replacement for Jordie here, I am grateful to have Charlie to drive me around the city. Without him I'd probably get myself hopelessly lost."

CHAPTER THREE

If the visit to *Maison Charles* next morning was a revelation to us, the bill we received at the end of it was a near knockout! Between the two of us we had just over fifteen hundred Rands, but Meredith was still obliged to write a cheque for the balance! I had brought only cash, and, having been warned of the risk of robbery while using banking machines, I was terrified to go and draw more money. This brought home to me very forcibly how fortunate we were that Merry's father had insisted that she have a bank account of her own, into which he had deposited quite a sizeable amount. Nevertheless, after we had enjoyed all that *Maison Charles* had to offer, I kept agonizing about whether or not there was enough money left in her account to cover everything, and I decided that it was high time I had credit card!

It did not take us long to conclude that Peg Jones who had done our hair in *Spoors-einde*, was hopelessly out-of-date. Those splendid corrugated iron waves of hers, and the corkscrew curls she unfailingly contrived for attendance at weddings and funerals, indisputably belonged to a different era. On the other hand, city hairdressers, in my opinion, were there chiefly to make curly hair straight. Then, added to this, it seemed to me, that the hair was not cut evenly, because the younger clients ended up with the ends of theirs looking as though it had been chewed off rather that trimmed. In spite of this, I finally had to concede that the result was most becoming. In the end they looked lovely, and, as a matter of fact, I didn't think that the two of us looked too bad, either!

There was the nicest little girl called Julia working for Mr. Charles. They called her a 'cosmetologist', or something like that, and we were thrilled to be informed that we could not only have 'facials' and be made up, right there in the salon, but would also be given advice when it came to the choice and subsequent use of suitable cosmetics. To tell the truth this was a tremendous relief to me—after tossing and turning half the night, wondering how one could just walk into a department store, and select what you needed from the intimidating assortment of stuff I had glimpsed during our previous visit to the shopping mall.

I must say that after the hairdresser and the cosmetician had concluded their ministrations I was more than satisfied with what they had done to me, and they were extremely judicious when it came to working with Meredith. While studying her from every angle, they went into raptures, pronouncing her hair to be so lovely that they were loath to cut it, and the final consensus of opinion was that it should just be shaped around her face, leaving one or two endearing wisps on either side, and the ends trimmed so that so that she could wear it loose. Moreover, they could not believe that, having lived in the desert for so long, her skin could be so flawless that only the lightest of make-up could be recommended.

"I seldom encounter a complexion as flawless as yours, Mrs. Connaught," Julia enthused. (Involuntarily I was reminded of the sunbonnets and the Baobab extracts!)—"I am not going to prescribe much more than a moisturizer, a sunscreen, a dusting of a good face powder, a sky blue eye shadow, and a rose lipstick. I shall also demonstrate the best methods of application. You would be surprised how many women simply do not know how to attain the best effect!"

And she would never be able to guess how grateful we were to find her so cooperative, because both Meredith and I would rather have died than disclose that, between the two of us, we did not possess a single cosmetic! Instead, we mumbled something about having had to leave the house so early that we had decided to come just as we were. My candid excuse would have had to be that, after Mark's death, I had given up on my appearance, and frankly had not cared because I had seen no reason to make the best of myself. Meredith, on the other hand, had never before had the opportunity to learn about such matters. Fortunately she was exquisite enough not to have been anything less than completely lovely, without any improvement.

At last, sporting all the recommended 'enhancements of beauty' Julia had shown us how to apply, we gaped at one another, open-mouthed and wordless! We were so bedazzled by our mutual magnificence that, as we strolled through the mall, we could hardly see where we were going, and had to stop repeatedly to take a good look at ourselves wherever there happened to be a mirror. After that we tackled the dress shops with remarkable confidence...feeling very pleased with ourselves.

Our sparkling new appearance lent us the courage to enter what looked to be a most exclusive boutique, and anyone who heard us would have taken us for members of the city's elite, without a second thought. One of the new dresses Meredith bought suited her so well that she decided to wear it home, and she was pleasantly surprised when the assistant suggested that her other parcels be delivered to her residence. Soon she had reason to be grateful for the confidence acquired through the transformation Julie had wrought, when, upon giving her name and home address, this caused the manageress to react quite gushingly with: "You are not Mrs. *Doctor* Connaught, are you?... Mrs. *Tristan* Connaught?"

Smiling shyly and with childlike pride, Merry responded affirmatively, and after this she could hardly wait to get home and show herself to Tristan. But we were not ready for the adventure to come to an end just yet. We first went and had the most amazing coffee in a place where every second woman looked to me like the film stars I had seen on the screen in *Spoors-einde.* After that I dialled the number I had been given for someone to fetch us, and could only hope that whoever passed the message on to Reg would not mention any of it to Tristan and spoil the surprise.

Acutely aware of our newfound glamour, we crept into the house and up into our bedrooms....I, to try on the spider web hose, and Meredith to practise applying the lipstick as she had been shown at *Maison Charles.* Twenty minutes later we descended the stairs in all our glory, and who should be the first person we encountered, but Reggie! He was in the hallway when he happened to look up at us, and it was deliciously gratifying that he was obliged to take a step backwards and exclaim: "Aunt Biddy! Meredith! What have you been doing to yourselves? You look marvellous! Meredith, your hair suits you wonderfully like that, and Aunt Biddy, you look *years* younger!"

We two, Meredith and I, were still standing there preening ourselves like peacocks, when Tristan suddenly appeared out of nowhere. One look at his face, and my heart sank—right down into my new shoes! His countenance was absolutely contorted with rage, and I don't think I have ever seen anyone so angry...

"Meredith, what on earth have you been up to?" he demanded furiously, and then addressed himself to me. "You, Aunt Biddy, are no doubt behind this, not so?"

I was a little nervous of him but couldn't hide a triumphant smirk. He was not displeased because Meredith's appearance was unattractive. She had never before looked quite as stunning, and I knew, beyond a doubt, that his ire stemmed from pure frustration!

He was seething because he had been thwarted! It immediately became evident that, by denying him the thrill of executing the 'transformation', the entire balance of the game had shifted. While I searched my mind for a suitable response, I could hardly believe my ears when, before I could say a word, Meredith flashed back with: "No Tristan! You are mistaken. **Adéle Bradshaw is!**"

CHAPTER FOUR

I t's wonderful how the state of one's appearance and the degree of one's self-confidence can go hand-in-hand! It seemed as though, when Meredith and I returned to that house, every vestige of uncertainty and nervousness, which had sometimes almost bordered on obsequiousness, had been left behind—in a shopping mall!

Before very long she was a new person! She walked with a new spring in her step and there was self-assurance in every line of her charming little figure. She held her head high and looked the world squarely in the face, and more than once Tristan was forcibly reminded of the first occasion on which she had unexpectedly revealed that underlying strength and determination.

"I don't see you keeling over or having convulsions because of it!"

Whenever he thought about it, he could again hear her lash out at him, defensively and with uncharacteristic vehemence. That day he had been made to recognize that such an outburst had been a rare occurrence, and that, away from any situation in which she felt totally safe and in complete control, she was insecure and vulnerable to a marked degree. Now, to his cost, he was frequently reminded—in no uncertain terms—that, sufficiently provoked, Meredith, the strange, unpredictable child-woman, was quite capable of diminishing further such desired triumphs, in the future!

There was no doubt that she had consistently been provoked, often beyond endurance, and it was inevitable that, because of this, she would become stronger and better able to cope; however I refrain from using the word 'hardened', for that she never could be. ...She had been so bitterly disillusioned that she grew to arm herself against any possibility of further disenchantment, but her nature was such that she remained vulnerable, and there would still be times when she would doubt herself, or tears would flow, no matter how hard she tried to steel herself against possible pain.

Here I must not forget to say that much of her newfound confidence would be due to the return of Jordan Ashton, and that in him she would find an ally even more solicitous than Reggie had been.

Of all things to be doing when Reggie's phone call reached him in Nelspruit, Jordan, having already listened delightedly to the heartbeat of his first nephew or niece, had his hand on his sister's abdomen, feeling the baby kick. And Ben Ashton, who had been watching the two of them lovingly, was quick to notice the bemused expression on his son's face fade, to give way to a frown of concern as the unduly long conversation proceeded, and the moment the caller rang off he asked concernedly, "What is it, son? You look worried!"

"I am," Jordan admitted. "That was Reg, and he has just told me of a situation in my home that has shaken me to the core. I just can't believe what I have heard...! It sounded like some bizarre storyline from a soap opera, and what concerns me most, is that the little Hilliard girl seems to be the victim of some diabolical ill use!"

"Whatever do you mean, Jordie?" Ben asked. "And which little Hilliard girl?"

"The older one.—Meredith. I had heard from Auntie Bid in *Spoors-einde* that, while Tristan was there visiting his great-uncle, Doc Hugo was called to the Hilliard spread because the younger one was so sick....Remember, Dad...the little kid who was so upset when she accidentally broke the Dresden shepherdess you had brought to be added to her mother's collection? Well, evidently Professor Hilliard telephoned for Doctor Hugo Connaught, and Tristan went in his place."

"The girls must be grown-up by now..."

"They are, Dad. But just wait 'til you hear this..."

"So far none of that sounds so diabolical to me, Jord," Zhaynie commented. "There must surely be more than that to it, for you to look so disturbed.—And what's your house got to do with it?"

Jordan, still frowning, shook his head as though with disbelief as he explained: "Auntie Bid told me, when I called to find out when I could count on Tristan's return, that he had married young Meredith and was bringing her back with him. The suddenness of it came as bit of a surprise, but I accepted this philosophically, thinking to myself, 'Well these things do happen. Obviously love at first sight!'—But now it appears that he has been treating her abominably! I can't believe it, and nor will you when you hear the extent of it! I know that Reggie does not approve of Tristan, and can be hard on him, but surely he can't be making all this up?"

"You mean 'physically', Jordie?" Zhaynie wanted to know. "Somehow I can't see old Tris doing anything like that!"

"No. It sounds to be more like deliberate mental and emotional abuse, belittling her and exposing her to the ridicule of his friends—especially to one of his patients with whom, according to Reg, he's having a more intimate relationship than he should! As I said, I simply can't believe that he would behave like that. I must go home and sort this out. I can't have things like that going on in my house!"

"What surprises me even more," his father said, "is that Meredith's parents would have permitted such a hasty marriage. Jasper Hilliard was always very protective of his girls, as I recall."

"He can't have been very enthusiastic about it, Dad, because Aunt Biddy was persuaded to accompany her, and, from all accounts, she, Auntie Bid, is also staying in the house. I'm told that Mrs. Hilliard died some years ago, so Auntie Bid has become a sort of mother figure to Meredith. It's a long, hardly credible story, but, according to Reg—whom I would trust with my life—Meredith would have never have been able to endure Tristan's treatment of her without Auntie Bid to be there for her....And now—to add to everything else—because a new development has made Reggie uncertain as to how long he might be available, he wants me to come home as soon as possible. I'm so glad we have the meeting behind us, because, in view of all this, I think I must leave as soon as possible."

"Of course," Ben said understandingly, "and, if you will have us, I think your mother and I will go with you. The drops you prescribed seem to be working, but you did say that, although you did not find anything too serious wrong with her eye, you would still like Doctor Fisher to give her a thorough examination....So how about us flying you there, and we'll get Matt to drive your car back to Bryanston for you?"

"Matt?" Jordan looked inquiringly at his father. "Perhaps you mean Uncle Willie, Dad?"

"Of course!" Ben corrected himself. "The boy manages so well with that prosthesis, that I am inclined to forget!" All of a sudden the bleakness returned to his handsome face, and his children were immediately aware of it. "If he were home in

Canada he'd have his own car, adapted to his needs, and the driver's seat would be on the opposite side!"

He sat silent for a few minutes after that, holding his hands to his face, and when he spoke again, the agony of his thoughts was audible to the two who loved him so dearly. Jordan was still sitting beside his sister on the couch, and he slipped his hand into hers when Ben said, "I can't understand why, after I have returned so often to the place I love best of all, this particular time should be so difficult for me! Perhaps because the possibility of having to leave it forever keeps looming up to torture me, memories come flooding back with an intensity I cannot find words to describe!

"Because of this, yesterday's meeting was extremely difficult for me, and, now in addition, I have to be reminded of my state of mind on the day I first met Tristan's father, and what that man would come to mean to me. That was also the day I first set eyes on Reggie, who worked part-time in the '*Seed and Feed*' store—to which I went to inquire about your Uncle Jamie. You know much of the story already, but you must indulge me today, my beloved children, because I cannot bear to relive these memories alone.

"If I had not gone there, I would never have discovered that my brother was dead, and Reggie's employer would not have driven me to the home of Father Clifford Connaught— who took me in when I was at the end of my tether...and, in so doing, lifted my foot onto the first rung of the ladder that led to salvation, and the knowledge of Jesus Christ.

"It was Clifford who introduced me to the De Beers, whose farm you were to inherit some day, Jordie, and for whom I named you 'Jordan', after the river near that farm; and it was Clifford and Thora Connaught who went to care for the children for whom your mother had founded the care centre in

Louisiana. Unfortunately Tristan has always been a source of concern to them, and we have all made allowances for the pre-natal and other influences that could have made him so. But now Timothy, their first-born and the one upon whom they can rely, has been called up, possibly soon to be sent to Iraq...! I don't know how Thora would be able to bear it if anything happened to him, and I pray to God that, if they have been advised of Tristan's marriage, they never find out about his latest transgression!"

Ben stared into space as though seeing things that were hidden from the other two, before he continued.

"Oh, the painful clarity of pictures that march before the eyes of memory! What I can see now is Antoinette—our chubby, three-year-old little Tony of those days—running towards my friend and priest, Peter Crawford, when he turned up unexpectedly to join us as we sat outside under the Syringa tree one Saturday. After a news flash that there had been casualties the day before, he had had a busy time, visiting and reassuring everyone in his parish who had a family member on the Angolan border—and there were many who were on tenterhooks at that time. Upon his arrival here, Antoinette immediately recognized him as the nice, friendly man who had visited her distraught mother the day before, and she ran up to him eagerly, throwing her arms around his legs, and screaming with glee at thus impeding his progress.

" 'Must be the red hair,' he laughed. Picking her up in his arms, he acknowledged almost shyly, 'But, for whatever reason, it's gratifying to know I made a good enough impression to be so warmly welcomed!' In response to which Tony's mother's disparaging observation was that the child was probably only missing her father!

"Greg was either in Angola or the Caprivi Strip at that time, and Marina made no secret of her resentment of the fact that, having been away when Tony was born, he would not be there for the birth of his second child, either. It was obvious that she was at the end of her tether. I can still hear her bursting out passionately at one stage: 'I'm telling you all, here and now, this is the last time...! I'm sick of it!...I told Greg, long ago that we should emigrate, and, by hook or by crook, no matter how we manage it, if this one is a boy, we're leaving, for sure!'— And that was the day she first said, 'I'm not bringing him into the world to be cannon fodder!'

"Your mother and I were keeping her company on New Year's Eve of that year, when Father Peter and Uncle Nico Olivier—who was still the local police sergeant at that time— came to the front door together, to bring Auntie Marina the news that her husband had been killed. Of course Marina went to pieces, upsetting Antoinette, and causing the child, when catching sight of the priest, to make straight for him. She had heard him addressed as 'Father', and supposing him to be hers, she hurled herself at him with whimpering little squeals of "*Fallah! Fallah!*", and then, somehow, managed to clamber up him like a frantic kitten scaling a tree. She locked her arms around his neck, and her chubby little legs around his waist, hid her face against his chest, sobbing, and could not be dislodged; not even after she had fallen asleep once more....You saw how she, now a grown woman, clung to him when he arrived here with you, Jordan. How very nice it must have been for you to have been able to bring her such a wonderful surprise!"

"It was, Dad," Jordan confirmed. "And it was quite moving to observe how hard Father Peter had to try to curb his impatience to see her again. She may be his step-daughter, but he certainly adores her!"

"It's mutual, I would say," Zhaynie remarked, with an indulgent chuckle. "It's just wonderful to see how well they all get along!"

"It is," Jordan agreed. "And I was actually given two great opportunities to make people happy. Uncle Willie Marais did not know that I was bringing Matt, either! We kept that a secret, too!"

Ben suddenly grinned and his face lit up. "I'll never forget how Willie used to pick me up for work each day, after I first arrived in this country—because he did not think I would be safe driving on the 'wrong side' of the road! He was always studiously polite because I happened to be 'the boss', until the day when he began to expound on the subject of rugby, his abiding passion. The more he became caught up in the telling, the more enthusiastic he became.

"The journey was far too short to get into every detail of the last moments of Southern Transvaal versus Western Province, but it lasted long enough for me to hear, for the first time, that excited 'Ach man, Ben man, I tell you…!' which I shall forever associate with my first experience of an uninhibited and passionate fan's post mortem of a rugby match.

"And so the ice was permanently broken. I bought his sons, who were equally passionate about the game, rugby boots for Christmas that year, and I guess that's why it was like a knife-thrust in my heart to learn that Matt had lost a leg during the same conflict that had taken the life of Tony's father."

" Dad," Zhaynie interposed gently, "that's why I said at the meeting yesterday, that I am not sure whether I want to go home to the States with you, to have my baby.…I know that this country is becoming more and more violent by the day, and I cannot say that I am not afraid, *but one cannot run away from danger altogether*! One can only pray!

"Take, for example, Uncle Willie's brother, André—the one who worked for the national airline—and his family, who emigrated to Canada after the plane on which he was flying was shot at over Luanda. Uncle Willie was telling me yesterday how he constantly kept encouraging his children to go and join them in Canada, but unfortunately for Matt, this country was embroiled in the Angola, South-West Africa, Namibia thing that seemed to go on forever, and eventually, before he could leave here to go to Canada, he was drafted. Later it was decided that he would go as soon as he was discharged from the army—which, as we know, finally came about through an injury....Now Matt is in Canada, a Canadian, but, if you come to think of it, it took the loss of his leg to accomplish that. He is safe, as Uncle Willie so ardently longed for him to be—but where is his Uncle Andre's youngest son now?...Fighting the Taliban with the Canadians in Afghanistan!

"If Dominic and I decide to do as you suggest, and relocate to the States, where you have such eminently suitable jobs waiting, both for him and his father on the California *Beauclaire* groves, that would be one, tempting option. On the other hand, if we decide to stay, and even though I might be willing to accept your offer to move us to Bushbuckridge, Graskop, or some other place, there would be nothing for Dominic and his father there! Years of training and experience, on their part, would be utterly wasted—not to speak of the heartbreak for us all, just thinking of how you laid every brick of this house with your own two hands!

"It's such a very difficult decision to make, Dad. So difficult that I have even thought of another possibility. If there's not enough money in the 'Land Reform' budget for this property to be purchased, you could perhaps donate it to the powers-that-be, and Dominic, his parents and I could continue to live here, and work along with the new, black owners. An arrangement that is already working well at Mataffin."

"Dearest," Jordan said affectionately, hugging her, "now you are talking absolute nonsense, and you know it! There is no way that would work. To be fair and just, the first people we'd need to hand these groves over to, would be the black family who have worked, and lived here, for longer than some of us can remember.—People like Phineas, Sarah, their immediate family and their relatives, because the alternative you suggest would never work for them....In the first place, having virtually been the 'seconds-in-command' for all these years, they would hate the playing field to be levelled to the extent that they are no longer esteemed above the rest. And as for the others, as things are at the moment, all are considered equal, and accustomed to taking orders only from either an Ashton or a Verwey. But, if this place were to be divided into separate farms, there is a very great likelihood of strife. Who would have first choice? At what? And so on...

"We have a great deal in common, my darling sister, because, like Tony, we were born here, and, even having grown up in the States, we feel as though we are South Africans; but, if I might advise you, think first of your precious child. Go back with Mom and Dad to the States. Go home to *Bentleigh*, have your baby there, and then make further decisions later. It's not doing you any good, Miss Eugenie, to have these concerns milling around in your head, right now!

"There will be plenty of time to sort things out later. In the meantime, you have heard what Uncle Willie Marais said, and what Dad agreed to be the best option. Although it will come as a blow to the Lowveld farmers who use our equipment, we'll start by going ahead with closing the Ashton facility, next door, move the entire inventory, and any employees who want to go along with it, back to Isando, and take stock of the situation from there.....I have a very strong feeling that it won't be long before Uncle Willie and Auntie Bets go to join the rest of their family in Canada!—Now, Dad, how about we pray about this together. Shall we pray for a healthy little addition to our family, perfect in every respect, an easy time for Zhaynie, and health and blessings for her husband and every member of his family?...For my precious mother's beautiful eyes to be protected, and for God's intervention in the lives of Meredith and Tristan?"

"Of course," his father promptly agreed. "But first let us give thanks for all the many blessings already showered upon us, and ask God's forgiveness for our needless—and fruitless—worrying about things that He is able to control far better than we can!"

"Right!" said Jordan. "And thinking of my own mother, I suddenly thought of the little Hilliard girl who doesn't have one, and I want to thank God for Aunt Biddy, and pray for her, too."

When the prayers came to an end, Eugenie rose awkwardly to her feet, with her brother's help, "Now let's go and join Mom and my dear mother-in-law on the stoep. I need to move.... This little blighter is kicking me to bits, and I'm sure I heard the rattle of teacups!" Later, while reclining on the *chaise longue*, she put the question very seriously to Jordan: " Do you think it'll be okay this time, dear brother-of-mine? What did your stethoscope tell you? Would my little one and I make it to the States safely, or have I left it too long?"

"You'll be fine, this time," he assured her earnestly. "You have never been able to carry a baby for this length of time before, and I heard some pretty healthy sounds coming from the little tyke. If you want to go home for the birth, though, you and Dominic will have to consider making tracks pretty soon. I have a strong suspicion that you're further along than you think, and you don't want to be delivering the first Ashton grandchild at some crowded airport—or worse, on an aeroplane!"

Just then, their attention was caught by the sound of the Jeep pulling up next to the house, and minutes later, Ben, who had gone straight from his talk with the children, to find Amy-Lee and give her a kiss, looked up to see his friend, Paul Verwey, coming up the steps, followed by Paul's son, Dominic, Zhaynie's husband.

"Heavens, how that takes me back, Paul!" he exclaimed. "This has indeed been a day of *déjà vu* for me! Amy-Lee and I were on the stoep, just like this, on the day you came up the steps and introduced yourself as the new citrus inspector! Who ever dreamt that we would be brothers-in-law some day! Neither of us even had children at that time!"

"And I wasn't even married!" Verwey laughed. "Nor would I be, without the machinations of your dear wife. Remember the day Rob Brink took Ash up in his plane, Amy-Lee, and, when they did not return on schedule, we thought they had crashed?"

"I do," Amy-Lee smiled. "And then I manoeuvred the situation so that you would have to take Stella home, and now she's my daughter's mother-in-law.—The rest, as we know very well, is history! Come here and give your own mother-in-law a hug, Dominic....When you have finished kissing your wife, that is!"

Jordan carried his father's teacup over to him and, as soon as he had fetched his own from the tray on the table, he sat down beside him, leant over, and confided in a low voice: "Dad, this thing with Tristan really is depressing me. We have all leant over backwards, over the years, to make him feel wanted and secure, and I invited him into my home and my practice because I believed in him. However, while jeopardizing his reputation by having an improper relationship with a patient, is one thing, hurting that little girl by his behaviour is another matter, altogether, and I'm not sure what to do about either of those problems. I am so grateful that you and Mom are coming back with me, because I just don't know how to handle the situation, and I can only hope that Reggie is mistaken. I can't picture anyone wanting to be anything but gentle with Meredith. I remember her as such a cute little thing!"

"You amaze me, Jordie," said his father. "What a memory you have! I wouldn't have thought that you would even be able to recall her name. It is so many years since we were there—you must have been in your early teens—and I doubt if she was more than ten or eleven years old. She must have made quite an impression on you, for you to remember that she was 'cute'!"

"She did, Dad, perhaps because she reminded me of some of the illustrations in that lovely, glossy book of Nursery Rhymes that Eugenie used to have, and from which Mom would sometimes read to me when I was small. Zhaynie had impressed on me, very emphatically, that I was never to touch the book with unwashed hands, and I was very careful never to 'dog-ear' any of the pages.

"I remember Meredith particularly, because, in her sunbonnet and apron, she could easily have been mistaken for Lucy Locket or Miss Muffet, and if I am concerned about her, it's perhaps because, when I was a child, I would have been horrified if any of those quaint little characters in the book had been similarly hurt or disillusioned..."

'*I know you would, my son,*' Ben thought to himself, '*because you are so immensely compassionate!*' Aloud he said, smiling at Jordan, "I remember that when you were about three, you did not like to think of Miss Muffet being harassed by the spider!...By the way, how is your clinic progressing?"

"Very well, thank you," Jordan replied. "I only wish I had more time to spend there, because then I could extend the hours. Perhaps some day I'll find someone to help me, in a voluntary capacity."

"We must talk about that some time," his father said. "Now it's high time I apprised your mother of the fact that we are going to Johannesburg tomorrow, and that she needs to get ready for an early departure. She'll be pleased to hear that Biddy is there because we haven't seen her for years!"

CHAPTER FIVE

I was thrilled to bits when Jordan phoned to tell me that he and his parents were on their way, and that I should send his driver, Charlie, to the airport to meet them. They were all high on my list of favourite people, and how nice it was to be filled in, later, on all the details of what had transpired in Nelspruit. I was deeply touched to learn that they had prayed for me, for I certainly needed it!

It was only natural that, at this end, we should all have been under a strain after the recent confrontation with Tristan, and, although it hurt Meredith, I was secretly glad that he was so seldom home. Reg was able to report that at least his colleague was in the office every day, to see patients, but what he did after consulting hours were over, we could only guess.

Things changed dramatically as soon as we learnt that Jordan was coming home, and that his parents would be with him. Meredith and I, for reasons of our own; and Reggie, not only because he was relieved at the prospect of being able to leave Jordie to sort out the drama in his house, but also because Felicity, his adopted mother, was due to have by-pass surgery in Bloemfontein, and he wanted to be there with her.

Jordan's servants were so well trained that there was nothing we needed to do to prepare for the visitors, even at such short notice—and, in any case the Ashtons would be accommodated on Jordie's side of the house. However, after diffident consultation with Reg, and Angelina, the Zulu cook,

Meredith took the liberty of bringing flowers from the garden and arranging them in the suite which, she had been told, was permanently reserved for '*Umnumzane* Ash' and his wife. She then went as far as to bake scones, which were much appreciated when the travellers arrived.

If she had been nervous, which she had every right to be—considering her tenuous position in Jordan's house—she need not have been. The Ashtons did not care how or why she happened to be there. They simply embraced her unconditionally—literally and figuratively—as was a characteristic of their warm, loving family. Jordan had not yet heard the barely credible story, Ash Ashton had only an inkling of it, and Amy-Lee knew nothing of it, other than that Meredith was Tristan's wife.

She, Amy-Lee, had heard about Professor Hilliard's daughters many years before, when her husband and Jordan had returned from their visit to *Blouspruit*, and Ben remembered her only as a sweet child, very much concerned about her little sister, but when Jordan saw her he looked as if he had either been winded, or had suddenly seen a dream image come to life before his very eyes.

"Meredith!" he exclaimed. "How lovely to see you! It's hard to believe that you are now a married lady! You have grown up to look exactly as I knew you would!—And I am so very sorry to hear about you mother!"

"Thank you Jordie! And I would have known you anywhere! I'll never forget how kind you were to try and console my little sister, Susan, when she had that mishap with the shepherdess." Then her voice changed as she asked guardedly: "What about my mother?...What did you hear?"

"Why, that she had passed away, of course!" Ben put in. "We only learnt that from Reggie yesterday, Meredith, and we were all sorry to hear that. I would certainly have written to your father to commiserate if I had known. Rosalie was an unusually lovely woman, and I know you must miss her tremendously!"

"Her death certainly changed our lives," was all that Meredith said, and it saddened me to detect the hidden bitterness in her response. Only the night before, when I thought that, like me, she was absorbed in the movie we were watching on television (a new experience for both of us) she had burst out with: "How is it possible for both my father and me to have been forced to suffer such let-downs, Aunt Biddy? Are so few people to be trusted?" And that was the first indication I was given, that she had somehow discovered the truth about Rosalie's desertion. I fumed inwardly at the possibility that Tristan might have blurted out what Doc Hugo had told him, on that fateful day when Jasper had telephoned for the doctor's help.

We were sad to see Reggie leave, and we prayed earnestly for his mother's surgery to go well. However, it soon proved that Jordie's parents could not have come at a better time. Having been to consult Doctor Fisher, and having been reassured that all was well, Ash and Amy-Lee went out of their way, for the remainder of their visit, to make Meredith and me feel at home. I was happy to reminisce with them about Bethlehem and the people we knew in common, and Meredith enjoyed being taken to see such attractions as were deemed to be comparatively safe to visit. Among other things, we saw the Government Buildings in Pretoria, and the breathtaking panorama of Jacarandas in bloom, and Jordan accompanied us whenever he was free. If his parents were mystified by the fact that Meredith's husband, who had known them for most of his life, was so seldom in evidence, they refrained from saying so.

Seldom did we return to the house without Ben expressing his sadness at seeing, for himself, the neglect and destruction of so much that had been fine and beautiful, and when he risked driving past what used to be the magnificent Joubert Park[12], once the jewel of Johannesburg, he was devastated. There, in days gone by, executives from nearby places of business were wont to bring a book through which to browse in the shade of lofty trees, while lesser employees enjoyed many a lunch break among the well-kept flowerbeds, ablaze with a riot of flowers. Students from the Art School had found the park to be an oasis in the city, where they could gather to eat their sandwiches on manicured lawns, and hear the cooing of turtledoves above the constant hum of traffic from the surrounding areas. Now, finding the trees and the flowers gone, the doves silent, and nothing but litter everywhere, Ash Ashton was overwhelmed.

His son, Jordan, lived in a fine, comparatively safe area, but he still feared for his safety, and constantly prayed for his protection.—Even more earnestly than ever, after he had been taken to visit the area in which Jordan's clinic was situated!

Gone were the days when a nurse, walking through a dangerous area was safe, as long as her uniform distinguished her; or a doctor would be protected by a white coat and the stethoscope around his neck. On the very steps of Johannesburg General Hospital, a young female physician on sabbatical from Britain had been stabbed—on three, different occasions!

Meanwhile, for the time being, Jordan hesitated to confront Tristan, preferring to see for himself what it was that had so disturbed Reg, but it was not long before he took me aside one day, and questioned me. He shared with me as much as Reggie had told him, and pleaded with me to be frank with him.

It was as though he had been wounded, personally, by all that Meredith had been through since her marriage, but somehow what dismayed him even more, was the fact of her mother's desertion. He hung onto every word I uttered, and the constantly changing expressions on his face reflected his intense compassion, as he listened to the story of how a mere child had been obliged to take her mother's place, be a companion to her bereft father, and help to raise a younger sibling. He put his hands together contemplatively, shaking his head incredulously as he learnt how she had accomplished all this while also assuming the role of housekeeper—with only the memories of her grandmother's example on which to rely, and her faithful Bushman servants to advise her.

I am sure that, had he known the full story then, Jordan would still not have condemned Jasper for what he had done. He would have sympathized with him, given him the benefit of the doubt, and, learning of the extent to which the girls had been educated, he would have commended their father for this. He was utterly amazed to learn of Merry's research, and the fact that she had, furthermore, been working on a thesis for a doctorate when Tristan had come on the scene.

"She must be thoroughly frustrated and desperately bored here!" he exclaimed. "I wonder what can be done about that? I must think of something to interest her…!"—He might have been given some inkling of it from what Reg had passed on to him, but I had not yet got to the part of the story where Tristan had begun to ridicule and humiliate her, and how bitterly he and Adéle Bradshaw had hurt her. When I did tell him, he was dumbfounded.

"It's all very well to have the talents and the extensive learning of which Meredith is entitled to boast, Jordie," I said forthrightly, "but it terrifies her that people might find out how little she knows of anything outside the environs of *Blouspruit*! She knows so much, technically, about so many things, but she does not even know what the Kalahari really looks like!

She remembers *Spoors-einde*—because she went to school there before her mother's death changed everything so drastically. She's familiar with the road from *Blouspruit* to there. With Upington—and what she saw on the way there—and then from there, to here; but, until Reggie took us to Sandton City, and, more recently, the outings with you and your family, that has been all!...She would be quite overcome with embarrassment if anyone were to question her—even about the immediate part of the desert that surrounded her home!"

"And Tristan takes advantage of that, does he?" he demanded disgustedly. "He actually allows her to be taunted?"

I nodded. "He promotes that, but in such a subtle manner that no one would suspect that the torment is deliberate. I think his initial plans were somewhat broader, but, unfortunately, in trying to help her, I may well not have done her any favours. She knows now that she can look the world in the face, with regard to her appearance, but I have realized too late that in helping her to lose her 'difference' I have probably caused her to lose whatever hold she had on him!"

"Well, what is to be done?" Jordan later asked of his parents, after he had relayed to them all that I had told him. "What should I do?"

"About Tristan's attitude towards her, my son? Very little," Ben told him, very wisely. "She is his wife, in the eyes of the law. If this were a case of physical abuse or anything like that, the law could intervene, but this sounds like too obscure a form of ill treatment to be dealt with by you or anyone else. You could, of course, demand that Tristan leave your home and your practice—but what happens to Meredith in such a case? As I see it, all you can do in the foreseeable future is to try and shield her from further derision and hurt.

"As far as his affair with Mrs. Bradshaw is concerned, however, you need to warn him in no uncertain terms, that he stands a chance of being disgraced. Threaten him with the certainty that you will report him, if he does not break that off immediately!"

"Dad," Jordan muttered, his head in his hands, "do you have any idea of how hard this is for me? I have never willingly got anyone into trouble in my life. How can I do this, now, to a man I have sheltered since we were children? He comes across as being so arrogant, but we all know how insecure he is inside!"

"We'll have to pray about this," Ben said, "but," he declared firmly, "I feel very strongly at this moment, that it is high time that Tristan Connaught learnt to stand on his own two feet. He is a grown man, and an experienced physician, and it's up to you to point out to him that you are perfectly capable of managing your practice on your own, rather than be associated with any scandal. Tell him unequivocally that you find his behaviour unacceptable!"

"And Meredith? What do I do about her, in the meantime?"

"All you can do to help her, is to affirm her and do your best to keep her occupied, Jordie," said his mother, offering her opinion for the first time. "I agree wholeheartedly with everything your father has said, and here's a suggestion.... Before I came in on this discussion, I happened to talk to Biddy. Meredith, she tells me, carried the entire responsibility for running her father's home, and did so very successfully. Here's your chance to make her happier, and at the same time turn your house into a home. Speak to the servants, explain that she has authority in your house, and then put it to Meredith that you would appreciate her help."

And so, for the time being, Meredith was happy. As happy as she could be, under the circumstances. Up until then, except for the scone-baking episode, she had been very careful not to behave as though her position in the house carried any weight. Considering how Jordan and Tristan had thus far succeeded in sharing the house amicably, cared for satisfactorily by their servants, she had refrained from intruding; and, particularly because of Tristan's attitude, she had felt much like a guest who might be outstaying her welcome. Now, encouraged by Jordan and his mother, she began, gradually, tactfully, and with her inherent gentleness, to make a few changes.

For the first time she began to feel as though she were indeed the lady of the house. She began by periodically bringing flowers from the garden, rejoicing in being where so many varieties—hitherto unknown to her—were there for the picking, and delighting in the privilege of arranging them. She consulted with the cook and, initially awe-struck by the range of products that could be purchased at the supermarkets—to which there always seemed to be someone willing to take her—periodically did some baking. One Thursday which, she was informed, was traditionally the day when black Christian women attended church, she prepared the entire meal for dinner, and was rewarded by generously expressed compliments.

It spoke well for her inborn diplomacy that none of Jordan's employees showed any signs of dissatisfaction with the new arrangement. In fact, I never saw any of them other than completely satisfied with the 'regime' of the *inkosikazi*, as they referred to her. Having grown up among Bushmen, she found Angelina, the buxom, well-spoken Zulu cook, rather intimidating at first, but the latter very soon became a firm and most spirited supporter of Doctor Tristan's wife—especially after Meredith showed such open interest in her.

Benjamin Ashton was responsible for enlightening Merry as far as the 'Thursday' arrangements were concerned, and also concerning Angelina's standard attire for the weekly religious observance. "It was Tristan's father, Clifford Connaught who first cautioned me," he related. 'Beware if you expect any black female person to work after twelve noon on a Thursday!' was what Clifford actually said. Of course I was baffled. 'Why on earth not?' I asked.

"I then learnt from him that they all go to church. 'Anglican, Methodist, Presbyterian...you name it!' he told me, and then went on to explain that was their 'shot in the arm' which charged their batteries for the rest of the week....Since then I have personally observed that what they get out of it is indeed far more than just 'church', and also that there is a very strict dress code; a special sort of uniform.—You should get Angelina to show you.

"Each denomination has its own, particular colour of blouse, drawn in at the waist with a girdle, over which they wear a large, white, starched collar—shaped a bit like an ephod—not unlike the ones the nuns used to wear with their habits, at the Mission in Lesotho where Father Clifford worked, before coming to be the rector of a little church in Bethlehem. They also wear a very characteristic white, starched cap. ...Sort of four-cornered, for want of a better description!"

Prompted by Ash, Meredith begged Angelina to come and show herself, before leaving the house on the following Thursday, and was so impressed, that she asked him to take a snapshot of Angelina, to be sent home to *Blouspruit* for Susie, Mieta and Malgas to see. This, of course, further endeared her to the woman who, having formerly held sway over the household, could very well have become an adversary. Instead she became an ally for life, and Ben, learning, for the first time, how very much Meredith missed the Bible Study and prayer time with her father and sister, promptly invited her to join him and his family in their oblations, starting that very evening.

An invitation was then also extended to me, and we gathered in the small, intimate sitting room of the senior Ashtons' private suite, where Ash, wanting to set Meredith at ease, very considerately started off by questioning her about the form her own family's Bible studies usually followed. This brought a wistful smile to her exquisite little face.

"It varied," she told him. "Each of us had a favourite passage or two, as I'm sure you do, too, Uncle Ben, but the times I liked best were when my father would ask us to name a verse that had particularly 'jumped out' of our daily readings from a little book called *Daily Light on the Daily Path*', which has set verses for morning and evening of every day in the year. For years we have marked anything that impacted us, noting the year and sometimes the circumstances, so that every time we get to that quotation again, we are able to reflect on what the special message was on a particular morning or evening, and the reason it made such a special impression.

"It's amazing how one can have read something repeatedly, year after year, without it making any impact, and then, one day, a certain verse—or even just a part of it—takes your breath away. Others would have had a different verse speak to each of them....Read it again, on another occasion, and it doesn't come across in the same way.—Something else does!"

"That's right!" Jordan agreed eagerly. "But there are some verses that never leave you, can be applied, over and over again, in varying circumstances, and still have that same significance!"

"Tell you what," Ash suggested, "let's do something different tonight. Why don't each of us take a turn to quote our own, very special verse, and then, if anyone wants prayer for someone—or something—go straight to prayer time?"

It was a source of indescribable pleasure to me, to witness the complete absence of self-consciousness in Meredith's demeanour. She spoke at some length, with sublime confidence, and I believe that in the company of this family she had suddenly found what she must have been missing acutely....The privilege to be herself, and feel completely at home with people who embraced her; who welcomed her into their midst without reservations. It gave me a lump in my throat to appreciate the extent to which she must have been missing her own family, and the degree of disillusionment with which she went to meet each new day. At the same time, the mental picture of Jasper and his daughters at prayer, made me want to weep. When I thought of Rosalie and how she had treated that fine, sensitive man, I winced as I thought of what he might have had to write in his own little book, over the years!

As though she, too, was thinking of her father, Meredith said with newfound perkiness, "I can tell you at once, what one of my father's is! We girls have had to hear it constantly.... Ecclesiastes nine, chapter ten: '*Whatsoever thy hand findeth to do—do it with thy might!*' My own is from Isaiah twenty-six, chapter three: '*Thou shalt keep him* (and her, of course) *in perfect peace, whose mind is stayed on Thee!*' "

"And mine," Jordan contributed promptly," is, '*Be careful for nothing: but in everything by prayer and supplication, make your requests known unto God. And the peace of God which passeth all understanding shall keep your hearts and minds through Jesus Christ.*' That's Philippians four, verses six and seven. And I have another, which is similar. '*In quietness and in confidence shall be your strength!*' Isaiah thirty, verse fifteen!"

And that's precisely what I, Biddy, had been seeing in him, more and more clearly with each passing year, since he was a boy!

I think that Meredith, his parents, and I, were equally disappointed when Jordan was called out to a nearby home shortly after that, to see a child with what sounded like a severe attack of asthma. We spent roughly another thirty minutes in prayer, and then, after enjoying a cup of 'bush' tea, known as *Rooibos*, we were treated to more first-class music by the other members of our own, private, 'in-house' orchestra.

Needless to say, these developments were not exactly pleasing to Tristan. Apart from the fact that his supposedly infatuated Meredith had betrayed no sign of exactly pining for him, of late, it must also be remembered that he considered himself to have first claim on the Ashtons, and she had virtually usurped his place! He sulked—but I was elated!

As I had told Jordan's mother, Amy-Lee, Merry had borne the sole responsibility for the smooth running of her father's ménage for many years. And, because, in leaving her home to be with Tristan, she had, in addition, also had to leave behind her lab and her music. I added that I had been immensely concerned about her enforced idleness, with the possibility of resultant boredom or, at worst, depression. I had to confess that, having been told by someone in *Spoors-einde* that, in the city, the employer was often dictated to by the employee, I was relieved to find that, in Jordan's house—where the domestic arrangements were based on mutual respect—that was clearly not the case. Meredith seemed happier, and, as a consequence, I was happier, too.

The Ashtons were a musical family. There were very few people in Bethlehem who had not known about Jamie Ashton's incredible talent, and how brilliantly he had been able play everything from Gospel music to New Orleans jazz on the clarinet, his body moving to the rhythm of some music that came to him from nowhere, as his fingers moved over the instrument with wondrous facility.

After Jamie's death, declaring that it was as if Jordan had the spirit of her 'dearest boy' in him, it had made Aunt Minnie de Beer weep with emotion the first time she heard him do the same, and, with equal passion—going off at improvisational tangents, the way Jamie would play jazz; weaving around the melody, sometimes swooping down below the basic tune, and sometimes soaring above it in the most glorious manner.

It was difficult enough to reconcile the image of Jordan, the dedicated physician, with the transported musician. Now I was to learn that Ash Ashton, head of a vast conglomerate and one of the wealthiest men in the world, was similarly gifted—a consummate pianist—which perhaps explained the fine Steinway grand in Jordan's living room.

It was an experience to hear father and son play together, but we were to be further transported with delight, when Jordan fetched his mother's cello from his parents' suite. Perhaps it was the excellence of the performance, or just the exquisite pain engendered by the particular piece of music, but, to our dismay, Meredith suddenly burst into tears, and ran from the room, sobbing. Jordan, greatly concerned, went after her to try and ascertain what the cause was, and I, hoping to reassure Ash and Amy-Lee, explained that Merry and her father were also musicians, and that perhaps it was that, particular composition, or the fact that Jasper, too, was a cellist, that had reminded her too poignantly of him.

What Jordan said to Meredith I'll never know, but she came back presently, looking a little sheepish, with him leading her by the hand. "Just a touch of homesickness," he kindly explained, on her behalf, and then suggested that it was time we had some refreshments. Later, upon learning that she, too, played, he persuaded Meredith that it was her turn, took up his clarinet, once more, while his mother drew her cello closer, and when Tristan came in, about half-an-hour later, it was to find, with no small measure of surprise, that his wife was happily making music with the Ashtons.

That night, when Jordan went to say goodnight to his parents, Benjamin happened to inquire how and where he had caught up with Meredith, after she had fled upstairs, and he seemed to find Jordie's answer significant. "I heard her," he replied, "and that's how I found her.... I found her in her bedroom, crying her eyes out!—Why do you ask?"

"*Her* bedroom? Not in Tristan's?" Amy-Lee exchanged an eloquent look with Ben. "It's just as I thought!"

"What are you suggesting, Mom?" Jordan was quick to ask. "What is just as you thought?"

"Those two don't live like married people, my son," she observed quietly, and, because I did not yet know the story of the early years of Amy-Lee's own marriage[13], it puzzled me that it should look suspiciously as though there were tears in her eyes. "That sweet young person! How could he have been so callous? I am still baffled by the situation, and much troubled, wondering what *really* made Tristan want to bring her here!"

This time Jordan filled in for his mother whatever he might previously have omitted from Meredith's story, leaving out nothing and making a point of including what I suspected as having been the basic reason behind Tristan's marrying her. And, as was to be expected, Amy-Lee was shocked!

Jordan was very quick to comment appreciatively on the evidence of Meredith's presence in his home. He could hardly credit it that so dainty a person could be passionate about gardening, but promptly gave her *carte blanche,* demonstrating his sincerity by immediately instructing the gardener, in her presence, that *Inkosikazi* Meredith was to be given all the help she desired.

More than once I was to hear how much he enjoyed having her there, and how he now realized that, as his mother had said, it indeed took a woman to make a house a home. Unfortunately Tristan—the one by whom Meredith secretly longed to be appreciated—chose to ignore her efforts. Meanwhile she and her father talked regularly on the telephone, and I communicated with Jasper, more than once, but by some sort of tacit agreement, neither of us saw fit to advise him of the true state of affairs. When Doc Hugo and I talked, I was happy to hear him say he was doing well, but of course said nothing to him about the situation, either.

The Ashtons, or I, also kept in constant touch with Reggie, as we were all anxious for news of Felicity, and we were relieved to learn that the surgery had gone well. When the time came for her to be taken back to Bethlehem, from Bloemfontein, Ash offered to fly her there, and kindly invited me to accompany them. It was a long time since I had set foot in the National Hospital in Bloemfontein—South Africa's 'centre city', where I had done my training—or been back to visit my old hometown, but, eager as I was to go, I did not want to leave Meredith. So it came about that she was included in the invitation, and the four of us accordingly went off together to the Free State, to fetch Reggie and his mother...on an errand that would have important consequences!

Anyone who meets Benjamin Ashton, or 'Ash' to his friends, will no doubt soon come to discern that he is a man of deep faith, that he believes in 'Divine Appointments' and most definitely does not believe in coincidence. Because she had never flown before, Meredith was seated up front, beside him, and as we were coming in to land in Bethlehem, he pointed out a windmill, and explained for her benefit, that the sprawling, red roofed buildings far below us, were all part of the *Eugenie Beauclaire* Centre, founded by his late brother, and named for their grandmother. A few minutes later he informed us with unconcealed excitement: "I've just been given the most wonderful inspiration!—Unquestionably the answer to a prayer!"

The next morning, after we had settled Felicity back in her little house, I took Meredith to meet some of my old friends, among them Tristan's still very English grandmother Burkett, who, after talking to Merry and making it known that she would not object to being addressed as 'Grandma', remarked with the forthrightness which is the prerogative of the elderly: "Probably the first sensible thing that rapscallion has ever done in his life! That boy truly has the devil in him!"

And I'll be darned if Meredith didn't go and stick up for the blighter with a sharp retort. "Only after having qualified as a physician, I'd say, Grandma Burkett!" was her defensive riposte, which tickled the old lady enough to make her pat Merry's hand and inform her that she thought she was going to like her. " Matter of fact young madam," she informed her, " I do, already!"

Back at Felicity's home, we found the patient lying on the couch, looking considerably more cheerful than she had appeared to be, immediately after arriving home the previous day. Ben, Amy-Lee and Reggie were there, having tea and keeping her company, and from the moment I entered the living room, I sensed that they were all in particularly good spirits.

Reggie was the first to speak, and, holding his mother's hand, he announced joyfully, "Aunt Biddy, with God's help, my immediate problems have all just been swept away. If Jordie agrees, and I have no doubt that he will, Uncle Ben has proposed that, as part of their philanthropic outreach, the Ashton Corporation sponsor Jordie's clinic—as their South African Aid project does with the *Eugenie Beauclaire* Centre— and I have been offered a job there as Jordan's assistant!"

"That's wonderful!" I cried, and Meredith concurred enthusiastically: "What a brilliant idea!"

"Jordie does not have the time or the resources to keep it open for as many hours a day, as he would like," Reggie went on, and, because the new arrangement would be of benefit to the underprivileged—to whom I have vowed to dedicate my life—it will not only provide me with an income, but will also mean that, by comparison with some of places I have served, I will be much closer to my mother."...Somehow there was nothing in that statement that came across as the least bit self-righteous, for that was honestly the way he lived his life. It was a tribute to Felicity, for that was how she lived hers, and to James Ashton the third, who had set the example.

"I promised Jordan that we would talk about this sometime, but I have selfishly kept postponing that conversation," Ash confessed. "For several reasons...among them a concern that if the scope of the clinic were to be broadened, and if Jordan did not find the right sort of person to help him, he would end up carrying a heavier burden than would be good for him. On the other hand, there was the certainty that he would not accept financial help from me. He has inherited a double dose of that stubborn desire for independence!...From my brother, Jamie, who gave up everything to come to this country, in order to prove that he could do without the help of his father, or the Ashton Corporation—and ended up caring for black children! And from me, Jordie's own father, once an insecure man, devoid of all faith, who wanted only to do whatever his big brother did. Who ended up establishing a citrus farm in South Africa—and nearly lost his precious wife in the process...!"

At that, Amy-Lee put her hand lovingly on his shoulder, as though to reassure him, and when he lifted it from there and held it to his mouth, I was suddenly given a small clue to the cause of the tears misting those beautiful blue eyes when she had asked about Meredith, and where she slept.

"I suspect that Jordan's heart is in the clinic, but he keeps up the practice in Sandton to support it. I firmly believe however, that no patient is ever short-changed there as a result," said his father.

"That's quite true, Uncle Ben," Reg concurred. "They adore him, and if anyone ever dared to say, in my presence, that he is another who panders to the 'rich and famous', I would only have to respond with his own words: "They get to be just as sick as anyone else, Reggie, and, rich or poor, all my people deserve the best medical care I can give them!"

Presently there were two phone calls for Ash; one from Jordie, and the other from Zhaynie. While Jordan was clearly touched by his father's offer, it took Ben some fast-talking to persuade him that agreeing to a philanthropic company's sponsorship of what could be known as the *Eugenie Beauclaire* clinic, was not the same as accepting money from his father, and that more people could be helped in the facility if it were extensively upgraded. "I know you derive enormous joy and satisfaction from having established all that by yourself, son," he pointed out, "but consider this....There could, perhaps, even be a soup kitchen or a free cafeteria for the patients."

So Jordie finally accepted the offer with gratitude, and I, Biddy, was left with the impression that it was the part about creating a position for Reggie on the staff that had helped to persuade him!

He had hardly rung off, when Zhaynie phoned, explaining that Angelina had told her where to find her parents. She sent her love to Felicity and the rest of us, and then announced that she and Dominic had decided to take the advice of those whom they had consulted, including that of his unselfish parents, and were prepared to return to Long Island with her parents, for the birth of their child.

"One thing saddens me greatly, Dad," she had to admit, however, "and it is that, by leaving, I shan't be able to have Uncle Dick Evans to deliver my baby. Not only is he our doctor, my godfather, and your other best friend, but he also brought both Jordie and me into the world, as well as every Crawford child, from Antoinette down to Gregory, Isobel, and their Benjamin!

"Re-living the golden days of my own childhood, being spoilt by Phineas and Sarah—who are still so dear to me— playing with their numerous grandchildren, whenever we were here, eating *putu*[14] and gravy with my fingers, on the grass— under the Syringa tree—and riding among the groves, on the tractors with you...that is what I dreamt of for the children I hoped to have! I wanted to sit on the stoep you built, and wait—as my mother did for you—for my fine, strong Dominic, wearing his big boots and floppy felt hat, smelling of the sun and the soil, to come home for tea....And, oh, Daddy, it hurts to let go of a dream!"

Her words triggered nostalgia of such heartbreaking proportions, that it constricted his chest and blurred his eyes. He had to go outside, to where he could be alone, and groan out loud, as he needed to do. So many memories, and so many emotions surged through his mind, that he could hardly bear it.

Zhaynie's reference to how her mother would sit on the stoep at *Beauclaire* to await his coming, took him right back to the day after Amy-Lee had first arrived from Britain to join him. He had been up since dawn, and, returning to the house in the fresh, early morning air, from where he had been working at the lower end of the orange orchard was the happiest moment of his life, thus far. When he saw her sitting on the stoep, the joy was so overwhelming that he could hardly breathe. He had vaulted over the side door of the Jeep like a teenager, and gone bounding up the steps, two at a time, calling out to her, "Hi, there, pretty lady! Good morning to you!"

She was still in her housecoat, sipping coffee, and she looked up with a smile when she heard his voice. Something was different about her. The beautiful hair, no longer confined, was a cascade of shining gold down to below her shoulder blades, and he was instantly taken back to another morning. The day he had come home from Harvard, especially to take her to her graduation ball. She had been waiting for him at the top of the steps at *Bentleigh*, his family's Long Island residence, smiling in welcome, grown into a stunningly beautiful, elegant young woman; her school days behind her. And years later, he was amazed that he had not been able to recognize that the rush of pleasure he had felt then, was love! On that occasion he had also leapt out of the vehicle and bounded up the steps exultantly, just as he would, again and again, and that spontaneous, embrace was what his lovely child would constantly see, remember, and want for herself.

He could understand so well why she loved their South African *Beauclaire,* where the perfume of orange blossoms, and the glory of all that flourished there, made every day glorious. Where the Southern Cross in the starry heavens, made each night magical. He knew that she and Dominic were as happy there as he and Amy-Lee had been. Theirs was a good marriage, a union of two beautiful people, deeply in love, by the Grace of God, and he was reminded of what Antoinette had written about the two of them, in her book...

The allusion to himself was embarrassing, but the rest of her description was very sweet. *"The middle Ashton child is called Eugenie. (Pronounced like 'Zhaynie'),"* she wrote. *"She is very, very beautiful. Just as nice as her mother is, but, strangely enough, is not one of the 'blonde' Ashtons. They say she looks more like the Beauclaires of Louisiana, and her hair—which is as long and shiny as her mother's—is as black as the poetic 'raven's wing'. She has her father's devastating smile and his intense blue eyes, though....Now, there's another case of 'love at first sight'!*

"Once every year the Ashtons go back and stay in the house Uncle Ash built there in the 1970's, and which has, of course, had to be enlarged over the years, to accommodate the children. In all that time, Dominic and Eugenie hardly saw each other. During this last visit to America, however, when the Verweys brought Dominic with them, it was as though they, Zhaynie and Dominic, had been struck by lightning! What will come of that, I don't know. I can't begin to imagine how Eugenie's family will feel about her marrying and going to live in South Africa—especially at a time when people are leaving there in droves! It's like my parents' story in reverse!"

And now the same 'lightning-struck' two were about to become parents—and he and the woman who still held every corner of his heart, the person with whom he was still as much in love as he had been when it was she, and not her daughter, who had sat on the stoep waiting for her man to come home, were about to become grandparents!

Somehow, here he was, again, in Bethlehem, where he had been led to take some pretty big steps in his pilgrimage towards the intimate knowledge of God.

He raised his eyes to the heavens, and offered up a fervent prayer...

We flew back to Johannesburg next morning, leaving Reg to take care of Felicity for a while longer, and this time it was Amy-Lee who sat in front with Ben. They did not talk loudly, and sometimes spoke to one another in the Louisiana French of their grand-mothers—which, of course I did not understand—but when they reverted to English, it was possible to catch snatches of their conversation, and I heard Amy-Lee make the observation to Ben, that he seemed to have shed some of the heaviness that had so obviously been oppressing him ever since he had been back to Nelspruit.

"What has been troubling you so awfully, my darling?" she asked him at one stage. "You, the one who always reassures the rest of us. Aren't you the same one who so readily quotes from Proverbs eighteen, verse ten? The one who reminds us that *'the name of the Lord is a strong tower and the righteous runneth into it and is safe'*...In times of anxiety, or if ever anyone tried to make you doubt the power of prayer you would unfailingly affirm, as Paul wrote to Timothy: *'I know whom I have believed, and I am persuaded...!'* Why can't you now?"

"I still believe that, dear heart," he said with conviction. "What you saw was not depression, fear or lack of faith. It was *sorrow*! I sometimes felt as though my heart could break for what was, and what can no longer be!...No one knows better than you do, how I have always cringed at the very mention of war, because of the effect it had on my childhood and my relationship with my father...and now it seems that there are few places in the world, where there is no war. Now a new generation is being sucked into the vortex, from which there seems to be no escape, but I accept and take comfort from the conviction that God knows all about it, and it's His business to worry about—not mine! He will sort it out according to His will!

"The fact that Willie's first-born has been maimed, remains a cause for mourning—despite the courageous manner in which Matt carries on with his life. It still sickens me that the rest of Willie's children have had to go away and leave him and Bets behind. It is sad that, if they go to join them in Canada, they have to leave behind the house that that family built, together! The house with so many memories. The house in which Willie's wonderful parents ministered to me, where the Lord touched me, and not only sent me back to Nelspruit, prepared to face the consequences of the court case, but later equipped me with the fortitude to go home and take up my responsibilities in the States once more. In His own time, He gave me you, and a fine son like James, to help me carry that burden, as I grow older! He gave me Jordan, whom I love so dearly, and of whom I am so proud; and he gave me a daughter who is as good as she is beautiful.

"I have hated to think of New Orleans devastated by Hurricane Katrina, and the damage that was done to your grandmother's home in Louisiana. But, thanks be to God, we were blessed to have my *Gran'mère* Beauclaire's plantation, and to make it available to the Crawfords and their precious charges—with no loss of life! We have many homes, my love.—How perverse I am to persist in allowing that, of them all, my heart still is with the one I may have to relinquish!...

My beloved home beneath the Southern Cross. My *Beauclaire* in Nelspruit!...Will you ever know the hurt of it, Amy-Lee? Our daughter does!"

"I will indeed. Because I feel the same, my dearest Ash," she said, so softly that I could barely hear her. "We found each other there, beloved, and there we conceived our first child. We dreamt of living there in our old age, surrounded by our sturdy grandchildren....How tragic that, as things are now, it is not even considered expedient for the first of them to be born there!...But we are not alone, and we are not the first. The Bible is crammed with stories about people who had had to go through worse than that..."

"I know," Ben agreed. "And now I will confess to you, as I have to my God, that I am deeply ashamed! You said that I seemed to be less despondent—and that is because not only have I been reminded in the twenty-second verse of Psalm fifty-five that I am to cast my burdens upon the Lord, but Jesus, himself, invited us to hand our burdens over to him. I have now done so! I have put all the self-pity, and every other problem, on the altar, and, having shared my concerns with Him, I am vastly comforted—for *I know whom I have believed, and I am persuaded...*!' Whatever happens now is His will!"

And, to this day, I catch my breath whenever I remember how, as we arrived back at Jordan's house, he came running towards his parents with his cell phone in his hand.

"I'm an uncle, praise God!" he cried. "Welcome home, *Grand-père* Ash and *Grand-mère* Amy-Lee. You have a bonny grandson! Young Benjamin Paul Verwey was born twenty minutes ago—at *Beauclaire*, would you believe it? By the Grace of God, Doc Evans and Aunt Trudy, surely the finest obstetric team anywhere, just happened to be visiting there. Everything is under control. They have asked me to give you their love, and to tell you that they will also extend the best of care to the overwhelmed new dad!"

For a moment or two Ben was too overcome to speak. Then he put his arms around his wife and son, and proclaimed, loudly and exultantly: *"The Lord has spoken*! We give Him thanks and praise!...Hallelujah!"

CHAPTER SIX

Aday or two before we'd left for Bethlehem, I had noticed that Tristan seemed to be a little more attentive to Meredith; even so what transpired at the breakfast table next morning was a surprise.

Jordan had taken his parents to the airport, and because they had snatched an early snack, there were only the three of us, Meredith, Tristan and I, at the table. Conversation was desultory, to say the least, and because I am one of the unfortunate people afflicted with a compulsion to speak lest silence becomes awkward, I had made some trite comment about how eager Ash and Amy-Lee must be to get to Nelspruit, and how fortunate they were to have their own plane, when— apropos absolutely nothing—Tristan looked up from buttering his toast, suddenly turned to Meredith, and tersely demanded, "Well did you miss me while you were gone, or was my old pal, Reginald, vying too eagerly for your attention?"

I held my breath, waiting for her to reply, and when she did so, I had to blink. "No, Tristan," she said flatly. "To answer both your questions…No!…Number one, I did not! And two, he certainly *was* not!…But I do miss my father, and occasionally I miss a man I left behind, in a Kalahari hotel!"—A rejoinder which, coming from an unsophisticated girl, who knew so little about men, I considered to be quite admirable.

Whether this was when he started stewing about a long-distance call he'd received the night before, I don't know, for, until then, he had not said a word about it to us. Anyway, after finishing his breakfast in sullen silence, he pushed his chair back with such force that it almost fell over, and then, without as much as excusing himself from the table, he turned to me and, in a tone of voice so icy that it boded no good, announced: "I'd like a word with you. Will you kindly come with me to my study!"

I smiled reassuringly at Merry, who looked alarmed; and understandably startled myself, I followed him with some trepidation. Feeling much like a child probably would, when summoned to the principal's office for committing a misdemeanour, I tried to predict what was coming, and allowed all manner of possibilities to flash through my mind. However, the reality of what I did encounter was the last thing I could have anticipated!

"How *dare* you!" he yelled at me, the moment I entered the room, "What the devil do my affairs have to do with you, Bridget Williams? And who asked you to take it upon yourself to go and introduce Meredith to my grandmother?...Was it not to be expected that she would immediately telephone my parents and tell them of your visit?"

"It never occurred to me that you would be displeased, Tristan!" I replied, bristling. "And I do not like to be reprimanded like a naughty child. Mrs. Burkett is an acquaintance of mine, and I thought it would give her pleasure to see how wisely you had chosen. I don't know why it should matter that she, in turn, reported the visit to your parents, and, in any case, don't you think that she would have heard about it, sooner or later—perhaps from Reggie's mother, or someone else?—Would she not have been affronted if her newly-acquired granddaughter had been in Bethlehem, and had not bothered to pay her as much as a courtesy call?"

"I knew from the beginning that it was a mistake to bring you here!" he flung at me. "You have been nothing but a troublemaker and an irritant to everyone in the house!"

"To you, you mean!" I responded furiously. "No one else has given me any indication that that might be the case. I know why I am such a thorn in your flesh, my boy," I went on, throwing all caution to the winds as my temper rose, and recklessly jumping in, feet first. "You know that I have been able to see through you from the first day you came to *Spoorseinde* as a teenager. I never thought that the sweet little child of two such wonderful parents could grow up to be such a disappointment!...Did you think that I was deceived, for one minute? I was well aware of what you were up to. I knew very well what you were planning to do with Meredith, and there was nothing I could do to stop you!"

That did it! "I'm not your 'boy' Mrs. Self-righteous Williams!" he retaliated, furiously kicking the door shut, and next thing we were going at it hammer and tongs! Meanwhile poor Meredith, who had never, in her entire life, heard a voice raised in anger, or a door purposely slammed, did what she would have done at *Blouspruit* when she needed to think. She snatched up the large straw hat that had replaced the sunbonnet, and was conveniently lying where she had left it on the front stoep, put on her sunglasses, and headed for the garden.

And it was there that Jordan, returning from seeing his parents off, found her.

"Good morning, Miss Muffet!" he called out cheerfully. "What a charming sight, on a beautiful summer's day. I miss the bonnet, though!"

She looked up from cutting the dead heads off the hydrangeas, and tried to smile, but it was hopeless. "Oh, Jordie!" The quivering of her lips made it difficult to get the words out, and he saw that tears were very close. "They're fighting in the house!"

"They're what? Who's fighting, Merry?" He was completely nonplussed, "In the *house?*"

"Aunt Biddy and Tristan! He's very cross with her about something, and they went into his study to have it out—but they soon began to shout at each other, so I ran out here. I think it's got something to do with Aunt Biddy, and me, and I would hate ever to be the cause of disunity in your home!...I know now that it is your home, Jordie, but I didn't when I brought Aunt Biddy with me. I should have asked you for permission to bring a visitor, and I apologize!"

"Meredith!" he was quick to reassure her, as she told me later. "I'm only too glad that you invited her! My parents are, too. And I love to come home and find the two of you here, waiting for me." He smiled, and like every one else at whom that smile was ever directed, she was warmed by it. "I love the inviting smells that come from the kitchen, I love the flowers in my house, and I love seeing a real, live, little Lucy Locket with garden shears in her pocket!"

"As I said before," she told him, a crooked smile beginning to light up her own face, "it's a never-ending source of delight to me to find that so much of what I was unable to plant in my own garden, grows here."—He noticed that the sweet mouth had stopped trembling and the tiny hands had stopped shaking.—"I only wish I knew the names, and could identify every single flower and shrub in your garden. I intend to buy a book, especially about the indigenous flowers and shrubs I have longed to see for myself, and perhaps, if the climate is suitable, you would let me plant a few of them here!"

"Most of what you see was already here when I bought the place," he admitted, "and I don't know all the names, myself, so I'd be interested too. When my dad goes into raptures about what he has in his *Beauclaire* garden in Nelspruit, I can't compete.—Tell you what," he said, "sounding just like his father, "how about I give you such a book for Christmas? You can choose it, yourself, if you like, and then maybe you, and Auntie Bid and I, can go to a nursery and buy whatever takes your fancy.—On second thoughts, why don't we get the book today, and then, when you've had time to decide what you want, we can go again, and get whatever you like, in time for Christmas!...I need to leave here soon, but the shops will still be open later, and maybe we could go then. I'll take my pager with me, in case I'm needed."

"I'd really enjoy that! Thank you, Jordie." Now her own, lovely smile was back, reflected in her eyes, and he was enchanted by it.

Seeing that she was obviously feeling much happier, he deemed it safe to go inside, and reluctantly left her to enjoy what she was doing, while he went to see what he could do to restore the peace. Also very wary now of doing anything that might further displease Tristan, he decided that he had better invite him to join in the excursion to the bookstore.

Wisely, when speaking to Jordan, Tristan skipped a few of the details concerning the cause of his anger, knowing that it would have been difficult for him to grasp why any man would take so long to advise his parents of his marriage. After due consideration, he must also have realized that Jordie would have thought it very odd that his, Tristan's, parents had had to learn from his grandmother that their son had 'taken a wife'. In addition, by the time Jordan came and spoke to me, I had calmed down. Despite the extent to which it had bothered me ever since, I had also had time to reflect, and consequently resolved to say nothing to him about that one part of what I had heard Tristan say to Reggie at the time of our arrival. Nevertheless, it would soon become apparent that, in spite of what both Tristan and I withheld from Jordan, he, too was troubled.

I realize now that, being the man he was, I should have shared with Jordie the range of circumstances that had begun to trouble me more and more, beginning with the shock that a bridegroom bringing home a new bride, should have phrased a request as Tristan had done. I had, in the first place, taken exception to his asking another man to show her to her room; but it was the '*her* bedroom' part of it that had become significant to me. Although I knew, mostly from the movies, that, throughout history, there had been married couples, especially wealthy ones, who each had their own room, but, in this day and age, it did not seem normal to me—unless, of course, there was a special set of circumstances that made such an arrangement necessary.

Then one night, when Merry and I were watching television—which was still a novelty to her—I don't know which shook me more, the unexpectedly daring and almost censorable scenes in one film we were watching, or Meredith's reaction to them.

"Good gracious, Aunt Biddy!" she exclaimed incredulously, covering her eyes with her hands. "Do people ever really behave like that?"

"If they're married, perhaps," I responded lamely.

"But do they actually *sleep* in the same room? *In the same bed*?"

For once in my life I was wordless. Inarticulate—until it struck me! Of course, Meredith would have no knowledge of such arrangements. Her parents had probably never shared a room, and here, because we lived at opposite sides of the house, she would not be aware that Ash and Amy-Lee did! My tactful little 'talk' in *Spoors-einde*, had clearly not covered the subject broadly enough. Having conscientiously stuck to my own room at that ghastly hotel, I now shrank from asking about the sleeping arrangements on her wedding night!

Right from the outset, Tristan's choice of words had seemed very odd to me, and now—strange as it may seem, and without my knowledge—Jordan had a similar concern. Having heard both sides of the story, one thing that had resulted from his talk with Tristan, was that he, Jordan, had been given cause to mull over some of his mother's remarks concerning the relationship between Tristan and his wife. And, not yet made aware of what was going through Jordan's mind, the more I thought about this, the more concerned I became, and I believed that there was no one with whom I could discuss my unease.

After the run-in with Tristan, I had only one desire, and that was to go home. I missed *Spoors-einde*. I missed my work, Doc Hugo, and—I finally owned up to this in my heart—I missed Jasper acutely; but I could not leave until I had found a solution to Tristan's bizarre behaviour. Nor could I expect Jordan to take the responsibility for the care of his partner's wife.

It was thus an enormous relief to learn that Ben Ashton was due back shortly. The Ashtons hated to be separated, but these circumstances were unique. Amy-Lee elected to be with her daughter and the new baby, while Ash had to be back for an urgent meeting in Isando, and would be staying with Jordan for about two days.

I had known him for many years, but was not aware, until I read what Antoinette Verwey had written about that in her book, that Benjamin Ashton would take time off from running a 'stupendous international conglomerate to conduct missions around the world.' He ministered, she said, in the market place, to his staff, and to some of the wealthiest—but often unhappiest—people with whom he did business. In that case, I reckoned, Ben Ashton, by the grace of God, had to be an experienced and trained counsellor, and would surely know what I should do. In the meantime I resolved to pray for guidance.

As we were soon to learn, I was not the only one who was pleased to hear the news that Ash was coming. Though it was not for the same reason that I rejoiced, or just because Jordan was anxious for news of his sister and his new, baby nephew, he was also openly impatient for his father to arrive.

As their offices closed early on Wednesdays, it was Tristan's custom to play golf on those afternoons, and when he made it known that he would not be home for dinner, Jordie reacted promptly. "How about we go to the Mall during the quieter time, after five, and I buy the ladies an early dinner, after we've done our shopping?" And of course we accepted readily.

I insisted on sitting on the back seat of Jordan's car, while Meredith sat beside him, in front, and, before very long, the two of them were chatting away happily, as only two people who feel completely comfortable with one another, can do.

"I'm so glad my dad is coming," he told Merry, " and I sincerely hope he isn't going to be tied up with so much business at the plant, that he doesn't have time to try out some music with me. Very often I just tootle away on the clarinet by myself, because I find it difficult to find an accompanist, and, because of my irregular hours, I can hardly inflict myself on a regular group. Now I'm dying to try out an exciting arrangement of 'Rhapsody in Blue', which was of course written to be a concerto for piano and orchestra, and, as I don't have an orchestra to back me, it presents me with a challenge. This is primarily why I find this arrangement so exciting. It provides me with an opportunity to play more than just the introduction on the clarinet.

"I love the music because it is such a masterful blend of jazz and what today would be know as 'pop' music, but I need my father to do the hard work. He plays the entire rhapsody as a piano solo from start to finish, brilliantly, and, what is usually the piano part, just as Gershwin himself would have played it—fast, fast, *fast*!—But I have fallen in love with a CD on which the pathos of the 'lead in' on the clarinet almost makes me want to weep.

"That is what it sounds like to me!...Sobbing!...One reviewer referred to that as 'wailing'—and that's *exactly* how I want to play it—with the intro sliding up the scale with that 'trilling' glissando, at such a pace that it takes one's breath away, and the heartrending sound of it tearing at one's heart like a cry for help! I can't wait to try that, with Dad providing the background in certain passages, and then taking over the solo part in the third movement. You'll enjoy that, I'm sure!"

"I know I shall, and I'm looking forward to hearing that. You are as blessed to have your father love music and be able to play well, as I am.... I know exactly what you mean by that sliding up the scale part. My father has a vinyl recording—by Paul Whiteman's orchestra, I think—and my sister and I have listened to that often on an old gramophone—or what you probably call a 'phonograph'. Although Susie has never seen either a mountain or snow, she says that clarinet conjures up a picture for her, of a skier going up a rise and then speeding down the other side!"

"Marvellous!" Jordan cried. " Yes! Yes!—It was the Boston train that inspired the furious rhythm that Gershwin introduces into the composition, but, after this, I'll also picture that skier, only, as he is going down, I'll see him turning somersaults!—Oh, Meredith, you must hear my father!"

"I've heard him play, if you recall, and, listening to that Chopin *Polonaise* the other night, I was quite sick with envy."

"He is great," Jordan agreed. "And what I find most amazing, is that his moods are so clearly reflected in his choice of music. What he plays is what he feels, so there's a more than remote chance that he may not feel like Gershwin when we do get started. He is a very accommodating man, and likes to oblige, but it's never the same when his heart is not in it; so, depending on how things go at the plant, there's a possibility that I may not be able to get him to do that."

All at once he shook his head compassionately, as a memory of what he had learnt about his father at another time, came to him.

"Phineas and Sarah, who have been with my dad since he first embarked on the citrus project near Nelspruit, have plenty of stories to tell about him; and many of those stories concern his despair during a time when my mother was not able to be there with him. When he was alone in the house, they will tell you, his presence was always betrayed by the desperate sound coming from the piano. I know, from the way they have described that music, that he must seldom have played any but the most complicated études, and when I questioned him, personally, about that time, I learnt that he did not play Debussy, or Chopin—unless it was a work like '*Marche Militaire*', which he could pound out, the way he played some of his choices from Wagner. No dreamy waltzes; but when he really got his teeth into jazz or '*Rhapsody in Blue*', the servants could only look at one another and raise their eyebrows questioningly.

" 'This was how he had played after the *kleinmiesies* (little missus) had had the accident,' they say. Sometimes after the *baas* had spoken to her on the telephone, the music would be kinder to the instrument, but once, when he had not heard from her for ten days, and was unable to reach her for himself, they knew all about it!"

"Your parents appear to be a singular couple, Jordie," Merry observed, "and you are a very blessed family!"

"We are, indeed," he agreed, "And how pleased I am that you did not say that we are 'lucky'! I get quite hot under the collar when Tristan says that to me, sometimes almost accusingly. Just as fervent as my father is in protesting the existence of 'coincidence', he, Dad, also passionately disputes the possibility of 'luck'."

"My father would agree, wholeheartedly," she said. "And I think it was your father who convinced him of that, when he visited us all those years ago."

"That's quite possible," he agreed. "And it was the father of his friend, Willie Marais who first impressed that upon him. You must have heard us speak of Matt Marais. Well his full name is 'Matthewis', the Afrikaans form of the name 'Matthew', and, as Dad tells it, when he went to Uncle Willie's house for the first time, the two boys, Matthewis and Markus could easily have been my uncle Jamie and himself, at that age, while the bright five-year-old Lucia—more often called Lucy—might have been 'little Amy-Lee', who is now my mother.

"Willie's father had explained to Dad that the boys were named for Matthew, Mark and Luke in the New Testament, and he, my dad, had no sooner asked why they had skipped 'John', when he regretted it. He felt that he had been facetious.... Even more so when Mr. Marais explained that there had been a 'John'—more precisely, a 'Johannes'—but he had died soon after birth, and because the doctors had told Uncle Willie and Auntie Bets that they couldn't have another child, Lucy was all the more precious. This was when my dad observed that they were very lucky."

"And then?" Merry wanted to know.

"Well apparently Jacob Marais was silent for a time before he responded thoughtfully, that he would rather put that as 'blessed'. In his vocabulary there were no such words as 'luck' or 'co-incidence'. He did not believe in 'ships passing in the night', either. That, in his opinion, made God too small! He believed implicitly, and now my father does, too, that God is bigger than mere chance. He, too, believes that we meet, and things happen, by Divine intervention!"

"What a riveting story, Jordie!" Meredith responded. "And I believe that, for some reasons I did not understand at that time, my father derived tremendous comfort from hearing it!"

By then Jordan had found a convenient parking spot, and, telling us to wait until he came around and opened our doors for us, he already had one foot on the ground when Meredith offered shyly: "I'd be happy to play the piano part with you, if your dad does not find an opportunity to do so, Jordie. My father maintains that my hands are too small, and that I lack the physical strength to bring that furious, nervous, typical Gershwin rhythm to the third movement, but then I'm quite comfortable with the subtle, more restrained, second.

"We shan't have the kettle drums to establish that characteristic jazz rhythm I am accustomed to hearing on other recordings, but from there it soon moves to the principal theme, which is where, I guess, you will also want to come in and replace the deeper bass sound of the bassoon, with that of your clarinet. If you are going to try an entirely different version from what I'm used to, it promises to be an exhilarating experience. A challenge to me to give it a go! I'll do my best!"

For the moment, Jordie forgot all about getting out of the car. "I've heard you, don't you forget that, either!" he responded eagerly. "And right, here and now, I'm taking you up on your offer! You play very well indeed, and it would be fantastic—beyond my wildest dreams—to have an accompanist 'on tap', as it were, right there, on the spot, in my very own house!…By the way, we also have an old 'gramophone'—I grew up in this country don't forget! It's stored in what we call the 'Garden Cottage.' "

"Is that the sweet little place I can see when I'm busy in the garden? Beyond the orchard? I stole a wonderful ripe peach, still warm from the sun, the other day, and I spotted the little house from where I was standing."

"Yes. It was one of the attractions of this place when I bought it, because I wanted to give my family their own space whenever they came to visit. A few years ago, we altered the main house, along the lines of what we have on Long Island. *Bentleigh*—where my brother James and his wife live—is about three times the size of this, but we did the best we could.

"My dad had the Long Island mansion remodelled in such a way that when the Crawfords—Antoinette's family—came to live with us, they would have a complete suite, almost like a separate cottage, and there are two smaller suites like theirs, for friends, missionaries on furlough, or others who need to make a fairly prolonged stay in New York. Now that Antoinette is married, and living in Pietermaritzburg with her husband, Stephen—another member of the Verwey family, and also a specialist in tropical diseases like herself, and his grandfather, *El-Hakim*—and her sister, Isobel, unfailingly called Izzie, which she hates, is married to my brother, the Crawfords have more room to accommodate others from time to time.

"Because my time is not exactly my own, and my parents did not come to South Africa then, as often as they are planning to do in the future, I wanted to be as close as I could to them, when they visited me, so they now have that suite in my house, and the cottage remains available for the use of whoever else needs it. In fact I am seriously thinking of offering it to Reggie, in case he wants to bring Aunt Felicity to come and live with him."

"What a lovely thing to do, Jordie! Apart from everything else, there's safety in numbers, isn't there? And I'm sure that, after spending so many years away from her, in so many dangerous places, it will be great for him to lead a more normal lifestyle, and be with her whenever he likes!"

"That's what I thought," Jordan said.

Both were silent for moment until Meredith pensively remarked, "How lovely to have people coming and going from your house all the time. I wish Susie and I...!"

She stopped so abruptly that Jordan was moved to ask: "You and Susie what?"

To his surprise, her response was a laconic, "I don't want to talk about it!" and her tone had noticeably changed.

"Why ever not, Merry? What's the matter? Have I said something to upset you?"

"No," she assured him fiercely, recovering herself. "I just don't want you also making fun of me as some sort of oddity!"

***

Because I looked at everything in the bookstore through Jasper's eyes, I could see nothing worthy of someone with his superior knowledge of literature and books of intrinsic value, so I gave up the search and went to join Merry and Jordan, who, with that moment of awkwardness forgotten, were having a thoroughly good time paging through book after magnificently illustrated book on '*Highveld*' gardening. And when she had finally made her choice, he took us to dinner in the most fabulous restaurant I have ever been in. The menu was so extensive that Jordan had to help us choose, but somehow we did not feel the least bit embarrassed about eliciting his advice. Both charming and attentive, he proved to be the superb host one would expect of Ash Ashton's son, and, as far as I was concerned, the excellent meal was enhanced by the absolute lack of self-consciousness or strain on our part. We just had a rattling good time!

At one stage a friend of his passed by our table and, when introduced to Meredith, stared at her with undisguised admiration. Jordan teased her about it, and she was highly amused at the very thought of such a thing, but again she exhibited no sign of the slightest discomfiture. As good as the food was, and despite the imposing décor, I could sense however, that they could hardly wait to get home and try out the music.

On the way, they took up the conversation in which they had been absorbed earlier that evening as if there had been no interruption. "We have quite an ensemble when we're all together at *Bentleigh*," I heard him telling her. "My dad and my sister are the keyboard people, my mom and my brother James—when he isn't up to his ears in high finance and board meetings—both play strings, and I am the only one who chose a wood-wind instrument."

"I wish I could hear you all together like that," she sighed wistfully. "I would also love to be able to play the kind of music you and your father were playing the other night. How do you do that, Jordie? You both seemed to be completely immersed in it. You improvise, and almost play around the melody at times. How did you learn to do that?"

He laughed delightedly. "By osmosis, I guess! Louisiana jazz!—Ah, New Orleans Jazz! One can't grow up in Louisiana, if you are at all musical, without being influenced by it. It just happens and, at times, the very soul seems to be dragged right out of your body to float on the wings of it. Once you get to be under the spell of it, you're hooked! No matter how you try to remain rigid, your body just has to move along with it, too...!"

"He gets it from his Uncle Jamie," I emerged sleepily from a doze long enough to interject. "And, like him, from the plantation folk among whom he spent so much time! If you like jazz, you'll enjoy Dixieland and Gospel! Get Ash and Jordie to play, and Ash to sing *Just a closer walk with Thee*, sometime, and you'll know exactly what I'm talking about!"

"But can anyone learn to play it?" Merry persisted. "Someone like me? *Rhapsody in Blue* is a form of jazz, isn't it? Only it sounds classical at times."

"Wait until my father comes, and he'll show you how and where to begin," Jordan promised. "Apart from blocked chords and nimble fingers, it takes soul, and a superb sense of rhythm to play jazz piano, I think, and he's an expert! Feel free, however, to go and look in the cottage—Angelina will give you the key—and listen to some of his records. Bear in mind that there is far more than those classical passages and the rhythmic jazz of Harlem's clubs in what we're going to be playing. My dad is very methodical, so look, among other recordings, too....For those of Scott Joplin's piano rags and the folk music of the Yiddish theatre. The days will be getting hotter and hotter for a while, and when you tire of the garden, you'll have the leisure to be able to experiment with new music, with no one to bother you! I predict that soon you'll be hooked, too…on Cajun and Jewish music, on Zydeco and Klesmer. The range is endless! Listen to the records, and to my dad—while he's here—and, before long, I promise you, you'll also be itching to play Dixieland and jazz!"

As I thought, they could not wait to try out the music arrangement about which Jordan was so enthusiastic. They were completely absorbed in what they were doing, and I made tea more than once, believing that they drank it abstractedly, until Jordan suddenly looked at his wristwatch and sighed.

"Now," he said, putting the clarinet back into its case, "I'll reluctantly have to call it a day. Clinic before seven, which means I must be on my way by six, if I want to avoid the traffic. It's been wonderful, Meredith, I must thank you. And thank you, Auntie Bid. It helps to be plied with refreshments when one's working so hard!"

"Jordie, before we go upstairs," Meredith said, as something suddenly occurred to her. "Tomorrow being Thursday, Angelina won't be here to cook, and your father will be here. Is there anything that he specially likes, and that I can prepare for dinner? What's his favourite? If necessary, I'll ask Aunt Biddy to help me, because I bet you'll name some wonderful American dish that I don't know how to make!"

Jordan laughed. "Not so! You'll be surprised. He likes roast beef and Yorkshire pudding!—There's a story attached to that, which I shall tell you some time. Otherwise he enjoys a plain and simple *braai* with *krummelpap*[15]! We have a gas barbeque, and we can use that, if you like.—Then the men can do the work, and you ladies can sit and watch us. The weather's very good for outdoor cooking right now!—So how about we do that?"

It was just like Jordan to stop us as we were going to our respective rooms, and say regretfully, "I'm sorry that I made that remark about Tris. Please forgive me! I should not be so critical of anyone, let alone someone who has had cause to feel so deprived." Glancing at Meredith, he went on to say, "Anyway, I'm happy for him that he has now found a reason to be less dissatisfied with his life!"

***

Ash and Reggie returned simultaneously, and somehow the presence of two more people in the house temporarily changed the ambience. Until a routine was established there was quite a holiday-like feeling about the place.

Ben, it seemed, had been given no option but to stay for a few days longer than he had intended, but having solved the problem, with the solid cooperation of the ever- resourceful Willie Marais, things were going so well in Isando that he was now able to proceed with negotiating some pretty good deals for his employees and the firm. Reggie, moving into the cottage, happily preparing for the time when his mother could join him, and just starting at the clinic, was in high spirits, and Jordan, finding himself progressively being relieved of some of the weight of what was formerly far too heavy a schedule, was enormously grateful for the freedom to work in two places, without having to neglect the one for the other.

With a wallet bulging with digital pictures of the new grandchild, his father's exuberance was reflected in the music they had the leisure to play together in the evenings; and it was at this stage, while Matt Marais was still in the country to help him, that Jordan embarked on a project to assist people suffering from Post Traumatic Stress Syndrome. Before long, he was to discover that this disorder did not only afflict veterans of war. He would come to know patients who had suffered unspeakable trauma, right there in the city, in the province, and further afield, which led him to begin recruiting colleagues, better equipped to deal with the problem than he was, to donate some of their time to the endeavour.

It was also at this time, while Meredith was in good hands, that I felt I could safely go home to *Spoors-einde*, and I lost no time in making my decision known. If it was gratifying that everyone except Tristan—who smirked with ill-disguised satisfaction—expressed regret upon learning this, it was very hard for me to witness the immediate change of expression on Meredith's beloved little face. We had several good cries together, and frankly, once, when she even went as far as to beg me not to leave, until she had been able to decide whether or not she should just give up and go home with me, I wondered why the heck she didn't go straight to her room and start packing! She was finally able to assure me, however, that she did understand my need to get back to work and resume my normal life. She had made up her mind, she said, to 'hang in there', as I think the saying went, and appreciated the fact that Doc Hugo was not eating properly. Furthermore, my friend, Sally, while competently helping out as his receptionist, reminded me tactfully that she had made it abundantly clear, when first approached, that her willingness to stand in for me was not to be regarded as a token that she was signing on for the long haul.

There was still some unfinished business to attend to, however, and I was determined not to leave Johannesburg until I had attended to that. Accordingly, I waited for an opportunity when Ash was alone in his sitting room, one evening before dinner, to get a few troubling things off my chest.

I found him sitting in an armchair, reading a book that he so frequently recommended to others—making me wonder if that might not be a good present for Jasper—and the lamp above his head made a halo of the golden hair which had not yet begun to fade, and showed hardly a vestige of grey, except around his temples. What a magnificent looking man he still was! This was not the first time I had thought how fortunate Jordan was to resemble his father so closely. The son had inherited the same stature, the same remarkable blue eyes, the flashing smile, and the same, generous nature, and it would not have surprised me to find that more than half of Jordan's female patients were in love with their physician!

"Come right in, Biddy," Ben said, before I could knock, catching sight of me standing in the doorway, and rose at once to greet me with a hug that immediately dispersed all possibility of awkwardness. This reminded me of an anecdote once told me by Trudy, the wife of Dick Evans, the doctor who had recently delivered Zhaynie's son. She, Trudy, and Dick had been invited for brunch on the day before Ben was to meet Amy-Lee, who was coming to visit his farm, and, upon their arrival at *Beauclaire*, they found that Nelspruit's most popular bachelor had been inundated with gifts of every kind, ranging from cakes to jams, pies and puddings, brought by neighbours and townspeople, to welcome the 'American lady'.

Trudy still laughs at the recollection of his embarrassment when, unable to resist the temptation to tease him, she remarked: *"Ach,* they may bring you presents, Ash, but they actually come for the hugs!"

We talked for some time about many things, including the reason why, whether he was alone or surrounded by his family, the daily reading during his 'quiet time' always included both the Bible and the Oswald Chambers book, '*My Utmost For His Highest*'—which I then became determined to buy for Jasper before I went home—and finally I found enough courage to pose the burning question...

"Ash, what would make a man want to marry a woman if he didn't intend to consummate the marriage?"

He clasped his hands between his knees and sat thoughtfully for a while, with his eyes closed, before he finally turned to me and said a strange thing. "Perhaps because he did not love her enough—or, on the other hand, perhaps because he simply loved her too much!"

I was quite naturally flummoxed, and, because I knew him so well, I felt free to respond without reticence. "Now come off it, Ash!" I protested. "Are you prevaricating, or is this supposed to be conundrum?" Those intense blue eyes were fixed very intently on my face and, to my surprise, when looking into them; I could find no evidence of jesting. "You're serious, aren't you?"

"What do you think, Biddy? Of course I'm serious!" he said. "Can you not believe that a man can revere someone so deeply, that it would seem as though consummation of the marriage would be a violation?—No? Well, I'm certain you have no problem believing the reverse! One only has to wait at the checkout in a supermarket to realize that marital strife sells! The tabloids are obsessed with stories about people who will ruthlessly marry—even though the spouse is detested to a degree which makes it impossible to share a bed with him or her—simply because the sole aim is to end up with a divorce and sue for money!...Tragically I could name numerous such cases, without even having to consult the gossip columns. I have personally counselled victims of such cruelty....And then, of course, there is the 'marriage of convenience' scenario, where a certain situation requires two people to be married, but not necessarily to live together!"

"You're right there," I conceded, "but, what if none of the situations you have presented is applicable? What about an instance where the spouse is both beautiful, and as lovable as she is sweet? What if he knows that she loves him? Would any man who is successful enough in his own right, not to have to marry for money, be so low as to go through the ceremony, while planning in advance to distance himself from his bride, *immediately after the ceremony?*"

"Perhaps because he is considerate enough to give her time to get used to being with him...?"

"No!" That was when I became emphatic. "What if he only becomes progressively colder towards her?"

"You are skirting around an actual situation aren't you, Biddy?" He put this to me so directly that I was compelled to nod. "You wouldn't by any chance, be talking about Tristan and Meredith, would you?"

He had taken my breath away, to the extent that, once again, all I could do was to nod. But then I *had* to know!

"What made you hit on that, Ash?"

"Because Jordan has come to his mother and me with certain concerns, and both Amy-Lee and I have tried to give him advice. Particularly on the score of a female patient with whom Tris seems to be far too friendly!"

"Adéle Bradshaw? I don't trust that situation too much, either, Ash, but it only began to niggle at me recently. I have actually been carrying the greater part of this burden around with me for months! Why do you think I was open to persuasion when Meredith begged me to come with her?

"I tried to talk to Doctor Hugo about my fears, but, although he has called him to account, himself, on a few occasions, when it comes to Tristan it's a waste of time for anyone else to say anything that is not totally complimentary....I could, of course, have confided in Meredith's father, but I doubt if he could have dissuaded her! In addition, the younger daughter, Susan, is similarly enamoured of her new brother-in-law, and unreservedly approves of Meredith's marriage.

"For all I know, Merry may genuinely have fallen in love with Tristan. Perhaps even passionately so, but frankly, my greatest fear is that, having little knowledge of men, she might merely have been fascinated by him. Mesmerized! You must admit that he is very attractive in his own way, and though it might have a *subliminal* motivation—I must be careful to stress that—she could have been further driven by a need to escape, although she categorically denied that when I confronted her!"

"And yet, she does not strike me in the least, as the sort of girl who would be devoid of the ability to decide for herself whether or not what she felt for a man, was love or sheer fascination," Ben remarked. "She possesses great charm, is physically beautiful enough not to have to feel anything other than serenely confident in the presence of both men and women, and from what I have gathered from both Reg and Jordan, she is extremely well-educated, with above average intelligence. Wasn't she halfway through a thesis for a doctorate? "

"You're correct, up to point, Ash. But certainly not when it comes her being unduly endowed with self-confidence! Being the daughter of Jasper Hilliard, she couldn't be anything but well educated. She is indeed brilliant, and she was working on a thesis—so, if she does decide to stick it out here with Tristan, the first thing I would recommend is the acquisition of a laptop. Evidently her physical research has been completed, and she can manage without her lab, but she cannot afford to let all that has already been written, go to waste. Soon gardening and house-keeping won't be enough for her!"

"Amy-Lee said the same thing to Jordan—about the need for Meredith to be kept occupied, I mean—but we were talking about naiveté! Somehow I can't reconcile that with research and a PhD. thesis, if you don't mind my saying so. I can of course take into consideration that, apart from her research, she did devote much of her time to keeping house for her family, and the care of her sister and father"—he raised his eyebrows sceptically—"but surely, Biddy...?"

That sentence, left hanging in the air, is what prompted me, at last, to tell the entire, unvarnished tragedy of *Blouspruit*, and how it had affected the lives of all who lived there! And by the time I came to the part about the self-imposed isolation of the Hilliard family and the guards at the gate, Ben was appalled.

"Twelve years!—*Mon Dieu! Il est terrible! Tragique!*" He murmured to himself in French, as he might have done if Amy-Lee were there. "If I had heard this from someone else, I would never have believed it!" he admitted to me. "Jasper must have been out of his mind to go to those lengths. To do that not only to himself, but to those helpless little girls!" He took my hand in his and said earnestly, "Forgive me, Biddy, for anything I have said, so far. Now I understand what you were trying to tell me!" Shaking his head, he muttered something else in French, and then, in English confessed: "I am still reeling at the enormity of what betrayal can do to someone....There you have an example of how a man, so clever that he borders on genius... a fine-looking man whose charisma is reflected in his exquisite daughter...so stricken by heartbreak and disillusionment, that even he can be driven to crazy lengths to protect his children from similar pain! Oh, my poor friend!

"I wonder what Jordan will say when he hears about this! Although it is a long time since he met him, he holds

Jasper Hilliard in high esteem. His dignity, fine work and vast knowledge of so many things, made a tremendous impression on the teenager my son was then, and Jordie has also retained unbelievably vivid memories of Meredith; particularly of her gentleness and inherent empathy with anyone who is hurt!...A trait already revealed when she was a mere child!"

"When I am in Jasper's company, which has quite often been the case of late," I confessed, "I find all this hard to believe, myself. I can't begin to imagine what it must have done to him when, in response to an emergency call, it was Tristan who came, and not Doc!"

"Please tell me about that, Biddy. Is that where he comes into the picture? And how do the rest of the pieces fit together?"

Well, I told the story just as I have already set it out in this account, trying hard not to sound too intolerant of Doc's attitude, but telling the truth about Tristan—from my point of view! I think that what overwhelmed Ash, was the resourcefulness of Meredith, how she had soldiered on, trying to fill the woman's place in that house, and how efficiently she had coped, while deprived of so much without which even mature women might have despaired. Tristan's derision, when learning of the lengths she went to, in order to provide for the everyday comfort of her family, sounded like poor fiction— but it was true. In my opinion, her resourcefulness could only have been compared with that of the pioneer women who had arrived in the far northwest of the province in covered wagons, more than a century before.—Except for a few, big differences. She did have a comfortable home, access to modern technology, the indigenous people were her friends and not her enemies, and she had been given every possible opportunity to exercise her exceptional brain!

Ash was as disgusted as I was, at the very thought of anyone wanting to exploit or make fun of a way of life Merry would never have chosen for herself, but had accepted with dignity and grace. "*She makes soap!*" When I repeated that my voice broke. My bitterness at the manner in which Tristan had said that to Adéle Bradshaw, was not lost on Benjamin Ashton.

"You really love that child, don't you, Biddy," he observed gently.

"I do!" I responded emotionally. "As if she were my very own, and I dread leaving her behind!"

A sudden 'pinging' sound went through the house, indicating that the front gates had been opened, and Ash smiled contentedly when, presently, Jordan's car could be seen coming up the driveway. Moments later a cheerful voice called out," Hi, Dad! Hi, Auntie Bid!" and soon after that a head as blond as his father's poked itself in at the door. Jordan gave his father a hug and bent over to kiss me on the cheek. "You two should not be looking so glum on this absolutely splendid day! I'm off to have a quick shower, while Merry makes me a cup of tea because, at my request, Angelina is trying to get dinner ready a little earlier than usual. I did tell Tris and I hope that suits everybody else!…I need to look in on a patient, after dinner, and then Reg and I have a meeting with the guy who is going to be installing the new security system at the clinic, and we were wondering, Dad, if you would come along and give us your opinion.

"By the way, you were quite right about the lack of adequate security, and now that I am virtually responsible for Reggie's safety, I want to take every possible precaution. He's all Aunt Felicity has got!"

Ash and I were continuing the discussion in which we had been involved before Jordan's intervention, when the lively strains of a dual piano and clarinet rendition of *'Saint Louis Blues'* reached us, and Jordan's father beamed! And when this was followed by *'The Birth Of the Blues'*, he became really enthusiastic. "She's a natural!" he cried delightedly. "She has a heart for the Blues and you'd think she had also been playing Dixieland and Ragtime all her life!

"What a joy to hear them!" he exclaimed a while later, as the music continued. "No dark undercurrents down there, right now, hey? 'Blues' or not, one can't do it like that unless your heart is in it! And just listen to her! Your little Meredith is getting right down into it, isn't she?...I only had to give her a few tips, and play along with her a few times, at Jordan's request—and now what a joy to hear the two of them! She now wants to be shown how I do the boogie bass for *'Alligator Crawl'*!

"In view of what you have just told me," he observed wryly, "I'd be interested to see what happens when Tristan comes home!—But, Biddy," he implored, "before you condemn Tris too harshly, you have to be able to understand him, and perhaps you will permit me to help you do that!"

"Benjamin Ashton," was my stubborn response, "I was present when that kid was born! And I've repeatedly had to pander to his moods ever since he first started spending holidays in *Spoors-einde* with Doc!—Trust me, if he is fed up about anything, he just won't come home—until he has given us all sufficient time to notice his absence!"

"I know about that, too," Ash agreed. "I have observed him dispassionately and analytically, as well as with affection, over the years—because of the great love I have for his parents—and I have prayed for insight into his very complex character, because of my great love for the One who made him. As a matter of fact, I was thinking about Tris, while reading Chambers, just before you came into the room. As often happens, I mistakenly read the page intended for another day, and it was this part that gripped me: *'Our Lord knows perfectly that when once His word is heard, it will bear fruit sooner or later. The terrible thing is that some of us prevent it bearing fruit in actual life.'* My prayers now are for the grace to be able to discern how that message applies to Tristan!"

"I have something to say to you about 'Discernment', Ash", was my firm response, "but I'll wait until I've heard all that you have to say. You were to expound on the complexities of this young man, remember? Perhaps we can pray together after that. For Meredith, for Tristan—and for Jordan?"

"What makes you put it like that, Biddy?" Startled, he regarded me with concern, instantly grasping my meaning. "Are you, like me, beginning to worry that my son is perhaps getting to be a tad too fond of that little girl?"

I had to nod. "I'm sure he does not realize that, himself—but, oh, Ash, if only she'd met him first!"

Neither of us spoke for some time after that, and while the lively music continued downstairs, the silence in the room was almost tangible. Then at last Ben said, "I have called Tristan a complex man, and he is. He could be an excellent physician—perhaps even better than Jordie—if only he cared enough! The kind of people he prefers to accept as patients provide a clue to everything that troubles him, and he is only comfortable socializing with people—generally very wealthy individuals—who have to hide their insecurities, and the dissatisfaction with their lives, behind the same brittle veneer that he wears. He sees right through them, because he knows what lies behind that veneer, and that makes him feel superior, because he can secretly despise them for it. At the same time, he has been known to get up to some pretty heartless shenanigans, because that draws attention to himself. He enjoys becoming a talking point among his associates!

"And there you have the crux of the matter! My family, who have grown up with him, all recognize that, but they don't hold it against him, because, they realize that he is afraid to let just anybody in behind that wall of sophistication, in case his insecurity might show. If you were to ask him outright what he wants out of life, and if he were prepared to give you an honest answer, he would say what he has repeatedly said to my children: 'I want to be first with someone! I want to be the only person in someone's life!'—And that of course comes directly from having had to share his parents."

"That's what Doc maintains," I said, "but that does not explain why he is the way he is, to a girl who was wholly prepared to put him first. What do you think he expected to get out of this marriage?"

Again there was a prolonged silence, until Ben said thoughtfully, "I think that might have something to do with my daughter. I have just had a flashback to a day when Jordan was about four. I was busy at my desk, and he and Tristan were building a Meccano model of a bridge, on the floor beside me, comparing notes and providing one another with a running commentary on progress, as the work proceeded. I can't remember exactly when the subject was changed or how it came up, because I wasn't paying that much attention, but then I heard Jordie announce emphatically, 'I'm going to marry my mother!' To which Tristan promptly responded, quite aggressively, 'Then I'll marry her, too!'

"'Two people can't marry the same girl, silly!'" Jordie protested. " 'You'll have to choose someone else!' "

" 'Then I'll take your sister, Eugenie!' " Tris promptly decided.

"I did not foresee then, that what Tristan had declared that day would become so firm and lasting an intention, until the boys were older and well past the 'birds and the bees' stage. Tristan would frequently re-iterate his intention to marry Zhaynie, which I regarded as nothing more serious than 'boy-talk', but evidently it wasn't. What he would also proclaim, more often than not, was, 'I want to have been a girl's first—and with Eugenie I can be sure of that!'

"For a time after she became engaged to Dominic, he never came near us, but Jordie did repeat to me once, what Tristan had told him after that. 'She's the prettiest girl, I have ever known,' he reportedly said, 'and I'm not going to settle for anything less. I'm determined to find one that's even prettier, adores me, and has brains as well as looks. I want one that's exceptional! So out of the ordinary, that people will stare—especially Eugenie—and if I can't find one who is precisely what I'm looking for, in every, single aspect, I'll *make* one into what I want her to be!' "

The dinner bell rang, and we rose to our feet, but, before we went downstairs, Ash said, "If you're thinking what I'm thinking, Biddy, I believe we've suddenly hit the nail on the head, and if that is so, God help that little girl!...We can't have Angelina being upset, so we'll have to go down now, but, if it suits you, how about we spend some time here, when the boys and I get back later. We need to pray, and you were going to tell me something about discernment, I believe..."

"Ash," I corrected him solemnly. "I wasn't talking just about 'discernment'. I meant 'Discernment' with a capital 'D'.... The *'Gift of Discernment'* for which I prayed many years ago, and I believe was graciously given to me by the Holy Spirit. I knew nothing of what you have just told me, but I could have told you, weeks ago, what Tristan Connaught had in mind!

"I know why he married Meredith and I have an idea why he seems to have lost interest in her. For that reason I do believe that, in doing what I have, out of love for her, I have done nothing to improve the situation for her!"

CHAPTER SIX

It could only have been the kindness and generous support she received from the Ashtons and Reggie, that made Meredith secure enough of her position to ask Tristan whether she might have a party for me before I left. And she must have steeled herself against any probable rebuff, not to have exhibited a vestige of surprise at his brusque response.

"Why the hell ask me? I only live here, remember! And, have no fear. You will doubtless be able to get all the support you need from the exemplary Doctors Ashton and Seymour!"

Inadvertently, or not, it turned out he was quite right! Upon approaching Jordie she learnt that, for good reason, he had done very little entertaining of late, and had been feeling guilty about taking so long to reciprocate the hospitality shown him by friends and colleagues. As he had been away in Nelspruit at the time of Adéle Bradshaw's shindig, and none of his own associates had been invited to that, he found the idea of a party for me to be a splendid one. It would provide him with an opportunity, he said, to invite some of his colleagues, their wives—and the girlfriends of those who had one—and, at the same time, he welcomed the chance to introduce Meredith to them. He went on to suggest that Tristan and Reg should be encouraged to add some of their own friends and colleagues to the list.

"High time," was his approving remark. To me, however, he confided that, having heard Merry's plans for the occasion, he was concerned about her taking on what, to him, sounded like a mammoth task in the kitchen.

"Let her, Jordan!" I said. "There's a lot at stake here for her, but she also wants to do this for us, because for so many years, the only way she has known to care for those she loves is cook, bake, and make their home a happy place for them....To work for them!...She knows no other way of demonstrating affection and gratitude than to *do* something for them....Haven't you noticed? That's because she was never able to go out and *buy* them anything. She'd polish your car and darn your socks, if need be—if you get my meaning. She'd chop wood and polish the floors for us, if we'd let her!"

Immediately after having blurted that out, in my eagerness, I could have bitten my tongue off, for nearly betraying the full circumstances of her past!

She had made it known that she would like to have the party for me, but I knew that there was more to it than that. How well I knew what went on in that beautiful blonde head! Not for her the 'store bought' confections with which Adéle and the other members of the smart set were content. After all the flattering remarks made by the other members of the Ashton household, concerning her baking and cooking skills, she, Meredith would make everything herself, and, in so doing, would keep a three-fold purpose in sight.

What good were all the lovely new clothes, and the newfound confidence derived from her improved appearance, if she could not put the 'new' Meredith to the test? Until she had tried out the effect on Adéle, she could never be wholly sure of herself. On that previous, so disastrous occasion, the other woman had held the spotlight; but she, Meredith, now felt herself to be better prepared to assert herself. She was ready to take her place as Tristan's wife, and, as a gracious confident hostess, she could not fail to make an impression,

I took note of how her cheeks glowed and her eyes sparkled, as she planned the entire scenario. Once she had weathered this, she would never again have to feel inferior in the company of either Adéle Bradshaw or Gloria Triblehorn! The reason she had been so stupidly intimidated by them was wholly due to the fact that she had looked and felt like a *backvelder*. A child of the bush! This time, well prepared, well groomed, and fashionably clothed, there was no reason for her not to feel sublimely confident.

I doubt whether she had ever before been to any party, other than the one on which she now based her preparations, so, in planning it with much care and forethought, she jotted down every last detail, giving a great deal of attention to food, how she would arrange the flowers, and even where the guests would leave their coats—if they brought any, in this weather. Meanwhile Tristan raised no objections, but did not seem to show much interest, either. This, I believed was because he could not understand why such a fuss should be made of a woman who was, after all, only his great-uncle's housekeeper! Perhaps he was embarrassed by the very thought of having to make it known that the party was being arranged in my honour!

And even as I pondered this, I began to notice an unfamiliar pucker between Merry's eyebrows, from time to time, and when I saw the worried look, which had at first only fleetingly crossed her expressive face, become more and more evident, I initially took this to be due to Tristan's lack of enthusiasm—until I questioned her outright about it and was able to draw out the real reason for her anxiety. Some might laugh at this but, recalling the heartrending sobs on a previous occasion, I could not blame her.

"Aunt Biddy," she burst out despairingly, "what if they want to dance again? I don't know how, and I can't bear the thought of such a possibility! Why didn't I think of this before?"

I had to consider the situation for a moment or two before the solution came to me.

"Wait here! Leave this to me," I instructed, and went off in search of Ash, who was out in the cottage, where Reg was helping him to pack the last of the items to be taken to the big house. "Meredith is in quite a state," I informed him bluntly. "She is terrified that she might have to dance at the party, and there's no one better to explain why, than Reggie. He'll tell you about the last time!

"Now, Ash," I continued firmly, "you're reputed to be such a hotshot dancer, so you'll have to drop whatever you're doing, and show her!"

At first he was taken aback—with good reason—but then he nearly laughed his head off. "You're priceless, Bridget Williams!" Still chuckling he asked, "So where are we supposed to do this, and when do we start?"

"Right here and now!" I commanded. "This matter is urgent! The party is in four days' time so she's got to start learning today! Wednesday! While Tristan goes to golf!— Reggie, will you please go and fetch her, and bring Jordan with you, too, while Mr. Ashton and I discuss the *modus operandi*— and, for heaven's sake, don't let Tristan get wind of this!"

"I love to dance," Ben admitted, "and I'd teach her with pleasure. Amy-Lee and I taught our kids, and I have danced with Eugenie and some of her contemporaries, but Biddy, the young people of today do all kinds of weird things like 'Hip Hop', and so on, which I certainly can't do!"

"Well perhaps Jordan and Reg may know how," I began uncertainly, but then a happy thought struck me, and I could heave a sigh of relief. " I don't see any of the people I'm thinking of—and you know whom I mean—doing any of that, either. None of them, except for three who live in this house, will exactly be under thirty!"

"Okay then," Ash agreed, grinning broadly. "Bring it on! With Meredith's sense of rhythm, we'll have her dancing like Ginger Rogers in no time! Unfortunately, the best music for my purpose is on those vinyls, and they, and the record player, have already been taken over to the main house—but, if necessary, I suppose I can play the little upright piano here in the cottage, and, once I've shown Meredith, Jordan, and Reggie—if he knows how—can take turns to dance with her!"

What fun that turned out to be! At times it was hilarious and I even got to dance with Ash while Jordie played, to demonstrate for Merry's benefit how one did a slow waltz. On reflection, I can hardly believe that I'd had the nerve...that I had actually ordered those men—one of the them the dynamic head of a gigantic conglomerate, one of the wealthiest men in the world—and the other two—both busy physicians—to participate in such a harebrained initiative. Whatever the case, they entered in with good grace and most endearing zeal. Jordan was absolutely fascinated to learn that Bushmen danced in the desert, and that Meredith and Susan, watching them as children, had sometimes participated in those dances, too.

"Imagine me doing that on Saturday!" Meredith spluttered, laughter beginning to bubble up in her, at the very thought. "In front of your worthy colleagues!" With that she exploded with mirth, and it warmed my heart to see to what extent that wonderful sense of humour had been restored...

"How about treating us to a performance, right here, on the spot, Merry," Jordan pleaded, egging her on—and I'm darned if she didn't oblige!

She was heartily applauded and the light-heartedness remained with us while an amused Angelina and I brought refreshments, and the afternoon wore on. Ben patiently had Merry go through the paces until she felt quite confident, and then it was time for the real thing. He went to the piano, instructing Jordan to be the first partner, and his son obediently went over to her and held out his hand. As he, Jordie, took Meredith in his arms, a shock went through his entire being, he closed his eyes, trying to still the wild beating of his heart—and, for Jordan Ashton, the world would never be the same again!

Immediately after dinner that evening, he went off, without a word to anyone, and sat, head-in-hands, in semi-darkness in his office, praying, and wondering what he was going to do about a surging emotion, more powerful than anything he had ever known in his life! He felt as though his heart would burst with love for the tiny, exquisite creature that was Meredith. A love of which the seed had lain dormant in his heart since he was a boy, and had now exploded with such power that he was overwhelmed by it and could hardly breathe.

***

At length, not able to deal with this on his own, it came to him that the best he could do was to take his shattering discovery to his father, and, fearing that Ben might already be asleep, he drove home to Bryanston as fast as the law permitted. Somehow, as he was getting out of the car, he was not surprised to see the tall figure striding towards him in the moonlight.

"Wherever have you been, Jordie?" his father asked anxiously. "It's not like you to go off without your pager, or telling someone where you can be found! One of your patients telephoned, and fortunately Reggie was able to go in your place!"

And all Jordan could say was, "Please get back into the car with me, Dad, I beg of you! I have to talk to you, and what I have to say to you must be said in private!"

As they sat, side-by-side in the dim light, Ben waited silently for his son to speak, but was finally driven to break the silence.

"What is it, Jordie? You know there's nothing you can't tell me!" And when he sensed that Jordan was having difficulty finding the right words, he suddenly knew!

"Is it Meredith, son?" And all he received in response was a hopeless nod, until, as though the words were wrung from him, Jordan cried: "It's not fair, Dad! Here I am, hopelessly, desperately in love for the first, and what I firmly believe will be the only time in my life, and she's beyond my reach!"

"I know all about that, Jordie, and, from my own experience I know, too, that when one falls deeply in love...when that love is real...it is either ecstasy or agony! I've been through that. I also could not have her, but, in my case, it was my own fault! It breaks my heart that you, who have done nothing to deserve this, should suffer in the same way!"

"I feel as if I could die," Jordan groaned. "And what makes it worse is that she's my partner's wife! I have to see him, every single day, while being aware that he is the person I know to be the least worthy of her!...Meredith is the only girl I have ever loved. It is clear to me that, if no other woman has ever stirred me like this before, it is because, without knowing it, I have loved her from the first moment I saw her!"

"But she was only a child, Jordie! You can't be serious!"

"It must run in the family, Dad. Like father, like son! Haven't you always told us how you have loved our mother since the day she was born?...What a bunch we Ashtons are! There you were, in your own kind of hell, until God in His mercy rescued you from it, and there was my uncle Jamie, who died without ever telling Aunt Felicity that he loved her. And what about my grandfather who was separated from the one he loved, by sickness?... Now here I am—with no hope of ever having the one person I want, to be my wife!...I've never envied James or Zhaynie, but at this moment I do.—Fervently!"

They sat in silence again for some time, dealing individually with the sadness of all this, and then Ben was reminded of a conversation he'd had with Meredith's father while Jordan was out.

"How strange this all is to me, my very dear son! Jasper Hilliard telephoned tonight to ask if one of us would kindly advise Meredith in the purchase of a laptop to replace the computer she has had to leave behind, so that she can continue her work. He's emailing the data, but, as a precaution, has also saved it as a back-up on a USB memory stick, which he will send to her, somehow; perhaps with a special delivery service, when he goes to Upington to fetch Aunt Biddy, or, otherwise, with a helicopter that lands at his place from time to time. He considers the post to be too 'iffy' these days.

"In the course of his conversation, he happened to mention that, when Tristan arrived at *Blouspruit* that first day, and mentioned that he found it necessary to call you for Stephen Verwey's phone number, Meredith's immediate reaction was to exclaim: 'I remember Jordan!' She was excited at the recollection. She said you'd been so nice to Susan and to her, and she remembered the day her sister, Susie, dropped and broke something I had brought for her mother, and which you tried to mend.—'Remember, Daddy,' she reminded him, 'when Mr. Ashton and Jordie came here with two men, one of whom had taken them to places they called *Rietfontein* and *Witdraai?*'

"Jordan, she did not forget you, either! What a crying shame that we never went back!"

They were walking pensively towards the house, after putting the car away, when Jordan stopped his father with a touch on his arm. "Dad," he said in a low voice, as though someone inside the house might hear him, "there's something else about which I shall be wrestling in the dark, and I must ask you about it. Perhaps you can shed some light on it or I shall be tossing and turning with a vengeance...!"

"What is it, my son?"

"When Merry, Auntie Bid and I were in the car together on our way home from the restaurant the other night, I was prompted to tell Merry about how you had remodelled *Bentleigh*, and what we have since done here. A little later, after not speaking for a while, Meredith, who must have been thinking about what I had told her, and having made a remark about how lovely it was to have people coming and going from one's house all the time, started to say something about 'I wish Susie and I...' but stopped so abruptly that I was moved to ask: 'You and Susie what?'

"To my surprise, her response was a terse, 'I don't want to talk about it!' and her tone had noticeably changed. After that, naturally concerned that I had said something to upset her, I asked her what the matter was, and whether I had said something to offend her. Again her response was very odd. 'No,' she said, 'I just don't want you also making fun of me as some sort of oddity!'—What do you make of that, Dad?"

"Let's sit here on the stoep for a moment, Jordie," Ash suggested. "I think I can explain." And he then proceeded to tell Jordan all that I had omitted from Meredith's story when I had spoken to Reggie about her. This meant that Jordan had not known the full, story, either.

"*Twelve years!*" Jordan was staggered. "How absolutely awful! Are you telling, me Dad, that, other than Merry's father and the elderly invigilator, Tristan Connaught was the first, the only, adult white man she had seen in all that time?" He buried his face in his hands, and when next he spoke his voice was muffled. "Oh, dear God," he muttered, "Why Tristan?... Dad, look at the time, and he hasn't come home yet! He hardly speaks to her!" In this impassioned cry, Ben heard the boy, Jordan; not the successful, confident physician, and as he did so, he recalled a day when, at precisely the same age as Jordie was now, he, Ben, had sat in the priest, Peter Crawford's, study and wept!

He put his arm around his son's shoulders and said nothing as they sat together, allowing Jordan time to absorb the immensity of what he had just learnt. Only Ash, who had endured similar agony, and one of the few people who completely understood the loving heart, the sensitivity and selflessness of the special, amazing, clean-living man his son had grown up to be, could have appreciated Jordan's agony of spirit at that moment.

He could only be grateful for the ability to be there with him at this time, when Jordan finally turned to him and, in a strangled voice asked—as though the words were wrung from him—"What can I do to keep her happy, Dad? How should I behave towards her, knowing all that I now know?"

"All I can say to you, Jordie, is do the best you can to shield her from further hurt. Only God knows why you are the one to have been placed in this unenviable position, but you can at least protect her from the spite of others who are more sophisticated, and better equipped than she is to ward off the barbs of malice to which she is easy prey.

"Biddy told me that, although Meredith is so extraordinarily knowledgeable about so many things, she is extremely sensitive about her background, and dreads any of the people here finding out how little she knows about the world immediately beyond the environs of her father's enclave.—Hence the remark about 'making fun of her as some sort of oddity'. This has most likely happened to her already, since she's been here, and that's one area in which you can guard her, particularly at the party on Saturday.

"My work here is just about done, for the time being, so I want to go back to *Beauclaire* in time to prepare for the baby's christening. God willing, Father Peter will be performing the baptism, and I have been asked to play the organ—which I have not done for some time. I would love it if you could be there, but whatever happens, just know that your mother and I shall be praying for you, constantly, as you steer Merry through the further disillusionments she is bound to suffer..."

He, Ash, spent more than an hour on his knees in his study, before deciding to turn in, and, noticing the beam of light coming from under the door of his son's bedroom, as he went towards his own, he padded down the passage, tapped softly on the door, and then hearing a whispered, "Come in, Dad, I know it's you!" he went into the room to find Jordan in his pyjamas, reading from '*My Utmost For His Highest*'. An open Bible, in which he had been referring to certain verses, lay on the bed next to him.

"I thought you'd be reading Chambers," Ben observed. "That's precisely what I have been doing. However, in addition to the passage for today, I turned to a reference, which, although we were far apart, had a tremendous effect on your mother and me. One November, long ago, when I was alone on the farm, reading it, and she was in Britain, it was Uncle Willie Marais' brother, André, who went to the hospital to see her, and quoted that very sentence to her. You may have a different edition, but if you turn to the reading for November the first, you'll find the relevant paragraph at the end of it. Way back then, because the words made such a powerful impression on me, I wrote down the date, the year and the reason for doing so, in the margin. Tonight I believe that the same message is intended for you, so now I am the one to quote:

" *'If through a broken heart God can bring his purposes to pass in the world, then thank Him for breaking your heart!'*

" Jordie, my son, some day you will indeed have cause to thank Him, I promise you! In the meantime, don't waste time being angry or resentful. Thank God that He has placed that dear girl in your home, and not somewhere alone in a place where there would be no one to turn to after Aunt Biddy leaves. Don't resent the situation. Thank God for the privilege of taking care of her, even if you can't be all that you long to be, to her. Pray for her, and for strength and guidance for yourself....That's what I had to do!"

He patted Jordan on his head and, as he was going out of the door, he said, "And maybe you should ask for Grace to be able to pray for Tristan, too."

Jordan was generally up by five on Thursdays, but on the day after bearing his soul to his father, and driven from the bed in which he had failed to find rest, he was up earlier than usual. He went for a swim, hoping to clear his head, dressed and made coffee, and was about to place a bowl of cereal on the table, when, through the breakfast room window, he caught sight of Meredith in her housecoat, out in the garden, carrying a notebook and pen.

Intrigued by this, he went out onto the stoep, intending to call out to her, but then changing his mind, he went down the steps, and strolled down the path to where she was standing on the lawn, barefoot.

"Good morning, Miss Muffet!" he greeted her. "You're up early today, and you seem to be very busy! What are you doing?—You're getting your feet wet, you know!"

"Morning, Jordie! Yes, I'm frequently up at this time of the day, and I love to walk in the dew. Actually I prefer to go barefoot, and it's safer to do that here, than at home....I know it seems silly, but I think that it sort of recharges one's batteries to make contact with the earth like this. I don't like to go back into the house with wet feet, so I leave my slippers at the front door, and put them on before I go back inside…

"I see that you are already dressed and ready to go, and I know it's your special clinic day, but aren't you also up earlier than usual?"

"It gets light so early at this time of the year, and the birds wake me," he explained. "I don't expect Angelina to make breakfast for me on my early day, and, as no one else is awake, I am usually obliged to have it on my own, so, since you are up, too, I would certainly enjoy your company this morning. I'm only having cereal, but can I persuade you to come inside and at least join me for a cup of coffee?"

How he succeeded in carrying on a half-normal conversation, he did not know, for his voice was thick and his heart beat as tumultuously as it had done when he had held her in his arms, to dance with her. All of a sudden he was reminded of what his father had told him about the day after Amy-Lee, his mother, had arrived to join him in South Africa. Of how, returning to his farmhouse in the fresh, early morning air, from where he had been working at the lower end of the orange orchard, he experienced the happiest moment of his life. When he saw Amy-Lee sitting on the stoep, his father said, the joy was so overwhelming that he could hardly breathe. He had vaulted over the side door of the Jeep like a teenager, and bounded up the steps, two at a time...

But for him, Jordan, their son, all he had felt since the moment he had seen Meredith with the sun shining on her hair, and her tiny bare feet on the grass, was agony!

"I'd really like that," she said, in reply to his invitation. "In fact, apropos your question about what I'm doing, I'd be glad to have a few moments to read to you what I've been writing. I keep a diary and write home every day. At the moment I'm trying to describe your garden at this time of the year, for the benefit of my father and sister, and it's only thanks to you that am I able to do this. Dad might have seen glory equal to this in Pretoria, when he lived there long ago, but except for the near 'Garden of Eden' that Susan was able to glimpse beside the river in Upington, she has never had the privilege.

"I tried to give them the best garden I could, at *Blouspruit*, where the desert and the dunes have a beauty all their own, but to produce something like this is near impossible! Without the magnificent book you bought for me, I would not know the names of half of what's in bloom right now."

"My father is amazing," Jordan told her, walking back towards the house with her. "He goes into raptures about his garden in Nelspruit, and can tell you the name of every tree, flower and shrub there, as well as at *Bentleigh*."

"I know," she said.

She sat down on a stoep chair, dried her small feet—which to him were the most beautiful he had ever seen—put on her slippers, and continued: "It was he who told me that the lovely blue shrub next to your garage is a Plumbago *Capensis*, and explained that it was a variety that grew in the Cape—hence the name."

In the breakfast room, he drew out a chair at the table for her, and with his hands unsteady, poured coffee for himself and for her, trying very hard not to spill. Then he sat down and said, "Please read your letter to me, Merry. It would give me great pleasure to share in what you have written."

"Very well then," she said, smiling at him shyly, "here goes. My dad will later translate all this into Afrikaans for the benefit of old Mieta, so I try to keep it simple…

"Dear Dad, Susie and Mieta," she read,

"I have found out that the bush I was trying to describe to you in yesterday's letter, is called a 'Plumbago'. All the roses have new buds, the 'Bougainvilleas' are covered in flowers and the 'Brunsfelsia' next to the gazebo is fragrant with big new flowers. (Remember I told you about its marvellous perfume, and how, it is also called 'Yesterday, today and tomorrow', because, when the blooms open, they're purple to begin with, next day they are mauve, and finally turn white. Well, that's how there come to be three kinds of flowers on it at once!—But then you may have had one in the garden in Pretoria long ago, Dad.

"There are some white 'Gardenias', which, I am told, will sadly, soon be scorched by the sun. The 'Impatiens' (busy lizzies) are magnificent, as are the 'Begonias'. The 'Gerberas'—'Barberton daisies' to Uncle Ash—are ablaze with flowers, but will soon also find the dry heat a bit much. Lots of bunches of grapes on all the vines around the dining-room patio, and also in front of the cottage where Jordan's friend, Reggie and his mom are going to live. (I wonder if the grapes

grown here can ever taste as sweet as the ones that come from near the Orange River!) There is a blackberry bush growing against an open-air shower, near the swimming pool, and the 'crocodile' wall is covered in berries. Angelina picks the ripe ones every morning to use in the fresh fruit 'smoothies', as she calls them, for Uncle Ash.—Yesterday she made me one; and Susie, after you've tasted this, you'll never again be quite as wild about those pink milkshakes in Spoors-einde!

"In case you don't know what a 'crocodile' wall is, Dad, when trees are cut down and planks sawn, the rounded outside ones that still have the bark left on them, are called 'crocodiles', because of the rough skin or bark on the one side. I think that they are certainly more attractive, and probably more suitable than concrete walls would be, although I don't know whether walls can grow mould here. In any case, I think that they somehow look more natural in this setting. There is a lemon tree, which, Uncle Ash, who grows them in Nelspruit, told me, is called a 'Eureka', and it has lots of new baby lemons on it. The grapefruit tree is also laden with small, new fruit.

"Soon I hope to plant an variety of herbs. If Jordie agrees—and it is, after all, his house!—I plan to have three large window boxes on the wall outside of the kitchen door. There I'll have fresh rosemary as well as brown, curly leaf lettuces, rocket, baby spinach, lots of shiny sweet basil, chives and lemon thyme. With so many herbs of all kinds to use in my cooking, I'll really be able to surprise you and Susie when you come to visit. Angelina says we shall even be able to make sage tea!

"There are a lot more 'Hydrangeas' coming into full bloom, also both white and blue 'Agapanthus'. Evenings and nights are beautiful. One can sit outside till midnight without a cardigan, and just enjoy the smells and sounds of Africa, even though we live in a world city. The tree ferns have grown amazingly with all the rain, and, as the sun sets, and the gorgeous light plays on the leaves, I praise God for being in such a lovely place, and for all His blessings!"

"As indeed we do!" Ash said from doorway. "I heard voices and thought I'd come and join you. I have been listening with great interest to what you were reading, Merry. And I like the idea of the herbs. Perhaps you could, in time cultivate a complete herb garden. You're a girl after my own heart! Wait until you come to 'Beauclaire' someday, and then it will be my pleasure to drive you around in my Jeep, and show you the glory of my Flame Trees, Flamboyants and others that have to be seen to be believed!—Any coffee left, Jordie?"

"Of course, Dad, How nice to have you join us! I presume you're off to the plant this morning?"

"I am. I guess that, having had your own car stolen twice when it was parked outside of the clinic, you'd rather have Charlie take you in the other one this morning, and then he can come back for me and take me to Isando?...Does that suit you?"

"Sounds like a plan, Dad!"—He turned to Meredith.— "And, if you'd like to come along with Reggie later, when he takes over from me, you can see the clinic?"

"Oh, may I?" she responded eagerly. "That would be great!—And may Aunt Biddy come, too?"

"You don't need to ask, Merry." He smiled. "I'd really like to have her opinion, and hear her comments, after all her years of working with Doc Hugo, in his!"

"Well then, I'll tell her as soon as she's awake....And, Jordie, wouldn't you like to have some of our own glorious blooms in your clinic? I'm sure they'll give your patients a great deal of pleasure, and I could bring them when I come!"

"What a lovely idea! " He thought for a moment. "See if you can find a suitable vase, too—and, on second thoughts, if you don't mind, bring enough flowers for me to give some to one of my little patients, Fransie, to take home to his grandmother."

An affectionate smile spread across Jordan's face. "He calls me *'Oom Dokter'* ('Uncle Doctor'), and comes to visit me religiously, whether he is sick or not, whenever I am there early, because he is able to do that before he goes to school. It brings me joy to know I'll find him waiting for me when I get there.

"While Reggie and I have been getting the other office ready, Fransie has been our faithful little helper!...He'll have gone by the time you get there today, but I'll tell him to come back later today, and fetch the flowers....He and his grandmother—and sometimes their next-door neighbour—are my only volunteers. Mrs. Viljoen comes and cleans for me, and, now that I am being sponsored, I am trying to persuade her to let me pay her.

"By the way, Meredith," he reprimanded her, as he was about to leave, "I can't believe that you have been mailing letters to your family, when there are four computers in this house! I don't want to hear of your ever doing that again....The first thing we'll do when I get home this evening, is to set up your email for you!"

Meredith and I were awed, as much as by the enormity of what Jordan had taken on, as by his gentleness, his remarkable command of Afrikaans, and the respectful manner in which he treated his patients—some of whom had probably not been able to have a good wash for months! Doc had repeatedly told me how indispensable he found me, because without a receptionist, no one to book appointments, and no one to keep records, he would have had to do all that by himself. Well, that's precisely what Jordie had been doing, on his own, for close on eighteen months! And I criticized Tristan in my heart, as it came to me that Jordan must have exercised considerable powers of persuasion, to get other physicians to fill in for him when he had come to Doc Hugo's assistance, at a time when, in fact, it was one of Tristan's own relatives who had needed him so desperately in *Spoors-einde!*

We only found out that morning, about how Jordan and his driver, Charlie, would stop on the way to the clinic, and load up the boot[16] of the car with buns, fruit, milk and juice. Upon arrival, Charlie would set out the paper cups and make an enormous urn of coffee.

Of course—as a result of the pressure exerted by Ash— there was the usual heavy security; of necessity even higher in this part of the city than where we were staying. The entrance was heavily barred, but once admitted, and immediately on being granted admittance, one of the main qualifications for access to treatment and refreshments, was the willingness of the patient to wash his or her hands. This could be done at one of the many large pumps of sanitizing gel, which had been conveniently placed, on strategically situated tables, on either side of the door, and in several other places around the waiting room.

Meredith found a perfect spot for the vase she had brought, arranged the flowers, which were much appreciated by the waiting patients, and then somehow, before she and I knew it, we found ourselves involved, and the time passed too quickly for us. This clinic and the people in it were very different from those who came and went in our *Spoors-einde* consulting rooms, but, having been Doc's receptionist for so many years, I somehow found myself marshalling people around, and felt sufficiently at home to offer to do a few injections and blood pressure tests, when I saw that Jordie was rushed off his feet. Of course I did not know then about the emotional upheaval or the sleeplessness of the night before, but I noticed that, by the time Reggie arrived with Charlie, at noon, Jordan appeared to be less jaunty than usual. Meanwhile, Meredith, who in addition to working—albeit temporarily—in a doctor's office, had perforce gained considerable experience in dealing with almost every kind of childhood malady, as well as having had to weather a wide range of family emergencies, was soon involved in filling out forms and taking care of some of the inevitable paperwork. Unfortunately we could not stay long enough to meet young Fransie, but we were told, later, that his grandmother was pleased with the flowers, especially because they had come to her straight from Doctor Jordan's own garden.

The time passed all too quickly for us, if not for the exhausted physician, and soon it was time for Charlie to drop him off at his Sandton practice, after which we were taken home. Meanwhile Meredith, thinking back on her brief stint in Doc Hugo's pharmacy, was set to speculating on how Jordie's prescriptions were filled, and wondering how those people at his clinic managed to pay for them. She made a mental note to ask Jordan about that. When she did raise the subject, at the dinner table, she was obliged to put the question to Reggie, however, because Jordan was not yet home, and learnt that an account had been opened at a nearby dispensary, by the Ashton Corporation, so that there would be no charge to the patients. Later, bearing in mind the fact that Reggie was earning a salary, probably through the good graces of the same group, she could not help wondering why the budget could not also run to covering the cost of a small number of office staff to help Jordan. Suggesting this, she found it incredible that no one wanted the job.

"Either too scared, or the location of the clinic does not appeal" Reggie told her. "Most of the people who do that kind of work are much in demand, I'm afraid, and prefer the more glamorous, air-conditioned places, with better prospects! Only people whose hearts are really in it, will seek employment in our place! One has to be as dedicated as Jordan is, to really want to work there!"

In studying Jordan that morning, immaculate in his white coat, which he wore as conscientiously in Greymont as he did in Sandton, and seeing the compassion and love he radiated, she, like me, had noticed how tired he looked, and I'm sure that it was then that she decided that, if the opportunity arose, she would volunteer permanently, and give to Jordie and Reg whatever help it was in her power, and within her capability to give. She had found her knowledge of medical terminology useful, and perhaps that would count for something.

***

On the afternoon of the great occasion, my party, all the preparations having been made, Meredith and I went back to *Maison Charles*, where we received the same excellent service as before; only this time Merry's hair was parted down the centre, but still allowed to hang loose at the sides, framing her face in a sort of curve around it. This, we were told, was how all the Hollywood starlets were currently wearing theirs, and the effect was wonderful. I could hardly take my eyes off her, and I doubted that even the embittered Tristan would be able to resist such utter loveliness.

When we climbed into the car that had been sent to fetch us, I reckoned we could have given some of those models a run for their money, and, for the first time, I really began to look forward to the night ahead. If Adéle and her cronies did not manage to prick the balloon for me at the party, I vowed that when I got back to *Spoors-einde*, I would never again allow myself to be intimidated by either Mrs. van der Vuywer or that busybody, Trix! I was good and ready for the fashion parade. And I would tell Peg Jones precisely how I wanted my hair cut in future...!

Of course I could still do with a bit of practice on the high heels, but I could hardly wait to see Jasper's face!

Later, while Merry and I soaked in perfumed water in our respective, luxurious bathrooms, I thought how marvellous it must be to be able to boast of more than one! In *Spoorseinde* there were still people who had to make do with a basin, an enamelled jug, and a few saucepans of hot water! And, in addition after all this cosseting of ourselves, we could take all the time we needed to dress! Boy, this was the life!

Merry's gorgeous, ankle-length dress was in the height of fashion—teal blue, with a skirt swinging from her narrow waist, to flare at the knee—and I really enjoyed seeing my own reflection in the mirror. Heavens! What those sheer stockings and high heels didn't do for a woman!

The two of us descended the staircase slowly, in stately manner, to where the men were gathered in the lobby, and when they saw Merry coming down, both Jordan and Reggie exclaimed with unconcealed enchantment! Involuntarily I glanced at Tristan, who, himself, looked like a second Matthew McConaughey in his tux and bow tie, and, to my immense satisfaction, I thought I saw a flame of interest in his eyes, and read an expression very close to bemusement, on his handsome, arrogant mug! I caught him looking down at Merry's dainty sandals, which matched her dress, and tried to guess what was going on his head. Could he possibly have been thinking of the first time he had seen her—in a shapeless tent of a dress, and *velskoens?*

No one who looked closely at Meredith that night, would have believed that she had spent the whole morning, and most of the previous day, in the kitchen. She would not hear of it that I should help—clearly because the success of the evening was to depend solely on her efforts—and I, who had already realized, on the occasion of my very first visit to *Blouspruit*, how capable she was, was amazed, nonetheless, at the wide variety of food she had prepared. When and where had she learned to do all this? Surely not from books! And certainly not from the television! I knew that she had stamina—anyone who could stand on a step stool for hours on end, making soap, had to be up to the task—and she got plenty of exercise in the garden; but despite all the effort she had put into the preparations for the party, she did not betray the slightest sign of fatigue. She looked as fresh as the morning dew, and I knew that this was probably because she was so excited and so happy!

She was not Jasper Hilliard's daughter for nothing! Every so often, when I was able to listen in on a conversation, I heard her talk intelligently, effortlessly holding the interest of people to whom Jordan or Reggie had specially introduced her. Having met some of them at Adéle's devastating event, quite a few of the guests were already known to her, and it must have been difficult for them to reconcile this exquisite, elegant and self-confident person, with the bewildered girl they remembered from that occasion.

It should be a foregone conclusion that my eyes would immediately seek out Adéle Bradshaw and Gloria Triblehorn. I exulted when I saw that both were visibly flabbergasted. I began to congratulate the two of us, the 'barbarians' from the Kalahari, on a total victory!

Before I go any further, however, I must make mention of Jordan's inestimable support; particularly as I suspected that, behind that mask of supreme confidence, Meredith was hiding the nervousness she most certainly must have endured.

Furthermore I, Biddy, was constantly on tenterhooks; unable to be quite so comfortable, because I carried my own concerns as well as Meredith's in my heart.—And added to that, my shoes were killing me!

Jordan saw to it that I had a seat where nothing could escape me, and he made a point of gravitating to Merry and myself at frequent intervals, as though he wished to assure us that he was there for us. His concern and regard were such a comfort. Meanwhile he also managed, with the co-operation of his father and Reggie, to make sure that everyone had a drink, and that no one was neglected in any way.

Many questions were fired at Meredith by people who were genuinely interested in both her work, and the Kalahari, and who, although they had lived in South Africa all their lives, had never been there and knew nothing about it. Having been forewarned by his father, it was nothing short of amazing how adroitly Jordan jumped in to rescue Meredith whenever he thought that she was in danger of floundering. Fortunately, because of her close association with the Bushmen at *Blouspruit,* and because of what she had learned from them, she was able to explain that, in this day and age, very few *KhoiSan* lived in the traditional way. Few were left of all the many *San*, or Bushmen, collectively known as *Basarwa* in Botswana, who had roamed southern Africa for a period believed to go back at least twenty-thousand years. But it was Jordan, who, having retained an interest in the area since his first visit there as a boy, was able to fill in the fact that their very sad fate had recently been brought starkly to mind by a furore that had erupted over the removal of two small, remaining communities—the *Gana* and the *Gwi*—from Botswana's Central Kalahari Game Reserve.

In response to the many questions with which, believe it or not, he, the 'American' among us, was bombarded, he went on to tell his fascinated audience, few of whom were not South Africans, that the Kalahari, which is the largest continuous area underlain by aeolian (wind-blown) sand in the world, stretches from just north of the Orange River, through Angola, and into the Congo. "As a matter of fact," he elaborated, "the Kalahari extends right up to the equator in some places. The red sand of the dunes in the south has been blown down to there from the Sahara, by the winds of eons, to cover the savannah, or 'veld', that lies beneath it.

"Until Meredith very recently came to grace us with her presence she could be said to have lived for all of her life, in the most north-westerly part of the North Cape Province, yet she is from the southern Kalahari *Duineveld*, which, I am told, is considered by many to be the 'Kalahari proper' or 'real Kalahari' This may be nearer the truth, although even then, a significant area of the southern Kalahari dune-veld lies within Namibia as well."

Merry glanced gratefully at him. "Yes," she took up the conversation from there, "the name *Kgalagadi*, to use the spelling nearest to its indigenous name, is the one used by the *Bakgalagadi* of Botswana, who in turn take their name from it, and from that, the name 'Kalahari Desert' is obviously derived.—The Kalahari sand."

"Is it the same, everywhere?" Doctor Chadwick Fisher, Amy-Lee Ashton's eye specialist, wanted to know. "I have always wanted to visit that area, but ever since my wife and I arrived from Britain to settle here, there never seems to have been an opportunity to do so."

"No, sir." Jordan responded. "To answer your question, Doctor, in the southern Kalahari, which is the driest part, the desert takes the form of a stationary dune veld.—By the way, while that is spelt with a 'v', it is actually pronounced 'felt'.— To the east and to the north of that, it becomes a flat, park-like terrain, or savannah. It is in the southern part that Meredith grew up, and where Auntie Bid, Mrs. Williams—tonight's guest of honour, whom you have just met—still lives. Tristan's great-uncle, an amazing man, also originally from England, is the only physician for miles around, and Auntie Bid, who formerly was a nurse in the Free State town from which my colleague, Reggie Seymour hails, is his most excellent and efficient receptionist-cum-nursing assistant."

"That's very interesting," Fisher said. "Perhaps knowing people there, will encourage us to make the trip sooner than planned!"

"You would be astounded at the many variations there are in the colour of the sand, Chadwick," Ash put in. "Very close to where Merry was raised, in fact all around her father's estate, there are dunes almost the deep red of tomato soup, and sometimes more than one colour can be seen in a single one! When Jordan and I once tried to climb up a dune, the texture of that sand was totally unexpected and it is difficult to describe.—If you ever do go," he advised, "Jordan and Biddy are the ones to ask about the best places to visit."

"And you must stay at *Blouspruit,* my family home, Doctor," Meredith added, now more confident, and thus quite assertive. "You and Mrs. Fisher would be made most welcome, and could, at the same time, find out first-hand what it is like to live in the desert."

"Indeed you must, sir," Jordan encouraged the specialist. "Meredith's father, Professor Hilliard, has had years of experience of living in the desert. He would welcome you, so please let Meredith know, if and when you decide, and she'll put you in touch with him!"

"That would be very kind of you," the doctor said, smiling at Meredith. "We'll take you up on that some day."

Unabashedly gloating, I considered that last small exchange, however unintentional, to have been nothing short of brilliant! In one fell swoop, Jordan and Ash had succeeded in elevating Meredith and me from being on a par with, say, the furniture, to people worth knowing. Her father a professor with a home worth visiting!...And I, a trained nurse and 'most excellent and efficient receptionist!'—Aha! I thought. 'Put that in your pipe and smoke it, Adele Bradshaw!' But that would not be the end of it....Far from it!

Meredith's field of expertise lay in what grew in the Kalahari, and the many uses to which the plants and shrubs were put. Her avid listeners were surprised to learn how much underground water there was, the necessity to dig deep wells in order to reach it, and how those wells were dug, but the ladies were interested, above all, in an appetite-suppressant which the Bushmen were said to have been using for thousands of generations; and, as she responded to the questions, they hung onto her every word.... Hadn't they heard something about that on Oprah? And how did it work?

That was right down Merry's street, and she explained that the drug, called B57, was based on a substance extracted from the desert plant *Hoodia gordinii*. The San, she informed them, had been chewing on a cactus they called *!khoba* (pronounced with a click) for thousands of years, to stave off hunger and thirst during their long hunting trips in the parched Kalahari. It was on this, that overweight individuals were pinning their hopes. Her own, personal hope, she said, was that, from this plant, the impoverished Bushmen would derive an income to improve their lot.

It was only after Jordan had left, that Merry and I realized to what extent we had depended on him. Just after ten, the phone rang, and a few moments later I saw one of the servants go and speak to Tris, only to be casually directed to Jordan. I could not hear what was being said, but I assumed that one of his patients had called, and I fumed at the manner in which he or she was being referred to Jordan, instead.—Not that I thought, for one minute, that the patient would be deprived. On the contrary! If I seethed it was because of the manner in which the younger physician's good nature was being taken for granted, and how shamelessly Tristan took advantage of him. It was beyond me that anyone could be so selfish, especially as this was Jordan's house, and he was the host of the party.

It was from that moment on that things began to go so terribly wrong...

Now seated between Adéle and Gloria, was a middle-aged, pleasant-faced woman who had arrived late, and whom I had not yet met, but she soon introduced herself as the matron of the Dawnview clinic, to which many of Doctor Connaught's, and also Doctor Ashton's patients, were referred. Discovering that we had a nursing background in common, we were soon comparing notes and chatting away like old friends, when Meredith, who had momentarily been out of the room, returned. Seeing a new face beside me, she was concerned lest the newcomer hadn't been offered anything to eat, and she immediately went over to her, carrying a platter of hot sausage rolls, a small plate and serviettes.

"Good evening, and welcome!" she said, smiling, and then introduced herself.

"How nice to meet you at last!" the other woman exclaimed. "I'm Dorothy Hunter, and I have already met your friend Mrs. Williams. Doctor Ashton has told me so much about you." She smiled back at Meredith, and pretended to feel guilty. "Thank you, I'm going to try one of these, because they have been recommended to me, but I confess that I was secretly hoping that there were some of those delicious tarts left. I had several of them—among other things—in the dining room when I was talking to a colleague there, and I think that I really disgraced myself!" At that Meredith, assuring her guest that it was no trouble, went out obligingly, soon to return with a silver basket of small, crescent-shaped jam tarts, which she offered to her new acquaintance.

"Mmm," Mrs. Hunter enthused, biting into one. "The crust simply melts in one's mouth. Is it true that you made all these goodies, yourself? Dr. Seymour tried to convince me of that just now, but I find it difficult to believe. You look far too young to be so capable!"

Meredith was extremely modest, but flattered by the sincerity in the older woman's voice, she blushed becomingly, and was about to make some laughing response to cover her embarrassment, when Adéle leant over, quite rudely I thought, to speak to Gloria, who was sitting on the other side of the Matron Hunter.

"I find domesticity in my acquaintances so boring, don't you?" she remarked in the drawling voice she assumed to illustrate how truly bored she was. "Heaven preserve me from ever becoming immersed in such mundane pursuits! I maintain that a woman who confines her interests to what is within the four walls of her house, sooner or later becomes caught in a relentless trap in which she can only end up deserted and alone. In my opinion, there's nothing that can drive a man so quickly into another woman's arms, as his wife's absorption with things in which he has not the slightest interest!"

"I quite agree, dahling," was Gloria's response, with a meaningful glance in Meredith's direction. "There's no doubt that the old adage about the way to a man's heart being through the stomach, is no longer valid in this, the twenty-first century.—The age of supermarkets and fast food. Why then have servants, for goodness sake? I mean to say, provided a man finds himself an attractive enough mate, he is surely quite content to leave the running of his house to the servants. If not, then why hire them in the first place?"

"Precisely!" was Adéle's affirmative view.

As happens, sooner or later at most parties, not all of the guests remained gathered in one room. We were in the lounge, but others, among them Ash—who was circulating and being sociable in his son's absence—had drifted around, into the kitchen, as well as the dining room, and I was sorry that he was not present at that moment, for Meredith could have done with his moral support.

The two thorns in Merry's flesh had been speaking so loudly that they had succeeded in catching the attention of almost everyone in the room, and while it was probably only Meredith and I—and perhaps Tristan—who could interpret the true meaning behind the words, Merry drew her breath in sharply, and the woman called Dorothy was just in time to catch the basket of tarts that Merry was holding, or it would have fallen to the floor.

"It definitely displays a lack of dignity for a woman to pay too much attention to the menial things in the house," Adéle carried on relentlessly, and then, waving a languid hand at Tristan, called out to him, "Or what do you say, Tris?"

Like Meredith, I held my breath as I waited for his rejoinder, and, when it came, I could cheerfully have murdered him. "Well, I'd say that, in the *backveld*, people would hold a different point of view!" There was derision in his grin as he said that, and my blood boiled at the way in which he emphasized the word 'backveld'—which is tantamount to saying the *bundu,* the boondocks or the stix!

If he had married Meredith because he genuinely loved her, her newfound self-confidence and elegance would have delighted him, because she had really done him proud. He would have nurtured that delicate sprig of confidence and have been very careful that nothing threatened it until it was well established and strong. I think that, to a certain degree, that had briefly still been the case when we first arrived in Johannesburg, because there had been times when, despite his self-absorption, he had taken the trouble to help her or give her advice when necessary. Then I had gained the impression it gratified him to play the master, and, when it suited him, to be sure of her dependence upon him, but things had now reached the stage where his manner very plainly indicated that, for all he cared, she was on her own.

Whether she sank or swam was now entirely up to her.

Ever since Meredith's bitter humiliation at Adele's party, I had secretly been quite proud of the steps I had taken to ensure that nothing like that ever happened again. Now, too late, I was to be provided with irrefutable confirmation of the fact that, if the insight I had been given that day in the *Spoors-einde* church was correct—and I believed that it was—my impulsivity had done her far more harm than good. As if Meredith was not feeling uncomfortable enough already, someone then had to go and suggest that it was time for dancing!

It seemed that one obstacle had hardly been overcome, than we were confronted by another! I was dismayed, as was to be expected, and my immediate reaction was to look at Meredith. I could read her thoughts like a book! What was to be done?

Jordan had gone out, Ash was nowhere to be seen, and I knew that, without one of them in the immediate vicinity, she would panic. Jasper may have provided his daughter with an excellent education, as far as mathematics, science, and many, many other spheres of higher education were concerned, and there was not another woman in the room who could hold candle to her in that respect, but, unfortunately this was not the time for relying on such accomplishments! None of what she had learnt would be of any value to her in this situation, and we could only hope that she would not be invited to dance....Fat chance!

"Will somebody put on that new tango CD!" I heard somebody call out. "The one with some of those pieces from that TV 'Dancing With The Stars' competition on it!" And when a voice cried, "You take Meredith, Tris! We need to see the two of you dance this together!" I knew at once who it was that challenged him...

Oh, dear! Where were the days of the slow waltz and the quick step, I thought despairingly. I had done the tango in my day. Even the Twist, the Locomotion and the La Conga would have been okay for a baby boomer like me, who, along with the other probationers had rocked with the Beatles, but I had never seen such mockery of what can be a marvellous dance to watch. This performance was downright cruel...

Some of the details of what occurred are mercifully a bit vague to me now, but I remember that smile on Tristan's face. How often had I not seen him like that, preparing himself, as a child, for yet another outrageous exploit! Egged on by Adéle, he grabbed the poor, pleading Meredith in his arms, and almost dragged her across the floor, to where, amid loud laughter and whistles of approval, she was subjected to the most grossly exaggerated movements of the dance. He made her do back-bends, thrust her away from him so violently at times that she almost fell over, and then having violently jerked her back towards him, swirled her slight body around until she was dizzy! I certainly believe that there were few people—besides, of course, Adéle and her cronies—who realized that Tristan was making a fool of his wife. It was more likely that most of them thought that they were clowning....That she was participating in this travesty of what could have been a very beautiful dance, purely for their entertainment; but to my gentle, defenceless and inexperienced Meredith, so ignorant of the ways of blasé, vindictive sophisticates such as Adéle and her associates, it was sheer torture. She tried in vain to break loose—which only encouraged more laughter—and the moment the music came to an end, she fled.

It is possible that Tristan intended to apologize, because he immediately went after her, and I still wonder what would have happened if Adéle had not run after him, and thrust her arm through his.

"Well, my dear Tris," she observed sarcastically, "your job is plainly not yet done, is it? It seems that there is more left for you to do, than simply to work on your little wife's appearance." She looked up, her gaze following Meredith dispassionately as she, Merry, ran up the stairs. "Isn't there an old saying that you cannot make a silk purse out of a sow's ear?"

In my consternation, I had also shot up from my seat to go to after Meredith, but as I reached the hallway, dismayed to find Adéle and Tristan there, I heard someone behind me, and turning around, I recognized Doctor Fisher.

"Mrs. Williams," he said apologetically, "I did not mean to startle you. I'm sorry! I was just looking for that fascinating young wife of Tristan's and I thought I saw her go in this direction. My wife is so taken with her, and is really keen to talk to her again..."

"How nice," I stammered nervously. "She has only popped upstairs for a minute to powder her nose, or something. I shall immediately go and tell her that Mrs. Fisher wishes to speak with her."

I found Meredith in her bedroom, in a dreadful state. She was completely beside herself with despair and embarrassment. I was destined to see her in tears many more times, but, at that moment, it would have been difficult to believe that she could ever again be quite so desperate, or so totally devoid of hope.

"Oh, Aunt Biddy," she sobbed, "How could he?...How could he do this to me?... To expose me to the mockery and contempt of others like that? Tristan took advantage of the fact that, as far as he knows, I do not know how to dance, and although Uncle Ash had taught me, there was no way I would have attempted to do so for the first time in front of other people, without him or Jordan! In any case, whatever that awful dance is called, it's certainly is not one that we have practised!"

Of course I sympathized with her, and inwardly I wept for her, but, once again, this was not the time for dwelling on problems. She was about to say more, but I very crisply interrupted her.

"Merry-love, there is still so much for you to learn, and to be able to hold your head high even at times like this, is the most important requirement of all. This has been a ghastly setback for you, especially when you have prepared everything so beautifully, but do you remember what I told you last time? Although I hope that nothing like this will ever happen to you again, this experience, awful as it may seem, must be used to equip and make you ready for the next time. To grow strong and be prepared for whatever life throws at you!"

"Yes, I remember what you said last time, and where has that got me?" she cried bitterly. "I am no match for that woman. She knows that I am a hopeless failure—and what's more she is aware that I know that, too!"

"Don't you ever say that again! You are not a failure! You are a beautiful, lovable and charming young woman, and you have many people who love and admire you!—Just think of how Uncle Ash and Jordan, and even Reggie, dropped everything they were doing, to try and help you.—How can you let one, selfish and cruel woman, override that? Meredith, I have had more experience of life than you have, and I promise you that, if you did not pose a threat to her, she would not have to go to so much trouble to make your life a misery!'

"But she's not the one I care about, Auntie. What hurts so much is that Tristan allows it! He seems to encourage her! You have to admit that he spends a great deal more time with her than he does with me! In fact he hardly ever speaks to me!"

I felt as though my heart could break! Every word she had said was true, and I felt so inadequate. How many more times was Rosalie's beautiful child supposed to endure such hurt? Nevertheless, in the little time I had left before going home, I had to concentrate on strengthening her. Little knowing that Ash had been a witness to similar, agonizing despair— Jordan's—not more then a few nights before, I did exactly what he did; and what came to me was a line of Scripture that Mark had often quoted to me.

"Remember, Merry-love," I said, kissing her forehead, "and never forget that, '*All things work together for good to them that love God*.' "

"Now," I said briskly, when the slender shoulders had stopped shaking, and she was no longer breathing with the heartrending hiccoughs of recent sobbing, you are going to comb you hair, powder your pretty little nose and put on some more lipstick, and then we're going downstairs. The people waiting down there, are there at your invitation—or at least the party was your idea—and you are not ceding the victory to Adele Bradshaw or any of her bunch, ever again! There is a very nice lady waiting to talk to you downstairs, and I can only hope that she has not left by now.

"Only Adéle and Tristan know where you have been, or why, and, if you can behave normally, let people see that lovely smile, and carry yourself confidently, you won't have to worry about Adéle, or Gloria. They'll see that you have your armour on, and you're ready to take them on!—But let's just have a quick prayer before we enter into the fray once more!—And don't forget, for one minute, that this is Jordan Ashton's home, and that you have been given the honour of playing the role of hostess to friends he has invited!"

Somehow I found the words, and I began to pray for this vulnerable child, this grown woman who, through no fault of her own, had the innocence of a child, and who had never known anything but love and acceptance, until she had come to this place. I asked the Lord to give her the courage she needed to go back and face whatever lay ahead.

As we were praying, I heard footsteps in the passage, and then there was a knock at the door. "Hey, Meredith are you in there?" came the voice of Benjamin Ashton. "Sorry I was on the phone so long. I'll tell you and Biddy about that later, but I just want you to know that I've taken my old record player downstairs. While I was talking to my wife, I heard music, and gathered, that, as you feared, the dancing had started so..."

Before he could complete the sentence, I had yanked open the door. "She won't be a minute, Ash," I informed him. "We're just putting on the old war paint, as women do, and we'll be right down."

"Then I'll wait and go down with the two of you," he said. "I went to apologize to the folks who are sitting in the dining room, for my long absence, and there encountered Mrs. Fisher who is anxious to have a word with Merry. I told her that when they had finished their chat, I would be waiting to have a dance with Meredith, because I'd hauled out a few recordings of my old favourites, and now it turns out that the Fishers and some of the others who are gathered there would like to dance, too."

"*Lord*!" I said under my breath. "*You are so clever*! (Of course He knew that already, but I think He likes us to acknowledge that we are aware of that fact! Besides, He's my father and my friend, and I often carry on such conversations with Him.)... "Thank you for your goodness and mercy!"

One obstacle remained to be eliminated, and that was Merry's crushing embarrassment. She had made a fool of herself, she insisted, and it took some doing to convince her that it may well have appeared that she and Tristan had put on that exhibition for the entertainment of the onlookers. Now I could not wait to see Tristan's face, when she and Ben Ashton glided onto the floor!

"Jordie also phoned," Ash told me when I joined him. "He's on his way home, and was pleased to hear that no one had left the party yet, because he says we still have to drink a toast to the lady of the hour—that's you, Biddy—and he claims the privilege of proposing that. I passed his message on to the Fishers and anyone else who might have been about to leave, so that they would wait, and because they know full well what a GP's life can be like, they're quite happy to do so.... It's not that late yet."

"Ash," I said in an undertone, "before Meredith comes, I need to ask you something urgently....Do you know what's wrong with Tristan? That's the man to whom his loving mother sang when he was only a few hours old, with tears dripping onto his face. How could he have grown up to be so objectionable?" And then I told him about the tango incident.

"I'd like to hear about that, too," I was startled to hear Meredith announce from right behind me. Having emerged from the bedroom, she had, without my knowledge, been standing right behind me all the time.

"I don't know," Ash acknowledged ruefully, "but, if he would subject himself to 'Inner Healing' ministry—which he continues to refuse—we'd soon find out. This is not like hypnotism or psychoanalysis, as Aunt Biddy will confirm. The Holy Spirit has the mind of God, and is able to reveal to Tristan whatever is hidden and suppressed inside of him, and then the healing will begin. This is also not like a medical or psychological procedure, where, even after analysis, the patient often needs to take medication for the rest of his or her life, and I suggest that we three pray very hard for Clifford and Thora's son to submit himself to that! They are possibly the ones who have been most hurt by his resentful attitude."

And so Meredith, squaring her shoulders and with a more relaxed expression on that lovely face, went down the stairs with Ash on one side of her, and me on the other. All she asked, on the way down was, "Aunt Biddy, do you think that my mother made my father feel as bad as Tristan constantly does me? In that case I must ask God to protect Susie. What if someday she does the same to someone who loves her?"

I could answer without having to stop and think. "That was a completely different situation, Merry-love, and your mother was not anything like Tris. She was my friend, a beautiful kind and loving person, in every other way, and I'm sure she hated herself for what she did you to your father.—How else could he have loved her right to the end? So much so, that he went in search of her and brought her home?

"This thing with Tris is not genetic, I can assure you. I only need to go back, in my mind, to both his parents, to be certain of that—and you only have to think of Doc Hugo, to conclude that whatever has embittered Tristan to the extent that he strikes out, even at those he loves, could not have been inherited from any of them."

Later she conversed confidently with Mrs. Fisher and some of the 'older' folk—meaning those who were about my age— none of whom had witnessed the tango disaster. In addition, following my advice, she was so charming to Adéle and Gloria that they did not know what had hit them.

Somehow, having just previously discussed Tristan, I found myself pitying him. I acknowledged that my attitude towards him had hardly been what Jesus would have wanted. In trying to protect Meredith, I had been equally spiteful and vindictive, and admitting that, I was made to renew my resolve to pray for him—and everyone else who had been involved in this diabolical movement to demoralize Meredith. However, despite what I had said to her, I was now consumed by the agonizing realization that Rosalie had felt herself to be trapped at *Blouspruit*, both before and after her marriage to Jasper, and if I had any influence whatsoever, on him, I would see to it that he did not keep Susan under too tight a leash.

Presently Ash put on a record, and it was a delight to see Meredith relaxed and plainly enjoying the dance with him. It was not the first time that it had amazed me that Ash, who was such a consummate, classical pianist—in my opinion, easily in the 'concert' pianist class—should have such a catholic taste in music.

When that record came to an end, he chose a recording of an old wartime song which had been a favourite with my parents, and which Jordie had played at his father's request on the Wednesday, when Ash was teaching Merry how to dance to that tempo. *"You'll never know..."* was the song the vocalist was singing, and they were just beginning the dance, when Jordie, not having had time to change before responding to that call, came in, looking so dashing in his evening clothes, that, if I had been young, and happened to be the patient he had gone to see, I would surely have swooned!

"Hey!" He called out to Meredith. "They're playing our song! Give me a minute to freshen up, Dad, and then I'm cutting in!"

As he returned and took Meredith in his arms, I did not realize how appropriate the words were, or how they tortured him...

"You'll never know just how much I love you..." sang Al Martino, the great Italian-American pop crooner... *"You'll never know just how much I care..."*

For some reason tears stung my eyes...

By the time the guests had left that night, we were still too wound up to go straight to bed, so I made tea, and all of us except Tristan, who had driven someone home, sat around the kitchen table to debrief, as it were. I was glad of the opportunity to express my thanks to everyone, before Ash went back to Nelspruit, and I had to tell Jordan how much I had appreciated his speech.

"You made me feel really special," I told him. "I'm glad I was also given a chance to say how very special I find all of you.

You have been so kind to both Meredith and me, and I shall have plenty to tell Doc, and Merry's father and sister, when I get home."

I then turned to Ben. "I hope you will remember to give my love to Amy-Lee, Ash, and also to Eugenie and Dominic, and to Dominic's family. Please tell the new parents that I'm proud of them, and will pray very hard for them. Especially for their precious little one. I'm sure that the baptism will be a joyful and memorable occasion for all of you! "

"I'll certainly do that, Biddy," Ash promised. "Now I must tell you about the phone calls tonight. It was actually Zhaynie who rang, the first time, and after that I spoke at length to my wife.—I loathe being away from Amy-Lee, and I have been missing her so much that I went to talk to her in my study.—I can only hope that none of the guests considered my prolonged absence to be discourteous!

"Anyhow, this is the gist of the two conversations. Zhaynie says that without you there, in person, as the godfather Jordie, nothing will seem right to her. She knows that it is not very long since you were at *Beauclaire*, but she begs you to come. I said that you would have to speak to her yourself, son, but that I felt sure that, with some careful reorganizing, that could be arranged. However, her second request makes that a little more difficult.—She dearly wants Tris and Meredith to be there on the great day, and she also wants us to persuade Biddy to postpone her return to *Spoors-einde* for a few days, and come, too...!"

No one spoke for a little while, and then Reg asked, "Why does that problem have to be insurmountable? This is a once-in-a-lifetime thing for your family, Uncle Ash, and I can understand why Zhaynie would also like to have her childhood friend there, and meet the girl he has married. It's a perfectly reasonable request. If it's Jordan's patients you are concerned about, I can carry the pager over the weekend."

"That's very kind of you, my friend," Jordan said. "I can hardly wait to see my little godson, and I would very much like to be there, but it's not more than a few weeks since you last covered for me!"

Reg brushed that aside. "*Ach*, come on now, Jord!...It isn't as if I lead a crazy social life, or anything, and I'm going to have to ask you to cover for me when I go and fetch my mother. As it is, I shall only be spending the weekend unpacking my stuff in the cottage. Your father can fly the four of you there and back, and if you leave here after your consulting hours on Friday, you can easily be back on time for a regular Monday at your office. If Aunt Biddy wants to take the flight to Upington, while you're still at the airport, that could also be done, I suppose, but you'd have to leave Nelspruit pretty early for her to make it in time!

"What are friends for, Jord? You'd do the same for me, and I'm not even an uncle! You wouldn't want a proxy godfather standing in for you at the baptism of the first Ashton grandchild, would you?"

Jordan looked doubtfully at his father. "Well, Dad...what do you think?"

"I thinks that's a capital idea, and I appreciate Reggie's offer. Now all we have to do is to discuss this with Tristan when he comes back tonight, in case he's still asleep when I leave in the morning. Then we'll hear from Meredith and Aunt Biddy, too.—But I have other news as well.

"This is for you and Meredith, Biddy. Amy-Lee says there is no way she's going back to the States without seeing you, Bid, and she'd like to see Doc Hugo and Jasper again, too....It's forty degrees Celsius in Upington at the moment, so, even if you do decide to come to *Beauclaire* for the baptism, how about we, Amy-Lee and I, come back here as soon as the weather cools down a bit, we pick up Merry and the Fishers, and we all go off to *Spoors-einde*, where Jasper can come and fetch his daughter for a visit, and then, when we go to *Blouspruit* to fetch Meredith again, we'll all have a visit?

"There was also a message from your father, Merry. I believe he has spoken to Tristan, who will take you to buy your computer, perhaps tomorrow, and he wanted you to know that he has put the money for it in the bank, because it is his and Susie's gift to you."

"That would be wonderful!" Meredith commented— abstractedly, almost tonelessly, I thought—momentarily emerging from a noticeable pre-occupation with something else. "What a great idea! If that can be arranged, I would greatly appreciate it." Immediately after that she turned to Jordan, and said the strangest thing...

"I didn't know that piece had words to it, Jordie! What a beautiful song that is!"

And enigmatic as her statement had been, Jordan must have been able to make sense of it, because his response was a solemn: "*I know!*"

Something bothered me about these two. There was nothing I could do about Jordan and I knew that, if he was troubled about anything, no matter what it was, he had the privilege of going straight to his father—they were that kind of family—so, before I climbed into bed, I, being all Meredith had, made the excuse that I wanted to tuck her in for the night, to go back to her room. After making small talk for a moment or two, I came straight out with it and asked her what the problem was. I thought that, when it came to her relationship with the man to whom she was supposedly married, nothing could surprise me, but what she said, certainly did!

"I can't go to Nelspruit," came the muffled voice as she attempted to draw the blankets up over her face

"Why ever not?"

She hid her face in the pillow. "Because I'd have to sleep in the same room as Tristan!"

Put yourself in my position. Wouldn't you have been confounded? But that was nothing compared to the shock of her explanation. I nearly fell off the bed! At first I thought I was not hearing properly, so I pulled the blanket away from her face and demanded that she repeat the last sentence. "I can't hear you when you cover you mouth, Merry!"

"I'm not ready to have a baby," she burst out, "and Tristan would make a rotten father. He might be cruel to it. When I have children, I don't want their father swinging them around by their arms or legs!"

"But Merry..." I began, but she cut me short.

"I had the wrong idea of what 'sleeping together' meant, but now I've seen on television, *with my own eyes*—to put it ungrammatically—what happens when the men come into the girls' rooms, and thank goodness, Tristan has never come to mine! I know how babies are made. I knew it scientifically, but I didn't know it was like *that*!...I'll have to warn Susie!"

Now, before I go any further, I had better explain that, once one reached the top of the stairs, in that house, Jordan's bedroom and bathroom were on the right, with his parents' suite beyond that. To the left was Tristan's, then my bedroom and bath, and, at the end of the corridor, in the corner, was Meredith's; and, as well as keeping her curtains open, so that, if she was ever wakeful, she could see the stars and the moonlit sky, she slept with her door ajar. I was the only one who ever went to check on her, which is why, when she heard a gentle tap at her door about twenty minutes after I had retired—still trying to get my head around this new development—she sleepily responded to the whispered, "Merry, are you asleep yet?" with an invitation to enter.

As I say, she was used to my coming to look in on her, from time to time, and it was only when Tristan sat down at the foot of her bed, after closing the door behind him, that she she realized who her visitor was, and she was instantly on her guard.

"Please go away!" she hissed, shrinking from him. "I know why you have come, and I want you to go!"

"Merry?" he exclaimed, taken back. "I came to tell you that I would be happy to go shopping with you tomorrow, but mainly to say how sorry I am. Not just about tonight, but for everything to which you have been subjected since you came here. I had time to think, as I was driving back here tonight, and thinking how lovely you looked when you were dancing, I could cheerfully have cut my throat!

"I could kick myself when I think of the time I have wasted. And how your opinion of me must have changed. I am not a good person, little Meredith, but I am going to try hard to be better. Uncle Ash has told me of Zhaynie's wish to have us at her baby's christening, and I'd like to go. You'll love her, and I am longing to show you off to her.

"Maybe we could start over, and spend some time alone together on the farm, where there are none of the distractions and horrors of the city.—I do hope you'll come with me..."

I wonder what he thought when she retorted: "I accept your apology, and I'll think about going.—But don't you think, for one moment, Tristan Connaught, that you are sleeping in the same room with me!" He had his hand on the door handle, when she added, "And, right now, it is doubtful that you ever will. I don't think I even like you any more!"

CHAPTER SEVEN

It must be made clear, that although I have been writing about how Jordan felt, and what he had confided to his father, and I have described many other details of their lives thoughts, and emotions, I was not yet, at that stage, in possession of all those facts about which I would only learn later. Of course I knew a great deal about Meredith's situation, because she shared so much with me, and I had overheard a conversation, here and there, but it was only when I learnt that Tristan and his father-in-law had been talking on the phone that I realized that Jasper very clearly knew nothing about any estrangement between the 'newly-weds'.

It had become obvious that he and Tristan were still on good terms, and also that Meredith did not tell her father about matters that might have distressed him. I ground my teeth as I contemplated how much he needed to be told when next I saw him! Was it better to leave him in the dark?

On the Sunday morning following the party, it was once again just the three of us, Meredith, Tristan and I, who sat down to breakfast. I had cut up the fruit while Merry made waffles, and she had put some of the batter into the fridge, so that she could make more for Reg and Jordan when they returned from taking Ash to the airport. Once again the atmosphere was strained—but there was a subtle difference.

This time it was Tristan who made the overtures, and Meredith who was noticeably distant. I had spoken on the phone to Doc, Sally Vercueil and Jasper, in the meantime, and it had been decided that, in the first place, there was no way we could be certain of my getting back to the Johannesburg airport after the visit to *Beauclaire*, in time to take the only flight to Upington; and, secondly, it would have meant lugging all the stuff I had accumulated while I was in Bryanston, to Nelspruit with me. Joking, as usual, Sally said she thought she could stick it out with Doc for another week, and was pleased to learn that Jasper would be meeting me in Upington, because Hennie's taxi was giving trouble and he had to wait for parts. Later he, Jasper, told me that he would have come for me, in any case.

One very important detail of which I was not aware—nor would be until a day came when Meredith told me—was that later that day, she sought out Jordan in his study, where he was busy writing medical reports, and put a very odd question to him. "Jordie," she asked, "what did your father mean when he said that the Lord had spoken?"

He sat for a while, with his brow puckered, and then replied, "Ah, now I think I know what you're talking about. Are you referring to his response when I told him that Zhaynie and Dominic's baby had arrived?"

She nodded, and then putting his hands together thoughtfully, he said, "Well, I guess he had put out a fleece!"

"You mean like Gideon did in Judges 6:36-40?"

"Yes, I think so....Yes, that's what I think he meant."

"But doesn't Scripture warn us, somewhere else, against asking for such signs? When we studied that once, my father told Susan and me that The Old Testament law prohibited putting God to the test!"

"He was right, Merry!—Why don't you sit down for a moment, while we talk?" Drawing out a chair for her, he continued earnestly: "Before we follow Gideon's example, we should take a closer look at some of the specific circumstances in his case, and then consider what other Scripture passages say about looking for a sign from the Lord. I believe, though, that it is important for me to define what I meant when I said that my dad had 'put out a fleece'.

"This is only my personal opinion, but I don't think it is wrong for someone to study a situation, very carefully, for general indications of God's leading.—Not as Gideon did by imposing a specific 'sign', and then demanding that He should give him instant guidance by satisfying that particular imposition. That, in my opinion, is putting God to the test in a way that is forbidden."

"Thank you for that, Jordie.—If it's not impertinent, may I ask you why you thought your father had done so, and what you think your father did?...You see," she explained quaintly, "I am thinking of doing something like that, myself, on two counts, so this is very important to me. I don't want to do anything wrong!"

He was immeasurably touched by her childlike humility, and overwhelmed by the fact that she should choose to share such an intimate thought with him. Here was the woman who, when questioned, had spoken so knowledgeably the previous evening, on so many subjects, that even Tristan had, at one stage, been moved to say to Gloria Triblehorn, "Shut up, Glow, I want to hear this!"

He put out his hand, and spontaneously ruffled her hair. "I believe that God heard my father's prayers for guidance, when he was in an agonizing turmoil, trying to decide whether to give up *Beauclaire*, and move the family out of South Africa. Eugenie was quite prepared to go back with him and my mother, and have her baby in the States, but God chose to let little Benjamin be born, right there, at *Beauclaire*! Not even in the hospital! My dad implicitly believes that to be God's sign to him, and he has told us all that *Beauclaire* is to be Benjamin's!"

"Praise God!" she cried. "What a wondrous thing to happen! I'm just blown away!—Thank you for telling me, Jordie, but I hope that does not mean that I am obliged to tell you about the signs I need—even if one of them concerns you!"

Shortly after that, she and Tristan went off to buy the laptop, only occasionally breaking the strained silence between them, and I went out into the garden in search of Jordan, whom I found sprawled out on a lawn chair, in shorts, with the '*Sunday Times*' over his face to keep the sun out of his eyes. He must have heard me approach, for he raised the paper and said, "I was wondering where you were and what you were doing.— Would you like a cold drink? Or tea? …I make quite a good cuppa, Auntie Bid!"

"I remember," I told him. "I have never forgotten how you brought my tea to me, in bed, one morning during the epidemic, when I was simply too tired to get up and make it myself.…But I don't need anything to drink right now thank you. What I would really like, however, is a few minutes of your time…"

"I'm at your disposal," he said gallantly. "Allow me to take the chairs into the shade, and then we can visit more comfortably. The sun has moved just enough to be too bright, and I was too pre-occupied to notice." After having carried the chairs to where we were shaded by a massive Plane tree, he invited me to sit down, and then asked, "Now what would you like to talk about?"

"Meredith," I said, without beating about the bush.

Now please remember that I have already said that there were matters, such as how Jordie felt about Merry, for instance, and what he had said to Ash about Tristan, that I did not know. If I had, I would never have spoken to him in quite the way I then proceeded to do. Anyhow, it's too late for regrets now, and there were things I badly needed to get off my chest before I went away. Jordan must have sensed this, because he favoured me with that amazing smile, and kindly said, "Go ahead, Auntie Bid. I'm all yours, for as long as you like. All afternoon if need be!"

"Jordie," I began hesitantly, "I don't know quite where to begin, so I'll start by confessing that I don't know how much of Meredith's story Tristan has told you, and I am doubtful that he has told you precisely how this marriage came about. He may not have told you how she and her sister were kept in seclusion—very congenial seclusion, I might add, but isolation nonetheless. Which is the reason she cannot be blamed for not being totally *au fait* with the customs and demands of the more urbane style of life she is required to lead here. She does very well, I'd say, but I believe that she hides a great deal of apprehension at times.

"She possesses talents, which she does not flaunt, and that many other women would envy, but that does not mean that she, on her part, does not envy every woman who has acquired that city-bred veneer....She's not the proverbial dumb blonde, Jordie. Her father has been responsible for developing her brain and nurturing those talents to a remarkable degree, and, if you could see her lab at *Blouspruit* you would be amazed...!"

"It's unnecessary to point this out to me, Auntie," he assured me solemnly. "I have discovered for myself what an extraordinary girl she is. And the very fact that she has not acquired the shallow attributes to which she might wish to aspire, contributes to her charm, in my opinion. Tristan has found himself a rare jewel, and she's exactly the kind of wife every doctor would want. She's not just intelligent and tactful, Auntie Bid. She is as sympathetic and caring as she is beautiful. She knows how to make a man's home comfortable and welcoming—a refuge to which to return, thankfully, after a tiring and sometimes depressing day!"

A time would come when it would suddenly strike me quite forcibly, how, as he warmed to the topic, he was actually putting into words precisely what I was trying to tell *him*! "Surely it must be clear to you," he added, "that Tristan realized that—or why else did he marry her?"

"Heaven only knows!" I exploded, and then had to compose myself. "I have my own opinion, which I have shared with your father, but I have difficulty in stating that categorically, to you, Jordie, just in case I am wrong. Moreover, my purpose in seeking you out today was not to talk about Tristan. It is the situation as it pertains to Meredith that has prompted me to come to you...

"She seems to be comparatively happy at the moment, but I have an awful feeling that it won't last long. You were not here to witness what happened last night, or to hear some of the barbs that were targeted at her, but I was; and I have to take steps to protect her from further humiliation and hurt like that, after I have left. Now that your father has returned to *Beauclaire*, that is something that cannot be done without your help and cooperation. There's only you, and I'm talking to you now, in case we don't have an opportunity to be alone like this again....Jordie, I cannot go away and leave her to the wolves!"

"I'm willing to do anything you can suggest, Auntie Bid," came the prompt and very kind response. "Just tell me what it is that you want me to do, and I'll help, where, and whenever I can..."

"If you only knew how much I am depending on you, Jordie!...I hope and pray that Tristan will gradually come to the realization of what he is doing to Merry, and what is expected of him. I hope he will come to find it in himself to give her the support which should be a joy to him. In the interim, until he is man enough to figure out what that entails and fulfil his duty, I have to beg you to help me find peace of mind. It is high time I went home, but, in order to go in peace, I must be sure that she has someone on whom to lean..."

Heaven forgive me!—If only I had known then what I was asking of him!

"And now," I croaked, "my throat is so dry that I'll have to take you up on that offer of something to drink. Water will do, please!"

When he returned with a crystal pitcher of Mango juice, ice, and two glasses, I drank thirstily from mine, before I could continue:

"Jordan, it won't help to try and convince Meredith that she is neither incapable nor inferior. She'd be the first to argue that scientific knowledge and above average housekeeping skills do not necessarily make her the most suitable wife for Tristan Connaught!...You were the one to raise the question of why he married her, and it might very well be that he saw something in her that is no longer there—or that he had hoped to mould her into precisely the woman he wanted her to be, and that he no longer finds that possible. ...Whatever the case, this marriage is not working, and I am surprised that Merry has not yet asked if she could return to the Kalahari with me! If she stays, she will have to lean heavily on you!"

He courteously refilled the glass which I held out to him.

"I would not ask this of you," I went on, " if I did not already know how unselfish you can be, and I would not have had the audacity to approach you if I didn't think that you would understand. Meredith has a wonderful sense of humour, but she is in danger of being robbed of that. She must be encouraged to laugh at herself more frequently, as she felt free to do when she did that dance for you the other day. Somehow, she seems to be completely unselfconscious when she is with you!

"Regard this as a medical issue, if you like. If need be, think of Merry as a patient in need of treatment for a colossal inferiority complex. Go to the lengths of flagrant flattery, if you deem that necessary, but instil in her, somehow, the confidence and trust she so desperately needs!"

His rejoinder was not at all what I anticipated. In fact I was quite shocked.

"I do not need to go to those lengths, Auntie Bid," he replied stiffly, and I thought his tone was unnecessarily cool. He almost sounded as if he were reprimanding me. "What you are asking of me is to go beyond the boundaries of ethical, professional conduct. As a nurse you should know better! No matter how I feel about the situation, Tristan happens to be my partner and a colleague, and you are virtually asking me to flirt with his wife! Besides, when I pay Meredith compliments, I mean them, and it would make me self-conscious if you were ever to think that, when I do so, it is only because you have asked this of me. That I was only being nice to Merry to please you!"

At that he rose abruptly from his chair, strode across the lawn, as far as the garage, and came back looking a little less agitated.

"I went to look at that blue Plumbago! She's right!" he remarked incongruously, with wonderment in his voice. "There are many things of spectacular beauty in my garden, and I have taken them for granted. I have admired them at a distance, and have been grateful to have a garden of my own, but she is teaching me to 'see' them; to know them! My senses are more alert since Meredith has come to live in my home.

"Like my father, I'm learning that every beautiful tree, flower and shrub, has a name! And now that she has access to a computer, I'm aware that the kind of weaver birds we have here, and what we call *'geel vinke'* or yellow finches, are busy once more making their nests in the big evergreen oak. And Meredith tells me that it is because the crested barbets have got chicks that they sit in the *Celtis africana*, the white Stinkwood, every morning, and sing that high-pitched note. They are announcing that they are now proud parents, and they chose the white Stinkwood because it is the best tree for insects. She notices things like that and brings them to my attention..."

He came over to me, and kissed my cheek. "Dear Auntie Bid, I'm sorry I flared up! You touched a very tender spot! It's just that I did not want to be asked to do what I could not refrain from doing, anyway! And, as I said just now, I never want you to think that when I say nice things to Merry, it is only because of you that I do so!

"What I will do, however, is to let Tristan know, in no uncertain terms, that I do not approve of his association with Mrs. Bradshaw—although I know perfectly well what he derives from it. She is slightly older than he is, and they have many interests in common. She is a golfer. They belong to the same club—where they have friends in common. They enjoy cocktail parties and such pursuits, and they are used to meeting at the club for sundowners—which I am not criticizing, only pointing out for your consideration. In addition, he needs a person who is totally focused on him, and, whatever her motives, Adéle seems to be focused alright!"

"I've heard something like this before—perhaps even from you, Jordie.—Does it mean that, in that respect, Meredith has failed him because, confronted with the newness of everything, her interests have perforce been too widespread?...And, that, because she has settled in here so well that she is not wholly absorbed in him, or completely dependent on him, she does not answer his purpose?...That he continues to cling to Adéle, just in case?...Is that what you are saying?"

"More or less, but there is more to this than I can fathom.... And I reckon that only God can sort that out, Auntie Bid. Let's wait and see what happens in Nelspruit."

"Meredith is still not sure whether she is going with us," I had to warn him. "And please don't ask me for the reason, because I cannot tell you that!"

I did not know then, but that was the second time in one day, that the females of his household had said something along those lines to him!

*   *   *

Meredith and Tristan arrived back with the long-awaited laptop, just after four, as Reg, Jordan and I were having afternoon tea. Our invitation for them to join us was politely refused, and I guessed that this was because Merry could not wait to try out the new acquisition, and she and Tristan—who was looking considerably more genial—went directly upstairs to unpack it.

Evidently Ash and Amy-Lee had decided that, as their visits would be shortened and less frequent in the foreseeable future, Meredith should be given the use of the study in their suite, and, at their instruction, Jordan had meanwhile cleared a filing cabinet and several drawers in Ben's desk for her use, put a new cartridge in the printer, and placed a generous supply of paper within easy reach. Consequently, as soon as he had emptied his teacup, he, with Reg hot on his heels, was quick to follow them, to see how she liked her new 'office'. She was so delighted that, in her excitement, she exuberantly threw her arms around Jordan's neck; then hugged Tristan, and Reg, in turn; and, when I came in, puffing, because I was still not used to the mile-high, Witwatersrand altitude, I was treated to the same enthusiastic reception.

"I am so thrilled!" she exclaimed blissfully. "I can't thank you all enough! It has been such a nice day, altogether! After we had found and bought what I wanted, Tris took me to the loveliest place, with a beautiful garden where there are all manner of little craft stores, and an outdoor restaurant, where they serve an excellent lunch. Most thrilling of all was that, at one stall, I found a man holding a Baobab pod, and he has given me a pamphlet about the lady in Botswana who sells, and will ship Baobab products—the proceeds of which will go to aid the Bushmen! Now that I have my own computer, and her email address, I shall write to her without delay!"

By this time she was almost out of breath with exuberance, but she continued animatedly: "And, Aunt Biddy, I was also given the name of a Mission in Botswana, from which even Bushman musical instruments can be purchased, and I'm going to make it my business to let people know about this! Just think, now that I am so well equipped, I might be able to help them, and also people who do this on our side of the border, to publicize their enterprises.—But first, I can't wait to access my email and see if my research data has come, and get started on my work!"

We shared in Merry's excitement as her data was transferred successfully to her computer. She immediately proceeded to pull up some of the documents onto the screen, amid expressions of admiration at the excellence of her illustrations, and it was interesting to observe how, just as Tristan, on the day he first arrived at *Blouspruit*, had taken pains to make Jasper and Meredith aware of his friendship with the Ashtons, he now showed off by, proceeding to impress upon Jordan and Reg, his intimate knowledge of Merry's work.

"I've seen her lab, of course" he observed self-importantly, "and it's quite remarkable what she is able to do there! In fact it is so well equipped that she was able to do a gram stain for me, in order to establish whether her sister's malaise was due to a virus or a bacterium!" This was followed by a further dissertation, accompanied by a knowing chuckle. "Her father was so worried that I might end up with designs on his daughter—quite correctly as it turned out—that, in order to get rid of me, he promptly listed all Meredith's qualifications for taking care of her sister, without my help. I tell you, what with listing CPR, home nursing, and the ability to give a good injection, he made her out to be a regular Florence Nightingale! And she attempted to prove this, by threatening to give her sister an enema, in my presence.—But that's another story!"

I have to confess that it had been a surprise to me that he should actually have been prepared to take her shopping. It then came to me that this was possibly because Jasper had specifically asked him to do so, and I spent a great deal of time wrestling with this. I finally came to the conclusion that Jasper's request had been gratifying, and had somehow, in Tristan's estimation, officially re-established his, Tristan's, position in Meredith's life. The very fact that he had taken her to lunch, and taken the trouble to find a place that she would find pleasing, was interesting, and there was something quite appealing, I thought, about the proprietary air he had adopted in taking the laptop upstairs for her.....But was there a catch?

To Meredith's joy, her father had also sent pictures of the lab, the house, of Susan and himself with the Bushmen, and very thoughtfully, one of her precious red rose—in order to prove that Susie was taking good care of it.

"*Ach*! Just look at them all!" she exclaimed, almost in tears. "How I miss *Blouspruit*!"

"I'm sure you do, Merry," Jordan said sympathetically, "and we shall all try our best to make you happy here!"

It might have been my imagination, but it was Tristan who did not look quite so happy after that!

What an enigma he remained to me! Thinking again of Meredith's outing with him, I had to admit to myself that I would not have expected such graciousness on his part, and the fact that he was soon scowling once again, did not escape me. Was he actually jealous? And, if so, did he really care for her?... It would be some time before I would discover that his main desire now was to show off his exquisite wife to the people in Nelspruit—despite the bitter realization that her evident poise and self-assurance had been acquired without his personal intervention in the process. That there had been so many other people quick and ready to do what he had considered to be his prerogative, must have stuck in his craw; nevertheless, not even in his wildest dreams had he expected her to become so much like the woman he had planned to create. In every aspect, as far as appearance and charm were concerned, she was all he had pictured, but it was infuriating that, just when her cooperation had become most crucial, he was faced with what might prove to be an insurmountable obstacle...

It would be the greatest disappointment he had suffered since Jordan's sister had married Dominic Verwey, if he, Tristan, could not parade his wife before Zhaynie, and pointedly lead Merry off to bed; and, distressingly, Meredith was not only digging her heels in as far as any such semblance of intimacy was concerned....She remained obdurate, and still refused to be pressured into going to *Beauclaire* with him!

He was due for greater disillusionment!.... When finally she did accompany us, the few days we spent on the Ashtons' citrus farm, would bring a revelation to Tristan Connaught that would knock him sideways....He would find that Eugenie, caught up in the running of her own home, and the all too precious experience of new motherhood, did not have time to make the anticipated fuss of him. And, worst of all, not only had his own wife become far more beautiful in his eyes, but Zhaynie's other attractions had also paled in comparison!

While we were gathered in Meredith's new 'office', the phone rang and, we heard Jordan discuss, with a colleague, their plans for a proposed meeting on the following Tuesday.

"*Ja*," he said, sounding amazingly South African, "it's a nice place and would be a good venue as it is close enough for most of us. I'll get my secretary to make the reservations, as soon as we're sure....Thanks...That makes nine with you, so far, and I'll find out whether any of the people in my house would like to be present, too...*Ja*, I'd like you all to have an opportunity to hear Matt speak, personally. He was to have left already, but now, as his folks are away, with his uncle in Canada, he will come with us to Nelspruit, in their place, to attend the baptism of my godson.

"He is also pleased to have the opportunity to talk to Father Peter Crawford, the priest who had to go and break bad news—not only to the lady who is now his wife, when her husband was killed, but several times to other families in the town. As some of you know, Marina Crawford has become quite an activist when it comes to Angolan vets."

"Oh, hell!" Tristan muttered. "Now we're going to hear about nothing but bloody Angola, General Dallaire and Post Traumatic Stress Disorder, all the way from here to the farm! Why doesn't Jordan put the man on Xanax and get him to shut up! I've been nagging at him to do that, for weeks!"

"Whatever this is all about," I said to Jordan, glaring at Tristan, "if it has anything to do with the kids who were in that war, you can count me in....For my husband's sake, if for no other reason!"

"Thank you, Auntie Bid," Jordan said, having heard me as he rang off. "I meant to tell you about the meeting sooner, but nothing had been confirmed as yet.

"Now," he went on, smiling at Merry, "in all the excitement about Meredith's computer, I also forgot to tell you that there's been a change of plan concerning the travel arrangements next Friday. Matt is going with us, as you have heard, and my brother, James, and his wife, are flying out, and will also be at *Beauclaire*. My mother apologizes for this, but, as the sleeping arrangements now have to be revised, she suggests that James and Isobel, Tris and I, bunk in the big house, and that you, Auntie Bid, and Merry, stay with my parents at their place.

"James and Isobel will be arriving on Thursday, but I don't know yet whether they will be spending the night here, or what other arrangements they have made."

What a bitter blow that must have been for Tristan! All his plans had gone up in smoke. It was mollifying, to a degree, that, by the sound of it, Zhaynie had decided that he was to be accommodated in her house, but, even if Meredith could be persuaded to accompany him to the farm, he and she would not even be under the same roof!

As I might have expected, he, Tristan went off, without a word, to have a sundowner with Adéle, Reg returned to the cottage, and I took a book from Jordan's excellent library, to see what I could find on the subject of Post Traumatic Stress Disorder. As there was a distinct possibility of renewing my acquaintance with Father Peter Crawford, and meeting his daughter, Tony, in Nelspruit, I was thinking of his wife, Marina, and trying to recall what she'd had to say about Angola when I had met her in Bethlehem, so long ago; long before I had heard anyone use that term. Now, thinking about how her first husband had been killed in Angola, and how the news had reached her only hours before the birth of her son, I could understand why she so repeatedly used an expression about not having wanted to raise him only to become what she called 'cannon fodder', like his father!'

I had since gathered—and had read a veiled reference to that fact in her daughter's book about 'The Samaritan of the Sahara'—that Marina Crawford was not an easy person to get along with. In one part, writing about the celebration of her, Tony's, engagement, she used the words, "Unfortunately this afternoon, my mother, who has this disconcerting way about her, had to go and disrupt it." And, in another, "I'm sure Marina Crawford must be the most outspoken, direct woman in the world.—Hardly what one would have expected of the rector's wife, back in Nelspruit!"—Could Marina possibly have become so hard as a result of her own 'post traumatic stress'? While vowing that her son would never go to war, had she not, at the same time, perhaps subconsciously, have been deciding never to expose herself to hurt again? Did she wear that hard shell to arm herself against the possibility of further pain?

But then all her children—Antoinette who was three at the time, and those of her second marriage—had turned out so well; whereas Thora Connaught, whose husband, though unjustly imprisoned, had been very much alive when Tristan was born, had produced a son who had been a constant worry to his parents.

I made a mental note and determined that, if an opportunity presented itself at Matt Marais' meeting, I would raise the question of how a formerly widowed woman like Marina, who had long since remarried, could still be affected, and I looked forward to hearing the views of people more learned than I! Meanwhile it baffled me that Matt, who had every reason to be bitter, was so completely contented with his lot, lived a full and useful life, and campaigned on behalf of others.... That, I felt, was a question for Ash Ashton.

While I was reading on the stoep, Meredith and Jordan remained in her office, looking at the photos Jasper had sent, Meredith eagerly studying every detail and pointing them out to Jordan, who remarked that Susie had grown so much as to be unrecognizable, but that he would have known her father anywhere. Because she had been totally absorbed in *Blouspruit* and its people, Jordan found it almost incongruous when, all at once, she turned to him and announced: "I've decided to go with you, Jordie, if your sister and parents will still have me!"

It took a moment for this statement to penetrate....Then his face lit up and he responded eagerly, "That's great, Merry. What made you change your mind?"

"I put out a fleece!" she said enigmatically.

CHAPTER EIGHT

If the return of the Ashton family to *Beauclaire* was a red-letter occasion for their friends and neighbours, their church, and the people on the estate, itself, it couldn't have been more memorable than it was for us. What pleasure to be there and to share in the joy of the family reunion!

After a near perfect flight from Johannesburg, in Ben's plane, we were brought from the Nelspruit airport in two cars—one driven by Ash, and the other by his brother-in-law, Doctor Paul Verwey, entomologist and former citrus inspector, who had joined Ash and Amy-Lee many years before, in the partnership which ran the Beauclaire Estates citrus organization so successfully. Upon our arrival at the farm, we found Amy-Lee Ashton, and her son-in-law, Dominic, on the wide stoep, together with Dominic's mother, Stella, waiting to give us a warm welcome the moment we appeared at the foot of that significant flight of steps. We, who were familiar with the story of Ash and Amy-Lee, knew that those must have been the very steps built with Ben's own hands, and which he'd so anxiously had to help Amy-Lee to climb more than thirty years before.

The pickers and other employees were also part of the 'welcoming committee', but it was to the grizzled Phineas Mohubedu, surrounded by his family—Sarah, his seventy-year-old wife, and daughter, Selina—that the privilege of actually doing the honours was awarded. The dignified, aging *Bapedi* man greeted James and Isobel Ashton, Matt Marais, Tristan, and me, in the lofty manner to be expected of a bishop of his church, but Jordan—and, for some reason, Merry, whom Jordie had just helped out of Ben's car—were treated to an emotional reception that made tears spring to my own eyes.

The old man raised his hat, which had been thoroughly dusted on his trousers, and extended his hand, but Jordan would have none of that! He threw his arms around him, and enveloped Phineas in a bear hug that must nearly have squeezed the breath out of the old chap.

"*Genoeg nou, lêdulêputswa! Onthou dis nou die nuwe Suid-Afrika!*" ("Enough now, grey beard! Remember, this is the new South Africa!") Jordie responded, visibly moved, himself. Whereupon Phineas retorted in Afrikaans: "*Baas Ash hy is my baas! En die miesies sy bly my miesies! Die kinders hulle bly my kleinbasies and my kleinnnonnies, tot die dag dat ek sterwe!*" ("Baas Ash he remains my baas, and the missus she remains my missus! The children they remain my small basies and my little missus, until the day I die!") "*Dumela, my kleinbasie! Ons is bly jy het teruggekom, kleinbaas Jordie!*" he muttered, sniffing.

"That means, 'Good day, little baas! We are pleased that you have come back,' Jordan translated for Meredith's benefit. To the old man he said, "*Dankie, Phineas. Ek is bly om weer hier te wees. Hierdie kleinmiesies is Nonnie Meredith. Sy kom van daar ver af. Van die Kalahari!*" ("I am pleased to be back!")

"*Dumela kleinmiesies,*" Phineas said, acknowledging Meredith. "*Dis goed dat die kleinmiesies saamgekom het! Ons het 'n nuwe kleinbasie ryker geword!*"

"Now he's greeting you, Merry...He says, 'Good day little missus and it is good that you have come, too! We have been enriched by a new little baas!'" Jordan again translated for Meredith, who then wanted to know, "What is the correct word to use for greeting, Jordie?...Do I also say, *Dumela?*" And

Jordan nodded, only to be surprised when she then turned to the old man and said, *"Dumela....Ek is ook bly om hier te wees, Phineas. Dis 'n baie mooi plek wat julle hier het! Ek wil graag die kleinbasie Benjamin sien!"* ("I am also happy to be here, Phineas. This is a very beautiful place that you have here! And I would very much like to see the little baas Benjamin!") After which she shook his hand.

"I was able to understand all that was said, thank you, Jordie, except the odd *Sepedi* word," she informed him later. "Most of our people speak Afrikaans, too, so I also know that you told him that I come from far away. From the Kalahari! What continues to astound me, Jordan, is that you are so fluent!"

"Don't forget that I was born here, Merry. I was educated in the USA, for the most part, because, before my brother, James, was sufficiently equipped to join the Board of the organization, my dad's main job was still with the Ashton Corporation in New York. But we came back here regularly—until my father began to divide his time between the Manhattan office, the New Jersey plant, and the Missions on which he began to go regularly with Uncle Peter Crawford. He, Uncle Peter, is a priest—whom you'll meet very soon, and it's his daughter, Isobel, mostly called Izzie who, as you now know, is married to my brother. Uncle Peter's eldest daughter, Antoinette, of whom you might have heard us speak, is a legend in this town, and her grandfather, Uncle Bert Mostert, gave my father his first job here in Nelspruit.

"You'll soon be able to figure out all these people, but the Verweys might confuse you to begin with, because so many of them are called Dominic. Sometime I'll have to tell you about the famous Dominic, known as *El-Hakim*, the doctor, and also often spoken of as the 'Samaritan of the Sahara.' He is the grandfather of Stephen, the husband of Antoinette, whom we call 'Tony'..."

"If I might digress for a minute, Jordie," Meredith intervened, "and getting back to your fluency in Afrikaans, I also find it interesting that you refer to 'Father Peter' one minute and 'Uncle Peter', the next. At the same time—while, probably because you are an American and therefore, provided you wished to do so, might be permitted to call even your parents by their first names—you are reluctant to have Phineas to refer to you as his 'kleinbasie'. This I find baffling because—like me—you, in the pursuit of courtesy, also observe that very South African practice of addressing any close, adult friend of the family, in fact any grown-up whose surname you don't know, as 'Uncle' or 'Auntie'!...So, by the same token, I believe that Phineas and the rest of these people revere your father so highly that you'll never get them out of it! When they speak to you like that, they are honouring you and your siblings as your father's children—and, in my opinion, it is also an endearing term of affection!"

"You are right, of course," Jordie acceded. "About all of this. But, to get back to Father Peter, I love the story about the first time he came here to visit my dad. He has fiery red hair, as you will soon see, and when Dad went to inform Sarah, Phineas's wife, that Peter, the priest, was coming to lunch, she was quite incredulous.

" *'Daardie kleinbasie met die rooi hare is 'n moruti? Auk!'* ('That young baas with the red hair is a priest!'), she cried, shaking her head incredulously, while exclaiming with approval, " *'Dis goed! Ons baas het so 'n vriend nodig!'* ('That's good! Our baas has need of such a friend!')"

"Phineas and his family had this proprietary attitude towards my father—in fact they still do. Dad once told Uncle Peter that they seemed more like parents to him, and he smiles at the recollection of how Sarah's eyes would widen when, no matter how rare the occasion, he opened a can of beer for himself. She would tilt her head and wag one finger; an indication that one was the limit!"

"I love it! How special for you all to have had such a long association with the people who work for you! We are blessed, too, in having our Mieta and Malgas, who have been at *Blouspruit* since my mother was a child, and they are like grandparents to me! I could never have left my father and sister alone, otherwise!"

"I've met them, don't forget, Meredith!" he reminded her, thinking of what his father had told him about her, and it delighted him when she replied, "I had not forgotten, Jordie! Just as I had never forgotten you!"

Amy-Lee, accompanied by Jordan, led the way to her house, where Meredith and I were being accommodated, and as soon as Jordie and the woman called Selina had brought our luggage, he took us to meet his sister. So eager was he that he would hardly allow us time to wash our hands, let alone have his mother show us the house Ash had built for her when the original farmhouse was given to Zhaynie and Dominic. We would have to wait until later to inspect that, but secretly, Meredith and I were as impatient to see the new mother and child, as he was...!

I had heard a great deal about Eugenie Ashton—now Eugenie Verwey—and I was not disappointed when I was finally privileged to meet her. This was the girl with the 'hair as long and shiny as her mother's, and as black as the poetic raven's wing', described by Antoinette Verwey in her book. Tony was right. Zhaynie, like her brother did have her father's 'devastating smile and intense his blue eyes'!

Of the three siblings, Jordan, the youngest, and Zhaynie, were no closer in age than she and James, the eldest, but there was an unmistakeable bond there, and whenever Jordie spoke of her, his affection was clearly reflected in his face. She was feeding her baby in her bedroom, and showed no self-consciousness when Meredith and I were taken by the impatient Jordan to meet her. He introduced us, and then knelt down on the floor beside his sister, kissed her, and gently rubbed his face against the infant's downy head. "He smells so nice, and he's so beautiful!" he murmured, "And so are you, dear one. I always used to tell you, that, after Mom, you were the prettiest girl I knew, and now you are even more beautiful than you were when I was little. You are a poster child for motherhood, Zhaynie!...Did you have a bad time, dearest?"

"No, it wasn't too bad", she assured him, stroking his cheek and smiling at us over his head. "Doc Evans said he'd never seen a baby—not even you or me—so impatient to be born! But I'm so glad you approve of your nephew, my darling Jordie," she answered lovingly, before saying to us, "And I am so very pleased to meet both of you, Auntie Bid, and Meredith. I asked Jordie to bring you to see me right away, because my little one takes forever to feed. I never got to Bethlehem to meet you, Auntie Bid, when the rest of the family went there, and,"—turning to Meredith—" I have been so intrigued and curious to see the wonder girl who managed to snare old Tris, that I could not wait to see you, either!"

She was charmingly outspoken, and her smile was so very much like Jordan's, that Merry was disarmed at once. "And now, Meredith," Zhaynie continued, "I can see why!...No wonder he fell for you like a ton of bricks!...My brother has described you so well, that I would have known you without any introduction."

"I think the same can be said for us, as far are you are concerned, Eugenie," I responded. "Congratulations on the birth of your baby!"

"And I am so happy to meet you at last, Zhaynie," Meredith said shyly. "Jordan talks about you all the time, and he has not exaggerated, but I think you overrate me! You, however, do indeed have a beautiful child! Do you think I might kiss him, too? And may I hold him some time?"

"Of course!" Zhaynie chuckled, "He won't break!"

"I'm reminded now of how small my little sister was when I first held her," Merry confided wistfully. "And now she's taller than I am." She dropped a kiss on Benjamin's head, and then impulsively kissed Eugenie on the cheek. "It makes me want to cry, to think of her. Except for the ones in Jordie's clinic, I don't think I have seen a white...!" She stopped abruptly, turning her head away, and because I—and possibly Jordan—understood that she was panic-stricken at having almost betrayed herself, I said hastily, "Well, I think it's time we left you and your brother to talk. He needs time to get acquainted with the new member of his family. Besides," I added lamely, Matt and Tristan must be wondering what has happened to us. See you in a little while, Zhaynie!"

"What a stunning girl!" Zhaynie remarked, once they were alone. "She's quite breathtaking! And so nice, Jordie!— Why did you allow old Tris to beat you to the draw?"

She had spoken lightly, and was dismayed when he unexpectedly slumped down on her bed, staring dismally at the floor. "That was my little Miss Muffet, Zhaynie," he told his sister in strangled voice. "My little girl in the sunbonnet! She was already married to Tristan by the time I saw her again....Oh, Zhaynie...!"

"You're not in love with her, Jord, are you?" She was alarmed by the way he had said that. "You sounded as if...?" And then she saw his harrowed face and held out her hand. "Come here, sweetheart.—Oh, Jordie!"

He was back on his knees beside her in one bound, she drew his head towards her, and so they remained for a while; he with his head on her lap, against the tiny warm body of her sleeping child.

"*Ach*, my dearest *boetie* (little brother)," she crooned over him. "And to have her in the house with you, and see her with Tristan all the time....It must be awful for you! I read it in your eyes! When we Ashtons fall in love, it's desperate, and it's for keeps! Tell me about it!...But why did she sound so disturbed when she was talking about her sister?"

He sat down then, with his legs outstretched and his back leaning against her knees as she stroked his hair with one hand while cuddling her baby with the other. "It's all even worse than you think Zhaynie!" he groaned. "I think I must tell you the whole story, so that you can appreciate the full extent of my misery!"

And then he told her, and she was able comprehend that what Merry had been about to say, was that the last white baby she remembered holding, was her sister, Susan.

"She has been like a mother to Susie," he went on, "since she, Meredith, was about eleven and Susan five, and she has never been close to a white child, other than Susie, for years!

"Unfortunately it is a source of tremendous embarrassment to her that her mother should have behaved so badly, and she does not want people to know, that, until three months ago, she had been secluded from the outside world for close on twelve years!

"Now she lights up my home and my life, Sis. She's changed my life! She's only been in my house for six weeks, and already it is empty if she leaves it for a moment! I never wake without hoping she'll be up early enough for me to catch even a glimpse of her before I have to leave....I cannot communicate in words, the way my heart lifts when I come home and she's there! I see her out in the garden, in the mornings, with her big hat on, and her notebook in her hand, planning what she is going to write to her father and sister that day, and suddenly it is difficult to put on the confident, self-assured, physician-face my staff expect to see when I get to my office..."

He rose to his feet when he saw that she needed to put the sleeping baby back in his crib, and, when she had done so, Zhaynie came to him and wrapped her arms around him,

"Dearest Jordie," his sister exclaimed, close to tears. "I can hardly believe what I have been hearing! That small, cute little creature really does seem to have wound herself around that great big heart of yours! I have never seen you in a state remotely resembling this....Never as much as a schoolboy crush! You were so wrapped up in your studies that I actually used to worry about you! Now all of a sudden I see you enchanted to the extent that your life seems to be entirely revolving around a girl! My heart aches for you, and I would do anything to make this easier for you, but looking at the situation as it stands, I can see no way to do so!"

"There *is* no way! She and I have so much in common— we even make music together—and while it is bittersweet and often agony to have her so close, I don't want Tristan to take her away—because my life would be empty....And besides, she needs me! You have no idea how he tramples on her feelings!"

"Does her father know that?"

"No.—But Aunty Bid does. And she has been like a mother hen, clucking around protectively to shield Merry; but she, Aunty Bid, has a life of her own to go back to, and then there will only be Reggie and me. I thank God that Aunt Felicity is coming, but they won't be in the same house!"

"And does Dad know?"

"Yes," he said miserably. "Also about how I feel about her. It must show, because he knew without my telling him!"

"And what did he say?"

"That we would have to pray about this!"

"Well then," his sister said, "that's what we'll do, my *boet*!"

"I'd appreciate that, Zhaynie.—And may I ask you to do something else for me?

"Just say the word..."

"Meredith does not lie, and nor does she indulge in idle words. If she said she was looking forward to meeting you, she meant it! So see if you can find out why she was so reluctant to come with us, at first, and what suddenly changed her mind!"

"You know I'd do anything for you, but I can't just go up to her and ask her why she didn't want to come, Jordie!" Eugenie protested.

"Well then ask Auntie Bid!"

"And what should I do with the information, if I can get it? Come straight to you?"

"No....Tell Dad! He'll know whether it is something I should know, or not!"

Zhaynie did come to me, and, because I was sick of subterfuges, and I knew that she had a good reason for asking, I told her straight: "I believe it was because of the likelihood that she might have had to share a bedroom with him—and she changed her mind when she learnt that she did not!"

"Oh, my goodness!" Zhaynie responded, visibly distressed. "Now what outrageous stunt has he pulled again? What has he done to mess up this time?... Meanwhile, his parents need his support badly. Reggie phoned this morning to tell us that Aunt Felicity had heard from Tristan's grandmother that his brother, Timothy, has been critically wounded in Iraq. His parents have been unable to get hold of Tris on the phone, but I suppose my dad will have told him by now! When they couldn't reach Tris, they also phoned here."

We had tea out on the stoep, and later moved to the side of the house, where a long, trestle table had been set up, and lunch was served in the shade of a gigantic Syringa tree. That was where I had the privilege of meeting the one and only Mrs. Nolte.

Felicity, who had come to Nelspruit in 1976 to give evidence in support of Ash, had been the first to tell me about the owner of the renowned tearoom, who had closed her establishment for an entire day, in order to attend his hearing in the local courtroom, and she, Felicity, had raved about the never-to-be-forgotten *braai*, organized by 'Mrs. N.' and her daughter, Mercia, to celebrate his acquittal.

More recently, Ben had shared with me the horrifying account of how the two women, having been robbed twice at knifepoint, had closed down the business for good, and he had expressed his concern at seeing how frail and depressed Mrs. Nolte had seemed to him during his recent visit to the farm. However, my first impression when I was introduced to her, was that this could not be the person of whom he had spoken. This buxom, apple cheeked, friendly, Afrikaans woman was simply bubbling over with *joie de vivre;* authoritative, confident and very much in control of the lunch arrangements. Refusing

Zhaynie admittance to her own kitchen, Mrs. N and Mercia, had been busy in the kitchen with Sarah and Selina, and treated us to a superb meal. When I happened to remark on the excellence of their catering, all I got in response was, "Just wait for the christening tomorrow...!"

It was young Dominic, the baby's father, who remarked, as an aside, "And you may be sure, Mrs. Williams, that no one will ever be able to forget it! You should have been here for our wedding! Recently Mrs. N went into some sort of decline, but she is not the same, depressed woman she was, even a month ago, and none of us can get over the miraculous change in both her health and her manner. I think she was just heartbroken at the thought of losing her 'blue-eyed boy', as she refers to my father-in-law, and I truly believe that his decision to retain *Beauclaire* was better than any medication Doctor Evans could have prescribed!...As a matter of fact, there is a different atmosphere everywhere in the vicinity. The cloud that hung over us at the very thought of this place without the Ashtons, has been dispelled, and we have all felt hopeful again, from the moment my little boy was born!"

As the table was being cleared after lunch, Mrs. Nolte announced authoritatively, "We'll be having tea when Doctor and Mrs. Evans get here, but you people will have to be content with cold chicken and salads for supper because my daughter, Mercia, and my son-in-law, Nico, will be otherwise occupied!... I've iced the cake and made the milk tarts for tomorrow, and now, Zhaynie, I need your kitchen to myself. Sarah and I need to make at least 200 crumpets, because you may be sure that the church will be packed, and very few members of the congregations will leave without coming into the hall for refreshments afterwards. Mercia and Nico are going to make the *koeksusters,* specially for Ash, at their place."

"Do you think that I might be permitted to help?" I was surprised to hear Meredith volunteer. "I don't know how to make them but I'd really like to learn…"

"I don't mean to brag, but *I* know how," said Ben airily, pretending to be very proud of himself; and gazing across at Matt Marais, he grinned. "I was given my first koeksuster by Willie, Matt's father, who was my very first friend in this country.—But, be prepared…it's quite a long story.

"When I visited South Africa for the very first ime, it was to introduce some new product, and ever since I'd been given the itinerary for the trip, I had wondered whether I might possibly be able to see my brother if I were the one who went. In the normal course of events, when new equipment was about to be launched, we would send at least a two-man team; an engineer to demonstrate its application and instruct the people in the plant in regard to assembly, and a marketing man to make the presentation and provide a course of instruction for the reps, who would have to go out and sell to both distributors and potential customers. As I was able to do both, I came, personally.

"After doing some of the inevitable PR, and attending numerous receptions, I finally got to doing what I liked best… working with my hands in the plant…and the presence of Willie was an added bonus. Here I must mention that Matt's mother, Bets, is an excellent cook, and she had no sooner heard from Willie about the poor, lonely American who had come to join the men in the workshops, than she took to sending me special treats. She was evidently up to her eyebrows in baking for Christmas, and this is how I came to be given my first slice of 'milk tart'. Soon after that, with her contrivance, I became addicted to the most delectable confectionery I had ever eaten, known for some strange reason as a *koeksuster*. It was only because Bets was thoughtful enough to include the recipe, 'in case my wife would like to try and make them', that I found out that they were made of dough plaited into braids, deep fried in boiling oil and then, while still piping hot, immediately dropped into ice-cold, ginger-flavoured syrup!

"Now I am blessed to have two *koeksuster* aficionados right on my doorstop, as it were!"

"I meant it when I said I'd very much like to learn how," Meredith told Mrs. Nolte eagerly. "May I come and help you? I love cooking and baking!"

"And she's really good at it," Ash informed Mercia and her mother. "You should take her up on the offer, Mrs. N!"

"You may be sure!" Nico Olivier spoke up, as he rose to go and join his wife and mother-in-law. "If you would like to come and help my wife and myself to plait the koeksusterrs, Miss Merredith, that would be wonderrful!"—He rolled his 'rr's' in a pronounced way, and Merry liked the way he said 'wonderrful!'—"I'll come and call you when we arre rready to go. The syrrup is made and in the frridge, so if you and I preparre them, Merrcia can starrt on cooking them!"

While he was speaking, that familiar little frown of concentration appeared between Meredith's eyebrows, but all of a sudden her brow cleared and she spontaneously went over to speak to him. "Why, I recognize you now! You are Sergeant Olivier! You came to *Blouspruit* once, with Uncle Ash and Jordie!"

It was his turn to look thoughtful for a moment, and then he exclaimed, "You can't be the professor's little girrl? *Ach*, wherre have the yearrs gone!...You have stayed just as prretty as you werre then! You got that from yourr motherr!...How arre yourr parrents? And when she told him that her father was fine, but that her mother had passed away, he seemed genuinely sorry to hear the news. But then he had to go and ask, "And what about that Brrady bloke? I just couldn't take to him!"

Meredith very smartly steered him the off the subject by telling him about a statue she had recently seen while driving through Upington, and asking whether it was true that there were still policemen who rode camels in the desert; to which the ex-sergeant replied that he had heard that there were a few in Botswana, but he couldn't be sure. He was surprised, he told her, that she had remembered that it was to *Witdraai* and *Rietfontein* that he had taken Ash and Jordie, and of course those camels had all been auctioned off many years ago.

All this time Tristan had been noticeably silent, as if he had deliberately withdrawn himself from the conversation, and I wondered briefly whether he was at least sparing a thought for his wounded brother, but the expression on his face was more like a sulk. So far Merry had been far too sure of herself for his liking. Had she purposely omitted to mention that it was on her wedding day that she had seen the statue, and that it was he who had driven her past it? However, after Nico had come to fetch her, and the subject of food and cooking somehow arose once more, he was provided with an excellent opportunity for making it clear that he had also spent time in the Kalahari with her, and to establish a prior claim to all knowledge concerning her culinary skills.—An opportunity appreciated all the more, since it was Jordan who had brought up the subject of the spread she had provided for the recent party at his house...

"Yes," he, Tristan, informed the company at large, "and what's nothing short of amazing, is how she makes such excellent use of what grows in the desert! *White Kambro* is good for dessert, you know, and she proved to me that *Haakdoring* gum was not only good to suck, but also good for starch. She uses *Kriedoring* berries or *Suring-uintjies*, boiled in milk, as a desert, and *Witboom roots*, stirred with a wooden spoon, burnt and mixed with milk and honey, when coffee is in short supply. She taught me that a brew from these roots was also a remedy for pulmonary problems!"

I knew I was being catty, but I just could not resist it. "And," I said looking him straight in the eye, "she even makes soap, doesn't she?"

I was looking forward to meeting Doctor Dick Evans and his wife, Trudy, two of Ben's closest friends, and had hoped that they would be there in time for lunch, but he, the doctor, evidently kept his consulting rooms open on Saturdays, and they did not arrive until just before four o'clock that afternoon. By the time they came, I had taken the opportunity to have forty winks, enjoy a quick shower and change, and when I returned to the main house, I found that the younger folk had moved to the stoep, so that Zhaynie could be within earshot of the baby, leaving the rest of the company still on the lawn at the side of the house. In my absence, Father Peter Crawford—or to give him his full title, the Reverend Doctor Peter Crawford—and the rest of that family had arrived, too, and from the gales of laughter that greeted me, I gathered that, like good friends of long standing, they were exchanging precious reminiscences.

"When Ash invited me to the *braai* to celebrate the completion of his house," Doctor Evans was saying," I told him that I was bringing the new vicar—namely our esteemed redheaded friend on my right—adding that I had a strong feeling that they would really hit it off. Little did I know that Ash, who was not a believer in those days, would shudder at the very thought!"

"You're dead right!" Ben chuckled. "I was definitely more than a little taken aback! I remember that you called after supper that evening, Sarah and her daughter were clearing up in the kitchen, and I was sitting on his stoep when I heard them singing. The words were in *Sepedi* but I recognized the doxology by the tune, which was no different from the one my grandmother had sung in French each morning. *"Praise God from whom all blessings flow!"* suddenly emanated from my kitchen, and I remember thinking, "Oh, no! Now I'll be having hymns in the kitchen, and a priest at my barbeque!—What the hell have I let myself in for?"

"Dad, you didn't!" James Ashton was horrified, and shot an anxious glance at his father-in-law. "How can you just come out with it like that, in front of Izzie and her father?"

"I assure you, my son, until now, this is the first time I have used that expression, and it will be the last! What I have just said was used purely as an illustration of how much my life has changed!"

"That's not what I meant, Dad," James protested. "You were referring to Isobel's father!"

But Peter Crawford was roaring with mirth. "Okay, Ash. You may as well go on from there....Own up! Tell them what you said later, while the barbeque was in progress; after I had seen the magazine with the photo of Amy-Lee, open on your desk, and had unwittingly said something that stirred you.... Tell them how you said, 'Peter,' pretending to be nonchalant, 'we have to talk some more.—I now must go and play host, but do you have anything planned for tomorrow? Can you come back then, to lunch?...I can fetch you, if you don't have a car. I'd really like to show you around!'—Gotcha, my friend!" Peter teased him. "You were suddenly so jolly keen to talk to the dreaded priest, some more, that you were actuality prepared to *fetch* me, if necessary!—And now you're my brother-in-law and my revered 'mission partner'!...How amazing is that?"

Well, something else had suddenly, and very visibly, stirred Benjamin Ashton, and none of us spoke as we witnessed a look of transcendent wonderment and awe begin to spread across his handsome face. He sat in silence for some minutes, with eyes closed and mouth half-open, and then slowly, as though waking from a dream, he said, "I have just experienced the most incredible insight! I am completely awestricken! We're told that this only happens when we confront death, but in a matter of seconds, my entire life seemed to flash by, before my eyes, and I was given the most overwhelming understanding of what some of the verses in Psalm 139 really mean! And strangely, in no particular order!

"It was verse sixteen that first came to mind...'*Thine eyes did see my substance, yet being unperfect; and in thy book all my members were written, which in continuance were fashioned, when as yet there were none of them!*'—And then, from fifteen, '*My substance was not hid from thee, when I was made in secret.*' What seemed to be of particular significance to me, as a new grandfather with that precious little one asleep nearby, was verse thirteen—'*For thou hast possessed my reins*'—which I should imagine means something like being 'knit' together. '*Thou hast covered me in my mother's womb.*'

" But then all once it was given to me to see myself in the light of the verse I had first been given. That was the one on which I was supposed to focus.... I had this image—as though I were looking down from above—of a Marathon runner setting off on a race, and I was able to see all the people who had been posted along the way, bearing water to refresh him. I understood clearly how, in God's race, every part of me, and the details of every other participant, had already been noted in His book. He knew how the race *should* end. He had intimately known every single cell, of every runner, when 'as yet there was none of them'.

"I had known the words so well, before, but all at once they have become meaningful—*full* of meaning—as never before! At that moment I was made acutely aware that His eyes had seen *my* substance, when 'yet being unperfect', as the psalmist says, and in that special book all *my* 'members were written, which in continuance were fashioned, when as yet there was none of them!' "

Nobody moved. We hardly breathed as he went on. "I saw every single one of you, and many others, who had been posted along the way, long, long, before I set out on my own race! I saw my mother and father, my brother, and even the faithful old Jenkins, our butler...." He fell silent briefly and then went on, "You know that I do not believe in coincidence...well, believe me, my beloved family and friends, *there is no such thing!*

"Willie Marais did not have to join the other members of the team from Isando, who came to meet me when I arrived at Jan Smuts airport that day.....He did not have to take me home with him to meet his parents, who would someday help me to find peace through 'inner healing' or healing of memories! When I was stranded in Parys, why was that grand old man there to fish in the Vaal River with me, and, in due course, take me to the railway station—which is no longer there, by the way—from where I set off for Bethlehem in search of my brother? And why, when I was at the end of my tether, did it have to be Tristan's father, Clifford, a priest, of all people— possibly the kind of person I most heartily reviled—who, together with the wonderful people I met with him, nurtured that little seed that had been sown in my soul, long before?... They had all been posted in strategic places!

"I could go on and on. About Uncle Charlie de Beer who first quoted my brother's words to me; words that I was blessed to proclaim, for myself, years later....'*I know that I know, that I know!*'...Bert Mostert, for whom Jordan is named, and who is now the grandfather-in-law of my son, James, is the man who hired me, when I arrived here, but, before he would commit himself, he first sent me for a medical to Dick Evans, who, in turn, brought Peter, the 'dreaded priest', to nurture that recalcitrant seed and till the hardened soil that was caked around it!...It goes on and on and on...I must not forget that, while I was waiting for my appointment with Bert, I went into a tearoom—where I met two people who have stood by me, ever since; nor must I overlook Phyllis, the most incredible telephone operator God ever made, and Nico, the police sergeant who was posted in precisely the right place, at the right time. There is Stella, who was my neighbour and became my friend; and her husband, Paul, the government inspector who had to bring me the unwelcome news that my trees might have red scale—and then they produced a son, to take my daughter off my hands…!"

This last was greeted with much laughter, but we did not want him to stop there. "Go on, please, Ash," Peter pleaded. "I have a sense that there is something very important that remains to be said."—And Ash, as though praying, held his hands to his mouth in the characteristic manner he adopts whenever he was deeply pondering something.

At last he said, "Yes, there is, Peter. There are still so many people I want to list. I have not yet told of the angelic little girl who followed me wherever I went, even at the risk of catching her beautiful long hair in the hedge, which separated our grandmothers' plantations in Louisiana, and never stopped loving me even though I hurt her so much….But, you're right, as usual…there is more…much, much more…

"Today, having been shown the pictures I have just mentioned—by the Holy Spirit, I believe—there is the glorious knowledge that the 'healing' of my memories is complete, and the conviction that I should be telling someone about this, is very powerful!

"Remember I used the words 'how the race *should* end'. Perhaps what I should have said was 'how He *wanted* it to end', but many of the people I saw in that vision, did not finish as He wanted them to! Some simply fell by the wayside, some disregarded the signposts, and others foolishly refused to accept the water! From then on, because they had only themselves to blame, they would become bitter, and the very mention of the water would make them angry.

"I see them now as the man I once was!…From the time I was about eight years old, I hated going to church, and I reviled the people who preached in them; in my case, not because I had fallen out of the race, but because I would not even be persuaded to enter it. I was terrified of doing so! Not only did I then disregard the most important rule, but I also refused to read the signs—and, what is worse, even when others managed to coax me into participating, I adamantly continued to refuse the living water!

" 'Refusal' is the keyword here. I am reminded of how, many years ago, I dreaded going to the service at Clifford Connaught's church, in Bethlehem and, having 'guilted' myself into attending for my brother's sake, I stubbornly closed my ears to everything but the music! Because I have been made to recall that day, I can now understand how something I read recently, does indeed pertain to someone who might profit by it...!"

"I know what you are about to tell us, Ash!" I burst out eagerly, before I could stop myself, and was rewarded by a nod and a gracious smile of acknowledgement.

"Recently I read a paragraph in Oswald Chambers' book, *'My Utmost For His Highest,'* " Ash continued, "which, after having read the same page at least once a year, for more years than I can remember, really 'spoke' to me that day. This is what I read: *'Our Lord knows perfectly that when once His word is heard, it will bear fruit sooner or later. The terrible thing is that some of us prevent it bearing fruit in actual life.'* Since reading those words, I have devoted a great deal of time to the consideration of them. I have had a strong sense that I am required to pass them on to someone else, at some stage, and I wanted to understand the thought behind them very thoroughly before I did so. Now I can interpret the 'water' in my vision, as being the 'word', in the context of Chambers' message, and the terrible thing that prevents it from bearing fruit, is the same as refusal of the water.

"What was the instruction that I personally disobeyed for so long, preventing the word from bearing fruit as it should?... Simple! I disregarded the wording on the signpost, which read, 'Forgive us, as we forgive those...!' But I was unable to do so, until I had been healed. I said I forgave, but I really couldn't! And it is because I was finally able to do so, that this has been such a powerful experience. Just as it was so wonderful when I was finally relieved of the burden of all that corrosive anger, that I am still always ready to give my testimony during the Missions with Peter. I am blessed to be able to do so!"

He grinned. "With Father Peter—that very same, once-dreaded priest!"

All the while Ash was speaking, I had been riveted to the extent that I had not noticed Meredith return and sit down near me, but I had, from time to time, glanced at Tristan, who stared fixedly at the floor. Spellbound, like everyone else who had been listening to Ash, I remained lost in thought for some time after he was done, and it was during that silence that I saw Tris get up and stride off into the orange groves.

Ash must have noticed that too, or perhaps he was just moved by the Spirit, for he suddenly said, "My friends, I think it is right that, in the midst of all the happiness we are sharing at this time, we should be quiet and remember Thora and Clifford in Louisiana. We need to pray for Tristan's brother, Timothy, who has been wounded in Iraq; for his parents and for Tris. We should also pray for all those children that Thora and Clifford have in their care, and for the people in and near New Orleans, as they are on the alert for the possibility of yet another natural disaster."

And so we remained in prayer for quite some time,

remembering, too, that baby Benjamin was to be baptized the following day, and giving thanks. It was Amy-Lee who, when asking a blessing on Willie Marais and his family, far away in Canada, included Matt, and asked for protection of his cousin who was with a Canadian regiment in Afghanistan.

"We praise you, O Lord, for sparing Matt's life and for giving him the grace to cope so wonderfully, and without bitterness, with a handicap which might have changed him forever. We pray a blessing on his wife and children, we pray that he goes home safely to Canada next week, and we pray a blessing on this project that is so close to his heart!"

"I pray for my father and my little sister," Meredith took up from there, in the circle, "and for the Bushmen of the Kalahari. Especially for those who remain so faithful to God and to the people of *Blouspruit*!"

"I pray for them, too," I said, when it was my turn, "and also for Doc Hugo that he might be blessed with the health and strength he needs as he soldiers on so bravely, and takes such good care of the people of *Spoors-einde* and those on the farms around it."

"I give thanks for my family and friends, Lord," was Jordan's prayer. "I praise you for the treasure you have given us in baby Benjamin, and everyone else who is here. I ask, in the Name of Jesus, that you will help Reggie to cope, that his mother will be none the worse for the transition, and that you will send someone to help in the clinic while he goes to fetch her!

"I also pray for all my patients, giving thanks and praise for answered prayer; especially that Fransie is doing so well!"

"And now," Ash announced, when everyone had been given a turn, "if you will excuse me for a little while, I'm off to keep a promise. I have a date with a charming young lady.....I'm going to bring the old Jeep around to the front, and then I'm taking Meredith on a short tour of *Beauclaire*—and Amy-Lee, sweetheart, if you and Biddy want to come, too, that would make it all the more enjoyable! I'll have three beautiful girls all to myself!

"God willing," he said to the others, "we can discuss final arrangements for Benjamin's baptism after supper, and, while I know that you have some distance to travel, and might not relish a late night, I invite anyone who wishes to learn more about Matt's ministry, for which Amy-Lee has prayed, to stay for that!"

Somehow I had not noticed, until I got up to go with Merry and Amy-Lee, that Tristan had long since come back from wherever he had been, and had been standing behind Meredith's chair all the time. He must have been gripping the back of it very hard, because his knuckles were noticeably white!

We three ladies waited at the foot of the steps for Ash to come, and were already seated in the Jeep when Matt Marais came hurrying towards us, as quickly as he was able. "Thank you for your prayers, Aunt Amy-Lee," he panted. "For my family and for me. To Ben he said, "I just want you to know, Uncle Ash, that I will always be grateful for those great rugby boots at a time when I could make the most of them, and that I thank God for my grandparents. It is because they believe in 'inner-healing' prayer, that you see me as I am. I would not otherwise be as well adjusted as you mentioned.

"Do not think for one moment, that I was always like this! And please, Uncle Ash, have no fear that my work at Ashtons' will suffer because I am dedicated to helping the people to whom I minister. I just long for them to have the same peace restored to them, that I have been blessed to find once more!" He handed Ash a slip of paper, explaining that the extract printed on it, had been copied from an essay written by his teenage daughter, Lucia, as part of an assignment entitled, *'When my father was young!'*

"I am so grateful that I was able to tell her about this part of it," he said to Ash, "unemotionally and without rancour.— There are no longer any buttons that dare not be pushed!" With a smile that might have been perceived as being apologetic, he added: "But I still wish that we had been allowed to finish the job! To have been withdrawn just when we were winning, makes it all so tragically futile, doesn't it?"

Ash would later pass on to me what Lucia had written, and I would be surprised at the choice of words. When I saw Jasper again I showed I to him, too, and I was able to discuss with him the sensitivity of a young girl who had chosen to write about her father's experience in Angola, and to have done it in this way...

"Conscripts, these boy-soldiers sometimes talked, whispered to one another about home, about war, about things and people they had known. Through each burning day the boys sought the enemy through the knee-length grass.

"For many days the boys saw blood and knew terror. They heard stories of horror from the rest of the war. In wakeful nights they had static conversations with themselves about the 'ifs' and 'buts' of it.

"Some had shot, hit and killed. Some had cried; others had died. The boys grew tired. They slithered through the bush with nervous eyes. They saw the rolling desert of straw, for it was the dry season on the Border. The grass stretched to the hazy horizon, vibrating in the distance. Flat, with stands of bushveld trees.

"The pans were dry, the rains were not yet due. That horizon was the limit of their earth. They could not gauge anything that existed beyond. The boys screwed their eyes like snakes; they cocked their ears like owls; scrutinizing stimuli to find the intruders, the Others.

"*Suddenly, halfway across a dried pan, it seemed the Others had found them!*

"*The sound loomed over them, a premonition of invincible danger. They had not the weapons to defeat this horror. No cover except the grass. The boys were like the buck of the Delta and could sense the peril, could smell it, and could taste its sourness. They could hear the sound of death creaking towards them: a tank—a T60 Russian tank!*

"*Fear brewed and curdled. The horrific sound persisted, it echoed and it surely promised death. The boys melted into Africa, but no comfort was found in the ground to which they had instinctively dropped for protection. This earth did not accept these boys....This earth did not want these boys.... Prone in the grass, their horizon was measured in feet.*

"*Some whimpered. Their bowels turned to water. Incontinence overcame the weakest...*"

***

But I had nothing heavy on my mind when I climbed in the Ben's Jeep, and what a pleasant drive that was! He had every reason to rave about the magnificence of the setting, and the beautiful things that grew on his beloved farm. Our excursion was all too brief, especially in view of the fact that he told us, confidentially for the time being, that he had a strong feeling that he and Amy-Lee would soon be needed in Louisiana, and that it might be some time before they were able to return to Nelspruit.

He did have time, though, after driving us around the farm, itself, to take us up to the *kopjie* or ridge, way up behind the house, from where we had a grand view of the orchards, saw the sun set over his groves, and breathed in the perfume of the orange blossoms in the warm summer air.

This, he confided, was his 'communing and listening to God' place. Far down to the right, was his 'talking to God' place. He pointed out a splash of mauve which, he said, was his favourite tree in all the earth. A Jacaranda against which he could lean and appreciate the feeling of the rough bark next to his cheek, when he needed to call out and petition God.

"My face was rubbed raw when Amy-Lee was in the clinic in London, I can tell you," he said, "but God in His mercy heard me! Because it is next to the gate that I went to lock every night—before Nico took over as our security chief and had the electronic gates installed—it became a good place to go, before I turned in....In the Northern Hemisphere I cannot see the Southern Cross, so, on a starry night, this is where I feel most at home. This for me, remains a very special place for giving thanks for answered prayers, and for all the blessings He constantly showers upon me!"

Was it any wonder, I reflected, that the children of such a man, were so special? I had always loved Jordie, and when I went to bed that night, I prayed that he, too, would find and some day marry a girl who would appreciate and be worthy of him!

When we returned, Ash dropped us at the foot of the steps and Meredith went directly to find Zhaynie, in order to check up on when the baby would be bathed, before going off to have her own bath and change before supper. Father Peter and family were sitting on the stoep, having a visit with his daughter, Isobel, and her husband, James, as the two of them were spending the night on the farm, and he would not see them until they met at the church next day. Meanwhile Ash had taken the Jeep round to the back door and then he came out onto the stoep, via the kitchen, to join the group gathered there.

In his father-in-law's absence, Dominic had seen to it that the men had a beer, and had poured a glass of wine for the ladies. It was Father Peter who was the first to notice that his daughter, Isobel, did not have in her glass what the rest of us were drinking, and the moment he commented on this, her shy smile gave her away. At the same time, James gave his father a meaningful look, and when Ash raised his eyebrows inquiringly, James nodded, and the next moment the two friends, Ash and Peter, were hugging each other and then the children, and there was so much excitement that Antoinette jumped to her feet to hug everyone in sight, tears ran down Isobel Mostert's cheeks, at the very thought of a great-grandchild at last, Bert Mostert thumped James on the back, and Amy-Lee Ashton came running to check on the cause of the commotion.

The first thing, Zhaynie wanted to know when she and Dominic appeared on the scene, was "When?"—Probably working out mentally whether her own baby would be old enough to be taken to the States by then.

"May!" Her brother responded, grinning broadly. His ears were red and he was blushing to the roots off his hair. "I'd have you people know that I have only just heard the news myself! Can you believe that there is a woman on earth capable of keeping anything so overwhelming to herself?"

"It was a very difficult decision," Isobel explained. "I wanted to make the announcement at just the right time. I wanted to wait until I could have all my family and James's, around me. This is so momentous for me," she said tearfully. "Can anyone imagine, for one second, how difficult it has been for me, during the past five years, to face the possibility that, for the first time in four generations, there was not going to be another James in the Ashton family? Ever since we arrived I have waited for just the right moment to bring the wonderful news to you, Uncle Ash, that your son will now possibly be able to present you, at the appointed time, with a James the fifth!

"For most of my life, I have heard about James the third—Jamie—and what a wonderful man he was, and I am able to state categorically that my James, James the fourth, is equally fine! ... After all, I have the privilege of being the closest to him, of all of you, so I know how wonderful it would be to have a son like him! There's no need to tell you that I have loved James since I was a schoolgirl. I'm grateful to God for giving him to me, and I to plan to hold on to him for the rest of my life!" Suddenly she smiled, and the solemn moment was past.—"Now it's up to the rest of you to do the praying, once you have made up your minds whether you want this child to have his father's blond, Ashton hair, or be another carrot top like us Crawfords!"

James was the least demonstrative of all the Ashtons, but he suddenly gave a shout of joy, as the reality really began to sink in. He caught his wife in his arms, and smothered whatever she was about to say next, with a kiss. "Stop that, you darling girl! he cried. "I don't care one way or another, whether it's a James or an Isobel, but I insist that he or she has that beautiful Titian hair and those amazing green eyes!"

"Imagine that," said Jordan, who was standing in the doorway. "Another small James and Benjamin to grow up together!"

"That means that you have the responsibility now, to provide us with another Amy-Lee, Jordie!" his sister-in-law remarked, teasing him.

"I'll first have to find a wife, won't I?" was his dry response, and only Zhaynie noticed the pain in his face.

It was at that stage that Stella and Paul Verwey, who had made a quick visit to their home on the adjoining farm, to fetch something, returned, and Meredith briefly rejoined us, before she went off with Zhaynie to watch the baby being bathed and fed. After that, she and Jordan went to find Doctor Evans, his wife and Matt, who had gone for a stroll. When Mrs. Nolte and Sarah, the maid, came to say that supper was ready, they were quite beside themselves upon learning the good news, and then we all sat down again to share a happy meal after Father Peter had said grace. Tristan managed to slip into the seat beside Meredith, and having taken a shower and changed into a fresh khaki shirt and shorts, he seemed in relatively good spirits,

It wouldn't have been possible for anyone to be glum for long in that company. There was not the slightest hint of a breeze, so we were able to enjoy another meal outdoors; this time by lamp- and candle-light, and when the moon rose, it was possible for Ash to forget all about the violence and the destruction that were seldom very far from our thoughts, and just savour the moment.

For Meredith this was yet another incredible happening. She was having the time of her life, and although I could not be sure, in that light, it seemed to me that her cheeks were glowing and her eyes sparkling. She found the unfamiliar experience of being included in such a large, warm group of people, whose love for one another was almost tangible; quite unforgettable. Teasing, saying the most outrageous things to one another, with no hidden meanings or malice, laughing hilariously at the repartee, was liberating. She felt free to join in without restraint, and even I, who was familiar with her sense of humour, was surprised to find how funny she could be.

It had been a long, crowded, but supremely happy day, and because we were all keen to hear what Matt had to say, we did not linger too long around the table. Excusing themselves because they had an important phone call to make, Isobel and James were the first to rise, bearing in mind the time difference between Nelspruit and Cincinnati, where Izzie's mother was holding a meeting; and Peter was saying, "Call me when you're done, please, I'd also like to speak to my wife, if she's reachable," when something happened that will always remain as one of the great experiences of my life—as I'm sure it will be for everyone else who was there.

We had been so engrossed in the delicious meal and the entertaining conversation, that we had not noticed that we were surrounded by black people, and looking around me, even I, a stranger, was able to recognize more than one face. Phineas and his family had joined hands, making room for many others, who began to squeeze into the circle, and I was not the only one with a lump in my throat at the sound of a few dozen African voices raised in glorious harmony.

This was not a first experience for three of the people at that supper table. It was a moment of almost heart-stopping *déjà vu* for Amy-Lee, Paul Verwey and his wife. Many years before, when they had learnt that Ash was safe, after it was feared that the plane in which he was flying had crashed, and while Paul and Stella were still estranged, the people of *Beauclaire's* 'Baas Ash' had done the same thing.

Amy-Lee was the first to reach the singers, to have her hand grasped immediately by Selina, her former caregiver, who drew her into the circle, too. We hastened to join her as, together with them, she sang the doxology....She, in French, the black people in *Sepedi*, Nico Olivier in Afrikaans, and the rest in whatever language the doxology was known to them.

Praise God from whom all blessings flow;
Praise him ye creatures here below;
Praise him above, ye heavenly host;
Praise Father, Son and Holy Ghost!

Stella's eyes blurred when she remembered how, when she had heard Paul's pleasant baritone voice beside her that night, she had, quite involuntarily, reached out and taken his hand. This time, as then, it did not seem at all strange that he should lift it to his lips, singing even as he kissed it...

And Benjamin Ashton's glorious voice rose above all the rest...

After this there was no need for any further discussion concerning details for how the baptismal service should proceed. Not after Peter had affirmed, "Ash, there isn't a person under the age of thirty at St. Margaret's, who will ever forget the day you confessed to the congregation who you really were, and then introduced Amy-Lee as your wife. I know I shan't...!" and this was greeted by a chorus of "Nor I!" from Ben's friends.

"I propose," Peter proceeded, "that, as you will be at the organ again, until you come down to participate in the actual baptism, you play the same processional and the same hymns as you did that day! Every one of them will be appropriate, and you will be bringing your brothers and sisters in the congregation more joy than you can imagine!"

"I'd be happy to do that, but it is not for me to decide," Ben said. "This will be Dominic and Zhaynie's day. I know they have already discussed the order of service and all other relevant details with you. Besides, Paul and Stella also have a say in this."

"Then, Dad," said Dominic, "I'll begin by saying, that that it is what we'd like, too, and my parents were the ones who first suggested this to Zhaynie and me." Suddenly he could not help smiling. "I don't want to be sacrilegious," he said, "but I've been told how you switched the order of the verses in the opening hymn that day, so that you could start with verse four and proclaim how little wealth mattered to you,...and that's also okay with me. But there must be something about you that makes you even hear verses in psalms, in the wrong order!" Then he immediately grew serious once more. "But I can tell you, I have never understood that particular psalm as I do now!"

"I agree," Antoinette said, but could also not hide the smile that was twitching the corners of her lips. "If everything is going to be the same, except for the baptism, of course," she pleaded mischievously, "may I please have permission to dash out from my seat to greet Fallah, as I used to do when I was three, and then sit on the altar steps, waiting to lead him out?"

"We could easily have put you into a red cassock, my darling," Peter Crawford said grinning affectionately at her, "and you could have carried the cross, since you're so keen to be in the procession, but even you can't be in two places at once!...Have you forgotten that you are going to be right up front with the godparents?"

Matt's meeting—attended by most of us, except Zhaynie, who went to feed her baby, and Izzie and Meredith who went with her—did not last long. Ash and Peter were talking outside on their respective cell phones as we assembled in the dining room, and both rejoined us with expressions so solemn that we knew at once that all was not well. Marina, Peter's wife, who had informed him that she had cut short her lecturing commitments in Cincinnati, and was on her way home to New York, had sounded almost demented with terror as she broke the news that their youngest, Ben's namesake, had been given orders to prepare for deployment to Iraq. Shortly before that, it seemed, Clifford Connaught, Tristan's father, had been informed that his wounded son, was in a military hospital in Germany, preparatory to being flown back to the States, once he had been stabilized.

It was difficult to grasp that two young people equally dear to us, with parents so close to our hearts, could simultaneously have become the cause of so much anguish....What are the chances of two people in one place, being dealt similar blows in so short a space of time? With Peter there with us, we were able to see that the normally cheerful, freckled face, had turned the colour of speckled, greyish marble. Tristan on the other hand was nowhere to be seen.

In the light of Izzie's recent, joyful announcement, Peter was reluctant to upset her, and it was decided that we would not tell her about her brother until after the christening celebration next evening. As to Peter, himself...all we could do was to take turns to hug him, and then sit down around the dining room table again, to pray for Timothy Connaught, young Benjamin Crawford, and for their distracted parents...

Peter, while appreciative of the prayers, was very prompt to assure us, however, that the two situations were very different. "My boy is mercifully still hale and hearty! He has not even left yet, and when he goes, he leaves with great anticipation, because this is what he wants to do, above all else. It is his mother who is causing me so much concern."

"I might have guessed," said Antoinette. "Don't forget, although I was only a child, I was there when she made the stipulation that she would not marry you, Fallah, as much as Greg and I pleaded with her, until she was positive that you would emigrate. The years we had to wait for those visas seemed interminable, and it still makes me want to cry when I think of the years that were wasted!"

Peter nodded. "I confess that I regret them, too. I am among friends, and you, Tony, are my friend, as well as a beloved daughter, so I believe that I can speak freely, and confess to you that I grow more concerned about Marina with each passing year. Having listened to Matt tonight, I can understand only too well, that people who have been in traumatic situations need more help than simply 'debriefing'. By the Grace of God, Tony and Stephen have come back with very few apparent scars, from dreadful places—to which they also went voluntarily— but Marina's state, is beyond me. I find no fault with what she does, or why she does it; only with the obsession that is destroying her!

"So many years have passed since Greg was killed, and we now have wonderful children between us, but her anger has only kept mounting, and it now possesses her to a degree that it is eating away at her—and at all human relationships. It consumes her, and her frantic campaigning is all that assuages that anger." He ran his hand through his hair with a despairing gesture. "I wonder if she'll even care about Isobel's pregnancy!"

By this time, Antoinette had risen to her feet. She stood beside him with her hand on his shoulder, and kissed the top of his head. "I've been a part of this journey, my dearest Fallah, ever since the day I first set eyes on you! I have walked beside you physically, mentally, and prayerfully, through all this, for so many years! Please don't give up hope now!"

She turned to the rest of us. "I beg of you, don't allow any of this to shadow Zhaynie and Dominic's glorious day. Please let us promise to keep this to ourselves until later!"

Some decisions had to be made, however. Peter was due to fly home to the States on the following Wednesday, in any case, and Ash made a snap decision, there and then, that he and Amy-Lee would have to go, too. Matt was on his way back to Canada, and it had already been decided that he would stay with Jordan on the Tuesday night, in to order attend the meeting as arranged by Jordie.

So we finally made a unanimous decision, and all promised not to distress anyone unnecessarily, until the time was right. We would get together the next evening, break the news to Isobel, her grandparent and Zhaynie then; and those of us who had to get back to Johannesburg, prior to going our separate ways from there, would all leave together, first thing on Monday morning. Matt would have plenty of time to talk to Peter during the flight.

After the last visitor had departed, Merry and I helped Amy-Lee and Zhaynie to wash and put away the few remaining dishes, as Sarah and Selina had long since been told to go to bed. Before long Ash came in to see if there was anything he could do, and when he found that he was not needed, he sat down at the kitchen table chatting about the events of this crowded day, until he remembered that he had not put the Jeep away. He went out right away, and was surprised when, as he was opening the door of the garage, he saw Tristan sitting in the vehicle, waiting to speak to him.

"Mr, Ashton," he said in a strange voice—though pointedly avoiding the 'uncle and auntie business' to which he only resorted when he was trying to get something out of someone—"as a physician I have to admit that all this 'inner healing' talk sounds like a load of crap to me, but, if you think it might be helpful, I'm willing to give it a shot! I don't know what it is supposed to do for me, but I do know that everyone else seems so happy, and I am not!—Can you do it for me?"

Ben was dumbfounded, but he collected himself sufficiently to say, "Tristan there is no one I would rather help than you, specially at this time, but you've got it wrong. I can do nothing! Only the Holy Spirit can do it, because He has the mind of God. I would willingly pray for you, here and now, but this is usually done in pairs. Preferably, two people need to be with you, so why don't I first ask Father Crawford to sit with you during the flight, after he and Matt have concluded their discussion, and explain how this works, and then we can talk further when we get to Bryanston. Due to some very worrying developments, he, Father Peter, my wife and I, have decided to return to the States as soon as possible."

"Well thanks for nothing!" was the curt response. "I've never in my life heard such utter bull, and if a clergyman has to be involved, you can count me out!"

"That is very sad, Tristan," Ben said gently. "Particularly as there is one I know of who could really do with your support at this time. The reason why Amy-Lee and I must cut our visit short is to relieve your parents of some of their responsibilities while they deal with the stress of your brother's condition. He is being flown back to America from the hospital in Germany, but I do not know where they will have to go in order to be close to him. This latest development is not good news. We should know by now, that only the seriously wounded are flown home for further treatment!...One thing of which I shall never be as sure as I am at this minute, is that you are desperately in need of God, and, once you discover that, we can talk again....In the meantime, be assured that you will be in my most earnest prayers!"

***

Oh, what a glorious, never-to-be forgotten experience that Baptismal service was! Mrs. Nolte had been right. Not only was the usual congregation present, in full force, but there were even people of different denominations....Nico, Mercia, Phyllis and her husband, who normally attended the Dutch Reformed church, Mrs. Nolte who was officially a Presbyterian, Len Coetzee the bank manager, who was a Baptist, and Phineas and family—members of the ZCC—the Zion Christian Church. Some of the people from the outlying parishes, who remembered Ash from the days when he had come to them with Peter, to provide the music at the monthly services, had travelled a long way to be present.

It was fondly recalled that, on more than one occasion— where there was no musician or the regular organist could not make it—Ash had played the hymns on a school piano, or crammed his long legs under the keyboard of an antiquated harmonium. Pumping the pedals with his feet while trying hard to maintain his dignity, he did so with all the gravity required to prevent provoking the vicar to 'unseemly mirth'! He laughs when he confesses that the first time he did this, he thought: "Oh, boy! If the Ashton's Board could see me now!"

We had to be at the church early, in order for Zhaynie to feed and change her baby, which she did in the rectory next door, and Ash needed time to locate and change into his red cassock, which it was really not necessary for him to wear as he was not serving at the altar. He wore it, however, chuckling as he pulled it over his head, because the one he had first been given to use when out in the country with Peter, had been little more than a shirt to someone of his stature, and a parishioner from one of those parishes had made this one specially for him. Benjamin Ashton is very tall, and the garment he had been obliged to wear before that, had been made for a much smaller man. The sleeves had hardly reached below his elbows, and the cassock, itself, barely came down to his knees. Peter's mouth frequently used to twitch, when he saw Ben in it; more than ever after he, Ben, had once referred to it as his church 'tutu'.

Looking at his family, who sat right in front, beside the organ, and recognizing so many old friends in the congregation, Ben's heart was very full. On the wings of memory he was taken back many years, to that other, special service. Today, as he again played some of his best-loved Bach voluntaries, and saw Peter, with the servers behind him, waiting, ready to enter, his heart soared with the processional hymn he had chosen. "Lift high the cross!" the people sang joyfully, the music swelled until the rafters rang, the crucifer lifted the cross as high as his arms would let him, and all that was different was that there was no little Tony Spencer, as Antoinette Verwey had been then, running out to march down the aisle with her adored 'Fallah'!

Both Father Peter and the Reverend Basil Cunningham, the present incumbent—who had been most cooperative in allowing the visiting priest to officiate—had been gracious enough to leave the choice of hymns to Ben. Each one had been chosen specially for the words, as well as for the music Ash so loved to play.—"To praise my God and to speak for me, the words I would say if I were able" as he had said to the people, on that memorable Sunday after the media had revealed that he was *the* Benjamin Ashton, one of the wealthiest men in the world.

"As we sing the next hymn," he had said that day, addressing the congregation, with Amy-Lee at his side, "it is my hope that it may convey something to you that I should like you to know about me. Something I cannot put into words, myself, because, especially in the light of certain disclosures which have recently been made concerning me, I find myself too embarrassed to try. ...I have chosen 'Be Thou my Vision'. We shall sing the whole hymn, but, if you would bear with me, may I ask you please to begin with verse four..."

Ben had kissed Amy-Lee's cheek as he took her back to her seat, and had then sat down again at the organ. The congregation had risen and together they sang, with Ben's voice soaring above the rest:

"Riches I heed not, nor man's empty praise,
Thou my inheritance, now and always;
Thou and Thou only, first in my heart,
High King of heaven, my treasure Thou art."

"Oh, God," he prayed silently on this Sunday morning, before he began to sing. "Bless our precious new baby, and be his vision, too. Give him the Grace to keep Thee, and Thou only, first in his heart, always....And please have mercy on Tristan Connaught!"

The retrospective view was more than favourable. It was unanimously agreed that the baptism, itself, had been a beautiful experience, and although Mrs. Nolte was not a member of the parish, she was so well known that she could well have been. The ladies of the church did not regard it as an intrusion when she virtually took over the kitchen, after the service, rallying the troops around her, as it were. Refreshments had been brought by others as well, and the people who faced a long drive home, certainly felt that ample provision had been made for everyone. No one left the hall hungry, and we *Beauclaire* folk returned to the farm feeling contented and enormously blessed.

The godparents, Stephen, Jordan and Antoinette were satisfied that they had made all the responses in an exemplary manner, and the parents were tired but happy. If the Ashton grandparents were feeling a little sad, it was probably at the thought that they, unlike Stella and Paul Verwey, would have to leave the next morning, and no one knew how much the little one might have grown before they could return. Meanwhile, Father Peter had gone home with Bert and Isobel Mostert, and most of that family, but would return for the barbeque, planned by Mrs. Nolte and others, for the late afternoon. It was arranged that, after the *braai*, Isobel and James would return to Nelspruit with Peter and his in-laws, Izzie's grandparents, to spend a few days with them there.

Somehow I had a feeling that Ben's subdued manner was a little more pronounced than the thought of leaving would have warranted, and it was only as he, Amy-Lee and I were on our way to their house to start packing, and the young people had gone off to relax in whichever way they chose, that he shared the cause of it with us. When he had gone to hang up the cassock he had been wearing that morning, and, thinking of the lady who had made it for him, he happened to remark to Father Cunningham that he missed the presence of Mrs. Bennett. It must have come as a dreadful shock to be informed: "She was murdered some time ago, Ash!

"That brought the number of killings among our congregants out on the farms, to four," Cunningham went on to tell him! "All in all, this has been a difficult time. Many of the young people, some together with their parents, have immigrated; some to Australia or Canada, and several to the

United States. Plans are now being launched, by the government to try and persuade people to come back."

Ben was excusably quiet after hearing this, and perhaps it was a good thing that this time it was not intended that the *braai* should in any way assume the proportions of what on another special occasion had turned out to be 'the barbeque above all barbeques'. Nevertheless many vehicles lined the avenue from the tractor gate to the front door, and more were parked between the main gate and the garage. As was to be expected, the sun had not yet set when people began to bring their folding tables and chairs from the cars, baskets were produced, and the ladies began to set out the fare they had brought, while the men saw to the fires.

And as was also anticipated, much delectable food was then consumed, many jokes told, and several appropriate speeches made. There was the usual good-natured ribbing, and Nico Olivier was quite bashful when it was recalled that he had, on that occasion, invited Mercia Nolte to see his trailer.

"It just goes to show how risky it is to accept such an invitation from ex-policemen!" Bert Mostert teased Mercia. "In the good old movies of my generation, the usual ploy was 'would you like to come up and see my etchings?' "

Presently the moon rose over the orange groves, the laughter and the small talk gradually began to die down, until there was only that comfortable, almost drowsy kind of chatter that comes after a good *braai*. From long experience, everyone had learnt that, once the children climb onto laps and nod, especially when people have to work next day, that is a clear sign that it is time to go home.

To Benjamin Ashton, in the light of what the priest had told him about Mrs. Bennett and others of the parish, the normalcy of that happy evening was poignant. He had to swallow hard with emotion, when, before all the guests left, his employees came to sing for them, and then everyone gathered around in a circle as Peter offered up a prayer of thanksgiving and blessing. After that, amid much good-natured leave-taking, one or two children crying, and loud slamming of car doors, their friends finally departed, leaving the people of *Beauclaire* to rest.

Zhaynie and her brother, were walking across the lawn to the main house, discussing the disturbing news about Tim Connaught, and Tony's brother, Benjamin Crawford, that had recently been told to her, when she caught sight of Merry and me on our way back to her parents' house, and she stopped in the pathway to call out to Meredith, inviting her to come and keep her company while she fed Benjamin.

"I don't know when we shall see each other again, Merry," came the friendly invitation. "I'd love to spend a little more time with you.—You can help me to stay awake, unless, of course, you are too tired?"

"Not at all!" Meredith assured her. "I'm not a bit tired, and I'd like that very much!"

"Well, Auntie Bid," Jordan said gallantly, "in that case allow me to escort you as far as my parents' place. I shall be busy for the greater part of the time we have left, before you go back to *Spoors-einde*, so let's make the best of it.—And Merry, if you'll wait with Zhaynie until I get there, I'll walk you back, too..."

Little did I know how important two conversations, about to ensue, would prove to be!

Meredith was quite wound up, bubbling over with elation after the events of the day.—In fact the entire time spent with the Ashtons on the *Beauclaire* estate had previously been unimaginable to her, and she was carried away to the extent that all reticence had dissolved like snow in the summer sun.

"Dear Zhaynie!" she burst out, as confidently as if it were Susie to whom she was speaking, "Thank you for inviting me to be with you one more time! I need to tell you that the last two days have been among the four happiest I have ever known in my life! I had never been in a proper church before, and never, ever, at such a ceremony. I could hardly breathe when your father played those hymns on the organ, and you all looked so marvellous! I dimly remember my little sister's christening in the garden of our home, long ago, when a visiting clergyman happened to stay over with us, but today was overwhelming! All the lovely people who surround you, the ambience here on the farm and...well...everything!"

All of a sudden her voice broke. "I'll never forget these last two days as long as I live, and I only wish they could last forever!" She seemed oblivious of the fact that she had just disclosed more about herself to Eugenie Ashton than she had to anyone else, thus far.

"What happened on those other two days to make them so happy for you, Merry?" Zhaynie asked, gently probing as she lifted Benjamin from his crib to change his diaper.—"Four days in your lifetime, however short it has been, aren't many, so to be included in them, the other two must have been extraordinary!"

"They were! I don't remember how that one day began, but it is memorable because, in the late afternoon, Jordie took me to choose a gardening book, and afterwards he took Aunt Biddy and me to dinner at a lovely restaurant, and I had a new dress to wear. Then, to top it all, when we went back to his house, he let me play *Rhapsody in Blue* with him. The other time was either when I helped out in his clinic, or when your father taught me how to dance. I danced with Jordie afterwards, so it is difficult to decide which day was better than the other!"

All the time she was listening, Eugenie was close to tears at the absolute innocence of this enchanting little person. She could well understand why Jordan loved her, and what tugged at her heart was that, while Jordan seemed to figure in every joyful reminiscence, Tristan's name did not come up once! Somehow, although she recognized that she might be treading on thin ice, she felt that the time was right to put a few questions to Meredith.

Searching for precisely the right words, the first thing she had to know was what had caused the girl's fear of revealing her past, and then to prod some more until she could find the cause of her reluctance to share a bedroom with Tristan. She could hardly believe it, when it was Merry herself who presented her with the perfect opportunity.

Benjie had fallen asleep, but, rather than putting him back to bed, right away, Zhaynie, rose to her feet, and, inviting Meredith to sit in the rocking hair she had just vacated, she said, placing the baby in Merry's arms. "You said you'd like to hold him, and this might be your last chance before you leave."

Meredith was thrilled. She kissed the rosy cheeks, the button nose and each tiny finger in turn, and then, looking around her, asked, "Where is Dominic's bedroom?"

Completely taken aback by the incongruity of the unexpected inquiry, Eugenie replied, "Why here, of course! Benjie's nursery is all prepared and ready for him, and we'll move him to there when he's a little older, but right now we feel happier to have him in the room with us!"

"That's not why I asked," Merry explained guilelessly.

"You already have your baby, and there seems to be plenty of room in this house, so why would Dominic have to be in here with you?"

Zhaynie could only stare at her for a moment or two, while she collected herself. "But that's what married people do, sweetheart! What a very strange question to ask! My parents have always shared a bed, and I have never known them to sleep apart, except when Dad is away on a trip. Even then he mostly takes her with him, because they hate to be separated."

"*All* married people?" Meredith was aghast. "You mean even James and Isobel?"

Zhaynie nodded. "Of course. Not everyone necessarily shares the one bed, but they generally sleep in the same room, unless there's a very good reason for doing otherwise." Meredith had to take her time digesting this, and that was when Zhaynie found the opening she had been seeking. "Did your parents never do that, Merry?" she asked, trying to choose the right words. "I mean after you and your sister were born. They must have done so, before that, otherwise you would not be here!" And she was alarmed when she saw the look on Meredith's face.

There was such agony there, that Zhaynie could not bear to witness it. "Don't look like that, Merry, dear! Why do you have to try so hard to hide your pain? I know your whole story! I know what your life has been like, and it is very tragic that two people could have drifted apart to the extent that your mother and father did, but none of it is your fault—and you don't have to be ashamed of any of it!"

All the time she kept hoping that Jordan would not come to call for Meredith too soon, Zhaynie kept praying for the right words to comfort the stricken girl, as she carefully took the sleeping child out of her arms and put him down in his crib.

"I thought they just stayed in separate rooms because they already had all the children they wanted!" Meredith sobbed. "I heard that expression on television, and I had entirely the wrong idea of what it meant to 'sleep together'!" After a while the storm passed, she dried her eyes, and faced Zhaynie defiantly. "Well, babies or not, Tristan is not sleeping with me! When I have babies some day, they will definitely not be his!... I suppose he's the one who told you about me. He knows I'm sensitive about having been cut off from the outside world and he takes advantage of it! I'm like some sort of artefact to him. His friends make fun of me, and he encourages them!"

"It wasn't Tristan," Zhaynie replied injudiciously, thinking that this would be of some consolation to the other girl "It was Jordie!"

The immediate reaction to this was not at all what she had anticipated. Meredith drew her breath in sharply and her eyes widened with horror. "*Jordan* knows?—So that's why he tries to be so nice to me! He also thinks I'm a freak, and because he's so kind-hearted, he indulges me!"

" No, no!" Zhaynie protested. "You have it all wrong! None of us is 'nice' to you, if that is what you consider us to be, for any reason other than that we love and care about you, Merry, and we want you to be able to feel how much you are loved by every one of us! Where you come from, and what happened before this, makes no difference to whom you are! I have only known you for two days, and I already wish you were my very own little sister!...When I say that we all love you, I mean it! Please believe me! Jordan would be most upset if he thought that I had caused you to think otherwise!"

"I love you, too Zhaynie. I love you all," Meredith replied, with that hint of a catch still there in her voice. "You make me feel safe and secure. I have felt accepted, and that is why I could not bear the thought that Jordan might also be deceiving me. I have already been misled and hurt to near breaking point. In fact, until I came here this weekend, I was seriously thinking of going back to the Kalahari with Aunt Biddy. All that was holding me back, was that I would miss Jordie and the music—and there was the secret hope that I could be of some use to him in his clinic. That is one place where I really feel that I have some worth."

Just then they heard Jordan approaching, humming as he came, and Meredith, taking Zhaynie's arm, whispered urgently: "Zhaynie, is what you told me, a prerequisite for being married? I mean is that what actually makes two people 'married'?

And when Zhaynie, perhaps misinterpreting the question, nodded, a look of the most powerful relief crossed Meredith's face.

"Oh," she said happily. "Then I'm definitely not married!" But her expression changed instantly as another troubling thought occurred to her, and visibly, crestfallen, she observed: "Oh, dear! But if I'm not really married to Tris, I can't stay in Jordan's house, can I? I shall be there under false pretences!"

Because I was so acutely aware of the short time I had left before returning to *Spoors-einde*, I was quite overcome with gratitude at being granted an opportunity to speak to Jordan in private, and with Merry out of earshot. While I had been there to keep Meredith company, she had coped, but now my main concern was that, although she had now acquired her own computer, and had her work and several other interests to keep her busy, these were all, to my mind, pursuits that would keep her as confined to one place as she had been at *Blouspruit*. I feared that, if Meredith decided to remain in Bryanston and had to be cooped up there, day after day, she could possibly become depressed.

She was not the type to sit with her hands folded, but she needed to find an additional interest, outside, where she could be useful, as she had been to Doc Hugo. Above all, she had to get out, and, although Felicity would soon be there, an outlet had to be sought for Merry—away from the house!

This is what, sitting on the stoep of Amy-Lee's home, I tried to convey to Jordan in a short space of time. "She must get out sometimes, Jordie. She has to be with people who need her, and where she can know that her life is worthwhile!" And he promised that he would give the matter some thought.

By the time he went to fetch Meredith, we had discussed her future so earnestly, that I forgot to preach to him about himself. I had still intended to caution him not to permit Tristan to take advantage of him so readily. I had meant to impress on him that it was high time that Tristan Connaught was made to respond to the telephone calls that came for him at night. Nevertheless, although I had omitted to do that, when I left Johannesburg a few days later, it was of great comfort to me that I had not left Jasper's child alone and deserted. I had been assured, and could trust Jordan to be Meredith's loyal friend and protector.

Someone less naïve than I, might well have foreseen this, but I wonder why it never occurred to me that the presence of Jordan, Tristan and Meredith, in the same house—and the close association into which their work at the clinic would bring Merry and Jordan—could possibly result in one of those eternal triangles about which romance writers love to tell!

He, Jordan, found a very preoccupied Meredith when he called for her at the main house, and it was difficult to decipher the message that his sister, with quizzically raised eyebrows, was trying to convey to him. Be that as it may, something made him say to Merry, as they walked together under the stars, amid the fragrance of the blossoms, "I hope that you won't be so homesick that you will want to go back to *Blouspruit*, and that you won't miss Auntie Bid too much, Merry. I promise that I'll do all I can to compensate, and Aunt Felicity will soon be close by, in the cottage. Unfortunately until Reg gets back I shall initially have to be away from the house more than I should have liked, and if I did not fear for your safety, I might have asked you to help at the clinic again. You made such a difference and the patients have asked after you!"

At that Meredith detained him by spontaneously grabbing him by the arm; stopping him in his tracks, and causing him to turn and face her in the moonlight.

"I'm not going home with Biddy, Jordan!" she announced. "And I am not afraid! Not if you'll be there!"

"That's wonderful news!" he cried, restraining himself from giving her a hug. "What made you change your mind, this time?"

"I put out a fleece," she said happily, and he could hear the jubilation in her voice. "Didn't I tell you that I had put out two, and that one of them concerned you?"

PART THREE

CHAPTER NINE

I t was really nice to be back home again. Jasper, who had spent the previous night in Upington, met me at the airport, and, after alternatively worrying about what he would have to say about my 'new look', and chiding myself for being a foolish woman, his remarks concerning my improved appearance, though guarded, were satisfactory.

What a considerate man he is! He first took me to have an early lunch, and then loaded the cool box in the truck with bottled water and various snacks, before we set off on the first leg of the long journey home. Naturally he wanted the latest news of Meredith, and because I had not yet decided to what degree I should enlighten him, I dwelt mainly on the happy weekend with the Ashtons, how kind everyone was to Meredith, and how there was a possibility that she would be helping Jordan in the clinic. I explained that, while my plane had left too early for Ben and Amy-Lee to be taken to the airport with me, it was a good time for Reggie to go off to Bethlehem, and we had been able to wait for our flights together. The Ashtons and Matt Marais would leave the next day, following a meeting, arranged by Jordan, for Matt to explain his concerns about post traumatic stress, and which I was sorry to have missed.

I did tell him that Reg had decided to fetch my friend, Felicity, a week earlier than had been planned, and, because old Mrs. Burkett was so distraught about her grandson's condition that Reg and his mother did not have the heart to leave her behind, she was coming too, and would be staying in the cottage with them for the time being. I made it sound as if it would be a good thing for Meredith to have Tristan's granny close by, told him about how greatly taken the old lady was with her, but assiduously avoided all mention of Tristan's reaction to the news of her coming.—This time he had not employed his favourite expletive. Instead, what he did say had been enough to turn the air blue! Evidently, after that he had immediately stormed off to his car, and when Jordan, just arriving home, asked, "Are you okay, Tris?" it was to be told: "No I'm not! My life is a bloody mess as it is, and now my bloody grandmother is coming, to make it worse!"

We broke the journey not too very far from *Witdraai*, at a lodge where there was a restaurant, and after tea and some discussion about whether to proceed or stay the night, we decided to press on; and, although we arrived in *Spoors-einde* very late, all the lights were on in Doc's house, where I received a welcome from both the old doctor and Susie that far exceeded my worth! How and where Sally and Doc had found the nasturtiums which had thoughtfully been arranged in my bedroom, I do not know, but there they were, and bless Katryntjie's heart, even a bed for Jasper had been made ready.

Having now come back to *Spoors-einde*, and about to return to my work in the doctor's surgery, I was suddenly self-conscious. I had to face the fact that perhaps the townspeople, and the farmers would think that I was a little too old for all the new-fangled fashions I had adopted, but my fears were unfounded. Even Jasper, whose compliments had been noticeably guarded upon my arrival, had recovered from the shock, to the extent that when we joined one another for breakfast before my first day back in harness, he, Doc, and

Susan were quite unanimously, and embarrassingly lavish in their approval. I was not used to compliments, and I felt a little embarrassed at those that were expressed, but, in the secret corners of my heart, I relished them!

Of course there was much that still remained to be told, but I stuck to my conviction that what they did not know would not hurt them, and all mention of Adéle and her cohorts was studiously avoided. Instead I described the gracious home where Merry now lived, told of her interest in the garden and the plants Jordan was taking her to buy, of the magnificent grand piano and how well she and Jordan played together—taking care to mention that Benjamin and Amy-Lee Ashton had their own suite in the house, and that they had obviously taken Meredith to their hearts. I succeeded in evoking uproarious mirth with my description of our first visit to the beauty parlour, and try as I might, I could not restrain myself from raving about Jordan and how dependable he was. I assured them unreservedly that it would be difficult to reconcile the new Meredith with their memories of the shy, uncertain little girl who had left there hardly six weeks before.

"You need never fear that Merry won't be an asset to Tristan in his practice," I told Jasper. "With her beauty and charming manner, she steals hearts at first glance. There is also no danger of her ever being bored. She is gradually taking over the running of the home, which will keep her busy, and Jordan constantly remarks on the difference it has made to have a woman holding the reins.

"Furthermore," I added, addressing Doc, "as I told Jasper yesterday, she is going to help out in Jordan's clinic and, what with completing her thesis, there won't be enough hours in the day for her!"

Feeling guilty about hiding the danger and violence in Johannesburg with innocuous euphemisms, I went on, "Tristan and Jordan have a very posh suite of offices in a prestigious building, away from all the hustle and bustle of the city, and, at Jordie's request, Merry has undertaken to see to it that there are always fresh flowers in the waiting room."

"Now about the walk-in clinic," I went on. "Jordan has established this in one of the poorer neighbourhoods. Reg works there, too, and Meredith is really looking forward to assisting them in any way she can. Your labours have not been in vain, Jasper. With her enthusiasm, and theoretical knowledge, in addition to the experience she has gained in taking care of her family, she will be a tremendous asset to them."

Before I knew it, it was time to open the door for the first patients. The time had passed too quickly. We walked out to the truck to see father and daughter off, but, lagging behind Susan and Doc, I was given a few minutes alone with Jasper. His remarks to me, then, were very disturbing.

"Biddy" he said, "I'm so glad that we have had this opportunity to be together, even for so short a time. You knew how anxious I was for news of Merry, and I have to thank you once again for your deeply appreciated gesture in accompanying my child to the city; but you now leave me far from happy. I have been listening very closely to all that you have related, and I don't know if you are aware of how frequently Jordan Ashton's name crops up in your conversation. I remember him as an admirable young man, but while you make him out to be this great source of support for Meredith, could he not, in time, possibly become a threat?"

My open mouth must have been an indication of my shocked surprise. "But Jasper," I protested, "weren't you the one who said that your one consolation in sanctioning this marriage, was that Jordan would be there to watch over Merry? What makes you even think of that?"—But in my heart I knew. Recalling Meredith's concerns about the possibility of her sister following in her mother's footsteps, I knew what was in Jasper's mind, and I pitied him. It was only natural that in Jordan Ashton he might suddenly see, and fear, the threat of another Scott Brady!

"Your wide eyes betray you, my dear Biddy," he said blankly, and with a deep sigh. "I know that you have grasped my meaning....Reading between the lines, it also bothers me that young Ashton seems to take far too much upon himself. Who is he to decide what is planted in Tristan's garden?"

He left me in a very troubled state. What if he should ever discover that I had personally encouraged Jordan?

After that, although I managed to get back into the saddle, and succeeded in the pretence of carrying on as normal, I just could not settle down. I was extremely anxious about Meredith, and I could not endure my guilt in deceiving Jasper. By the time Saturday came around I was so uptight that I persuaded Doc that it was time to pay a visit to *Blouspruit*. However, once there, my courage failed me. Somehow, by virtue of the fact that both men would be troubled—Jasper because of Meredith, and Doc, because his pride in Tristan would be shaken—I just could not bring myself to tell either of them how bitterly Merry had been disillusioned. One thing I did put straight, though, and that was that Tristan was not the owner of the house.... That it was at Jordan's invitation that Tristan shared both his home and his practice.

We did get around to discussing Christmas, and Doc's invitation to Jasper and Susan to come to us, was gracefully declined with the information that they had been invited by

Jordan to spend it with Meredith in Johannesburg. It was, however decided that, in the most unlikely event that Susan's examination results did not prove to be satisfactory, she would, in the new year, come to live in *Spoors-einde* during the week, as Meredith had done long ago, and would repeat her final year of school there. I looked forward to seeing Jasper regularly again, as had been the case when Mark was alive.

Meredith faithfully kept in touch. Her emails to her father, and letters to me, were cheerful and filled with news of exciting things that she was seeing and doing, and mention was invariably made of the little boy, Fransie, whom, it appeared, now shadowed Meredith wherever she went when he was in the clinic.

"Jordan often calls me 'Miss Muffet'" she wrote, and I could picture her smiling, "but in the clinic I'm mostly referred as 'Mary with the little lamb', and I miss him when he does not come.

"The peaches and other deciduous fruit in Jordie's garden are ripening at quite an overwhelming rate, so we take basketfuls of peaches and plums to the clinic these days, and that sweet little kid, always carries away a bag or two for children who live near his grandma's house. Jordie has arranged for him to have therapy at a clinic in Sandton now, and Charlie takes him there. Sometimes I go with him, when I am able to do so."

She went into raptures about her first visit to a large theatre to see an overseas production—which caused me no end of concern, as I was not told where or with whom she had gone. I could only hope that it was with Jordan, because he would know better than anyone else whether or not the places to which she was being taken were in a relatively safe area.

How ironic *that* hope turned out to be, when in a letter to me, but conspicuously omitted from any communication to Jasper, I learned that Angelina had been stabbed and robbed, getting out of a taxi right at Jordan's front gate! When Meredith phoned with the sad news that Timothy Connaught had died of his wounds, she took good care not to let on that Tristan's response had been, "Well, now they're stuck with only me.—And if being buried with the Stars and Stripes draped over my coffin, is what it would take to get their attention, I'm damned if I would want it!"

She, Merry, wrote enthusiastically and in great detail about her part-time work at the clinic, and, on the surface all appeared to be well, but, in regularly comparing notes, Jasper Hilliard and I could read more between the lines than she could ever have guessed. Our reasons for being uneasy were very different however! For instance, all Jasper was told, with no reference whatsoever to the reason for Angelina's absence, was that, for the first time in her life, and despite the heat, Meredith, was going to attempt the roasting of a Christmas turkey....Grandma Burkett, who was in a dreadful state about Timothy, had expressed a yearning for a *pukka* English dinner with all the trimmings! At Jordan's request, Boxing Day would, however, be spent beside the pool, with lashings of watermelon and iced fruit drinks.

That all seemed harmless, enough, but what upset her father was that there was hardly a communication from Meredith in which Jordan did not feature. If she was not enthusing about the clinic, it was about a film they had seen together, or an art exhibition they had attended. Eventually I became accustomed to the smothered expressions of concern that reached me over the phone.—Stifled in case Trix Hoffman might be listening in!

I knew that poor Jasper was having sleepless nights as a result. He had not ceased to be concerned because Meredith had married the first young man she had met, and was worried sick that the charming young Doctor Ashton might drive a wedge in between Tristan and his wife. He repeatedly tortured himself by pointing out how much younger Jordan was than Tristan, and I, unshakeably loyal to Jordie, refused to listen. My view all along, had been, and remained unchanged, that if Tristan had done his duty by Meredith it would have been unnecessary for her to lean on Jordan.

Despite the cheerful letters, Meredith did not seem contented to me. When I left I had not been at all optimistic, but had hoped for the best. Don't forget that there were many things of which I was still ignorant, and that spark of interest I had discerned in Tristan's eyes at my farewell party had, though slight, remained as the only source of hope to me, but not once did I discern in Merry's letters that Tristan had somehow reverted to being the romantic and passionate Romeo he'd appeared to be while he was at *Blouspruit.*

There were many aspects of Meredith's letters that I did not discuss with Jasper. As I have already said, I carefully avoided all mention of Adéle, considering it unnecessary to keep fuelling the poor man's misery. Moreover, now that I'd had time to think about it, I no longer perceived the overbearing Mrs. Bradshaw to be quite the threat that Meredith believed her to be—although she, Adéle, might well have wished it to be so! Meanwhile Jasper, fearing that Jordan represented a temptation to Meredith and that she might be fickle enough to transfer her affections to him, was not sleeping well. Merry, on the other hand was burdened by the conviction that it was Adéle who had been responsible, in the first place, for the waning of Tristan's interest in her, and, instead of being angry with the woman, now focused her hurt and disillusionment squarely on Tristan.

The way I looked at it, and what neither Jasper nor Meredith realized, was that there had never, on Tristan's side, been any real love to wane! If Tristan had been as madly in love with Merry as he had pretended to be, he would long ago have put Adéle in her place. As it was, the only time Merry was truly free of the burden of that stress, was when she was with Jordan. He affirmed her, and she was happy when he was near.

Then, in the September of that year, desperately needing a break, Doc finally succeeded in finding a locum, and went on a visit to 'the children' in Johannesburg, while I took as good care as I could of the young physician who temporarily replaced him. During Doc's absence, I had my hands full. Now that her sister's marriage had delivered Susan from years of virtual captivity, she had only one thought in mind, and that was to go to University in Gauteng. She would be close to Meredith who could keep an eye on her, as I pointed out to Jasper, and, as tactfully as I could, made him face the fact that time had not stood still. Both his daughters were grown up and Susie, having had a taste of freedom, was not prepared to have her wings clipped. She wanted her own chance at life!

Having devoted a great deal of time to discussion of the matter—amicably, of course—once the decision was made, Susan sat for the university entrance examination in *Spoorseinde*, and after indescribable suspense for all three of us, the news came that she had passed with flying colours. Meanwhile, because Doc was in Johannesburg with Meredith, I was temporarily free of serious concerns about Merry, believing that the dear old man would see to it that Tristan toed the line and did not neglect her.

I was not destined to push my problems aside for too long, however. Doc came back unexpectedly one day, and the moment he walked in at the front door, I could read the signs of distress on his face. He did not leave me in ignorance for long, either. After dinner that same night, he invited me to come to his study, where I encountered him with his head in his hands.

"Biddy," he plunged right in without beating about the bush, "I am so worried about the children that I do not know how I can go about my work tomorrow. It is essential for a physician to have his head clear of personal concerns in order to give his patients the attention that is their due, but this thing with Tristan and Meredith keeps pounding through my head so that I don't know which way to turn!"

"What's wrong?" I was alarmed. "What has happened that I'm not aware of?"

"I wish it were possible to tell you, in a word, precisely what has distressed me so, Biddy, but I'm sure there is little I can tell you that you don't know already. The situation must have been much like that when you were there, and I am afraid there is a great deal that you have hidden from me!

"No, no!" he gestured with his hands. "I am not reproaching you! I know that you withheld these things from me for my own good, to ensure my peace of mind. And, in any case, such a state of affairs would be very difficult to describe. What is amiss there, is too subtle for description, and I don't know what to say to Jasper. One has to be there!"

I could only nod. He had already put it better than I could have done. We remained, deep in unhappy thought, and without speaking, for quite some time after that, and when Doc broke the silence, he did so, shaking his head in disbelief. Without being aware of it, he gestured in a manner that suggested repelling of the unpleasant. As though pushing the hurt away from him.

"Biddy, how sadly one can be blinded by love!" he muttered. "How is it that I would never see Tristan as he really is? An unprincipled, selfish man—a good-for-nothing!" His bitterness was extreme, and my heart bled for the saintly old doctor. "It's hard to be rudely awakened isn't it?" he asked, obviously without expecting a reply. "Clifford's father, my brother, Harry, gave his life for his country. Now Timothy, Cliff's son, has made the same sacrifice, and—may God forgive me!—I keep asking myself why it was not rather Tristan. Timothy was of great value to many, and will be sadly missed...whereas...!"

While I understood where he was coming from, I was suddenly too poignantly reminded of a tearful Thora singing '*When Irish eyes are smiling*', to allow this. "Please Doc," I pleaded, "don't talk like that! God's ways are not our ways. As the Scriptures tell us, 'it is not in man that walketh to direct his ways!' Please, I beg of you, repent of that and pray for Tris—for he is all that Thora and Clifford have left!"

"But Biddy, Tristan's ways are surely not God's ways! That supposedly brilliant physician is not a physician's foot!...I can see that I shock you, but why did he ever choose medicine? It's not a job or a career! It should be a calling! Of course I'm not criticizing his ability. I'm talking about his attitude!"

Doctor Hugo swallowed a few times as though he had something stuck in his throat, "Biddy," he whispered hoarsely, looking me straight in the eye, "do you know that Tristan never accepts messages, and he certainly does not respond to an emergency call after hours? Even if it's his turn to be on call, he ignores his pager. That, in a family practice! Are you aware that he keeps strict business hours, and anything beyond that is automatically palmed off onto Jordan?"

"Shouldn't we perhaps blame Jordie for that?" I hedged. "Perhaps it is he, who with his unselfishness and dedication, has spoilt Tristan! I'm sure that if he would simply refuse point-blank to carry Tristan's load, and not do his 'dirty work', as I have heard Tristan refer it, our friend would be compelled to do it himself!"

"No, Biddy," the old man replied hopelessly. "You don't have to make excuses for him to try and make me feel better. You know as well as I do that Jordan goes because he knows that if he doesn't, nobody else will! Tristan would simply unplug the phone and disregard messages. While I was there, Meredith took messages several times, and when she pleaded with him, he turned a deaf ear. On each occasion she was obliged to turn to Jordan.... Tristan's behaviour suggests that he is drinking far more these days than I ever remember his doing before, and I believe that Jordan responds because he is afraid of what might happen once Tristan gets behind the wheel.

"Then there's another thing. His behaviour is so unpredictable that I fail to see how Meredith can tolerate it! Of an evening he mostly sits morosely slumped in his chair, but there were times when I saw him grab hold of Meredith, even though there was no music, scoop her off her chair and dance around with her as though she were a rag doll. She is such a slight little thing, and he is so much bigger and stronger than she is, that I have on occasion feared that he might hurt her!" (*As if I didn't know all about that!*)

"No, Biddy," he said again, "Until you know the whole story, do not lay the blame on young Ashton. You know perfectly well that he does not sacrifice himself for Tristan. He does what he does because he is a doctor after my own heart...!"

Again I could only nod. Had I not often wished that Tristan could be like Jordan? I had never before seen Doctor

Hugo as distraught as he was at that moment, and I could cheerfully have kicked Tristan Connaught for the pain he was causing a man who had put his trust in him. At one stage Doc took a handkerchief out of his pocket to wipe his eyes, and I could see that the gentle old hand was shaking.

"Biddy, promise me something," he requested all at once. "Promise me that you will say nothing about the situation to Jasper!"

"But how on earth can we hope to hide this from him?" I demanded impatiently. To deceive Jasper Hilliard was absolutely the last thing I wanted to do. "He's going to Johannesburg himself soon, to take Susie to Meredith, and he does, after all, have eyes in his head!"

"I grant you that," he acknowledged despairingly, "but I am not suggesting that we deceive him indefinitely. Only that we postpone the evil day for a while. Can you not perceive how wretched I am? On the one side there is a young man whom I have foolishly idolized and put on a pedestal—and, on the other, an old friend with a tragic history, who put so much trust in me that, against his better judgment, he allowed his precious daughter to marry a worthless individual....All because I was so plainly taken with the idea...Gracious heaven! That essential need for a yardstick of which Jasper spoke that day, and which Meredith so fatally lacked. Why, why, of all the young men in the world, did it have to be Tristan?"

I had so often asked myself that question, that I could empathize, and I could not bear to see the old man in that state. Yet all of sudden, for no accountable reason, I felt so overwhelmingly sorry for Tristan. There was this person, outwardly and physically so attractive, and yet so warped within. Surely no one gets to be so horrid by choice! What made him like that? And what was it in him that would want someone like Jordie to reach out to him, protect him, and endure his 'awfulness'?—I could think of no other word!

From all accounts, Tristan was hardly more than a toddler when he somehow managed to escape through the fence to be with the Ashtons whenever they were in residence next door, and perhaps it was then that Jordan, as young as he was, had acquired this enduring habit of shielding Tris.—What was it that Ben had said about Tristan's declaration that he would marry Amy-Lee when he grew up? And if he could not have her, he would settle for Eugenie? Was it simply because he wanted everything in his life to be like that of the Ashtons? To be a part of their family? Why was it that he was content to sit on the floor, playing with Meccano in Ben's study, and not in that of his own father?...All I was left with was the realization that, whatever the cause, while he seemed to be consumed with hatred for the world, in general, he hated no one more than himself. In hurting others, he was only hurting himself more!

I spoke to Jordan on the phone, twice before Christmas. On the first occasion he was able to tell me that Clifford and Thora had been quite overcome when Ash and Amy-Lee arrived in Louisiana so unexpectedly. There had been no need for words. They had simply clung to one another, and wept. Afterwards the two bereaved parents had not been able to find words to thank them for coming. They just could not get over it!

But, speaking to his son later, Ash recalled the night when he, an unshaved, distraught, and exhausted stranger, had been taken to a small house in Bethlehem, in the open doorway of which had stood a tall, spare young man in a black cassock. Stretching out his hand to take the suitcase from Ben with one hand, and gesturing welcomingly with the other, he had led

Ben to a small, but cosy living room where he set down the case for him. "If you need to use the bathroom," he said, "it's just across the hall—I'll just go and put some clean towels out for you..."

"Oh, Jordie," Ben said to Jordan, his voice thick, "I can never thank him enough for all he has meant to me over the years!—And he thinks it's such a big deal that I have come...! My dear son, few men have ever cast their bread upon the water, as Tristan's father has. Why can't that tortured young man find it in his heart to come to him?" And Jordan echoed that, at the same time remarking what a fine man Tristan's brother, Timothy, had turned out to be, and what happy times they had enjoyed together as families, whenever the Ashtons had returned to Louisiana, to spend holidays at the other *Beauclaire*, right next door to the Crawfords.

The second time I called, I was told that the plans for Christmas Eve were well underway in Jordan's house, and that Meredith was excitedly planning for the visit of her father and sister. Fortuitously, as Felicity and Mrs. Burkett happened to be there too, I was able to speak to everyone in the house, and finally to Jordie, who told me that his parents were remaining in Louisiana, and, instead of celebrating Christmas in their own home, they were spending it over at the Crawfords', where a party had been arranged for the staff and the children.

He also told me of several new developments. Ben and Amy-Lee, whose original intention had been to return to South Africa, for Easter, had offered to give Clifford and Thora a trip to the Bahamas or any other place they would like to go, for a change of scene, suggesting that they, the Ashtons, stand in as 'house parents' for the two, but the plans were changed again when the Crawfords decided that, in view of the expected arrival of several, still homeless small victims of the hurricane, they would prefer to stay where they were, and welcome the children.

In view of this, the latest news was that Jordan's parents would go to Nelspruit at Easter, after all, and then, when the time came, would take Mrs. Burkett back to the States with them, to visit with her daughter and son-law. What gladdened Jasper's heart was that Ben wished to keep a promise made to Doctor and Mrs. Fisher at my birthday party. While in South Africa, he would bring them to the Kalahari, which meant that Merry could be at *Blouspruit* in time for Easter.

Strange how things happen! When I had left Doc Hugo's study on the night he had besought me not to tell Jasper the cold, hard truth, I had wondered why he wanted me to refrain from doing so. I had agreed to wait, but I could not help wondering what that would profit anyone. Perhaps he hoped and prayed that some miraculous change would occur before Jasper and Susan arrived in Johannesburg.

It was only once I was alone in my bedroom that night, that I thought of how much I still needed to know and had neglected to ask. We had not even obliquely touched on the one aspect that I considered to be the most important of all....The question of the current relationship between Tristan and Meredith! It was odd that, except for the remark about her pleading with Tristan to take phone calls, he had not told me how she was, and had not said a word about how she and Tristan were getting along.

At last, exhausted, I turned off my light and lay down, only to wrestle in the dark with my concerns. Of course it was possible that, being first and foremost a physician, he had confessed, solely from a doctor's point of view, how his loving old heart was ready to break at the discovery of Tristan's unworthiness, but, intuitively I knew that there was more to his reticence that met the eye. Without the vestige of a doubt, I knew that Doc feared that Jasper would be beside himself, when he became a witness to Tristan's cavalier treatment of Meredith. He would be shocked to find how different the real Tristan was, from the disarming young man to whom he had entrusted his beloved daughter not many months before.

But what good would it do to keep Jasper in the dark? I kept asking myself. To wait until he and Susan arrived at Jordan's house? Would it not be kinder to prepare him gradually? How much misery might not perhaps have been prevented if I had frankly and honestly revealed the truth of what I had discovered? How foolish Doctor Hugo was to wish, wait, and hope for a miracle to make everything right before Christmas!

Early next morning, when Katryntjie took Doc's coffee to him, it was to discover what had been hidden behind the old man's request. Upon receiving no response to her repeated knocking, the faithful old maid opened the door and went in. Moments later her hysterical shrieks sent me, barefooted and startled, to investigate.

It seems that one can exist for a very long time with a broken leg or arm, but a broken heart is another matter altogether...

As soon as the exchange came on duty, and, regretting that I had forgotten to recharge my cell phone, I called *Blouspruit* and requested Jasper to hurry to my assistance. Then I had to arrange with the district surgeon, who was a fair distance away, to come and issue the death certificate, and I was quite tearful with gratitude when Jasper arrived, bringing Susie with him. It was no slight relief to have him telephone Tristan and Meredith, besides attending to such matters as were beyond me, and which, when Mark had died, had thankfully been handed over to dear old Doc to do for me. I left it to Jasper to discuss with Tristan whether he thought it necessary to notify Thora and Clifford in Louisiana. They'd had enough bad news to cope with recently, but Doc, Clifford's uncle, had been his last remaining relative.

While Jasper spoke to Doctor Prinsloo, the young man who had 'locumed' for Doc, and who fortunately still happened to be visiting an aunt in Askam, I went about my duties mechanically, attended to such patients as I could help without a doctor's presence, and then, putting a notice on the door, made it known that the consulting room would be closed until further notice. And all the time I was doing this, I could not get out of my mind the one question that seemed to be written in capital letters on every wall, door and window of that house, and would not cease from hammering through my brain.

I now knew why Doc had asked that Merry's father should not immediately be told that all was not well. He must have known that his days were numbered, and had hoped to postpone Jasper Hilliard's disillusionment until he would no longer be there to have to witness it! *But what had Doctor Hugo seen in Johannesburg that had made him so unhappy?*

Once Doctor Prinsloo had expressed himself to be still available, and willing to return, Jasper then arranged for Hennie Vercueil to go and fetch him. As Katryntjie, was completely out of it—justifiably so—she was of little help to me, and I was thus extremely grateful when, Sally came over as soon as she had sent Hennie off in the taxi.

She and Susie, together, were of great help to me, and, during that time of sorrow and anxiety, it was heart-warming to discover just how much Susan had matured in a few, short months. Together with Sally, she did shopping, answered the phone, and was simply marvellous in the way she helped to ply endless streams of people who kept dropping by, with tea and coffee. Another amazing thing was how people rallied around me. One of the most touching expressions of sympathy came from Van der Merwe's store, in the form of several boxes of groceries, and a list of other possible requirements that I only had to mark with a tick, for the order to be refilled immediately upon receipt—at no charge!

The outside temperature had reached forty-four degrees centigrade when Hennie's taxi dropped Adriaan Prinsloo off, shortly after five o'clock; yet, bless him, as tired and dusty as the young man must have felt, he washed his hands and face in cold water, and then went straight to the surgery next door to respond to urgent phone messages there.

I gave thanks for the presence of the doctor when one of the messages was from Klaas van Bruggen whose wife was expected to give birth soon, and for the first time, at the age of forty-two. He just wanted reassurance, and I was happy to see that when Doctor Prinsloo came back into the house, he did exactly what Doctor Hugo would have done. He checked his medical bag, to make sure that he had all that he might possibly need if he were required to go out on call.

Busy making supper, I invited him to go and look in Doc's bag, in the study, to see whether there was anything there that his own lacked, and which needed replenishing after the weeks he had already spent with us so very recently, and he presently came into the kitchen, bringing with him a note addressed to me. Not having time to open it right away, I went and put it on the dressing table in my bedroom, to read once my people had eaten.

We had thought that Hennie Vercueil would have to be contacted for a second time that day, with a request to fetch

Tristan and Meredith from Upington airport in the morning, but not long after Jasper had notified Tristan of Doc's demise, Merry let us know that they had decided to rent a car and drive to *Spoors-einde*, themselves; and once more I had to be grateful for Susie's help, when she went off to get a room ready for them. I did not think it at all strange that, suggesting that it would be an opportunity for the kind of 'girl talk' that sisters enjoyed, Merry should have asked to share the bedroom which, because she came to stay so frequently, Susan now claimed as her own.

Two days later the funeral took place—surely the biggest that Spoors-einde's cemetery had ever known—and Doc's will was read before Tris and Merry returned to Gauteng. Tristan had, of course, inherited the house and the practice, and I was surprised, moved to tears, and completely undone when it was revealed that my dear old friend and employer had left me one-hundred-thousand pounds sterling!—Money he had begun to deposit in a British bank soon after WW2, long before he came to live in South Africa, had accumulated to this extent!

Finally everyone went his or her separate ways, and I was left alone with Doctor Prinsloo, to mourn a venerable, truly great man. It had been decided that, at all costs, the locum doctor should be prevailed upon to remain for as long as possible, because our remote *dorp* could not be left without a physician, and there was but slender hope of Tristan's being able to sell the practice anytime soon. Those of us who remained in that place did so because we loved the Kalahari, but not many doctors were exactly clamouring to spend the rest of their lives in the arid isolation that is known as *Spoors-einde*—and for good reason!

My head was splitting by the time I could finally go and put my feet up for a while, and, sitting down to remove my shoes, I saw the note that had been left lying on the dressing table all this time, for no other reason than I had been too rushed to have a look at it.

"FOR THE SOLE AND PERSONAL ATTENTION OF BRIDGET DEWEY."—I recognized Doc's handwriting at once, and beginning to read what he had written, I was moved by the realization that he must have set these thoughts down in the final hours of his life—but I was soon to regret opening that envelope. Having done so, I would know little peace of mind for a long time to come!

"*Isaiah 38:14,*" I read, and reached for my Bible to check the reference before reading the rest. "*O, Lord, I am oppressed; undertake for me.*"

"*Psalm 61:1,2. Hear my cry, O God; attend unto my prayer. From the end of the earth will I cry unto thee, when my heart is overwhelmed: lead me to the rock that is higher than I...*"

And below those words was scrawled, almost illegibly, "*O, God, my God, Harry's great-grandson is a drug addict! How can this be?*"

How I managed to sleep that night, and how I managed to carry on with my work in the surgery and the house, I'll never know. I found myself in an exceedingly unenviable position from which there seemed little escape.

I was grateful for the presence of Adriaan Prinsloo (he pronounced it 'Ah-dree-ahn'), but as had been my experience with Doc, he was kept busy and did not often find time to 'visit'. When he was not seeing patients in the surgery, he was out on calls, which because the distances were great, took up a great deal of his time. Doc's Jeep was not air-conditioned, and even for a Kalahari-born boy, Doctor Prinsloo found the heat extreme. I had always maintained that after December 21st, the longest day of the year, the heat seemed to grow more intense.

Be that as it may, with Christmas approaching fast, and seeing little of young Doctor Prinsloo, it was towards sunset every day that I found the depression into which Doc's note had plunged me, to be even less bearable than usual. I had, moreover, been spoilt by having so many people around me, and now there was no one.

One evening after sunset I could not stand the heat in the house, and although it was no better outside, the very fact of being in the open air made my whole situation seem less oppressive than it was indoors. Adriaan was away on the Van Bruggen farm, where a difficult delivery was anticipated, and I did not expect him back till early morning. How long I sat on the garden bench under the Camel Thorn tree, with my hands folded listlessly on my lap, I cannot say, but the light had begun to fade, the stars were beginning to twinkle, and the moon was rising, when I heard footsteps on the gravel path, and, turning my head, I saw Jasper Hilliard coming towards me.

He sat down next to me, not saying a word, and we remained without speaking for some time until he finally asked, "And now what, Biddy? What do you plan to do with your life?"

The question was unexpected, but not difficult to answer. "I shall probably have to stay on and keep house for the new doctor, whoever he turns out to be, for a little while after the practice is taken over, but I am no longer obliged to do that. Doctor Hugo's generosity has made it possible for me to go away for a while, perhaps have a good holiday somewhere, before I look for something else to keep me busy. All I am sure of at the moment, is that I do want to return to the Kalahari eventually..."

"I see," he answered expressionlessly, and then he did something I would never have expected of him. He took my hand in his and it wasn't so dark that I could not see the hitherto inconceivable expression on his face.

"Biddy," he said softly, in that beautiful voice which had, for a long time, had the most powerful effect on the rate of my heartbeat. "Dearest, Biddy, I wanted so much to ask you this, long ago, but I feared that it would be too unfair to Hugo. Don't go away, precious little woman. Please!—Marry me and come and live at *Blouspruit* with me!"

They say that people of our age can no longer be romantic! Don't you believe it for one minute! (Anyway I'm sure that Richard Gere is a fair bit older than Jasper is!) Let me tell you that when Jasper spoke like that, I could hardly rely on my own voice. My first impulse was to throw my arms around his neck, and yell, 'Yes, yes Jasper, of course I'll marry you!' but something held me back.

Instead I said earnestly, "Jasper, I know that I can rely on you to be completely honest with me, and I expect you to answer this question truthfully, so I shall not be insulted, no matter what your response..."

"Well, what is it?" he asked, mystified. "What is it that you want to know?"

"Life must be lonely enough for you already, with Meredith gone," I began, choosing my words carefully, "and once Susan goes off to university, you'll be completely alone. Are you sure that you are not just asking me to marry you as a hedge against loneliness? To alleviate the silence?...I know I talk a lot..."

I was not permitted to proceed. He threw his head back and laughed so hard that he would not have heard me, even had I tried to say more. He laughed until he had me quite worried.

"What's the matter?" I demanded.

"Oh, Biddy," he spluttered, " you must be the best antidote for boredom that I know of. No wonder you...that you think..."

"Please, Jasper," I pleaded in a small voice. " I don't know what is so funny!"

He was instantly serious once more. "Forgive me, my dearest," he said, and I felt a thrill flood my whole being when he addressed me like that. "I did not mean to offend you! It's just that you put things so comically! My darling girl, do you think, for one moment, that I would ever ask you to be my wife if I did not love you with my whole heart?"

"Oh, Jasper," I sighed ecstatically...and I can't remember too much about the rest of the evening after that. All that comes back, vaguely, is that he again explained that the reason he had waited for such a long time to ask me, was that he was concerned about what would happen to Doc. And he told me something else that made me wonder if I might be dreaming.

He first asked me if I had any idea of how difficult it had been for him to break free of all shackles after more than ten years; not only letting Meredith come to *Spoors-einde*, but, worst of all, having to make his own appearance in a town where he was likely to be regarded as some sort of museum piece.

"And how do you think I found the courage to do so, Biddy, darling? Well, I'll tell you....After you and Hugo had been to the farm that afternoon, I took a deep breath and made up my mind that I'd have to make a plan quickly or I might not see you again. I knew that if I did not get that 'hermit' image behind me as smartly as possible, I would regret it for the rest of my life. I pretended that I was willing to change for Merry's sake, but you and I now know otherwise, don't we, sweetheart?"

Wasn't that the nicest thing for him to say?

We were walking back to the house, when all of a sudden I had a worrisome thought. "Where is Susie? You surely didn't leave her alone at *Blouspruit?*"

"I most certainly did not!" he assured me, chuckling. "I left her playing Scrabble with Sally Vercueil, and said I'd fetch her later. When I told Sally where I was going, I gave her a sly wink, and I have no doubt that that was why she said I could come back to fetch my daughter as late as I liked. Besides, it's a long way home, and I reckoned that if I had to stay the night in Hugo's house with you,"—his grin made the corners of his eyes crinkle up most adorably—"it would be better for *Spoors-einde* and its people to know that we had a chaperone in the house!"

We went to pick up Susie together but, before we left Doc's house, I fetched the 'Chambers' book I had bought for Jasper in Sandton. "I wanted to bring something special home for you," I told him shyly, " and this is what I chose."

"Are you telling me that I was actually on your mind in the midst of all the lights and the sight of the city?"

"What do you think?" I shot back cheekily.

***

Spoors-einde did not have its own newspaper, but we did have Trix Hoffman, and, in some ways, she was better. The town's latest news was received straight from the horse's mouth, as it were, and if one really wanted to have information broadcast urgently, she was also better than any town crier. When Jasper asked me to go with him to Johannesburg for Christmas, she was invaluable. I had no sooner breathed the word in her ear that the nice little doctor was back, and might have to be on his own at Christmas, than Adriaan was flooded with invitations—most of them from mothers of marriageable daughters—and he was probably far better fed while I was away, than he could possibly have been if I'd been there. And fortunately there was no better time for me to leave him to cope alone, because, with four holidays thrown in, the period between the last week in December, and the first in January, was traditionally a slow time for us in the surgery.

I was on cloud nine for most of the time—but not all of it! Wasn't I the most blessed woman in the world? I was soon to be married to the nicest man I knew, and have two lovely daughters to call my own, but I could not help dwelling anxiously on the problem of how, remembering my last conversation with Doc, I would be able to bear even looking at Tristan. Conversely, how would he receive me as a future mother-in-law? If one came to think of it, I had been his surrogate mother for more years than he had spent with Thora, but I was far from optimistic that he would see the present situation in that light.

I was actually very grateful that Susan, who sat behind her father on the plane from Upington, and had a window seat, kept leaning over his shoulder to comment excitedly on everything she could see from the air, because I had so much to think about that Jasper, who was accustomed to endless chatter from me, would periodically ask if I was alright. What kept me too preoccupied to want to talk much, was what weighed heaviest of all on my heart.—The question of how I was going to make a clean breast of all that I had been hiding!...How was I ever going to find the courage to tell him how his son-in-law had broken Doc Hugo's heart? How did one convey the tragedy that the dear old doctor's final note had revealed?

I was extremely nervous by the time we landed at the Johannesburg airport, where it was Charlie who met us, but, by the time the car drew up in front of Jordan's house, something so frightful had occurred that all other thoughts were instantly driven from our minds!

It seemed strange to me that there were so few people waiting on the front stoep of Jordan's house, and that I did not see Meredith among them. She was, after all, expecting us, and I had sort of half-expected her to give us—particularly her father and Susie—a royal welcome. How astonished I was when I saw Adéle and Gloria—of all people—come running towards us as we got out of the car, with Mrs. Burkett and Felicity, who was not yet able to run, following more slowly.

Adéle, that outwardly hard, ruthless woman, had tears streaming down her face on that day. Her lipstick was smudged and rivulets of mascara lent her an almost clown-like appearance. As she reached me, she flung her arms around my neck, weeping hysterically.

"Oh, Mrs. Williams," she sobbed, "the most terrible thing has happened! We tried to contact you, when we heard the news early this morning, but you were in transit! Meredith, Tristan, and some little boy, were involved in a dreadful accident a few hours ago, and Reggie told Felicity that it is uncertain whether Tristan will survive!"

"Oh, dear God!" I thought, my knees so weak that they would hardly support me. *"Doc prayed that Jasper would be spared a disillusionment, but he would not have wanted it to happen like this!"*

"And Meredith?" I heard Jasper's strangled voice beside me. "What of Meredith?"

"Jordan is at the hospital with them, Professor Hilliard," Gloria tried to reassure him. "All three are still in Emergency, so Jordan can't say for sure, yet, but he asked us to tell you that she does not appear to be seriously hurt. He can't say for sure until further tests are done. Evidently she may have suffered a mild concussion, and is of course, suffering from shock."

"The clinic has had to be closed for the time being," Adéle, still sniffing, took up from there, "and Reggie is waiting for transport, to take a family member of the injured boy— the grandmother, I think—to the hospital, to be with him while the child's condition is being assessed. Meanwhile the staff in Sandton are frantically contacting patients to postpone appointments."

By this time, Felicity had reached me, and having been introduced to Jasper and Susan, and expressing her regret that they should have been met with bad news, she told us that Jordan had given instructions that we were first to be given lunch, and after that he would personally come and take us to the hospital. There was no point in coming right away, he had stressed, because we would not be able to see any of them for the time being, and he, himself, could do nothing more until all the test results were in. It appeared that Charlie had already been despatched, immediately upon our arrival, to fetch Reggie and the injured child's grandmother, who had been told where to meet us.

"Jordan also said that you would know which was your bedroom, Bid—and Professor Hilliard and Susan are to have the Ashtons' suite.

Grandma Burkett, when I hugged her, could only keep repeating. "My dearest Thora! My poor Clifford! First his son, then his uncle and now this!—How will they be able to bear yet another disaster? I thank God that Ben Ashton is there with them!"

We had hardly eaten and freshened up to some extent when Jordie phoned from his car to say that he was on his way, and I was surprised when Felicity, who had taken the call, handed the phone over to me. "He wants to speak to you,

Biddy," she said, and I took it from her with some trepidation, praying that I was not to be given more bad news to pass on to the others.

"Aunty Bid?" he asked, when I spoke. "I thank God that you have come, but I'm afraid you may be in for a thin time. With Angelina still in hospital, and a house full of people, I can only ask you please to help me get through this time. I'll tell you more, later, but right now, can you please do me a favour?

"If they have not yet left, do your best to detain those two women, Adéle and Gloria, until I arrive. And please also make it clear to them, to Aunt Felicity and particularly to Tristan's grandmother, that there will be no point in their coming to the hospital for the time being. I have instructed that signs be posted on Tristan and Meredith's doors, as soon as they are brought to their respective wards, and no visitors other than you and Merry's family will be allowed.—I'll explain later."

Not fifteen minutes after that, the familiar 'ping' told me that he was coming up through the gate, and, having passed on his request, I marshalled everybody into the hallway, so that we could be ready to leave the moment he was ready to go. His face was grim, but he gave me a warm hug, shook Jasper's hand, and after giving him an encouraging pat on the back, made a point of speaking kindly to Susie, who was visibly upset.

"Welcome to my home, Susan. I am so pleased to meet you and your father again, You were very small when I saw you last, and I must tell you that even a callow youth such as I was at that time, was able recognize what a cute pair you and Merry made! Now, if you and Mrs., Burkett would excuse us, Aunt Felicity, and if you and your dad would go ahead, Susan—and wait for me in my car—I'll just have a quick word with Mrs. Bradshaw and Mrs. Triblehorn, and then I'll join you!...Aunty Bid, would you stay, please."

Jasper was sensible enough not to take offence at being thus dismissed, and he co-operated by taking Susan's arm, and walking with her to the car

"This way please, ladies," Jordan said briskly, leading us into his study and, closing the door, he apologized for not asking us to sit down. "I'm in a tearing hurry, as you can imagine," he explained, "so I'll get right to the point! I am about to transgress the patient confidentiality regulations, and may lose my licence for this, but if that is the price I have to pay, to sort out this sorry mess, so be it!

"I have not yet had the results of Tristan's blood tests, but I am puzzled about several things—which I don't have time to get into right now, so I'll just ask you outright.—Adéle and Gloria, is Tristan, to your knowledge on drugs, and, if so, do you know what they might be?"

When neither responded, he prodded them impatiently. "Come on, make it snappy! I have to know, if I am to give him the correct medication, and I don't have time to stand here waiting for you to answer me!"

This was a Jordan I had never seen before. This was an authoritative man, completely sure of himself, and determined not to tolerate nonsense.

It was Gloria who first broke the stubborn silence. "Well," she began hesitantly, "Tris has been known to chew a leaf or two sometimes, and then the three of us—and a bunch of other friends—do frequently smoke a few joints together of an evening..."

"You mean *dagga*? (Marihuana)"

"Yes. He gets it from a coloured guy. A painter at the General. And if you'd gone and looked in the back corner of your garden, on the other side of the pool, before last week, you'd have found quite a few plants. Tris thinks it's hilarious that Meredith believed them to be marigolds.—I don't think that the leaves look very similar, and maybe there's more than one kind of marigold, but how can someone who is supposedly working towards a doctorate on weeds or something, be that dumb? ! She..."

I saw that Jordan's hackles were rising.

"I don't have time to listen to that!" he snapped. "What else does he use?...Come on, ladies! Don't you understand that Tristan might be in serious trouble! Does he do any other drugs that you know of....? Does he ever, to your knowledge, inject himself or sniff something?"

"Pills," Adéle finally managed to blurt out. "We have had a few prescriptions filled for him, but I don't think they can be too bad. He's given us one or two, on occasion, and *we* didn't go running people over in our cars or anything!"

"But what were they? I must know!"

"I don't know!" was the similar response from both women. "He has them in his medical bag. I have never seen him go anywhere without it!"

"Well, thank you anyway," Jordie said brusquely. "Come, Aunty Bid!" And as we walked towards the car, he explained, "I wanted you there for reasons I shall later explain, but I am hoping that you can help me shed some light on this. You must have noticed his peculiar behaviour at times!"

"I have indeed," I said decisively, "and when we come back later I'll give you a note from Doc Hugo, which makes it clear that he did, too. You were kidding about some of the things you said to those women, weren't you? For instance, you are very well aware that you could look for puncture marks on Tristan's arms, and the blood tests will tell you what else you need to know!"

"Yes, they'll tell what is in his system now, but not what he might have been doing over a period of time. I could have told them about the 'pot', because he reeks of it—and the booze—but it's strange that I have never known him to drink excessively until lately!"

"That's exactly what Doc Hugo said," I told him breathlessly, almost having to run in order to keep up with his long strides. "And talking of 'bags'...I can soon find out more about that when the telephone exchange opens in *Spoorseinde* tomorrow morning. By the way, I remember wondering, when I noticed that Doc's was still on his desk after Tris had left to go off to *Blouspruit*, that first time, how he thought he would manage without a medical bag; and then last week, I noticed that, even when Tristan came with Meredith to attend the funeral, he brought his own with him; keeping it close to himself at all times!—I thought he was just being conscientious!"

In the car, on the way to the hospital, Jordan gave Meredith's father a report on her condition, as it had been when he had left there some forty-five minutes before, and was, furthermore, able to provide us with the details of the accident. This he was able to do, as he had witnessed it, and I saw his hands tighten on the steering wheel as he related, how Meredith and Fransie, hand-in-hand, had just stepped off the curb, in front of the clinic, when he had noticed this car come barrelling down the one-way street, at high speed.

"The whole thing was so, bizarre," he observed emotionally, finding it difficult even to talk about it. "I had been with them moments before, about to drive them from my clinic to where Fransie goes for treatment—which is why Charlie was sent to meet you—and the automatic security gate had already closed behind me, when, hearing Reggie call out something to me from inside, I hesitated, waiting on the sidewalk for him to come to the door and tell me what he wanted.

"It was like something from the worst possible nightmare, when first the edge of the bumper sent Fransie flying right into the path of the oncoming traffic, and I was horror-struck when, immediately after that, I saw that Merry had been hurt, too. The driver then swerved violently to the right, bashed into a parked vehicle—I think it was a truck—and was then hit by yet another vehicle, as his own car came to a standstill about two hundred yards down the street. He was pulled out of it, unconscious...

"It was awful, because even when Reg, having waited for the gate to open, came to my assistance, it was difficult to attend to three patients at once. I considered it risky to try and extract the driver of the vehicle, myself, until the right equipment was available, but, by the Grace of God, emergency vehicles responded quickly to my phone call, and the experts were left to extricate him from the wreckage."

"Do they know who the man is?" Jasper wanted to know. "Can he be identified?"

"I am sorry to have to tell you, sir," Jordan said reluctantly, " but I guess you have a right to be told. The driver was Tristan!"

We followed him like three lost sheep, through the door of the underground parking, into a building which, by the smell, alone, was so familiar to me that, even with my eyes shut, I would have recognised as a hospital. He stood aside for us to enter what he still called the elevator, and we, the 'lift', and once inside, he put his arm around Jasper. "Don't worry, Professor," he said kindly. "She's very precious to me, too, and I won't let anything happen to her. I know it embarrasses Tristan that I pray over my patients, but, today I prayed for him as I did for Meredith and for Fransie, whether he would have liked it or not. I also anointed the three of them, and laid hands on them, as we are told to do in the fifth chapter of the book of James, and as I, over the years, have seen my dad and Father Peter do…"

Jordie had used the word 'bizarre', to describe the accident itself, and that is all I can say about what followed. A nurse kindly went ahead of us, to show us where the two had been taken, from the ER, and we now found them—in separate rooms as Jordan had instructed. As we were about to enter Merry's ward, the nurse remarked to Jordan, "How strange is this, Doctor Ashton? … Your one patient, Mrs. Connaught, who is not yet fully conscious, keeps calling out for 'Jordie', and Doctor Connaught next door, can only mumble the name of someone called 'Biddy!' "

To make that already strange situation even more weird, when Merry did open her eyes, the first words she said were, "Jordie, please keep his grandmother away from Tris! They hate each other, and she terrifies him!" And the next were, "Was Fransie hurt?"

Her concern for 'Mary's little lamb' was natural, and what she had said about Tristan made it easier to understand why Jordan had left the puzzling admonition that Mrs. Burkett, Tristan's only remaining, close relative in this country, was not to come to the hospital. When I questioned Jordan later, he explained: "I had suspected for some time that Tris was on drugs, and alcohol exacerbated his erratic behaviour, but I only recalled this morning, when I smelled the drink on his breath so early in the day, how extremely upset he was when he heard that his grandmother was coming to stay. I believe that he only began drinking to excess after her arrival.

"I don't know why this should be, but, what I do know now, is that he must have hit the bottle the moment he woke up this morning. However, why he was in the vicinity of the clinic, at that time of the morning, I cannot understand!"

Jordan and I left Jasper to be alone with his children while we went in search of Fransie, and we were enormously relieved to learn from Reggie, who, with the child's grandmother, was sitting beside his bed, that the boy's injuries, while severe, were not as critical as we had feared. The main concern was that, in view of the fact that he was so frail, and already receiving treatment for a chronic condition, Fransie would have to be kept in the hospital for an indeterminate length of time.

Having hugged Mrs. Viljoen, and, holding the boy's hand, Jordan was quick to assure her that all expenses would be taken care of, and that, although her grandson was now in a different place, the treatment which was proving to be so beneficial to him, would somehow be continued.—Right there in the hospital, for the time being, and later, if necessary, transport would be provided for him to attend the former clinic.

The child was not so drowsy that he could not follow our conversation. *"Sonder die tannie?"* ("Without the auntie?"), he protested, trying to sit up. And then anxiously: *"Het die tannie ook seergekry?...Waar is sy?* ("Was the auntie also hurt?...Where is she?")

"Sy het 'n bietjie seergekry," Jordan told him, *"maar sy sal môre vir jou kom kuier!"* ("She was slightly hurt...but she will come and see you tomorrow!")

Meredith was brought home the following day, Christmas Eve, but it was only on the seventeenth day after Christmas that Tristan fully regained consciousness. And it was only after the specialist, whom Jordan had called in as a 'consult', was able to venture the opinion that Tris would live at all, that we knew that his spinal cord had been affected. His legs were paralysed, and the damage to his spine was such that he might never walk again. Tristan Connaught, the handsome, self-sufficient, sportsman...twice champion of his golf club...would probably have to spend the rest of his life in a wheelchair!

CHAPTER TEN

And so that is how Bridget Williams, born Dewey, and Jasper Hilliard came to start off their married life in Bryanston, Gauteng; in the home of Jordan Ashton—in his parents' suite!

When Jasper and I went with Jordan to fetch Meredith home from the hospital, she was wide awake, and well aware of all that had happened, and it was one of the supreme moments of my own life, when, with tears streaming down her cheeks and standing unsteadily on her own feet, she reached up to put her good arm around my neck, and said to her father: "Thank you for giving me a mother, Daddy! I hope you showed her my email, to let her know how much Susie and I love her, and how very blessed we are to have such a resourceful, discriminating father!"

By the time she was done, we were both crying; and after such a speech, she subsided willingly into the wheelchair Jordie had brought for her. I'm sure that was the first time the staff of that institution had seen Doctor Ashton personally wheel a patient into the elevator. If any of them had accompanied us all the way to the underground parking of the hospital, they might have been as touched as I was to see with what tenderness he lifted her from the chair, and how carefully he set her down on the pillows he had placed in the car, to ensure that the pain of her dislocated shoulder was not aggravated. Back at his home, I watched him almost reverently lift her out of the car again, and then—with Jasper going ahead to open doors—carry her into the house, up the stairs, and lay her down gently on her bed.

"There now, Miss Muffet," he said, smiling, as he removed her slippers for her, "you're safely in your own bed now, and I shan't let any big spiders come and frighten you away!" They seemed to be talking a secret language, but the scene was so poignant, and his gentleness so moving, that I did not want to spoil the moment by thinking too much about what it meant.

I watched her being settled as comfortably as was possible for her, under the circumstances, and, then, kneeling down next to her bed, I felt that there was something I should make clear to her, and to Jordie.

"I am not your mother yet, Merry-love—although I can't wait to be. Your father and I have not eloped in the meantime, without your knowledge...!"

It was after that, that Jordan came to where Jasper and I had gone to sit quietly for a while in the suite that had been made available to him, Jasper, and Susan, for their use, and the expression on Jordie's face prepared us for something serious.

"Auntie Bid, and Professor," he said earnestly, "there is something I have to confess to you. In desperation I have had to share this with my parents and my sister—which I somehow found myself doing in a weak moment, when the burden was simply too great for me to carry alone—but I can assure you that Meredith knows nothing of this.

"First I have to apologize for any undue affection I showed towards Merry just now, but I just could not restrain myself. I am deeply in love with Meredith—no, more than that—I *love* Meredith! She means more than life itself to me, but I promise you that I shall curb myself in future—which will not be easy. I shall also make it a priority to find her another physician.

Someone in whom I have confidence and in whose hands she will be safe!"

Later that evening, when the roundtable discussions began, concerning how Tristan was to be cared for in the foreseeable future, we could come up with only one, feasible plan. He would need a private nurse in the house, I was a nurse, and I also happened to be the person for whom he kept calling, in his delirium. Other plans could be made later.

Jasper saw the sense in this, and was prepared to let Mieta and his reliable Bushmen, some of whom had been there long before he had come on the scene, take care of *Blouspruit,* but that could not be a permanent arrangement. Among other responsibilities, he had a contract to fulfil. The only realistic plan was thus that we would remain in Johannesburg until Tristan was ready to travel, and then Jasper and I would take him home with us, and care for him on the farm—which would mean that Meredith would have to come back, too.

My Jasper is nothing if not decisive. I was quite shocked when, out of the blue, he took my hand and announced, very firmly, "Look, my dear people, I'm willing to be flexible, and will try to be as accommodating as I possibly can, but I have waited for longer than you know, to marry this woman, and even if I have to marry her right here, in this house, we're getting married! Now kindly make all your other plans around that contingency!"

As surprised as I was, I was not too overcome to say my piece.

"I'd like nothing better!" I said, and I knew that I was blushing. "But then I'll need you all to pray for Adriaan Prinsloo to find someone to replace me, permanently!"

"I think your prayers are about to be answered, my darling," Jasper said, with a twinkle in his eye, and giving me a squeeze in front of all those people. "I'm afraid the North Pole is too far from here for your Christmas present to arrive by sleigh, but would it do if it were to be dropped off in the Kalahari by helicopter? And perhaps a few days late?

"I have not bought your present yet, because, rather than do so in *Spoors-einde*, I had looked forward to taking you shopping in some, big, exclusive store—and of course making a stop at a jewellers' on the way—but circumstances have made that impossible for the moment. Anyway if you will marry me soon, I promise to provide your little doctor with a treasure; albeit not one as valuable as you. An old friend in Pretoria, who was once very helpful to me when we...when we...when there was sickness at *Blouspruit*, has been on the alert for someone who is capable, adventurous, impervious-to-extreme-heat, and preferably a middle-aged lady—we don't want your Adriaan led into temptation now, do we?—and he thinks he has found her!"

We did not have the turkey for Christmas dinner, and Boxing Day was not spent around the pool with watermelon and iced drinks! Felicity, Jordan, and Susie, with Jasper's help, did the best they could, to see that we were all fed, while I was obliged to stay close to Tristan's bedside. It was not so bad when he was in a deep coma, but for some reason I could not fathom, as he began to surface from it, his very obvious torment was only alleviated by having me sit at his bedside, holding his hand, and talking unremittingly. This went on for many days...

I've used the word 'torment', but perhaps 'terror' would be a better one, for I had never seen a grown man—not even when confronted by a snake in the Kalahari—quite so petrified as Tristan would periodically become. I did not know that a man could actually shriek, but Tristan certainly did!—He shrieked with fear! Many times! Then I would see him again as a small child, and, helpless to assuage his fear, I could only smooth the hair away from his burning forehead, hold his hand, and sometimes kiss his cheek. My heart bled for Thora as I did this, because her son seemed to find some respite from the horror when I kept repeating, "I'm here, Tris, just as I was on the day you were born. I'll take care of you, lovey! Don't you be afraid!"—But all that really helped was when I prayed for him to find peace, which I did, constantly.

In caring for Tristan, I think Jordan had the biggest problem of us all, because it was difficult for him to prescribe any kind of narcotic or other habit-forming painkiller, knowing that Tris was already addicted to so many different drugs. I had telephoned Adriaan Prinsloo in *Spoors-einde*, as promised, and because I knew very well how meticulous Doc had been about where he put what, in his medical bag, I was able to tell Adriaan exactly what I wanted him to check. Because, on some farms, there was only the light provided by candles or paraffin lamps by which to work, and Doc's eyesight was no longer of the best, everything always had to be put in the same place, and in the correct order, and whenever I had to restock his supplies for him, I had adhered strictly to the routine.

When Adriaan came back to the telephone and told me that there was no morphine in the bag, and that some other narcotics—including palliatives which Doc carried for cancer and other terminal patients—were missing, that was precisely what I had expected. I felt quite sick when I recalled that Tristan had been there for Doc's funeral, and realized what ready access there had been to a bag that was always kept in the same place.—On Doc Hugo's desk!

I admit that there were still times when I wanted to yell: "*Stop the world I want to get off!*" But I was given the strength to stick it out with Tristan. As stunned as I was by the confirmation of what I had suspected, I could no longer be as disgusted with Tris as I had been before. In the past I had told him frankly when I found his behaviour despicable! I had berated him for his shortcomings on many occasions, but somehow, sitting by him in that ward, hour after hour, any recollection of past transgressions vanished. Instead I felt every bit as protective of him as I had done long ago, when he had only been Thora's baby with the smiling, Irish eyes!

I knew that addicts in withdrawal suffered abominably, but never, in many years of nursing, had I seen anything like what this man was going through, and very soon my murmurings of love and care were no longer contrived to suit a purpose. They were sincere and I meant them. When I kissed that poor, bruised and swollen face, or gently wiped his brow, it was because I wanted to, and could not do otherwise.

One morning very early, as I waited for Jordan to come and take me home for a shower and breakfast, I began to pray earnestly that I might be given the discernment to understand Tristan's agony, and suddenly I knew, clearly, that we had been putting the cart before the horse. Tristan was not going through this grossly abnormal purgatory because he had used drugs. He had resorted to them, in the first place, to numb him; to render him insensible to the torture of something else! And, even as a young child, Jordan had been the only person in the world who had sensed that torture!

That night, as we were sitting round the dining room table enjoying the cottage pie that Mrs. Burkett had made for us, I began to report on my day with Tristan—merely speaking of his pain, which others might consider normal after such an accident, and making no mention whatsoever of drug addiction or withdrawal symptoms. I did not expect any comments other than profound sympathy for a seriously injured person, but, sad to say, Tristan's grandmother was, as usual, of a different mind.

It disturbed Meredith whenever she heard Mrs. Burkett say this, and I was furious with the old lady when she remarked, as she had done for the umpteenth time before: "I'm not surprised! *That boy has had the devil in him since the day he was born!*" This time I was astonished when Merry, who had come down to join us at the meal, suddenly flared up. "That is a dreadful thing to say about anyone, Grandma! How can you be so cruel?"

Taken aback, the old lady stuck out her chin and responded, angrily: "And that is not very respectful of you, young lady! That boy is possessed, I tell you. *Bewitched!*—And the sooner you face it the better!" With that she pushed her chair back so violently that it banged against the dresser behind her, and stalked out.

Something compelled me to look at Felicity just then. She met my gaze, and, opening her eyes wide, nodded significantly at me.

"Remember Jamie," was all she said, and I knew exactly what she meant!

"And Clifford!" was my laconic reply. "And Ash!"

***

How many times had I not prayed for guidance during the course of my life, and had my prayers wondrously answered! I was not surprised that the woman who had loved Jamie Ashton—'James Ashton the third'—and I, Bridget, would simultaneously connect Mrs. Burkett's spiteful words about

Tristan, with Jamie. I knew that Jordan was not fazed by this, either. Having spent many hours volunteering at the *Eugenie Beauclaire* centre near Bethlehem, he was well acquainted with the story of how his uncle's dedication to the betterment of black children, had contributed to the imprisonment, and later self-imposed exile of Clifford Connaught, Tristan's father. He knew very well how, in time, that had also led to the wrongful arrest of his own father, Benjamin Ashton. What was least surprising to me was the prompt answer to my earnest prayer that I might be helped to understand Tristan's agony...

During the apartheid years in South Africa, the very fact that an American would come to live in the country, and devote his life to black people, was immediately suspect. As far as the government was concerned, there had already been too much interference, and Clifford, the British-born rector of a church in a black area, erred only in his close friendship with that American with whom he had once worked at a Mission station in Lesotho—where, it was believed, refugees fleeing South Africa were being sheltered.

It was more than ten years after the day on which units of *Umkhonto we Sizwe* ('Spear of the Nation'), then a new, independent body, formed by Africans, and regarded by the authorities as the militant wing of the ANC, had carried out the first of its planned attacks against government installations, particularly those connected with the policy of apartheid and race discrimination. In its manifesto of 1961, this body had declared, *"Umkhonto we Sizwe"* will be at the front line of the people's defence. It will be the fighting arm of the people against the government and its policies of race oppression."

It became common knowledge that members of the unit were being sent out of the country to Zambia, Russia—and, it was said, to China—for training as terrorists, and, among them, were three young men, talented musicians, befriended by Jamie Ashton, from the time they were little more than children. They returned from Zambia after some years, blew up a power station and bombed a few other installations, at a time when violence had led to fear, fear to paranoia, then to more violence, and so it had continued. The young men, influenced by their mothers, claimed to have been bewitched, and coerced into doing this, by Jamie, who had died a few years earlier.

This also happened to be a time when several Anglican priests, and church leaders of other denominations, had been arrested. Clifford Crawford was immediately suspected of collaboration with the young malefactors, because of the liberality of his church, the fact that they had once been parishioners, and, mainly, because of his close association with what later came to be known as the *Eugenie Beauclaire Centre*, and its patron—James Ashton!

It would be difficult for anyone who was not born in this country, to understand how, and why, Felicity and I, and, especially Benjamin Ashton's son, a physician and man of science, would connect any of this with Tristan Connaught's pitiable state. We knew that we had to tell Meredith and her father the truth, and, without adequate explanation, what we believed to be the case might have been dismissed as balderdash! I believe, however, that what we revealed, though tragic, finally brought a measure of comfort to Merry, whose mounting depression was being ascribed to shock. Little did we know how bitterly she was suffering; consumed with guilt for an almost incomprehensible reason!

The three of us, Jasper, Felicity and I, were alone with her when she first admitted this, and I'm sure she would never have done so in Jordan's presence. But he was out on a call, while Reg sat with Tristan at the hospital. I had earlier helped Meredith into bed, while Susie was taking a shower, and Jasper was reading to Merry when we came to talk.

I began by trying to describe what Tristan was going through, and was thoroughly alarmed when this caused Meredith to burst into a storm of weeping that bordered on the hysterical.

"Hush now, Merry-love." I tried to soothe her, but sitting beside her on the bed, it was difficult to hold her too close in case I hurt her shoulder. "There, there. We know that this has been a dreadful time for you!…Have a good cry and perhaps you'll feel better!" Her father's jaw was clenched as he helplessly watched his daughter writhe in distress.

"It was all my fault!" she repeatedly cried out. "None of this would have happened if I had not been so cruel!"

"What do you mean sweetheart," Jasper kept asking anxiously. "What did you do that was so terrible?"

"I pushed Tristan aside when he tried to kiss me the night before. Oh, Daddy, I don't know what has come over him! He was never like this when were at *Blouspruit*, although he did kiss me once or twice, but since we have come back from visiting Zhaynie, he won't leave me alone.—And, oh, God forgive me, how am I going to tell you this? I don't love him, Daddy! I don't even like him any more. I love Jordie, and even though he will never know how much, Tristan suspected it. He kept accusing me of it, and then he would grab hold of me, so tightly that I could not escape, and almost smother me with kisses—which made me sick to my stomach because he smelled so ghastly. But I need not have been cruel! If I had been less angry, more tactful, or perhaps more gentle, he would not have been driven to do what he did!"

We were baffled, and I interjected. "What do you mean, Merry. How do mean that he smelled bad?"

Her response was staggering.

"*Dagga*," she said. "I had smelt this before, but was always able to repel him, until recently!"

"You could recognize that?" My mouth hung open!

"Of course," she said, looking puzzled, but no longer crying. "I have a few samples of it in my lab. In fact I have written about my analysis of the various components in 'pot', in my thesis, as I have about the common or garden Khaki weed, *Tagetes minuta*, which is of the genus known as marigold. Because neither is essentially a Kalahari plant, I may not use what I have written, but I have tried to compare the oils in cannabis with those of the Baobab and Khaki weed. The Khaki weed, although in its raw state it smells worse than marihuana—particularly when you walk on it!—has many therapeutic uses, unlike *Cannabis Sativa* from which *dagga* is derived. While it may be remedial for cancer patients, *dagga* is a poison not to be indulged in lightly by others!"

I was completely transfixed. Once Meredith got started on her favourite topic, her research, there was no stopping her, and I was grateful to see that she had temporarily been diverted from the cause of her distress.

"I didn't start off to study cannabis," she explained, "again because it is not part of what I hope to submit, but my interest was piqued when Mieta came to me one day, greatly concerned because one of Platjie's relatives smoked it, and had smuggled some into *Blouspruit*. And so I began a study of it, which I might weave into my thesis somehow. Tristan didn't necessarily have to come too close for me to notice it, and when I detected the odour of it in his clothes, and even in his hair, I was more scared than repelled, but I went about it the wrong way.

"I had read about court cases and other incidences during the course of which it had been proved, over and over again, that in most cases, addiction to more serious drugs had begun by experimentation with *dagga,* and the worst of it is, that it takes about a month for the body to rid itself of a complex substance called THC, contained in even one cigarette. I won't go into an explanation right now of what THC is, but research has shown that, because it is so slowly metabolized, it can, in certain parts of the body, take up to six months!

"I have learned that Tristan gets furious if anyone dares to find fault with him, or criticize anything he does, so I did nothing about it, but, one day, when I was right at the back of Jordie's garden, deciding where to start the herb garden Uncle Ash had suggested to me, I came across several plants, which I recognized instantly, and I pulled them out. I had just thrown them away when Tristan got out of the pool and saw me, and rather than upset him, I started to talk very fast about the herbs I intended planting, and how I was sorry to have to lose the marigolds which seemed to be thriving there!"

"That explains something I heard Gloria telling Jordan, but,"—and I hated having to do this to her—"what was it that made you think that you had somehow contributed to Tristan's behaviour on the day of the accident. What led up to that?"

She remained thoughtfully silent for a minute, and the trembling of her mouth was evidence of the fact that her distress went very deep. Finally, when she replied, it was at her father she looked, while responding.

"Daddy, I feel so bad about Tris! I don't love him and I never will. I heard Zhaynie and other girls discuss schoolgirl crushes when I was in Nelspruit, and what struck me painfully was that the reminiscences of experiences which reduced them to helpless laughter, were those of long ago; some before they were even teenagers. Antoinette had them all laughing about the little boy who had kissed her behind the piano in Grade One—but my first experience came at the age of twenty-three! You were so right to talk about my having no yardstick by which to compare Tristan, or what I felt about him. A crush is all that it was, Daddy, and now it's too late! I love Jordie, and this time I'm sure...as sure as I'm alive...but no matter what it takes, I'll stand by Tris because I am to blame for what happened to him!"

"But how?" Felicity, who had been listening intently, made herself heard for the first time.

"I have had time to think about Tristan's behaviour the night before. Now I realize that his unpleasant clutching at me, was desperate. He clung to me for a reason I could not define and I told him that I found him repulsive! I have sensed, too late, that Tris lives in terror every moment of his life. He resorts to boasting, outrageous behaviour, and fast cars—anything that will provide him with a measure of self-esteem and distraction—because otherwise he would feel himself drowning in something he does not understand! I haven't had much experience of life, but I think that he is the saddest, most desperate, and most pathetic person I have ever come across!

"When I pushed him away, with the excuse that I had to go to bed early in order to be up in time to get to the clinic, he forbade me to go. In my ignorance I retaliated. I should have known better, because he was not himself, and I had begun to recognize the signs. But it was then that, with good reason, he began to accuse me of being in love with Jordan, and, as I struggled free of him, and rushed towards the door, he shouted after me: "You're not going there tomorrow, young lady, and you're not working in that clinic with Jordan any more, even if I have to come and stop you, myself!"

It was difficult to offer any comment that would have been appropriate at that moment, and none of the rest of us saw Jordan in the doorway, but Meredith suddenly did. She put her hand over her mouth with profound dismay at what she had just disclosed, wincing with physical pain as she did so. She knew that he had heard her, and when I saw the look that passed between them, I felt as though my heart would break.

Again it was Felicity who broke the silence. "It must have been dreadful for anyone to hear, over and over again, for most of your life, that you are possessed of the devil. Jamie always maintained that one does not say to a child, 'You are a liar!...You will never amount to anything!' or use other words that are damning. I admire you for taking issue with Tristan's grandmother on that, Merry. Has she not realized that what she has so often said directly to Tris, and about him to others, could prove to be a self-fulfilling prophecy? It is a curse! And no matter how we are all feeling about ourselves, and everything else at this moment, we have to get Mrs. Burkett away from here before Tristan comes home!...Someone must speak to Ash or Father Peter about this, and we're going to have to pray incessantly for protection!"

Finding it in himself to think of Tristan, while having to recover from the inner storm that must have been raging in him since overhearing Meredith's declaration, Jordan valiantly pulled himself together, came in, and sat down with us.

"Curses are real," he affirmed, "and I believe what you are saying, Aunt Felicity. So would my father. To say that anyone is 'possessed' means that he or she is 'owned' by the devil, and that cannot be. It is as vindictive to say so, as it is cruel and dangerous!

"Having lived here, and in Louisiana, and after being on missions in many other countries, my dad has often spoken of this. It is an expression he abhors! In this modern day and age, the word 'demon' has been substituted for 'devil' and I believe it is possible for people to be *oppressed* by demons. They can be said to be 'demonized', but they cannot be 'possessed'...

"Aunt Felicity, as you were the closest of anyone, to my uncle, Jamie, will you please explain to us what you consider to have led to the accusation of his having 'bewitched' the three 'terrorists', how he might have incurred the wrath of some of the *Sangomas*, and how you think that this is connected to the cursing of Tristan....After that, if you don't mind, Auntie Bid, I'm sure we would all like your opinion. You were one of the people who went to see Aunt Thora on the De Beers' farm regularly, while she and Timothy—who must have been about three years old then—and Aunt Felicity were living there, after Uncle Clifford had been obliged to go into exile. As you were also present at Tristan's birth, I shall ask you please to tell us about the day you visited Aunt Thora, about the day the young men were executed, and about a subsequent visit by their mothers to aunt Thora...

"Please take your time, because this is all very important. I've done some phoning, and have been to speak to a colleague, on my way home from seeing my patient, so several matters have now been settled, which I hope will make life easier for all. Now so I suggest that we just take one step at a time, and see how far that gets us!"

"Well," said Felicity, "perhaps I should start with the day when Jamie first saw the children. He had come, one Saturday, to the library where I worked, and asked me for help finding a book. I didn't have it, but promised to order for him, and next thing I found myself accepting his invitation to join him for lunch. Those Ashton genes are very strong, I might tell you. If you see Jordan, you see his father. And if you see his father, you would have seen Jamie. For me I think that was love at first sight.

"After lunch, we emerged from the steak house to find a crowd gathered on the sidewalk, and there we saw three small, black children—thereafter referred to lovingly by Jamie as his 'piccanins'; not being derogatory at all, but because that is what he would affectionately have called them in Louisiana. One was playing a 'slap bass', ingeniously manufactured from an empty, three-ply tea crate, a broom handle, and with one string—probably a fishing line or some other kind of twine. The notes were changed by simply moving the broom handle back and forth, to vary the tension, and the boy succeeded amazingly well in providing the rhythm accompaniment for another child, who was playing some African kwela tune on a penny whistle. A third danced with all the abandon of undisguised delight.

"Some years later, when I met Jordan's father, and described the scene and the sound, Ash said it was as if he had been there in person. He could relive his own childhood ecstasy when Jamie and the black folk had made music, and he could instantly picture his brother's reaction that day.

" 'I'll bet you anything,' Ash exclaimed, 'that Jamie said he wished he had his clarinet with him!' "

"And that's exactly what he did say!" Felicity smiled at the memory. "He emptied his pockets into their hat—but that wasn't all!...If he didn't then persuade the children—having established that they lived quite near to the De Beer's farm—to get into Aunt Minnie de Beer's truck and go home with him!

" It was Tristan's father who told Ben that the kids hadn't taken much persuading to stay long enough for them to teach him the song they had been playing, and then for him to jam with them on his clarinet!"—She looked across at Jordan, smiling affectionately at him. "I can see you doing exactly the same, Jordie, given the chance!

"Sadly it was those same children, whom he loved so much, who were later brainwashed to the extent that they would commit sabotage; but the greatest tragedy of all was that Jamie should in any way have been connected to that—years after his death!

"Even greater than his passion for music, was his love of God. Of Christ. Ash described to me once how he, walking about in Jamie's centre, could at times only stop in amazement at some of what he saw. He was not yet a believer, himself, and while he found the many religious exhortations like *'Love thy neighbour as thyself'* and *'Seek ye first the kingdom of God and all else shall be added unto thee,'*—in three different languages—a bit much, and felt himself growing uptight, he had to admit that his brother had certainly gone all out to carry out whatever 'mandate' he had been given.

"Soon Ash, the American businessman, fresh out of the States, was learning a great deal about why his brother had all those exhortations pasted up on the walls of the centre, and why the children had to recite them every day.

"It was Clifford Connaught who told him, 'There's a lot one has to know about African people. Every tribe, every nation has 'exactly the same, only different' practices, beliefs and superstitions—as some comedian I once heard, might have put it. Ritual murders still occur in Lesotho from time to time, and I know that many members of the Mission congregation there, who, having come to the priest for help with some domestic situation or another, would still, immediately after that, go in search of the *dilaoli*, the soothsayer, to 'throw the bones' in order to divine the origin of the problem.'

"Thora, Tristan's mother, having been born and bred in what was then called Basutoland, by the whites, loved and knew a great deal about these people, too, but Clifford and Jamie had lived and worked among them, across the border of the Free State.

They knew that the *Sotho*, like every other tribe, were ever on their guard against spirits and would tell of *Moremo, the evil one,* from whom the spirit is only free after death, and of *Mosimo,* the beautiful place where the dead will find happiness.

"One of the things that particularly stabbed Jamie to the heart, while he had worked with Clifford, in *Hlotse*, perhaps better known to us older folk as *Leribe,* and which greatly influenced what he did at the centre, was that, despite one-hundred-and-forty years of dedicated work on the part of missionaries, ancestor worship in various forms still survived and still does, albeit with Christian teachings. He took all this, what he saw as confusion, terribly to heart. For instance, their supreme being, known as *Molimo,* may only be approached through the intercession of the spirits of the ancestors. That was why his, Jamie's, own prayer of thanksgiving—for the knowledge that we can 'come boldly to the throne of Grace', because of Jesus Christ—was written in so many languages in this centre. It is why so much of what was posted there, was also recited daily—for the benefit of those who could not read.

"Jamie, as you must know, greatly revered Our Lady, the mother of Jesus, but he took every line that 'jumped out' at him from Scripture, as a personal instruction, and could never be convinced that it was necessary to go to God through an intermediary—no matter how special or how holy! He would always refer anyone who believed otherwise, to the promise that Jesus is already interceding for us, and quote Paul's assurance that, when we do not know how to pray, the Holy Spirit makes intercession for us 'with groanings that cannot be uttered.' "

"What is a *Sangoma*, Aunt Felicity?" Meredith asked, apologizing for the interruption. "I'm wondering if there are such beings among the Bushmen. I must find out!"

"Although called 'witchdoctors' by some, in most cases *Sangomas* are seen as herbalists and healers, Merry. I'm sure Jordie can tell you that in South Africa a large percentage of the black population still consult a traditional healer, or *Sangoma*, before approaching a western medical facility, and it is being recognized that they can be an important resource to ensure that people get the right information about HIV/AIDS. But what incurred the wrath of some of them in the vicinity of the care centre, was the philosophy that was being ingrained there. Ancestor worship is very strong. It is the belief, among all tribes and clans, that ancestors are only seen in dreams, and the *Sangomas*, alone, are said to have the special powers to communicate with them. They were there to be consulted when anyone wished to communicate with a departed ancestor—while Jamie taught that through Jesus we could come boldly to the throne of grace. Who knows how much he and the centre were hated, and through them, Clifford, when, as the rector of the local church, he was made responsible for administration of the centre, which had been left to the parish in Jamie's will.

"Now it's Biddy's turn," Felicity announced—and mine was the truly painful information to impart!

"On the day that the young men were executed," I took up the story, "Thora was already showing signs of going into labour, when a crowd of women turned up at the De Beers' farm.—Do you remember the awful sounds they made, Felicity?" I asked her, and she nodded. "Some ululating and others shouting, and they would not leave until three of them were admitted to where Thora was sitting in the kitchen of the farm. They virtually swarmed her, muttering in *Sesotho*. One of the women looked her in the eye and spat on her. Another spat on the floor, intoning, 'The agony of your son will be greater than mine, this day!' And a third chanted, over and over, pressing her hand to Thora's abdomen and speaking to the unborn child, *'You will bring only sorrow to your mother!'* And yet another hissed, *'Cursed be the child you carry in your belly this day! He will never find rest!'*

"Only much later, when Thora was already in the hospital, did Uncle Charlie, who knew the language better than we did, translate for us. But Thora, rocking back and forth, in great distress must certainly have understood all that was said, and I'm sure she must have been in abject terror. She seemed afraid even to repeat those words. Perhaps she feared that saying the words out loud would make her nightmare real. That spittle on her face was very, very real, and she kept trying to wash it off.

"After Uncle Charlie had, for our benefit, interpreted what had been said, we made a point of being very casual about the occurrence, trying to persuade her that none of what had taken place was to be taken seriously, but I firmly believe that nothing so frightening could ever be forgotten!

"You know," it occurred to me suddenly, "Mrs. Burkett might have been cruel in putting it like that. But she was there, with her daughter, that day. She has lived among people who performed ritual murders. She knows of *Sangomas* who collected body parts of children, and she has become exceedingly superstitious. Who knows how terrified she might have been of Tristan's mere presence in her house—as if he could contaminate her! Imagine that poor, confused little kid being sent to live with her—of all people—when he was still so small!

"What I'd like to know," I added, thinking aloud, "is why his parents would dream of sending such a young child away from them at all! It is not something I would have expected either Clifford or Thora to do, without very good reason!"

"I think they must have done so out of sheer desperation," Jordie observed thoughtfully. "He hated being there with them! He was never happy in Louisiana, except when he was with us. Although I was younger, I never knew Tris to be anything but afraid, but I could never fathom precisely what it was that scared him—and if I couldn't, I'm positive that his folks couldn't either. He seldom confided in anyone other than my father and me, and although I tried to understand some of what he would sometimes quite involuntarily come out with, it was far too difficult for a kid like me to take seriously.

"Let me give you an example.... He was terrified of Spanish Moss, and it took a great deal of courage to make his way through it to our house. Only now that I am older can I appreciate how brave it was of him to go with me to my favourite place, and how much he must have wanted to be with me, to venture there, because he said that there were always eyes looking out of the trees at him.

"Perhaps I should explain that Spanish moss, hanging in strands, sometimes up to six feet long, can grow so thickly on the limbs of trees that it blocks out sunlight, and can be quite creepy for anyone. Even more so to a nervous child trying to fight his way through it. In our part of Louisiana it is often associated with Southern Gothic imagery because of the rather 'gothic' effect is has on the area around it.

"Well, there's a place with a dense canopy of overhanging Spanish moss, where, in the damp heat, and like my uncle, I like to go and play music. It was in this special place, which is protected by a dense wall of cypress, and encircled by live oak and elm, that my uncle Jamie would play his clarinet, and I often regret taking Tris there, because I notice that, even now, when he's outside on the golf course, if he lands up among the trees he can't get out quickly enough!"

Jordan then, as promised, filled us in on the 'matters' he had managed to settle.

"I have spoken to Theuns van Schalkwyk, a first-class physician, and one of the people joining us in Matt's proposed support program for persons suffering from PTSD. He will be looking after Meredith from now on, and will come and check up on her tomorrow, and every day after that, until he is satisfied that her shoulder is back to normal, and that she is not showing any signs of delayed shock. One of the saddest parts of all this, is that, even when she is once more able to move her arm freely, she and I will not have the joy of playing music together anymore.

"No one knows what the future holds for any of us, so the best Doctor van Schalkwyk and I can come up with, in the present circumstances and at short notice, is to combine our practices, sharing Tristan's patient load between us. Theuns has always admired our premises, and will be happy to move into Tristan's offices.

"Provision will soon have to be made for Tristan.—He will need a special bed and other apparatus. Fortunately he is in good physical shape, despite what he has been doing to himself, and golf has made his upper body strong.—In time he will have to use his arms a great deal, as he learns how to hoist himself out of one place to another. Once he commences therapy, providing he comes out of the coma soon, his strength can still be a point in his favour, in his rehabilitation. There is no way he can be taken to *Blouspruit*, until that has been completed. Even after that it is going to take someone with a great deal more physical strength than Merry's, to care for him. But we'll meet that eventuality when we come to it.

"Now," he went on, as dispassionately as he could—and I don't know that I had ever felt as sorry for anyone, or seen a man's face so ravaged—"about Meredith and me...This has indeed been a night of disclosures and discoveries. I'm afraid you have been left in no doubt as to our mutual feelings for one another. It appears that we both love one another...." He stared fixedly through the window and I saw his face working as he tried to disguise his emotion. He was close to tears. "This will be hard for us....I promise you that I have never kissed her, except perhaps to wish her a Merry Christmas. Never as a lover—which does not mean that I did not want to—but we shall have to face the fact that nothing can come of this.

"In the circumstances, I believe that it would be best for us, and the most fair to Tristan and Merry, both, if she and he can go back to *Blouspruit*, as soon as possible, but that again will depend on Tristan's progress."

"I agree with everything you have said, Jordan," Jasper said, clearly moved and shaking his head in bewilderment. "May I tell you how much I admire and respect you, and how grateful Biddy and I are for your unselfishness, and the practical manner in which you are conducting yourself—in a situation unequalled by anything I have ever heard of before! I am in awe!"

In spite of the sling, Meredith had her hands over her face, so that none of us could see her expression, but her shoulders were shaking convulsively, and I was swallowing hard. I wondered when I would be permitted to wake from the nightmare of all this!

But Jordan was speaking again, and he had become so authoritative that when he spoke we all listened. "My father and I, together, will see that Merry and Tris are provided for, and I know of no place where they will be better off than with

449

you, Auntie Bid, and you, Uncle Jasper." This was the first time he had addressed Jasper in this manner. And again I came close to bawling when he said, "I only wish that you two were going to be *my* parents-in-law!"

Then he shrugged his shoulders, and stood up. "I think it's time I got you back at the hospital, Auntie Bid, to take over from Reg. He has a full day tomorrow!"

"I'm coming with you," said Felicity.

"And so am I," said Jasper.

"Thank you. All three of you," Jordie said. "And while you go to be with Tris, I'll look in briefly on Fransie. Perhaps Susie would like to come for the ride, and see him, too. I'm sure the young fellah would like that! Especially when he learns that she is his favourite *'tannie's'* sister."

Outside of Merry's bedroom, he drew us aside and remarked brokenly, "She should not be going through this, especially after having lived such a sheltered life! Meredith is far too young to have to carry such an enormous burden!"

"If it is anyone's fault," Jasper replied, with a crack in his own voice, "it is mine, and mine alone! If I had not insisted that Tristan marry her, before taking her away, this would never have happened. No, I withdraw that!...I should never have let her come under any circumstances!"

"Then," said Jordie, with a crooked smile, "I should never have grown to know and love her. Nor would I have had the pleasure of having you in my home!"

Once Reg, and then Felicity and Jasper, had spent time in the ward with me, and their presence had not appeared to disturb Tristan, life became easier for me. He, Tristan remained unconscious, but heretofore he had seemed to know when other people were there, and his agitation had increased.

He tolerated it when Felicity ventured to kiss him, but while Reggie's presence did not appear to upset him, he screamed when he felt his hands on him. It was strangely different with Jordan, who did not take a lunch break, had been popping in on his way to and from work each day, stopped to examine Tris while he was on rounds, and then came again after supper every night. What was so astonishing was that Tristan stopped writhing, and a noticeable peace came over the poor, tortured man, the moment Jordie laid hands on him!

One afternoon we were surprised by the news that, as an elder of his church, Jordan had been able to arrange with his vicar, for Jasper and me to be married there, on the following Saturday, and arrangements were made accordingly.

Reggie sat with Tris at the hospital, to set my mind at rest, but Jordan was there to give me away. I was also blessed to have two lovely daughters to be my bridesmaids, and Felicity for a matron-of-honour, when I was married to Jasper Hilliard. While we spent one night in a very nice hotel, Susie moved into the bedroom I had been using, and then, until we were able to return to the Kalahari, Jasper and I lived together in Ash and Amy-Lee's suite.

There are many details of my happy wedding day that I shall never forget. Of course there is the memory of my amazing new husband, and the look on his face when he slipped the ring onto my finger. I tell you, listening to that man making his vows beside me, in that beautiful voice, my knees were weak! I had a sense of Mark looking down on us to give us his blessing, but I was in awe when Jasper later told me, in our hotel suite, that he had felt the same presence, and it was as though Mark were there, saying to him, "I'm happy that she has you to take care of her for me, my friend. Treasure her always!"

Of course I shed a few tears when he told me that, but any other tears, apart from those of joy, were precipitated by the look on Jordan's face when, erect and well turned-out, as usual, he stood behind us at the altar, with Meredith at his side. When it was time for me to hand her my bouquet, she, trying to take hold of it with one hand—as she had insisted she was able to do—fumbled, and Jordan took it from her, just in time. Hearing her smothered gasp I involuntarily turned around, to see them holding onto the flowers together, and to have to witness them looking at one another, at that moment, as though time stood still, was excruciating!

During the time Jasper and I were away from the house on our 'one-day honeymoon', Jordan had again consulted his father; and Ash, who was back in the States, at *Bentleigh* on Long Island, had to explain apologetically that he was unable to change his plans, and that he could not come sooner. James and Isobel were still with Antoinette in Pietermaritzburg, and James was enjoying his last long break from responsibility, before Ash could finally retire, and hand over the responsibility of running the Ashton consortium, to him.

Ben said that, in any case, no matter when Tristan regained consciousness, this was not, in his opinion, the time to attempt deliverance. Tristan would be too frail, and a hospital, where other patients could well be disturbed, was not a good place for this to be done, either. "Even healing of memories and the severance of generational ties can be disruptive sometimes," he had said to Jordan. "And I don't think that when Tris comes round, he will be up to it, so we'll have to leave that for the moment. I do suggest, however, that you contact Matt Marais' grandparents in the meantime, and discuss this with them. I know that they are back in Kempton Park, from Canada, and I can think of no people more suitable.

"If they can have been instrumental in sorting out your mixed-up father," he went on to say to Jordie, "they can be relied upon to be extremely helpful to Tris. My problems were nowhere near the same, but I was in a mess, and I would not be as happy as I am today; nor at peace, to the extent that I am, if it had not been for those two. God uses them mightily...

"Now about Mrs. Burkett. I'm flying a young man out from the Isando office, for training, and you know how your mother is about these things. She insists that his wife must be with him, so what I suggest, is that we arrange for Mrs. Burkett to come with them as far as New York, stay here with us for a week or so, at *Bentleigh*, and then be taken to be with her children in Louisiana."

"He emailed this to me, for you, Auntie Bid," Jordie said, handing me a page he had printed out for me. "These are the healing prayers my grandfather prayed for my grandmother, and which my dad later prayed over my mother every night, and he asks that whoever sits with Tris should please do the same.

"Here are also a few verses of Scripture for you to use as prayers, praying them on his behalf as though he were speaking them himself!

" 'Isaiah 38:14 *O, Lord, I am oppressed; undertake for me.*'

" 'From Psalm 61: *Hear my cry, O God; attend unto my prayer...when my heart is overwhelmed; lead me to the rock that is higher than I...*'

" 'This can repeatedly be read to him,' Ben wrote: 'Exodus 15: verse 26. *I am the Lord that healeth thee!*' But the one that keeps coming to mind as I pray for Clifford's son, is John 11: verse 4. *'This sickness is not unto death, but for the glory of God!'* "

CHAPTER ELEVEN

When applied to the vicissitudes of the next few months, there was much truth to be found in those much-quoted sentiments about how the best laid plans of mice and men 'were apt to go awry'. Our plans constantly did. In fact I found that expression applicable in so many instances, and quoted it so often, that it bothered me that I could not remember who had coined the expression. Of course my clever Jasper knew at once. "Robbie Burns, my love," he answered promptly. "From his 'Ode to the small mouse' whose nest he had dug up with a plough, and the correct words are actually *'gang aft agley'*—but I'll grant you that they appear to be very apt in the sense in which you use them!"

What a good man he is! I often wondered whether, if he had known to what extent his life was to be disrupted, he would ever have married me, but then he was quick to assure me that it was not his marrying me that had set the chain of events in motion. When one came to think of it, he said, it had all begun when Susie took ill, and then he gave me a kiss and said that, although it hurt him to have to see so much unhappiness around him, the one bright spot was that he had met me again!

I had really expected to be back in the Kalahari well before Easter, and I so looked forward to living at *Blouspruit* with Jasper! I longed to take care of him, in his own home, and I was bothered about leaving my stuff to clutter up Doc's house at a time when Mrs. Gresham, Jasper's specified 'capable, adventurous, impervious-to-extreme-heat, and preferably middle-aged lady' was trying to settle in to her new home and job.

Adriaan, who, professed himself to be more than satisfied with her, assured me, however, that neither she nor he were being inconvenienced in any way. They were very sympathetic, wished only the very best for Jasper and me, and wanted us to be assured that their thoughts were with all of us in Bryanston at this trying time. Apparently Sally Vercueil, bless her kind heart, was rallying around, and had spent a week in the office to show Margaret Gresham where everything was kept, and induct her into the routine. She, Sally, later told me that, needless to say, the corporate tongue of the *dorp* had done much wagging when the news that I was married to Jasper had leaked out, but then again there was no one who did not wish us well. In fact, she said, most of the people had actually remarked, very kindly, that they missed me. She also told me that Adriaan had made it clear that, although he would remain in *Spoors-einde* for the foreseeable future, he did not wish to buy the practice as he was planning to emigrate.

Be that as it may, Jasper and I finally decided, during the third week in January, that the time had come to go home for a few days, and with heavy hearts we left the children in the loving care of Felicity. But I'm running on here! Much had transpired before we actually left.

First of all, flattered and excited at the prospect of flying to the States at the expense and special invitation of Benjamin Ashton, Mrs. Burkett became all fluttery, and anxiously took off for Bethlehem, to go and get her affairs in order, as she put it, in preparation for the great adventure. Another welcome development was that Doctor Theuns, as we called him, was, even while still preparing to move into Tristan's offices, already seeing most of his patients, and the result of this was that Jordan no longer had to respond to another pager in addition to his own.

I was really pleased when Matt Marais' grandparents began to visit Tristan, because we were all beginning to feel the strain, and I not only appreciated the lightening of my own responsibility, but also the effect their prayers were having on Tris. Even in his unconscious state, what happened was almost inconceivable! He would calm down and sometimes seemed to be listening, although only someone who had spent so much time with him during the worst periods of his raving, would have noticed this.

Sometimes he would make a sort of humming sound as he exhaled, which did not emanate from his lips, but seemed to come from within. The closest I can come to a description of this amazing phenomenon was perhaps to compare it with the purring of a kitten. There was one drawback, however, and that was that, immediately after their departure, he would often shout more loudly than before. People who have no experience with demonic oppression would have scoffed at Jacob Marais' explanation that the demons within Tris, determined to make it evident that they were there to stay, would deliberately remain silent while kept at bay by a greater power, only to make their presence known once more, when they felt that covering removed.

This was when I understood Felicity's pertinent injunction that we should 'pray constantly for protection'. She and I had attended every lecture Peter Crawford had given in Bethlehem. We had never missed a seminar conducted by Peter or Ash, and we had gone as far as Bloemfontein to attend a conference at which both had spoken. Yet only now was I was made to recall a statement made once by Ash, in which, referring to the marking of the Israelite dwellings in Egypt with the blood of sheep, on the night of the Passover, to protect them when the angel of death came to kill the first-born of the Egyptians, just so Christians could claim the blood of the Lamb, Jesus Christ, for their protection. This was clearly what Jordan did—for spiritual, not physical protection—and this is what all of us did, after being reminded of those words, by Joey and Jacob Marais.

Tristan has a very dark beard and was rapidly assuming the appearance of a pirate in a Johnny Depp film, except that he looked extremely 'wild', and I was deeply moved when I arrived at the hospital early one morning, to find Jordan giving him a shave. Whereas Tris would scream in the horrifying way that sent chills down the spines of the nurses who attempted to do this, he appeared to tolerate Jordie's ministrations. I ascribed this to the gentle crooning that accompanied the operation, and of which I'm sure Jordan, himself, was unaware.

My admiration for Jordan Ashton mounted by the day! Jasper felt the same. Where that visibly exhausted young man, whose face was often harrowed with his own pain, found the grace to keep doing all he did, and the strength to carry on, could only have been drawn from the source of his tremendous faith. He walked in faith as I have seen few people do. If anyone wore the Armour of God, as St. Paul had instructed us to do, daily, it was Jordie.

It was Meredith who caused us the most grief. She had changed immeasurably, and plainly found it difficult to emerge from the deep pit of depression into which she had descended. Nothing we could say or do for her would temper her guilt. She carried it with her, constantly, like some appendage attached permanently to her, body and soul. I knew very well that all it would have taken was for Jordan to hold her close and comfort her, but she appeared to avoid him for that very reason, and the tension between them was like a living thing. They studiously avoided looking at one another, even at meals, and never risked being alone together, anywhere. Her misery was obvious to us all. The bruise on her cheek had darkened, to make the lovely little face seem even more tragic, but we were grateful that X-rays of the cheekbone, itself, had shown no evidence of serious damage. As painful as the shoulder was, it had taken the brunt of the fall.

Jasper and I went back to the Kalahari twice in the next month-and-a-half. On the first occasion, and with help of Hennie and Sally Vercueil, we moved most of my possessions to *Blouspruit,* where, I am happy to say, Jasper's Bushmen welcomed me most encouragingly. Mieta seemed to be surprised, but pleased, when I gave her a hug.

The faithful Malgas had kept the Landrover going by driving it around the property in Jasper's absence, and when he and Jasper went in it to fetch the rest of my belongings, I had a few hours alone to myself, to unpack what we had already brought, and to settle in and review my new home.

Wandering through Merry's lab, I felt a nigh unbearable sadness. All I could see was that sad little face, and the suffering in Jordan's. In this blessed silence I tried not to hear Tristan's terrified screams. This drove me to walk through every room in the house, cleansing it in the Lord's name, and praying that Rosalie might rest in peace. I asked for blessings upon the home, and that, from every nook and cranny in it, all memories of the sorrow that had invaded it long ago might be erased. I spent a long time in Jasper's 'lab', too. I had never seen it before, and was overwhelmed by the evidence of the meticulous care it must have taken to produce such exquisite work.

On the way back to Johannesburg, we did not get Hennie to take us to Upington in the taxi, as had been the custom in the past. Instead, in preparation for the time when we would have to bring Tris back with us, we decided to take the 4X4, and leave it in a garage owned by one of Mark's former pupils, before catching the plane back to Johannesburg.

As we set out from *Blouspruit,* completely alone at last, what was uppermost in our minds was the recollection of the last time we had travelled together like this—on Meredith's wedding day—and we were often silent. Then the children had been with us, but now there were just the two of us, and with every mile we covered, along every inch of the road which had been so very familiar to Jasper in the years gone by, it began to seem more and more as if this was the day our new life was really beginning.

Many things might perhaps have caused him to think of that peculiar saying 'the more things change, the more they stay the same!' But there was much that had indeed changed. Optimistically contemplating the years that might yet lie ahead for us, our spirits lifted, and we did not allow the problem of how we would cope with Tristan, or the possibility of other troubles, to cloud our happiness. Many more miles of the road had been paved, and since the day Jasper had withdrawn from the world around him, parts of it had taken new turnings, and the dunes had been carved into different formations by the winds of change; but, like the rest of life's blessings, the same animal species were to be seen, provided one looked hard enough for them against the wondrous variations in the colours of the sand that provided their protective camouflage.

Once or twice we stopped, holding hands wordlessly, as we drank in the stark, awesome beauty of it all, and praised God that we could be doing this together. As though we had never seen them before, we marvelled anew at the huge communal nests, constructed as 'apartment blocks' by the sociable weaver birds, to house hundreds of 'couples'. Occasionally hosting the odd snake or two, the nests hung from almost every Camel Thorn, Quiver, or other tree. Sometimes also from telephone poles, power line pylons and windmill platforms, and if one looked up at them from below, the minute entrances could be seen like myriads of little black polka dots in the basements of their haystack-like condominiums.

Sharing the Kalahari with Jasper made the whole world seem more spectacular, and more awe-inspiring, and somehow I found myself telling him about the day I had taken the right-hand turn from the gates of the Kgalagadi, to go and stand at his gates.

I told him why I had spent my weekend retreat in the park, and about the decision I had made not to return to nursing in Bethlehem. "I had become too used to the vastness," I confessed, breathing in the fresh, clear desert air. "I am a Kalahari woman, my love. I feel content, and perversely far less fearful among the lions and the snakes than anywhere else on earth!"

"And now those gates are open, my darling!" he said exultantly. "I've been set free, and the whole world is welcome to come and see what I have found!...The treasure I have brought home to share my life there with me!"

***

There is more than one kind of weaver, and more than one kind of nest. About the size of a coconut, those of the golden finches in Jordan's garden were smaller, and possibly the most intricately woven of all, but the little birds have much in common with their Kalahari cousins. As is the case with the sociable weavers, the tube like entrances to their nests are usually at the bottom or the side, to make them less vulnerable to intrusion by snakes and other predators.

Reflecting on this, as I write, I am suddenly reminded of the day Meredith had mentioned them in a letter to her father, which she had read to Jordie before posting it, and of a conversation which had sprung from that when Jordie came home that afternoon. The two of them had then embarked on an animated discussion of this phenomenon, with Meredith giggling and suggesting that, as there were no stairs to climb, the birds would have to be equipped with radar in order to aim straight for their front doors, and also had to be able to overcome gravity, in order to propel themselves, up through the holes and into the nests. Jordan maintained laughingly that they simply flew up, but Merry, then teasing him, demanded to know how, although the birds were so tiny, he thought there was enough room in the tunnel for the flapping of wings.

"I can't answer that," was Jordan's quick rejoinder, laughing at her. "I'll ask them next time I talk to them!...I'll bet that you'd be small enough to fly up any very small entrance, so you'd never need a very big nest, yourself!"

That was back in the days when both were happy, carefree and completely at ease with one another. But what a difference a few seconds can make. In an instant, while Tristan had wounded himself critically, and hurt others less severely—on the surface—the relaxed, happy camaraderie between Jordan and Meredith had been shattered.

I recall the afternoon when Merry and I were sitting on the front stoep, having tea, when Jordan emerged carrying a brightly wrapped package, and handed it to Meredith, without looking at her.

"I chose this for you, with great care, Merry," he told her. "It was meant to be a part of your Christmas present. The rest of it we were to have chosen together, but unfortunately that could not happen and you were not sufficiently conscious on the big day, for me to give this to you. Perhaps you would like it now?"

I watched her try to open it with clumsy fingers, and then close her eyes, breathing deeply as she fought for control of herself when she saw what he had given her. "Thank you, Jordie," she said, setting the recording of 'Rhapsody in Blue' aside and keeping her head down. Looking at the other CD, her only comment was, "Perhaps it was because I used to play Scott Joplin too fast, or it may have been that I was in an upbeat mood, for this music to have seemed so cheerful. When played at the correct tempo, some of the rags can actually be heartbreakingly sad, can't they?"

One morning while Jasper and I were away at *Blouspruit*, Jordie, who was up early, as usual, watched her walk dejectedly on the wet grass, down to the tree where the weaver finches had built their nests. She no longer carried the notebook in which she would diligently have recorded impressions for her father and Susie every day. He missed having her read her notes to him while they had coffee together, and it tore at his heart when he remembered her reading one day, *"The weaver birds, also called 'geel vinke' (yellow finches) are busy, once more, making their nests in the big evergreen oak, and the crested barbets have got chicks. They sit in the white stinkwood every morning and sing that high-pitched note announcing that they are now proud parents!"*

Lost in this reverie, he stared through the window, coffee-cup in hand, and still keeping an eye on Meredith, he was horrified when he saw her suddenly pitch forward, and disappear behind a tall shrub. He almost upset his coffee in his haste to set the cup down and go to her, thinking only of how, having her arm in the sling, it would be impossible for her to break her fall; and running to find her, he prayed that she had not done herself further harm.

To his even greater consternation, he was to discover that she had not fallen, but had flung herself to her knees, sobbing as though her heart would break. Upon reaching her, he saw that she was holding in her right hand a weaver nest which had probably fallen from the tree.

"Oh, Merry, my darling," he cried before he could stop himself, and totally disregarding the fact that he was dressed in his favourite suit, he went down on his knees beside her.

"My darling!" he cried again, gathering her into his arms as he stood up, and raising her to her feet with him. "What's the matter?"

She held out the nest to him, her small body wracked with sorrow. "Just look at this!" she sobbed. "Isn't life awful sometimes? I've heard it said the nests are deserted once strange birds have been inside of them. Is this what my mother did to my father?—And, Jordie, am I turning out to be like her? I thought Tristan was what I wanted, but I was so wrong! I never felt like this about him! Now I don't know how to live without *you*!...I am such a sinner. Will God ever forgive me?"

There was no way he could restrain himself after that. He tilted her chin and kissed the sweet mouth that haunted his dreams. He kissed her face, her hands and even her ears. He held her as close to him as he could without hurting her shoulder, buried his face in her hair, and wept with her.

"Oh, my dearest darling," he groaned. "I am the greater sinner! I break the tenth commandment constantly. I covet my neighbour's wife and I can't fight this any longer!—God help us! What are we going to do?"

It was noticing how wet her feet were, that brought him to his senses. Her resistance was probably low, and the last thing he wanted at this time was for her to be ill. He put his arm around her and, bending over to put his cheek gently against hers, he murmured, "Dearest Merry, I have never before felt like this about anyone. I have never made love to a girl before, and now that I know what it is like to adore someone, no matter how hard this is, I can face anything. Just knowing that I am blessed to have your love in return, will sustain me. In return I promise you that you can be sure of mine as long as we live!

"And now we are going to have to pull ourselves together, and somehow face the days ahead. I am bitterly ashamed of breaking my word to your father." He grinned tenderly. "You've got grass stains on your knees. Please go now and change your shoes and that damp housecoat. Then come down and have coffee with me, and we'll decide what our next step has to be!"

They lingered over their coffee, and feeling free to talk openly to him at last, she unburdened herself of some of her guilt.

"You have no idea of some of the unkind things I have said to Tristan, Jordie. He cornered me shortly before we went to Nelspruit, and when he told me that he was longing to show me off to Zhaynie, I guessed why he was so determined that I should go, too.

"He had never before come to my bedroom. In fact never having been on my own—and not ever away from home, except to stay with Aunt Biddy—I was bitterly hurt that he did not even take the trouble to see if I was alright, in that hotel where we stayed the night after our marriage. I was lonely and scared stiff, and if I had known which room was Aunt Biddy's I would have run to her.

"I was used to having Aunt Biddy coming to look in on me, from time to time. More regularly since we came to live in this house, and it was only when Tristan sat down at the foot of my bed, after closing the door behind him, that I realized who my visitor was....He tried to entice me to go to Nelspruit with him by telling me how we could start over and spend some time alone together at *Beauclaire*, and I blame myself now for being so angry that I could only rant at him. I told him, in no uncertain terms, that he was not to think, for one moment, that he would be sleeping in the same room with me! I told him that I did not even like him anymore—and the worst of it is that I spoke the truth! God forgive me! Because he was habitually so self-assured and arrogant, I did not know how needy he was!

"Can you understand why I was furious enough with him, to tell Zhaynie that if I ever had babies, they would most certainly not be Tristan Connaughts? Now what haunts me is that Tristan will never have children!...Was I cursing him?"

Reaching across the table, he took her hand. "No, my dearest. I'm sure you were not. And, because you are human, you must have been bitterly hurt at the insinuation that he only wanted you with him, to flaunt you in front of my sister! It makes me angry too!"

He kissed her fingertips and looked earnestly into her eyes. "Put all that behind you now, sweetheart. After today, we can never again talk to one another like this, so I'm going to kiss you one more time, but how about you get ready now, we have some breakfast in the hospital cafeteria, and then you go and visit Tristan? Dawnview is probably the best private hospital in Gauteng, so I can recommend the breakfast, and Dorothy Hunter, who was so taken with you at Aunt Biddy's party, would be pleased to see you, too."

"Jordie, when you say that it is time, I'm ready to go and see Tris. Whether he meant his vows or not, I thought I did, at the time, and whether it would have been less despicable to have broken them by leaving before this, I don't know; but one thing of which I am sure, is that we could never know a moment of happiness if I were to do so, now that he is so helpless. You must have had good reason for not wanting me to visit him before, and I'm not sure that I could have faced that, anyway; but now, with God's help and the knowledge of your love to sustain me, I'm ready to take on whatever responsibilities are demanded of me...

"I am embarrassed to go to the hospital after all this time, though. What must the nurses be thinking of a wife who has neglected her husband for so long?"

"That was not for you to decide, my darling. I gave implicit instructions that only people approved by me, were to be admitted—and, trust me, Merry, the stress of being in the room with him would have been too much for you. Dorothy Hunter knows that and so do the staff. Susie was quite miffed when she was turned away.

"Reg had taken her to see Fransie, and while she was in the hospital she went up to Tristan's floor, but the staff nurse on duty made it clear to her that the 'No visitors' sign was to be strictly adhered to. As it is, I need to spend a few minutes with him by myself, before I can allow you to enter! Now go and dress yourself most beautifully, so that they can all see what a lovely wife Doctor Connaught has..." He smiled ruefully, "And maybe I can show off with you and have the people in the cafeteria think that you're Mrs. Ashton! Call me if Susie is still asleep—and if you have trouble with zippers or anything else, I'll come and help you....Theuns thinks you should be ready for physio soon!"

As she rose to go upstairs and dress, he reached out, took her hand and drew her closer. "I asked for one last kiss, remember, and this will have to be a very special one, because it will be the last. I will have to remember it for the rest of my life. You will read it in my eyes, my darling, but, after today, no more talk of love!"

Later she would tell me of how, over breakfast in the cafeteria they talked of many other things. About *Blouspruit* and how much she missed the Kalahari and her lab. About the house in *Spoors-einde,* and the practice that Doc had left to

Tristan, and what should be done about them once Adriaan's emigration was approved. Then, getting more personal, she had to know why he had chosen to use words like 'before I can allow you to enter', and it was not easy for him to describe to her how bad it had been, and how afraid he was that Tristan's often alarming distress might upset her.

"He has longer periods between the episodes now. Of course we continue to be very careful not to do anything that might set him off, but no matter how careful everyone is, one very distressing mannerism remains. He makes very few other movements, Meredith, but I find it extremely stressful to see the frantic manner in which he constantly keeps brushing his hands across his face, and you mustn't allow that to get to you!

"When he has too much stubble on his face, I shave him very carefully, so as not to touch any part that might be tender, and it seems to soothe him, but whether it is a relief for him to be shot of that beard, or just the stroking of his face, I have not been able to ascertain. Nevertheless, I want to go and do that for him, before you go in, in the hope that he will be calm while you are with him, and not frighten you."

"Can't the nurses do it, Jordie?"

"No. Evidently not! He won't tolerate that, and as it is, they have a dreadful job washing him, because it aggravates his distress. Other than myself, he does not appear to mind Biddy or Matt Marais' parents touching him, but that's about it. I want him to start having physiotherapy for those legs, but I dread to think of the disturbance *that* might cause! Perhaps we shall have to wait until he gets home!"

Meredith waited in the visitors' lounge until Jordan came to call her, and she had hardly entered Tristan's ward, before Tris began to roar—and then the most bizarre scene was played out before her eyes. No one could be sure when Tristan was awake or asleep, and it was uncertain whether his eyes could focus; however, to this day, Meredith becomes emotional when she recalls how she had to watch Jordan approach her husband as one would when confronting a terrified wild creature. Jordie moved slowly forward, with his hands up, before very carefully touching Tristan's arm.

"I'm here, Tris....This is Jordie....I won't let anything harm you....I have brought Merry to see you, so now please be calm and don't frighten her!...She is not angry with you....No one is angry with you....We love you and we want you to be better!"

This he repeated over and over until finally there was peace in the room. Merry looked at Jordie beseechingly, and he nodded his reassurance.

"It's okay now, Meredith." He drew a chair closer to the bed for her. "Just hold his hand and keep talking. Pray, whenever you feel moved to do so. Keep telling him you are not angry. No one is angry, and no one will harm him!

"I'll go and do my rounds now, and I don't anticipate any trouble; but if you need help, you only need to press the button and one of the nurses will come running ...Okay?"

Once she was alone with Tristan, Meredith tried to talk to Tristan as Jordan had instructed her to do, but it was awkward at first. The man on the bed seemed alien to her; hardly recognizable as the good-looking, debonair young physician who had arrived at *Blouspruit* one day, to disrupt the lives of everyone there. But, after a while, studying the gaunt face, and distressed by the mechanical, near frantic manner in which he kept wiping his face, her heart went out to him, and she found herself murmuring to him: "You will be better soon, Tris....You will be handsome, and walking in the sunshine again some day, because you have parents who love you, and you have many friends who are praying for you. ...You'll get better, you'll see!"

After about an hour, Jordan came back to see how she was doing and he had hardly sat down to take a short break and get an update from her, when his priest, the one who had performed our marriage, came into the ward.

"Good morning Meredith." Recognizing her, he seemed surprised. " I thought I would find your mother here. She's often here on Tuesdays when I bring the Sacrament to the patients. I usually anoint Doctor Connaught, and then I give your mother Communion." He turned to Jordan. "But since Biddy is not here, and you are, Jordan, would you and Meredith like to receive the Eucharist while I am here?...Ah," he observed, " I see your patient is more restful today, Jordie. I also see that he is still on a drip, but do you think it would do any harm if I were just to dip the host in the chalice, and hold it to his lips. Communicate him by intinction, as it were?"

Meredith, well acquainted with Tristan's antipathy towards the clergy, in general, was instantly tense, and, unsure of how to respond, she instinctively looked at Jordan for guidance. He nodded, and she relaxed. Little did they know that within minutes, they were to be momentarily rendered speechless!

She and Jordan knelt on either side of Tristan's bed, while Father Palmer gave them their Communion, and then each took hold of one of Tristan's hands, as the priest, touched the wine-soaked, 'intincted' wafer to the sick man's lips. To their astonishment he opened his mouth to receive it, swallowing the tiny, sanctified morsel; his first food in nearly two months! Meredith and Jordan were exchanging looks of wonder, when Tristan's body was suddenly wracked with convulsions. His back was arched so that his head was forced deep into his pillows, while a dreadful grimace contorted his face.

As his lips parted, exposing his teeth, he emitted a series of snarls and howls such as none of us had ever heard before, and wished never to hear again. Unearthly shrieks that made the blood run cold, caused the nurses at the desk, some distance down the corridor, to drop whatever they were doing, and stand transfixed, listening in horror. Dorothy Hunter, waiting in the doorway of the ward, was flung sideways against the doorframe, as something like a blast of hot, sulphurous wind swept past her—and then peace descended, and the ensuing silence was so profound that for some moments no one moved...

It did not surprise me to learn, when Jordie fetched us to the hospital that night, that, until Jacob and Joey Marais turned up to take over the 'watch', the only people who had immediately recognized that a deliverance had taken place, were Jordie and the priest. When we discussed this later, Felicity and I had to admit that we had never known it happen like that, but Willie Marais' parents, albeit extolling God, were almost nonchalant, as though they took this incredible happening for granted. Hadn't that been exactly what they had petitioned the Lord, over and over and over again, to do, while they rebuked the demons? They were not reluctant, either, to apply the word 'miracle' to what had transpired.

"We have seldom found the resistance so strong, or known the process to take so long," they told us, " but this is what we prayed for, and the Lord has heard us! Praise His Holy Name!"

When Jordie fetched us to the hospital that night, I found it weird that, although Tristan's eyes no longer appeared sightless, he did not look around him in awe or even stupefaction. "Surely he cannot know where he is," was my first, thought—until I noticed that his gaze was fixed on Meredith. For a long time he simply stared at her face, but did not say a word. This, in turn, gave me cause me to wonder whether he was fully conscious, or had possibly lost his memory. Imagine our concern, when Jacob Marais reached Jordie on his cell phone as we were on our way home. Covering the phone with his hand, Jordie told us that Jacob sounded bewildered, concerned, but also excited.

"He is talking," Jacob reported. "Almost raving. We can recognize only one word of what he is saying, and that is Meredith's name.—He is really agitated, Jordan. He has tears running down his cheeks, and I think you should come back here as soon as possible!"

Merry and Jordan had both had a long and emotional day—far more so than the rest of us put together—but there was no way they could disregard the urgency in the old man's voice! This dear old gentleman who, with his wife, thought nothing of travelling all the way to that hospital from Kempton Park, to do the Lord's work!

"I'll turn around at the first, suitable off ramp, *Oom* Jacob," Jordan said, and about twenty-five minutes later we were back in the ward with Tris.

Meredith knelt down beside his bed, and Tristan, touching first her bruised face, and then, indicating the sling, ceased from weeping long enough to utter a sentence, haltingly and in a voice rendered so hoarse by all the yelling, that Jordan was concerned that his vocal chords might have been permanently damaged. But Jacob was right. Tristan was not speaking either English or Afrikaans. What he kept repeating hysterically was definitely in a foreign tongue. One of the phrases he kept using sounded much like '*mais oui*' which, of course meant 'but yes' in French, but did not make sense in the context of what he was so desperate to convey.

" *Me'wy*," he sobbed "*je suis désolé, chéyi! Pa'done moi!*"

Three of the people in the ward knew what he was saying. Meredith, her father and Jordan, who were all able to speak French fluently, succeeded in grasping the meaning of Tristan's words without too much difficulty, although they were spoken in a manner different from the French that Jasper and Meredith knew. Only Jordan was able to pinpoint the origin of the strange pronunciation, and it was obvious that he was immeasurably moved by this. He was obliged to wipe his eyes a few times with his handkerchief as he interpreted.

"What Tristan is saying," he translated for the benefit of the rest of us, is, 'I am very sorry, Merry, beloved—or darling. Please forgive me!.... In Parisian French: *'Merry, je suis désolé, chéri! Pardone moi!'* However, if you listen carefully—and I'll repeat both versions for you—you will detect that what is significant, is the missing 'R' in some of the words. This is typical of *Créole Lalouisiane*, a French-based Creole language spoken in Louisiana. There, for instance, 'parle' is commonly pronounced as 'pa'le'.

"How I know this, is because it is spoken by the people with whom I have played music; people loved by my uncle, Jamie. That is the language in which my mother will sing a doxology, for instance. She learnt it from her grandmother, who owned the house next-door to *Beauclaire*—which belonged to my dad's grandmother—and it is a form of French they learnt as children. Even today my parents resort to it when they want to communicate loving secrets to one another.

"*Créole Lalouisiane* is what would be spoken just north of New Orleans, along the *Bayou Lacombe* in St Tammany Parish, which is where our beloved *Beauclaire* is situated! Next-door to where Tristan's parents now live!—People, do you know what this means? It means that Tristan is speaking the language of his very early childhood! The very first language he would have learnt as a little boy.....We spoke it when we played games, and even on the rare occasions when we quarrelled!...Then the English of our parents became secondary!

"What has happened to Tristan is rare, but not unique. There are documented cases of similar occurrences, after severe head trauma and prolonged periods of unconsciousness. Sometimes the patient will even speak in a language entirely new. Hitherto unknown to him or her!...

"Speak to him now, in French, Merry. He will understand you, even if your grammar and syntax sound poor, and your accent seems peculiar to him. Perhaps you can pacify him sufficiently to help him sleep! If not, I think the time has come when it is safe to give him a sedative."

We were all so exhausted by that time that I don't know how we made it to Bryanston, undressed and climbed into bed. But it was difficult, at first, to relax. As we had gone from the ward, leaving Tristan with a nurse to check on him, we had done so with different words now ringing in our ears, and we went to sleep with the sound of Tristan's voice, pleading in his Louisiana French, *"Take me home, Merry! I want to go home!"*

CHAPTER TWELVE

Tristan's ongoing and heartrending pleas to be taken home finally got to us. Meredith could not stand this much longer, and Jordan's face was haggard, from both fatigue and the strain of bearing Tristan's distress in addition to Meredith's growing dejection. There came a day when, as a last resort, Tris was brought home in an ambulance. The physiotherapist came to Jordan's house and, when Tris could finally use a wheelchair, what had formerly been his study was reorganized to become his bedroom, as it was difficult to keep taking him upstairs.

His specialists were initially against having him moved, but, as Jordan told them, there were two doctors and a nurse in the house, which shed a different perspective on the situation, and then came another red-letter day, for all of us, when Angelina, recovered from the stab wounds, was pronounced fit enough to return to work. This meant less housework for Meredith and me, while Jordan was blessedly relieved of the necessity to make visits to the faithful Zulu lady, in yet another hospital.

What none of us realized was that Meredith's pronounced loss of weight was what troubled Jordie most. His heart ached for her, and there were times when it became almost too hard to abide by his resolve! Moments when he could gladly have thrown all caution to the wind and kissed the very breath out of her!

To be out of the hospital, and able to move around in the wheelchair, seemed to make Tristan more content, but the disturbing, compulsive wiping of his face did not cease, and he could still perpetually be heard begging Meredith to take him home. Zhaynie and Dominic came, bringing the baby to visit him, but he was completely apathetic, and it was fortunate that she, like all the Ashtons, was able to speak to him in Creole, because at least he listened attentively, and was quiet.—Still, when he did react, the only response she elicited, was a plea for Meredith to take him home. And he kept brushing his hands across his face!

Jordan had telephoned his father on the very next day after the amazing episode in the hospital, and kept him up to date on any changes in Tristan's condition. He was able to tell Ash that there was some improvement, in that there had been no recurrence of the screeching, and that Tristan was quite pathetically docile, but Ash was concerned about the continuation of the other two manifestations.

"I believe that the deliverance is complete my son," he told Jordan, "but there is clearly some healing to be done. Father Peter has been asked to speak at a healing conference in Pietermaritzburg, before Easter, and is thrilled at the prospect of seeing Antoinette and Stephen at the same time. I'll talk this over with him today, and, if James and I can complete the arrangements for the take-over of the company, sooner than was anticipated, I think that your mother and I must come with Peter."

This happened on the same day that Meredith spoke to Jordan, in Tristan's presence, and said in French, so that Tris would understand: "Jordie, to say that you have been wonderful, would be a gross understatement, but we can't stay here in your house any longer! Tristan is no longer your partner, and to expect you to have five of my family, including Tris, here, is now becoming an imposition. Furthermore, having given the matter much thought, I think it is time I took Tristan home with me, as he wishes. Perhaps he will be at peace and, please God, maybe we shall all be better off!"

"Meredith," he had to tell her, not knowing whether he was making things worse for her, or not, "no matter what you would like to do, Tris cannot possibly be moved just yet. And you know that I most certainly do not regard your being here, as an imposition. Please just wait until my father gets here, and perhaps by then we shall have figured out some way of getting Tristan to *Blouspruit!*"

At the very first opportunity we went to Kempton Park to thank Jacob and Joey Marais for the time they had so selflessly devoted to Tristan, and they were adamant about the need to read the Bible to him as frequently as possible. "Remember that we are told in Psalm 119: verse 130, that the 'entrance to God's words giveth light' " said Jacob; which immediatelty reminded us of all that Ash had said about that same psalm, in Nelspruit. It would be some weeks before we would be able to see clearly what the connection was, and I don't know how the old gentleman knew this, but we were also specifically told to concentrate on the first two verses of the Gospel according to John 14:2, 2 Corinthians 5:17, and Luke 15:11-32.

Past experience had taught us that this would probably prove to be a fruitless exercise, and we fully expected Tristan to protest. However, taking the Marais' admonition seriously, as soon as Jordan had a free moment to do so, he went in search of a suitable version of the Bible at the bookstore where he and Meredith had bought her gardening book, and he was well known. A French edition was hardly an item routinely kept in stock, but Doctor Ashton's request sounded so urgent that the book was promptly 'special-ordered'.

What Tris would derive from this was difficult to assume, and none of us honestly expected any results; mainly because the Bible that finally arrived was, as anticipated, in regular French. Despite the fact that the language is linked to the Cajun spoken in Canada and is regarded by many as French, and not a regional dialect without a literary tradition, no one could tell us if a Creole translation existed, and we finally accepted that perhaps, even if there was one, it was doubtful if it would have been available in South Africa. Because of this, it was encouraging to discover that, although Tristan only communicated in short sentences, expressed himself only in Louisiana French, and knew what Jordan said to him, he also appeared to understand Merry and Jasper when they spoke or read to him.

Contrary to all expectations, Tristan sat quietly in his wheelchair, no matter which verses were read to him, but, unfortunately we all noticed that, after having listened to the passages prescribed by Jacob and Joey, and more often after the verses from John's, Gospel, his pleas for Merry to take him home became even more heartrending. He seldom yelled or screamed any more, but he would frequently weep, and it was pitiful to see him sit, staring silently into space, with tears running down his cheeks. A pall of sadness hung over the entire house; made worse when we sometimes heard Jordan playing the clarinet, alone in his bedroom. When Ash arrived, some weeks later, looking forward to making music with his son, he was disappointed when Jordie said he had 'gone off' *Rhapsody in Blue;* and long after Meredith's shoulder no longer prohibited piano playing, it was not unexpected to discover that she, too, had somehow 'gone off' it!

It would take several chapters of this story to describe how the special bath and other things, listed as necessities by the physiotherapist, were finally put in place at *Blouspruit* before we went home, at last. Of course, right from the start, we had faced the fact that permanent arrangements would have to be made in the house for the care of Tris, and, knowing that we would soon be back there, it did not seem feasible to install too much special equipment in Jordie's house. Other than a few essentials like, for instance, a hospital type bed, we made do in the best way we could, while preparations were underway on our farm, against the day when we would be back there.

Merry had never seen a man's naked body, and while she had, on occasion had to bath her younger sister, she was, in her present state, still not able to use her left arm too much, and already far too exhausted to attempt doing this for Tris; so, while he was still confined to bed, I bathed him, doing as I would have done for a bedridden patient in the hospital. In time, a new routine was adopted. Jordie and Reg, between them, would take him into the shower, and I don't know how they did it, but always, after having water gush down upon him like that, the face wiping would stop for a while.

Then, one particularly hot Saturday afternoon, when Tris had reached the stage where he could be taken outside in his wheelchair, he sat wistfully watching Jordie and Reggie who, making the most of the summer while it lasted, were swimming and sunbathing. This was the way the three of them had often spent leisure time together during their university days, and all at once Jordan and Reg were overcome with compassion.

Stripping Tris down to his underwear, they contrived a way to lower him into the water, made almost tepid by the sun, and then, supporting him, and on the alert against possible problems, they got him to hang onto the side of the pool, raising and lowering himself to start the process of restoring muscle tone to his upper body. His enjoyment was childlike, and, until the end of March when there was a definite change in the weather, this was done whenever they were free. As often happened on the Highveld, an icy wind came blowing in one day, without warning, sending Johannesburgers scrambling to find their winter coats, but by then we were packing to return home.

During this time, my birthday had come and gone, but, thanks to Jordie—and Doctor Theuns and his wife, who kindly stayed with Tristan—it had been a happy one. Jordan had Charlie take Jasper and me to a very nice mall, where we paid the long-promised visit to a jeweller, and proudly wearing my sparkling Kimberley diamond next to the wedding ring on my finger, we later met Jordie, Felicity, Susan and Reg for dinner, before we all went together to see a movie.—The kind of movie everyone should see, on such a special night, with a loved one to hold your hand. It must, however, have been excruciating for Merry and Jordie, sitting side-by-side, and I did not think badly of them when I saw him take her hand and raise it to his lips. He did not let go of it after that, either.

As we were walking back to the house from the garage, after the show, Reggie surprised us by asking: "By the way, has anyone heard anything from Adéle or the rest of Tristan's 'in' crowd?...No. I didn't think so! I'm actually grateful that none of them can afford to talk too much without implicating themselves...

"I'm not going to be hard on Tris, ever again. I sincerely believe that he could not help himself....He was driven!"

CHAPTER THIRTEEN

While we took each day as it came, as far as Tristan was concerned, we now had to worry about Susan. With nearly the first quarter of the year already past, no permanent decision regarding her studies had yet been reached. None of the information derived from the brochures we had read together, before coming to Johannesburg, was of any use to us, as she could no longer decide what she wanted to do with her life. At one stage, saddened by Tristan's condition, and admiring the nurses in the hospital, she, too, wanted to be a nurse. A science degree, settled upon one day, gave way to a degree in nursing, the next. Now suddenly very much taken with the good-looking young man who came to give Tristan physio, she was going to be a physiotherapist. There was only one thing of which she was sure, and that was that she was not ready to return to the isolation of *Blouspruit.*

As it became obvious that she needed more time to grow up, and to enjoy the freedom of the outside world a while longer, we were grateful for an invitation for her to visit Nelspruit, extended by Zhaynie, who had met Susie, during her, Zhaynie's visit to Tris. Guessing correctly that this had secretly been prompted by Ash, and because Susie was excited at the prospect, we did not hesitate to take advantage of the opportunity. When Peter Crawford, Ash and Amy-Lee arrived from New York shortly after that, the priest went directly to see his daughter, Amy-Lee went ahead to Nelspruit, and

Susie went with her, leaving Ash with us—to spend time with Tristan

Although both Ash and Amy-Lee had insisted that Jasper and I should continue to occupy the suite they had so kindly given to us for our use, we had already begun packing a week or two before that, and most of our and Tristan's belongings had been sent ahead. A few days after Ash arrived, ready to fly us as far as Upington, we helped Meredith to get ready for the homeward journey. Many special preparations had to be made for Tristan to travel with relative ease, and what we would have done without Ash and Jordie to help us, I do not know. Having to make several stops along the way, Merry and I went ahead from Upington, in Hennie Vercueil's new taxi, with most of the luggage, while Ash, Jordie and Jasper followed in the 4X4, in which they had settled Tristan as comfortably as possible.

And so Jasper and I took our weary daughter and our maimed son-in-law home with us, and thus began my life as the *chatelaine* of *Blouspruit*. With the help of Jordan and his father, we put the patient down to sleep in his special new bed, Jordie gave him a sedative, and then, because no one felt like anything more, we had tea before we went off to shower or bath, and then fell into our respective beds. Hennie Vercueil was persuaded to stay the night, as he had a long day behind him, and would be driving the Ashtons back to Upington within a few days.

Jordan had elected to sleep in the same room with Tristan, in case the sick man needed help in the night, and I have no words to describe how much we appreciated everyone who pitched in to make this transition a little less problematical for Merry, her father and me. Mieta had prepared every bedroom as requested, and feeling a need to go and thank her again, before I turned in, I was to be reminded, and, not for the first time, of the uncanny intuition of the Bushmen people.

"Daai kleinbasie issie lekke nie. Ekke praat'ie vannie liggaam nie. Hy issie binne lekke nie!" she observed in the kind of Afrikaans I had come to understand over the years. "That young baas is not happy (or right). I do not speak of his body. It is inside that he is not right!"

How right *she* was! Jordie was woken in the early hours by Tristan's sorrowful whimpering. *"Timmee!...Timmee, mon fwe'...! Timmee!"* he groaned, now belatedly mourning for Timothy, his brother...

The following day dawned bright and cloudless as only a perfect Kalahari day can be and, with Tristan apparently sitting contentedly, and temporarily at peace in his wheelchair, we enjoyed breakfast on the back stoep; still a little tired, but happy, and overwhelmingly thankful for the respite from strain. Having been blessed to come home, at last, to where I hoped to spend the rest of my life, with someone I loved so dearly, I was anxious to start unpacking, and Jordan had expressed an interest in seeing Meredith's lab, but we had no sooner risen from the table, than we were riveted to the spot by the most agonized wailing.

"I want to go home!" Tristan implored. *"Me'wy, take me home!"*

At the end of her tether, Meredith clapped her hands over her ears, closed her eyes and stood still as though she were praying, but she was valiantly fighting for self-control. Then, suddenly, she went to pieces, and, bursting into stormy tears, and almost screaming, herself, cried out: ***"Stop it, Tristan! For heaven's sake!*** *Arrêt*! Stop it!...I've *brought* you home! What more must I do?...God help me, this is more then I can bear!" With that she rushed indoors and Jordan, reacting instinctively, ran after her, and found her curled up on her bed, sobbing hysterically.

This was too much for him. He gathered her in his arms, sat her on his lap, and, cradled her as if she were a small child. Following him, Jasper and I looked in at the door, and our hearts bled for them. Like cowards we had fled, leaving poor Ash alone on the stoep to deal with Tristan, who was, by now, completely beside himself, clawing at his face until it was scored with angry, red scratches. And then Ash, who had begun to pray for all he was worth, and had apparently been given a sudden inspiration, came rushing into the house, calling for me. Looking in at Meredith's door, and seeing his son with the inconsolable Merredith on his lap, he relived the agony of a night when he had been moved to hold Amy-Lee like that.

"Auntie Bid...Uncle Jasper..." Jordie pleaded, "please don't think badly of me. There is nothing amorous about this, I promise you. I just can't bear this either!"

Ash could not permit himself to dwell on the pathos of the situation at this moment. "Biddy," he requested urgently, "please bring me a Bible, out on the stoep, if you have one handy! I have put mine back in my valise, and I need one immediately!"

I did as I was bade, and handed him my own, which had small, yellow 'Post-it' notes protruding from the pages which I had marked for reading, at the instruction of Jacob Marais, and noting the order in which they should be read. Opening the Bible at the first of those pages, Ash began to go through them systematically, starting with the seventeenth verse of the fifth chapter of Paul's second letter to the Corinthians, in which we are told about how, if any man is in Christ, old things are passed away and all are made new. Carrying on stoically, he went on to the fifteenth chapter of Luke's Gospel, reading from verse eleven to thirty-two, the story of the Prodigal son. Tristan stopped wailing long enough to listen to how the son had decided, when in abject despair, to 'arise and go' to his father, in verse eighteen, and of how the father, seeing him, had not only had compassion on him but had kissed him.

Ash was astonished at the wrapt expression he saw creeping across Tristan's face, but the silence was not destined to endure. The moment he, Ash, began to read the second verse of the fourteenth chapter of the Gospel according to John, where mention is made of how there are many mansions in the Father's house, he provoked a renewed flood of tearful, desperate frustration. *"I want to go home! Take me home!"* Tris besought Ash...this time adding: *"La maison mon pe'! (Père)— My father's house!"*

Stunned, and hardly knowing how to tell us this, Ash came to find Jasper and me. He asked Jasper to advise Meredith of this new development, hardly knowing how to tell her, himself, and then said to me, "Biddy, my dear friend, I would give a great deal to have Peter here with me today, but you have some experience of this, so, although I realize that you have much to do, I am now going to ask you to partner with me in the 'inner healing' procedure for Tris.—Is there any place we can take him, where we can be quiet and completely alone with him?"

"Merry's lab is the best place I can think of, Ash," I said after due consideration. "It is at the other end of the house, and it is unlikely that anyone would disturb us at the moment. Our poor little Meredith is probably busy trying to deal with the devastating knowledge that, after having succeeded in bringing Tristan so far, all the way to *Blouspruit*, she will now have to take him home to his parents, if he is ever going to be in a position to resume any kind of normal life again! She will need a great deal of prayer, herself!"

We wheeled Tristan into Merry's lab, without turning on the very bright lights Jasper had installed to aid her in her research, and, having shut the door, Ash drew up two chairs and we sat, facing Tristan. He, Ash, rested his hand on the shoulder of the tormented man while I took Tristan's hand. The welts on his face were visible, even in this dim light.

"Now, my dear boy," Ash said gently, speaking to Tris in Creole French, "there is no need to be afraid. This is what you asked for when I found you sitting in my car in Nelspruit. Today, with the help of the Holy Spirit you are going to be set free, and your life will be changed forever. I promise you, that if you are patient, and God willing, you will, return to your father's house, even if I have to take you there, myself!" He then began to pray in the Spirit, under his breath so as not to alarm Tris, and I did the same.

"The Holy Spirit will help you as you try to recall a time, long ago, when this terror began for you, Tristan! Take as long as you like. You don't have to work too hard at it. Don't try to contrive something to please me. Just wait!" And as we, too, waited, Tristan became more and more agitated,

"Where are you, now, Tris?" Ash questioned him, very gently.

"In the dark!" Tris said, squirming as he did so. "I am in the dark and it is difficult to breathe. Burning, malevolent eyes are staring at me!"—This was the longest sentence we had heard him utter in weeks. "There is so much noise...Dreadful noise! Hideous noise! It is always in my head. I hear it constantly. It cannot be drowned out, and there's no running away from it! Sometimes I think I shall go mad of it does not stop!"

"Can you describe it?"

"No....It is too evil for words. So bad that it is impossible to be with children who yell and scream at me!"

"What is making the noise, Tris?"

"I can't see! It is coming from outside!"

"Outside where?"

"*Outside*!" he repeated impatiently.

"Can you see anyone there?"

"No....But I know my mother is there! She is very frightened, and she is trying to take away the bad stuff!...It's all over her face and it is sticking to her!"

"What bad stuff, son? How do you know, if you can't see her?"

"I can feel her trying to wipe it off!" he shuddered. "It is on me too!"

"What do you mean you can feel her doing this, but you can't see her?" I wanted to know—and, all at once a light went up for Ash...

"*Thou hast covered me in my mother's womb.*

"*Thine eyes did see my substance, yet being unperfect*" he quoted the words from Psalm 139, which had been given him that day in Nelspruit.

"*And the entrance to God's words giveth light,*" I added, excitedly. " Psalm 119: verse 130. That is what Jacob Marais urged us to read to Tristan.—Ash, Tristan is talking about things that happened before he was born!"

"You're right," Ben agreed. "Tris, now listen carefully to what I am telling you. You say you don't believe in Jesus, but your mother does. Can you see Him anywhere near her?"

"Yes." he said after some hesitation. "Yes, I see Him now! I see Him. He is wiping her eyes and her face, and he is bringing me out of the darkness, into the light! I am breathing better now. He is kissing my face, and giving me to my mother!"

"Where are the bad people now, Tris?" I asked him.

"They have gone..."

"Is anyone else there?"

"Yes, you are!"

"Now Tris, tell us about the bad stuff on your own face?" Ben took over from me. "What does it look like?"

"Spanish Moss!" He began to cringe, "It is all over my face!...Take it away! I can't see when it gets in the way. It makes everything so dark again!"

"Would you like to ask Jesus to take it away, Tris?"

"Yes! Yes! Please," he begged brokenly, "It is killing me!"

"Well now, how about you ask Jesus to do that for you. He can, and He will..."

Incredulous, myself, I heard Tristan obey; plainly finding little difficulty in doing so. Then there was a long silence, during which he breathed deeply, and then sighed.

"What is He doing now, Tristan?"

"He is reaching up, as far as he can, and cutting it down with a huge pair of scissors!"

"What does He do with it?"

"He is throwing it onto a fire, and burning it to ashes!"

Mention has been made of my having had some experience of Inner Healing Prayer Ministry, and Ash had not only befitted by it, himself, but, as a result, had also travelled far and wide ministering to people in many places, in this way. By now we had learned to be well prepared, and I had brought with me a full box of tissues.—A wise precaution, because by this time we were all three in tears...

Tristan was praising God and alternately leaning forward to hug Ash and me. He had stopped wiping his face and he was radiant, but exhausted. After that we took him to lie down on his bed, and he slept soundly until late that afternoon!

Jasper and I were ready for a siesta after lunch, Meredith and Tristan were both fast asleep, and I was on my way to my bedroom, when Ash caught up with me, looking bemused. "Biddy," he said, " for me, what happened this morning has not begun to sink in fully, yet, and perhaps you have still not quite grasped the enormity of it, either—but have you realized that you spoke to Tristan in English—and that he understood what you were saying?"

Jordan and his father must have been as tired as we were, but any time that could be spent together was too precious to waste. Instead of napping, father and son preferred to stay chatting on the stoep, and I dozed off contentedly listening to the quiet, gentle hum of their voices outside my window.

They talked for a while about their previous visit to *Blouspruit*, discussing the visit to *Witdraai* with Nico Olivier, the former 'camel cop', as his wife Mercia would affectionately refer to him on occasion; of how pleasant it had been to have Willie Marais with them on that trip, and how inestimable a part his parents had played in Tristan's recovery, thus far. They dwelt briefly on Rosalie Hilliard's undeniable beauty, and agonized about the lasting effect her desertion had had on her husband and the girls. This led them to recall the incident of the broken ornament, and to discuss how caring, Meredith, the exquisite child, had been even then.

This was too much for Jordan, and his heartache got the better of him.

"Dad," he confided despairingly to Ash, "I am responsible for my patients, and must put that responsibility ahead of my own desires, but God only knows how hard it is going to be to leave here tomorrow!—I've had so many reprieves already! Vowed so many times that I would distance myself from her. Every kiss is always supposed to be the last!

"Now brutal reality has suddenly washed over me like a tidal wave....If Merry is going to have to take Tristan back to Louisiana, I might never see her again! And even if I did, what good would that do? If I took leave, some day, and went to the Louisiana *Beauclaire*, it would only be rubbing salt into my wounds. To see her there, with a husband and in-laws would be more that I could bear! For two pins, just for the remote possibility of seeing her outside in her sunbonnet, I'd take another day off, and go back home on Sunday, but circumstances have lately contrived to make me take too much time off already!"

This was when Ash decided that it was time for a strict talk to his son!

"Here and now I'm putting my foot down, Jordan Ashton! It makes me see red when I hear you make apologies for taking a few days off, here and there. One or two trips to Nelspruit, and closing your clinic for a few hours, once in a blue moon, is hardly what I would describe as 'taking too much time off'! How you equate closing the clinic in an emergency, in order to tear off to see a patient somewhere else, as 'time off' is beyond me!

"It is years since you had a proper holiday! When you rushed over here to *Spoors-einde*, to help out Hugo Connaught, was that, to your mind, taking time off, too?

"You're not even thirty, my boy, but you're beginning to show the strain! You are at the beck and call of everyone who needs you, day or night, and I cannot allow this to continue. Jordie, you are a grown man, and you need not pay any attention to me, but I love you, I care about you, and I'm warning you.

You are burning yourself out. You have too many irons in the fire, and your mother and I are worried sick about you!

"I am going to be selfish about this, because, as much as I care about my fellow man—or woman—you, my beloved son, with the rest of my family, come first in my heart. And the problem with you is that your heart is too big. On occasion I have wished that James had more of it, but yours will be the death of you if you don't stop and think—right now! My latest concern is that, instead of hitting the bottle as some people do when they're miserable, you might try drowning your sorrows in even more work!"

Nodding, and biting his lower lip, Jordan thought about that for a few moments before he asked, "So what do you suggest I do about that, Dad? You are the strategist, the master planner of business operations, and you know how to analyse and provide solutions...so please tell me, now, how one applies business ethics and strategies when it come to human beings?"

"To begin with, your practice is too big and you need to bring in another physician—perhaps one who is willing to work in Sandton, and also put in time at the clinic. You know that there is money in the Ashtons' budget for that....You will have to purchase some sort of bus, or other suitable conveyance, to take the clinic patients for special treatment....I don't want to make you feel bad, but Merry should never have been allowed to do that, and nor should you!"

Again Jordan remained silent, but finally nodded, as before. "You are quite right, I know. I acknowledge that, and I promise that I shall take your advice, as soon as I get my current and most pressing problems behind me....Now that Meredith and her parents have brought Tristan here—which was hardly an easy operation, let's face it—he can't be moved back to Gauteng. If and when he recovers, he won't have been the first physician to practise from a wheelchair, but bridges were burnt on the day we brought Theuns in to take his place, and even if I wanted to take in a third partner—as you suggest—possible prosecution still hangs over him like the sword of Damocles.

"It is perhaps a blessing that I—who understand, and am fully aware of what drove him to do what he did—was the attending doctor at the scene—and he, himself, was the main victim of the crash. Furthermore, the wheels of justice grind very slowly here, these days, and so, as I should not imagine that Adéle Bradshaw and the others would be too anxious to talk, and neither Merry nor Mrs. Viljoen would want to press charges, I trust that this will blow over and someday be forgotten by all concerned—except for my poor friend, himself, and Meredith!"

" I agree," said Ash. " So what's next on your list of concerns?"

"I'm not sure about Tristan's condition. I know it is possible, though not probable, that because of nerve damage, he should feel no pain, but I am not a hundred percent sure of the specialist's diagnosis. Tris is going to need further tests and follow-up treatment before he can be taken to Louisiana, and he can't get that here, Dad....In Upington, perhaps, and when he gets to New York, as you have promised, I am sure you can arrange for him to be checked out there—but it makes my toes curl to think of my tiny Meredith periodically battling to get him even as far as Upington from here!"

Ash rose to his feet and walked to the edge of the stoep, looking out over the dunes to the west of him, and, ahead, at the endless expanse of desert that stretched from *Blouspruit*, as far as the eye could see. As far as the horizon, itself.

"Leave it to the—what did you call me? Leave it to the 'strategist and master planner of business operations'. I asked

Jasper once, when he mentioned how he had arranged for Biddy's replacement to be brought here, and evidently the helicopter that drops off emergency supplies and picks up his completed scrolls and other manuscripts, from time to time, is owned by a company that takes tourists on flights over the Kalahari. It is not exactly inexpensive, and one can't get it to land here at any special time, on request, but provided medical appointments can be made for Tristan, to fit in with the established schedule, it should not be difficult to organize that.—So tick that one off the list!" He chuckled affectionately and ruffled Jordan's golden mop that was so very like his own. "That's two down!...How many more can you think of?...Oh, yes, there's another...difficult, but not insurmountable, when you've got *the* 'planner of business operations', the one time 'kid tycoon', on your team!...Leave it to me, and I'll tell you about that later!"

Jordie shook his head, smiling at his father with equal affection.

"I look forward to hearing about that. I love you, Dad! You're incredible, but how I wish you could make it possible for me to live here forever. It is years since I was last in the Kalahari, but didn't someone say that, once you have held the red sand in your hands, and let it trickle through your fingers, you would never lose the longing to return. Even one more day would be an immeasurable gift!"

While some of the present generation drink coffee to the extent that they even carry cartons of it around with them, it is still my firm conviction that, in any self-respecting South African household, four o'clock in the afternoon, means 'tea-time'!

True to form, Mieta appeared promptly at four, carrying the tray and the teacups, and, following her, came a somewhat bleary-eyed Meredith, bearing the milk and sugar, and a batch of cheese scones, fresh from the oven. Tired as she was, my girlie seemed every bit as happy at being back in her old home, as the doting old servant was to have her there.

I emerged, lethargic, and rubbing my eyes, but also very happy to be there in time to overhear Jordan's statement about the yearning to return to the Kalahari, and I couldn't agree more.

"I am living proof of that," I said.

"And so am I," Meredith acknowledged. "Like the poem about the mermaid that ever calls from the deep, so the Kalahari forever calls to those who have once trodden its dunes! On the way here, as tired as I was, my heart leapt at my first sight of a Gemsbok and a meerkat, and it was thrilling to be able to discern ostriches, almost invisible as they were, against the background of a small *kopjie*. Last night, as we were driving through *Spoors-einde*, I told my mother that I loved that funny place second only to *Blouspruit*, and that I would never again be disparaging about Van der Merwe's store, no matter what city dwellers might think of it!"

"You know, Merry," Jordan said, coming forward to take his cup from her, " that was part of the pleasure of spending time here whenever I came to help Doc Hugo. It made me feel so important when little old Miss van der Merwe would take the trouble to let me know that a fresh batch of liquorice allsorts had arrived, because she knew I liked them. I loved the way people would call out a greeting from across the street, and how elderly gentlemen would tip their hats to me, even after an absence of nearly fifteen months! I never came away from any farm empty-handed, even if I was only given a small bag of the *Cucumis africanus*, Kalahari cucumbers—with instructions as to how I might find them useful—and once an ostrich egg to take home for Auntie Bid!"

"Yes. They do that! I remember, from my time spent with Doc," Meredith enthusiastically took over from there. "And I only need to think of the blessed freedom of walking to Van der Merwe's or to the butcher's with Aunt Biddy, as she was then, unafraid and smiling at the numerous people who seemed to know her, to get a lump in my throat....I really did burst into tears when I was in the kitchen, earlier, and the first of the Bushman people to come across the border were there, at the door, waiting to bid me welcome, and laden with gifts like berries, Baobab pods, and leaves, that they know I appreciate.

"They are uncanny! They must have known that I was planning to stay, because while they have brought many things that I like to eat and use in cooking, there is much that I had planned to study for the completion of my thesis, and with which I can now replace specimens that have either shrivelled up, or decayed."

"Did you know that Saartjie's new baby has come?" I asked her.

"I saw him!" she smiled. "He's adorable! And Platjie looks happier than any man who has ever won a lottery! It's hard to believe that Saartjie and I played together as children." She turned to Jordan, explaining, "Susie and the Bushman kids were my only childhood companions for years!"

"I'd like to see Saartjie—and her family," Jordie exclaimed eagerly. "Are they there now?"

"If they're not still at the back door, they won't be too far away, I assure you!...They're probably checking us out right at this moment. I must first go and see how Tris is doing, and then I'll come back and take you to meet them. I'm glad to see you have your boots on, Jordie."

"Indeed I have. Doc Hugo was a strict mentor during my earliest sojourns in these parts. And I'd really like it if you would take me to meet your little *'Saasi'* family," he said, "but I think that, as soon as I have emptied my cup, I must first go with you, in case Tristan is awake and needs help getting up. He may be ready to be brought out here.—Please remind me to talk to your dad about ways and means of making it possible for Tris to take a shower. He enjoys that so much!"

"Well, here I am." Jasper announced, emerging from the house to join us on the stoep. "Am I in time for tea?"

"If it's cold, dear husband of mine, it will be my pleasure to make a fresh pot. You were sleeping so peacefully that I did not want to wake you," I explained.

He felt the teapot. "No, it seems fine to me. Water seems to stay hot a good deal longer here that on the Witwatersrand. I suppose it's because it boils so quickly there.—But where is Ash? I thought I heard his voice out here a while ago..."

Looking around him, Jordan was surprised. "He was. I wonder where's he's gone. Perhaps he's with Merry, checking on Tristan. I'm just about to go and look in on Tris, myself!"

They came back without Ash, however. When Merry, carrying her own boots, returned to the stoep with Jordan, to report that Tristan was still sound asleep, he, Ash was already there, looking very pleased with himself.

"Listen to this, good people," he announced cheerfully, " I have just made a deal, and if it suits you, and you can stand another two nights of us, Jordie has been granted an extra day of leisure! When I went earlier, to investigate what was causing so much excitement in the kitchen, Meredith promised that if I could swing this, she and Mieta—and Biddy, if she were willing—would cook us dinner tomorrow night, the way her grandmother taught her, and I took her up on it. I'm sure

Jordie wouldn't want to miss a meal prepared from genuine Kalahari bounty!"

"And surely you would not doubt, for one moment, that you are welcome, Ash!" Jasper remarked. "This is wonderful news! If none of the strings on my cello have snapped during my absence, perhaps we could have some music. It would be such a pleasure to play with a pianist as accomplished as you are.—Would it be too much to hope that you have brought your clarinet, Jordan?"

Jordie looked almost bashful. "I did, in fact. I thought I would have only today here, and I was beginning to give up hope of playing a few pieces with you, because everyone is still so tired, and we don't know what tonight might bring, as far as Tris is concerned. He has slept so much, already!—Merry, did you really make that pact with my father?" There was nothing but sheer delight to be discerned in those blue, Ashton eyes now!

"Well..." She was noticeably blushing. "Not exactly in those terms, Jordie!"

"We had a really interesting chat," his father broke in, saving her from further embarrassment. "It was I who made the suggestion, to begin with. Merry disputes the belief held by some, that the Kalahari is really a '*dorsland*' (thirst land) rather than a true desert. However, she is willing to grant that if an area has, among other requirements, to be devoid of almost all plant and animal life, in order to be classified as a desert, the Kalahari would actually not qualify—because of the numerous plants and animals, that flourish here.—And, if anyone should know this, it is she. I plan to spend a good part of my extra day here, in a conducted tour of her lab."

I can't begin to imagine how bittersweet the rest of Jordie's 'reprieve' must have been for the two of them. I only know what Merry has confided to me, and later to Jordie's father and Jasper. There must have been other things too precious to share with anyone, but I could guess—and so could the rest of us, I'm sure—that the two of them would hardly be out of sight before they'd be in each other's arms, and we did not think any less of them for it! And, if the Bushmen were somewhere about, and saw them, I'm sure that they would only have looked kindly upon them. Mieta had already expressed the opinion that Jordan and his father were 'goeie mense'! (Good people.)

For Jordie and Meredith there was no immediate need for words. They simply clung together as if they would never let go, and kissed as neither of them had ever done before. There was nowhere they could really sit down on the ground, where they were, so, while we remained talking over second cups of tea—and thirds—they went around the house, and through the front door, into Jasper's study.

There they sat down together on the couch, and Jordie took her in his arms once more. His voice was husky when he spoke.

"Meredith, the consuming love I have for you, is making it difficult for me to breathe. I have a haze before my eyes, at the realization that there is nothing to prevent me from sneaking into your bedroom tonight, when everyone is asleep, except that we both know that it is not in us to carry on a clandestine love affair....It's the very word 'sneak' that would detract from the wonder; the awesomeness of the experience!"

"I would not stop you, Jordie," she admitted, whispering. "And I can't believe that I have said that. It can only be that, at last, I understand what drives people to want to do that....My own heart is beating so much that I couldn't bear it if you let go of me. I doubt if I could stand up right now!...I now know what you mean...I talked to Zhaynie about that once, and she tried to explain—but now I *know*!"

"I, too, could never have believed that I would ever feel like this, my love!" Jordan confessed, speaking softly with his mouth close to her ear as he pressed his cheek to hers. "I also poured out my heart to my sister.... In Nelspruit, and again when she came to visit Tristan. She confirmed what I had suspected, that your marriage has never been consummated, and I had never as much as kissed a girl until you came along, so I lie awake nights, longing to hold you in my arms, and wondering if there is any way your marriage could be annulled—only to end up feeling ashamed of myself!"

"I know all about that, too!" she cried. "I torment myself with more than that. For two pins I would throw all caution to the winds and run away with you, right now, but I would never be at peace, and nor would you! In the first place, Zhaynie could not say which countries accept non-consummation of marriage as grounds for annulment—although that would not be difficult to ascertain—but I have greater impediments to deal with, than that!"

"What impediments, my dearest? What others can there possibly be?"

"In the first place, what my mother did to my father. And, in the second, I could have left Tris before; but to leave him, now that he is utterly helpless, and so vulnerable, would be unspeakable!"

When Jordan, being the gentleman he was, confided to their fathers, individually, that he and Merry had toyed with the idea of seeking annulment of her marriage, but had immediately rejected all thought of it, he gave both of them Meredith's reason for not wanting to leave Tristan; but only to Ash did he repeat what she had said about her mother. He,

Jordan's father understood perfectly, and it was indisputable evidence of his trust in Meredith, and the mutual respect they had for one another, that he was able to go to her directly, and assure her of how much he admired her decision and appreciated the heartache this was causing her. At the same time, he assured her that no one—her father least of all— would dare to compare her recently awakened love for Jordan with that of Rosalie's desertion of her husband and family.

CHAPTER FOURTEEN

The day that both his earthly father, and the Father in heaven—for it is He who determines whether or not we wake at all—had given Jordan, could not have been more perfect. He had slept better than he could have hoped, and rose early, to be rewarded with the sight of his beloved 'Miss Muffet' in her ridiculously tiny boots and large sunbonnet, walking out in the garden, from which she hoped to erase all evidence of recent neglect. When she reached a place she obviously knew well, and where there was one of very few convenient rocks to sit on, she briefly removed the boots and walked barefoot in the dew, constantly on the alert against a lurking scorpion. Every so often she would bend over a plant or shrub, examining it closely, in the hope that it might be redeemable, and if she looked sad at times, it was because she was ever aware of the fact that this, for her, was a temporary, futile enterprise.

The knowledge that before very long she would be living in Louisiana, weighed heavily upon her; not because she had anything against the place, but due to the realization that, if ever she were taken to New Orleans, it would only intensify her longing for Jordie. As it was she could not listen to jazz without shedding tears. She tried not to dwell on all she would be leaving behind, but having so very recently been away, she loved her home, the Kalahari, and her people, all the more.

The radiant joy that lit up her sweet face the moment she caught sight of Jordan gladdened his heart. All depressing thoughts were instantly banished, and knowing that Tristan was not where he could see and be hurt, and having bared their hearts to us, Jordie felt free to run to her. They embraced one another, openly, and then they walked hand-in-hand together in the fresh, morning air.

Later that day, after a good breakfast, with Tristan seated in his wheelchair at the table with us, she and I helped Mieta to clear away and stack the dishes, and then we went about our individual duties for the day. We both had a great deal of unpacking to do, but she put off anything that could be left until after Jordie had gone, because the time with him was too precious to waste. The most urgent task, to be carried out, with Jasper's help, was the arrangement of Tristan's room. She put away his clothes and then, with Jordan to advise them, they worked out the most efficient arrangement of all essentials for the patient's everyday care. This had to be accomplished in the most efficient manner possible, so that everything that would be used daily, and on a permanent basis, would be within easy reach.

After that, the three men, Ash, Jordan and Jasper, put their heads together to discuss the best way to make it possible for Tristan to be taken into the shower. Only Malgas, the former gatekeeper, was remotely tall enough to assist Jasper, so the consensus was that the method formerly employed by Jordan and Reg would not be feasible. It was finally decided that Jasper and Ash, who were both good with their hands, would make a device in which Tris could be seated, while being sprayed with the 'telephone' shower. Jordan, who had heard somewhere, that just the water it took to brush one's teeth was enough to keep a Bushman going for two days, was concerned about how much would be going down the drain, but Jasper was able to assure him that there was a good deal of underground water at *Blouspruit*, and that, despite the laborious process involved, he had sunk more than one well.

This settled, Meredith and Jordan took Tristan to be with them while she showed Jordie around her lab, and, forgetting for a moment that Tris might not be able to follow the conversation, she explained what still had to be done before she was ready to submit her thesis. She could hardly believe it when, after listening to her, Tristan began to relate in Creole, hesitantly, but with quite a proprietary air, how she had once done a gram stain for him. His comprehension of English was excellent, and she hoped that this could lead to his ability to speak fluently again, regain other knowledge, and, in time, perhaps to resume the practice of medicine.

In the afternoon we 'elders' put our feet up again until four o'clock, when the tea came, and Tristan slept until he was brought out to the stoep to join us. This had given Jordie and Meredith a few more, precious hours to be alone together and renew promises. Each time they said goodbye, it was never enough, and, it seemed could never be final. If he could come to *Blouspruit* just one more time, before she went off to the States, he would endeavour to do so, he promised; and, perhaps, if she and Tris could come to *Bentleigh* at Christmas, she could see snow for the first time, and he could take her tobogganing. Both knew that the promises might well be idle, but they found consolation in envisaging the possibility.

True to Merry's bargain with Benjamin Ashton, she, Mieta and I cooked a dinner to be remembered by anyone who had never before eaten such fare. After a sundowner on the stoep, we went into the dining room, where Jasper said grace, and then our visitors were given, for the main course, a choice of roast venison, served with a coulee made from berries Platjie had brought; and a casserole of ostrich, prepared with Kalahari truffles. Merry also made good use of the *Kriedoring* berries, to concoct a delicious dessert, and there were other delicacies like apricots, from Upington, stewed with a root of elusive flavour, which tasted not unlike ginger. We then retired to the living room for coffee that she had made from the roasted roots of the *Boscia albitrunca*, the Shepherd's tree, after which we were treated to a concert of chamber music, provided by Ash, Jasper and Jordan.

Before going to bed, Jordan sought out his father, and finding him in the bathroom, brushing his teeth, he sat down on the edge of the bath, waiting until he had finished before he spoke. And, when he did, there was no one else on earth who would have been better able to understand than his father, Ben Ashton, who had once endured similar heartache.

"Dad," Jordan said, " I just want to thank you with all my heart for the gift of this day. I shall remember it for the rest of my life….I shall have to!…I made promises to Meredith today that I have now decided would not be fair to keep, and it's going to be difficult to explain why I have made this decision. I'll put you in the picture later. Meanwhile I thank God that we have to leave here before dawn tomorrow, because if I were to stay longer, I would not be able to abide by this resolution.—Have you ever seen anything as cute as those little feet in *velskoens?* That is a picture I shall carry with me forever, and wherever I go! One good look at her tomorrow, and I shall never want to leave her again!"

True to his word, he did tell Merry next day!

Jasper had decided to spare Hennie Vercueil the additional forty miles he would have had to cover, in order to fetch Ash and Jordie. For Hennie it would have meant sleeping the night at *Blouspruit*, if they wanted to be on their way by four in the morning, and it would be far more sensible, and far kinder to the taxi driver, if we took the Ashtons, father and son, as far as *Spoors-einde*, where we could have breakfast with Sally and, when the shops opened, lay in a few supplies before returning to the farm.

Meredith, who had hardly closed an eye all night, was up, but came in her bathrobe and *velskoens* to see us off, and Jordan managed to draw her aside, letting the rest of us go on ahead to start putting the luggage in the truck. And it must have been one of the most difficult things he had ever had to do in his life, to say to her, "My sweetheart, this time it's really 'goodbye'! There can be no more 'next times'! There are many reasons for doing this, and God only knows how painful this is for me....I'm sure you have slept very little, and I have hardly slept at all, but I know that I am doing what is right. We have drawn comfort from dreams, but now must face up to the stark reality that we can't go on like this!"

She was so shocked that she could hardly speak, but she did manage to cry out, "*Why, Jordie? Why?*"

He heard the anguish in her voice, and it was an echo of what was in his own heart. "There are many reasons, my dear one, but what has finally brought me to my senses, was the look on Tristan's face yesterday, when we were with you in your lab. I fervently hope he didn't suspect anything, but there were tears in his eyes!

"Meredith, we have so much! We have the knowledge of how deeply we love, and I know that I shall never change—but what is left in life for that man? He can't walk, he has lost his profession, and he has even been deprived of the ability to communicate freely with people; but that does not mean that his brain is impaired.—Tristan Connaught is no fool.—And the tragedy of it is, that he has never known real peace or joy in his entire life!

"Other friends have often criticized me for 'humouring Tris' as they put it, but, as I stand here today, and knowing what I know now, I would like to think that I might have made his tortured life a little more bearable for him....Now that everything else has been taken from him, I can't take his wife from him, too!"

She did not immediately respond because there was nothing to say, until she succeeded in asking him, in strangled voice, "But what about you, Jordie? Don't you also want the most out of life for yourself? You sacrifice yourself daily for other people. Your whole life is one of service to others!"

He tipped her chin so that he could look deeply into her eyes. "All I want now, my dear one, is something that belongs to you—and please don't deny me this....Give me your little *velskoens* to take with me!"

That must have been the very last thing she would have expected, but she was so bewildered that she complied automatically, took off the shoes and gave them to him. As he wrapped them in his handkerchief, and put them in his pocket, he told her: "I shall hang them in my office, and whenever life gets to be a bit too much for me, I'll be able to look at them, and say to myself, 'Jordan Ashton, the most beautiful girl in the world once honoured you with her love—and she wore those on her dear little feet!' "

Now almost hoarse with emotion, he gave her a hug, holding her close for a minute or two, kissed her, and then he ran to the waiting truck without looking back!

***

Jasper was wonderfully unselfish and understanding during the difficult period that followed. Because Meredith lacked the physical strength for many things that had to be done, her father was always there to help, and she knew that I was readily available; nevertheless the heaviest responsibility was hers. Jasper worked steadily on the translation for which he had been commissioned, and I ran the house, so to speak, while Meredith put in as many hours as she could in her lab—but seldom without having Tristan there. Jasper made a tray that could be flipped aside when it was not needed, and once this became Tristan's tray table, it was touching to see how willing he was to help with some of the manual procedures required in the lab.

Her father and I were so proud of Meredith. What went on in her heart and thoughts, and how she suffered, we had no way of knowing, but all the time she was there in the lab with Tris, she kept up a running commentary, keeping him abreast of what she was doing, but also encouraging him. She would talk as though she were confident of the future, about how he might someday have his own practice again, and of things they might do when they arrived in Louisiana. Of how she looked forward to meeting his parents, and to seeing all he could show her there. She boldly risked mention of places where the Spanish moss grew, and asked whether it would be possible for a wheelchair to be pushed from where his parents lived, to *Beauclaire*, next-door. None of these references appeared to upset him, and this was added to the list of other blessings.

Often, in his bedroom, or sometimes out in the sun— before the weather grew too cold—she would massage his legs with Baobab oil, and other agents she prepared in her lab, commenting, from time to time, to encourage him, that she saw none of the severe wasting of those muscles that, being a physician, he knew enough to expect...and dreaded to the extent that it depressed him. Many times, when she was kneeling at Tristan's feet, he would put his hand on her hair, thanking her in his language, or he would catch hold of her hand and kiss it. She urged him to use his arms, to wheel his chair, himself, and Jasper stood by, ready to help, as Tristan made the first attempts at getting himself out of bed, and into the chair. I saw to other, more intimate needs as I had learned to do in hospitals, in the past.

Very soon Tris became used to the little people that came and went, and often sat clicking away cheerfully at him out on the stoep, as though to assure him that all was right with the world, and he missed them if they did not come. Mieta, having long since upgraded her opinion of him, went out of her way to spoil him.

It was a happy diversion when Ash and Amy-Lee arrived with Doctor and Mrs. Fisher. We have a big house, and Mieta and I liked having all the bedrooms in use, as much as we all enjoyed the stimulating chatter going on all around us. This was particularly pleasant for my dear Jasper, who willingly turned off the lights over his scrolls and quills, to sit in the sun on the stoep and visit with these delightful, interesting visitors—all of whom were intrigued with both Jasper's work and Merry's. What was most amazing, the first time we heard this, was that Tris managed to say few words in English to the Fishers who knew no French!

Life was never boring for us, however, and although we missed our delightful guests, and the breath of the outside world that they represented, everything carried on as before, when they left.

We only made use of the helicopter twice. The first time, for Jasper to take Tris for a check-up in Upington, and the second, to attend Meredith's convocation in Gauteng. I think that Tristan, sitting in his chair in the aisle beside us, in the Great Hall was as proud of her at that moment as we were. Standing on the platform in her cap and gown as her doctorate was conferred upon her, she saw us and smiled, but I noticed that her eyes kept searching, until she located the Ashtons, and I detected from her expression that her heart sang when she noticed that Jordan was with them. However, when his parents came to congratulate her afterwards, he was nowhere to be seen, and with that golden head had gone the joy, and the big day was irrevocably ruined for her. His message of pride and good wishes, were conveyed to her by his mother, but her lips were so stiff that she could hardly express her thanks.

We met after the luncheon, to discuss final arrangements for Tristan to be taken to America, and Merry, who was already strained to the utmost, hurting with disappointment because Jordan had left without speaking to her, was quite overcome when Ben Ashton outlined his plans. Accompanied by himself and Amy-Lee, she and Tristan would be taken in the Ashton company jet, as far as London, and from there they would fly, first class, to New York. In due course, after having spent a few days at *Bentleigh*, Ash planned to take Tristan to undergo a battery of tests at a facility specializing in spinal chord injury.

"I propose," he told us, "to have Tristan admitted to a hospital, perhaps the Helen Hayes, in West Haverstraw, which has an excellent rehabilitation program for the treatment of the complex effects of spinal chord injury, as well as the emotional and psychological issues related to adjustment to a new way of life. Our aim will be to help Tristan to resume an active, independent life, physically and emotionally, as well as vocationally!"

It was a good thing that a number of other people in the hall that day, probably parents and students, had been noticeably affected by the proceedings, unashamedly shedding tears of joy—or perhaps disappointment, who knows? I believe that, as a consequence, we were not as conspicuous as we might otherwise have been, when both Tristan and Meredith broke down. I was sniffing, and Jasper suddenly had something in his eye that required the urgent use of his handkerchief!

Tristan was naturally the most overwhelmed, and he was fortunate to be able to speak freely, because I am willing to wager that no one in that place, besides himself, Ben and Amy-Lee, could understand a word of *Créole Lalouisiane*! As it was, even Meredith and Jasper did not catch everything Tristan said, but from their translation for my benefit, later, what they were able to follow was enough to stun the lot of us!

"Why would you want to do this for me, Uncle Ben?" Tristan demanded of Ash, weeping unrestrainedly. His stammering speech made what was to follow, even more heartrending. "I have given many people endless trouble, over the years—your son more than any other, perhaps—and yet you have consistently shown me nothing but love and kindness. Now, here I am, crippled through nothing but my own reckless, sinful behaviour, and still you reach out to me! Meredith and Jordan do not realize that I know how much they love one another—but I have wrecked their lives. They are caught up now, with me, in the mess I have made of my life, but they have neither reproached nor berated me. They have not failed to care for me!

"I have broken the hearts of my parents, and I have cursed my brother—and in selfishly keeping Merry and Jordan apart, I have literally destroyed three lives, one of them my own.— And still they reach out to me in love! Meredith, with those small hands, rubs oil into my legs, Aunt Biddy attends to my needs, overlooking past transgressions, and Uncle Jasper has not permitted the heartbreak I have brought upon his daughter, to deter him from ministering to me, too.—Dear God in heaven, how do you manage to do this? Why do you not cast me out in the street, and leave me to suffer all that I deserve?"

I could see, by the way Ben's face and eyes were screwed up, although he was neither frowning nor scowling, and by the way Amy-Lee and Meredith tensely waited for him to deal with this, that Benjamin Ashton was having a hard time trying to compose himself before responding. Finally, with eyes overflowing, and taking short, panting breaths, as he struggled not to break down, as well, he replied: "Jesus said, 'Love one another as I have loved you!'—What can I say to you, Tristan, that would improve on that?...And do you realize my dear boy, that you have just emulated the Prodigal Son?

"I must also tell you that, because I love your father like a brother, and because he came to me once in a London hospital where I was ready to die of misery, also as a result of a heart broken by my own foolishness, I intend to give you back to him, personally, and in the best shape possible!—Now let's all give each other a hug before we go our separate ways, and prepare for the journey." To Jasper, he said, " I believe you intend staying at an hotel until the helicopter is available? If you still want to do that, I shall understand, but our house is open to you. I am available to fly you back to Upington whenever you like!"

He gave Meredith a special kiss, and told her again how proud he was of her, and she, barely able to speak, told him, "I would not be where I am today either, Uncle Ben, were it not for all of you. I would like to add something to that, however. When I first began my research, I had to set my work aside frequently, because I had my sister, my beloved father, and the house to take care of. This time, I had a most wonderful mother who freed me to concentrate on my work, and to her I owe more than I can say!"

I don't believe that I was the only one who understood why Jordan had left so soon, and it was for that reason that we did not accept the kind invitation to stay in his house. In fact, I don't think that Ash had really expected us to do so. He was just being Ash, as courteous as ever, but he had a child who was hurting as much as ours was, and none of us wanted to subject our children to the ordeal of pretence again...

CHAPTER FIFTEEN.

The house at *Blouspruit* seemed very empty after all the children had gone. Susie was having the time of her life and was in no hurry to come home, and, strange to say, we even missed Tristan. Jasper, who believed, like Benjamin Ashton, that there is no such thing as co-incidence, did not bear grudges, and there was no resentment in his heart towards Tris...the cause of the upheaval in our lives.

Perhaps because of the work in which he delighted, Jasper, and possibly his children, spoke in ways that people who did not know them, might have considered pedantic, but it thrilled me when he talked to me like that. Sometimes while we sat on the stoep having tea, he would unexpectedly come over and kiss me. Or if we lay in bed reading, he might put down his book and say something like, "Beloved, the Lord knew that I needed you in my life!" I loved the times when, as I sat quietly knitting while he worked on a manuscript, he would look up to recite special lines of poetry to me, and I'll never forget the day he stretched out his hand to take mine, and quoted from Robert Browning's poem about Abraham ibn Ezra:

"Grow old along with me! The best is yet to be..."

Our dear, discerning Meredith knew that we would worry about her, and because, bless her heart, she wanted no clouds to sully our joy, she wrote almost every day—using her laptop to keep a diary while they were in transit. She sent this off to us as soon as she arrived at the Ashtons' home in New York, and after that my husband and I awaited her emails so impatiently that we would constantly check to see whether another had come.

New York in July and August can be perfectly ghastly, I have been told, but having spent most of her life in the Kalahari, Merry did not mind the heat. What disconcerted her was the length of the days. "When it gets to nine o'clock of an evening and the sun has not set," she wrote, "I am in awe of these people! I ask them how they stand it, but Uncle Ash just laughs. He told me, teasing me, that it was not until he arrived in South Africa that he could figure out how the word 'nightfall' must have originated. When he discovered how little 'twilight' there was, he began to appreciate how apt an expression like 'night fell', is in our country. He says it's because it really does 'fall'—so suddenly that he almost expects it come down with a thump!"

Every email was full of admiration for Ben Ashton, and her gratitude to him and to Amy-Lee was boundless. She described *Bentleigh* in detail, explaining how it had been remodelled so that Father Crawford and his family could live as independently as if they had their own apartment. She gave a vivid description of where James Ashton—who was now, in principal, the owner of the mansion—and his wife, Isobel lived, and where Ben and Amy-Lee now had their suite. Evidently she, Merry and Tris, were being accommodated in the part in which the Ashton parents resided, and she could not help wondering how it happened that, instead of being allocated Zhaynie's very feminine bedroom and bathroom, she occupied a suite that belonged to Jordie.

Somehow, I inferred that, being kind and very insightful, Amy-Lee must have known that Merry would feel comfortable among the school and university photos, pennants and other souvenirs of Jordan's life before she had met him. There was one picture of him in his white coat, posing on the steps of a hospital with other interns, and my eyes misted when, reading a message from her, I came to her innocent observation that Jordan stood out from the rest. It appeared that he was the tallest, his hair was the fairest and, according to her, his smile was the warmest. All in all, what she was really trying to say was that, in her eyes, he was out and out the best looking, and I knew that he was the closest to her heart!

Reading between the lines, my own heart bled for her. I was left with no doubt that, even if she devoted the rest of her life to Tristan, she would never get over Jordan Ashton, and her glowing accounts of how very nice James and Isobel were to her, convinced me that they suspected this, and were sympathetic. She had come to terms with Jordan's decision to make a clean break and not to see her any more, but there was hardly a letter from her in which she did not ask if we had heard from him.

There was one more email describing places she had visited—in which she made the observation that it was hard to believe how much a little Kalahari girl like her had experienced, in less than a year—and she told of how tremendously impressed she had been during a visit to the Ashton building in downtown Manhattan. Tristan had of course often been there before, but when, during a brief visit to James, Ash had taken her with him to pick up something from what had formerly been his office, she had been completely overawed.

"*Many of his citations are still on the walls,*" she related. "*There are pictures of him with some of the rulers and crowned heads of Europe and the Orient, and several with African leaders; and I saw others taken with people carrying out humanitarian work around the world, some clearly during Christian missions.*"

"I knew that he was a remarkable man before I came here, but it boggles my mind that he, with the onerous responsibility of running the consortium, could have given so much time to others!...I only have to think of what he has done and will yet do, for Tris, and how gentle he is with me, to want to cry. Think of the magnificent father-in-law some fortunate girl will have some day! I know it can never be a girl called Meredith, but whoever she is, I pray that she will appreciate both this father and his son!"

After the first three weeks, the letters were usually about Isobel Ashton's new baby and how taken she, Merry, was with young James Benjamin, or about Tristan and the hospital to which he had been admitted. She spent the greater part of each day with him, and, while she did not say so, I suspected that, in spite of this, it was good to have no responsibilities for the time being. Then, one day, there came an email containing the most amazing information...

At the time of the occurrence, she wrote, she was in the ward with Tristan, sitting at a small table which was just the right height for the precious laptop. She thought that he was asleep until, somehow sensing that he was watching her, she turned her head to discover that his eyes were open.

"How long have you been awake, Tris?" she asked him.

"Long time....I like to watch you when you are writing, because I try to read the expressions on your face. They change from sunshine to shadow, and back, as happens when the sun goes behind the clouds, and comes out again. Then I try to guess what you are thinking... Please come over here and sit closer. I want to tell you something."

She rose obediently, but before sitting down on the chair nearest to his bed, she smoothed his hair back from his forehead, noticing again how gaunt his face had become.

"Is there anything you need? Would you like some water, or juice, perhaps?"

"Nothing, thank you—except just you, here, right beside me!" By this time, she told us, she had begun to understand his speech quite well, and experienced little trouble following him, although on this day some of the subject matter was, at times quite difficult to interpret.

"As I was watching you," he began, "I thought of the day I took you to buy that laptop....Do you remember, *Me'wy?*" She nodded, and he went on: "I have been thinking about how, when we brought it home, it was brand new with no memory in it, except what you put into it—by choice! Data emailed to you for your thesis, and information downloaded onto that USB Flash Drive by your father, from your desktop computer at home, so that you could then access it on your laptop."

"I remember it all, Tris, but why go into that right now?"

"Because," he said ruefully, taking her hand and holding it tightly, "that was what I tried to do to you, *chéyi!* Please try to understand the analogy, because I am desperate to get this off my chest, and that is what occurred to me, watching you just now....When I met you, it was almost the same for me as it was for you to have a brand new laptop. You were as 'new' to me as anyone I had ever come across. You were so clean, and there was still so much 'memory space', that you represented an irresistible challenge. No...more an opportunity than a challenge! I wanted to be the one to install every new experience! Perhaps to be able to dress you the way Zhaynie used to do with her paper dolls!"

"But why would you want to do that, Tris? What did you hope to gain from that?

"That is difficult for me to put into words now…but I wanted…if I may again use the laptop analogy, I think I wanted to 'program' you, so that everything in your life from then onward would be associated with me! As I lie here, today, I would give everything I possess to be able to erase those memories from your mind, but, hard as I find it to get everything straight in my own mind now, I must at that stage—and most cruelly—have been trying to ensure that you would neither need, nor want, anything more than to be with me! You would be completely dependent and find no fault in me, no matter what I did…

"You have no idea how closely I watched you that day we came out of church in *Spoors-einde*! Do you know how rare it was to find a girl who was not jealous—but not because she did not care! Because she was so proud of me that she enjoyed witnessing the adulation of other women? A girl who would not be put off by my inevitable mood swings or crazy moments, because she knew no better!—Adéle and the people I called friends were generally so out of it themselves, that they did not even notice when I was! I did some pretty wild stuff to keep them guessing, and they were fascinated because they thrived on my exploits, vicariously sharing in my stunts, never knowing what I would be up to next!

"Before I found you, no one in his or her right mind had tolerated me for very long. They weren't able to! Friends—that is 'normal' friends—all except Jordan, very quickly abandoned me, probably for good reason, and that only contrived to make me more objectionable. I hid behind a veil of arrogance, and I tried to outdo my peers in every way, to get my own back! What I am not sure of now, though, is whom I wished to punish by doing this. It appears that it turned out to be none other than myself, and, in the process I hurt *you*!…I also underestimated you...You were too intelligent to remain gullible indefinitely, and, what's more, you had a powerful ally in Aunt Biddy!"

He kept quiet for a time, fighting for control of himself.

"Go on!" she said at last. "I'm listening!"

"Never during all this time, was the noise gone from my head. I once heard of an elephant that sucked tadpoles up its trunk with the water it was drinking, and when they finally turned into frogs, they made such a loud noise in its head that it kept bashing it against the trees to try and kill itself, or the noise!—Again I don't know which, and I don't know if the story is true, but I can empathise!

"Never, from as far back as I can remember, could I go anywhere to escape for long, from either the noise or those eyes that stared so malevolently at me. It was worse in the darkness, and particularly bad when, in addition, all those children where my parents live, looked at me with their big eyes. That made the noise louder and louder, until I would run blindly to *Beauclaire*, fighting my way through the Spanish moss, and trying not to notice the burning eyes that were everywhere in it. Once I got myself to where Jordie and his father were, I felt safe, and I never wanted to go home. Even when they were not at *Beauclaire* for a time, I would still go to hide there!"

"Oh, Tris," she murmured, aghast! "Didn't anyone ever guess? And if not, why didn't you tell someone? How old were you when this started?"

He thought for a while. "How do you tell grown-ups something like that when you are little—especially if you can't explain it to yourself? I think it started from the moment we got to Louisiana, because some of the black people must have reminded me of something in Bethlehem, and then there were always children yelling and screaming around me.

"It felt so good to be in the peace of Uncle Ben's office, and Jordie invariably played so tranquilly. He never fought about toys. He seemed to sense that I just wanted not to be hassled. His father would work away quietly, sometimes smile or give us a candy, or stop to admire what we had built. Now that I am grown-up and have been released from the nightmare, I have been able to figure this out, and I know that I was a different child when I was with them. The best was when I could stay with them at *Bentleigh*, however, because *there* I was free, for a while, of the things that scared me, and the older Ashton kids were also so nice to be with! There was no competition for attention, no noise, no children screaming, and, best of all, no moss or eyes to haunt me!"

There was another prolonged silence after that, and then all Meredith could say was, "Oh, Tris, how dreadful for you! And what made your parents decide to send you to Bethlehem? To your grandmother?"

"Heaven only knows! It is a very nice town, I know, but for me, it turned out to be the worst, possible place I could have been sent. Just as I now know that Bethlehem was just too closely associated with my nightmares, and that the black people in Louisiana were neither bad nor threatening. Jordie loved them—but it was all in my head, don't you see? And my brother, Timothy, represented another threat because he was so *normal*! Every parent's dream! It is small wonder that I was so intolerant of Matt Marais, and so jealous of Jordie's admiration for him. I resented all that talk of Post Traumatic Stress Disorder, because while I was so crazy, he was so normal!

"Whatever made me choose Medicine, I shall never know. Perhaps just because that is what Reg and Jordie did. I hated sick people, and I could not bear to enter a palliative care ward! In my practice I tried to stick to whatever relieved me of that!"

"Don't use that word again, Tris! You were not crazy! Just an innocent target of diabolical hatred before you were born!"

"I know that now, but we are talking about *then*! When I was finally palmed off on Uncle Hugo, things were better. He doted on me—I have realized too late—and, although Aunt Biddy was quite strict, I knew where I was with her. I felt safe, but I was bent on driving her to distraction!...Why? I don't know! Just as I don't know why I was not just left there permanently!

"I have had so much time for reflection lately. How is it that Aunt Biddy, who is a nurse, did not suspect when I began to take drugs? My behaviour was so irrational!"

All at once Meredith jumped up and walked over to the window, looking at the trees and the skyscrapers outside, without actually seeing them. "Why, Tris? Why didn't you want me?"

It was a strange question, coming out of the blue as it did, but he knew at once what she was talking about.

"You have every right to ask the question, and I'm going to be honest about this, even if you hold it against me forever. You were meant to be an experiment, and I did not want to be tied down. I wanted to put you to the test, and if you did not live up to expectations, and my experiment did not work out, I would have sent you home. I did not want to sleep with you, and no matter what you might have thought, I was not sleeping with Adéle. I did not have affairs! All I wanted was to be perpetually stoned. Wasted—but preferably not alone! Not by myself! It was sheer hell to be in that room by myself!

"Would you believe that, when I was at *Blouspruit*, a few nights before we were married, I was desperate enough to try chewing some of the leaves you had in your lab—in case I ran out of the dope I had in my medical bag? I did not realize until we went to Nelspruit for the baptism of Zhaynie's baby, that I was actually in love with you, and then I almost overdosed!...

"Now I think I would like that glass of water, if you don't mind!"

When she brought the water to him, he thanked her, drank it thirstily and observed, with wonder in his voice: "How very strange that the Lord would use Aunt Biddy and Uncle Ben Ashton as the instruments to free me from all that torment! And praise God it was Jordan who found me after the accident. Remembering that, I can never be thankful enough! On the other hand, I wish that there was some way in which the pain I have caused you could somehow be erased from my mind—and I'm not only talking about your shoulder, *mignon*! Please believe me, if there were any way I could make it up to you, I would.

"I have suddenly begun to pray, and it is beyond comprehension how I can remember so many words my father used, as well as most of the prayers he would offer up for the children in his care; Timmy and I among them! There are some he would have us all recite each day, like, *'Lord to whom all hearts be open, all desires known and from whom no secrets are hidden,'* and you might say, 'Well it's probably because you to learnt to say them, by heart,'—but, *chéyi*, how is it possible that, after all this time, I hear myself, quite involuntarily praying them again?"

"Why don't you ask Uncle Ash, when he fetches me, where those words come from and why this is happening? I assure you that he already has the answer."

"I do not doubt that....Before he arrives, will you promise me that, when the time comes, you will go to Louisiana with me?"

"Of course, Tris.—I am your wife!"

"No, you're not, my sweet!" He sounded adamant. "In the eyes of the law, maybe, but not in reality! If I could put all this right, I would, God only knows!—I ask myself constantly how things can be as they are, and I wish I knew how it is possible that I could have repaid Benjamin Ashton, the man who has always been there to make me feel safe, in the way I have!...How I, that boy whom he lovingly protected, to whom he willingly ministered and whom he helped to set free, could now have rewarded him for that, by taking from his son what he values more than his life itself?

"Stop that, Tristan!" Meredith exclaimed sharply. "We're not going there? That subject is closed, not to be opened again!"

In her next email, Merry went on to tell us that, when Ash came, Tristan did put those questions to him, and, as she had assured Tris, Ash did indeed have the answer!

He told about the night that he and I, Biddy, had prayed for Tris, and how he, Ben, had been thinking about him, while reading *'My Utmost For His Highest'* by Oswald Chambers, just before I came into the room. He related how he had said to me. "Because of the great love I have for his parents—and because of my great love for the One who made him, I have prayed for insight into Tristan's very complex character. As a matter of fact, as often happens, I mistakenly read the page intended for another day, and it was this part that gripped me: *'Our Lord knows perfectly that when once His word is heard, it will bear fruit sooner or later. The terrible thing is that some of us prevent it bearing fruit in actual life.'*

"My prayers on that night," he told Tris, "were for the grace to be able to discern how that message applied to you,

Tris, and they have been answered! I know now how those words applied to you, and I thank God that they will no longer be prevented from bearing fruit in your life!"

CHAPTER SIXTEEN

In the year Meredith Hilliard turned twenty-four, she came into her own. That was the year she began to write the children's books many of you have probably read to your children, but I shall tell more about that later. However, I must add that Jasper and I were not surprised in the least that she was moved to do so. In constructing her interesting, detailed emails to us, each day, she'd become really adept at recording her thoughts and experiences, and, in telling about the people she knew best, homesickness and heartache were, to some extent, assuaged.

Once she arrived in Louisiana, it was of course not feasible—in fact it was impossible—for her to continue with further research in regard to the plants of the Kalahari, but there was nothing to prevent her from writing about its people. She needed neither notes, nor encyclopaedias. Within the environs of *Blouspruit*, alone, she most likely had a more intimate relationship with *San* children than any acknowledged expert, for they and their Bushman cousins had been her playmates from the time she was born.

In one of her emails to us, she described her arrival in Louisiana, with Tristan and the ever-caring Ashtons, stressing that Ash had given Clifford and Thora Connaught no warning, and had also made his family promise not to let them know that he and Amy-Lee were bringing their son to them. Having parked his car as close as possible to the front door of the children's home, established by his wife, and leaving Tris, Amy-Lee, Meredith and Isaiah, one of the *Beauclaire* servants in the car, Ash went ahead, and asked one of the children to tell Father Clifford that Mr. Ashton had arrived, and was waiting in the office for him.

Of course the exuberance of the welcome he received was what he had learned to expect, and he was hardly surprised when Thora, calling out an excited greeting, came running downstairs, too. Ben kept the two of them talking long enough for Isaiah, Merry, and Amy-Lee to get Tris out of the car, and to bring him as far as the door of the office, and the way Meredith described what ensued had both Jasper and me close to tears.

Carefully orchestrated, the reunion of Tris and his parents must have been quite dramatic. Ben rose to his feet when Amy-Lee entered the office, and he then said to the priest: "Clifford, my very dear friend, once when I was travel-worn and badly in need of a shave, you welcomed a dishevelled stranger into your home. You brought me a clean towel and showed me to a shower. I was heartbroken, and you comforted me. I was hungry and you fed me!

"Once I was thirsty and you gave me water. Actually…"— he grinned mischievously—"I seem to recall, more correctly, that it was brandy, because I was on the verge of collapse! The Lord only knows how thankful I am that, tonight, after all these years, I can bring you and Thora a gift that will, I pray, not only help to quench your thirst, relieve some of the pain in your hearts, but also restore your joy and your hope!…Because of your love and loyalty to my brother, you were imprisoned and missed precious time with your young family. I pray that I can help to restore some of the years that the locusts have eaten."

Meredith said that she was very emotional, and old Isaiah was sniffing, as he wheeled Tristan into the room, with her, Merry, walking beside Tris and holding his hand. She was crying openly by the time Tristan—having first, wordlessly, and with his hands to his mouth, regarded the prematurely grey, barely recognizable man in the black cassock, and the tall, pretty woman with him—managed at last to whisper in his language, "Father!...Mother!"

There was no need for Tristan to repeat the broken confession he had made after Meredith's convocation. He was not given a chance to say anything more, anyhow, before his father was on his knees beside the chair, clasping his son's head to his breast and weeping over him so that his tears dripped down onto those dark, Connaught curls. Thora was on the other side, holding Tristan's hand, alternately kissing it and, looking up at Ben, and from him to Amy-Lee and the other two, and crying out: "Thank you! Thank you! Oh, praise God! Surely I am dreaming...!"

If Tris had ever longed for a welcome to compare with that of the Prodigal Son, he certainly received it that night. I tried also to imagine the reaction of his parents when they were introduced to the beautiful girl their son had brought home to them as his wife, but she mentioned little apart from describing how kindly Ben had performed the introduction, telling them, "This is Meredith—Doctor Meredith Hilliard, to be exact. A daughter-in-law any parent would cherish!"—And Merry confided to us that she hoped that they had read nothing significant in what he had added to that...."A daughter-in-law such as I would dearly have wanted for myself!" What she did describe, in detail however, was how Tris, struggling mightily to do so, suddenly succeeded in jerking himself upright, and out of the wheelchair, and, supported by his brace and callipers, took his first steps. Walking very slowly, half stumbling towards her, he said: "I owe much to my Lord, and to everyone in this room—but I would not have made the effort to live, and to be here, if I had not loved this girl enough to try!"

Of course there was plenty of hugging, crying and kissing after that, and it was touching to Ash and Amy-Lee to see the love and gratitude with which Tristan's parents welcomed and embraced Tristan's wife. Clearly Meredith's outburst had been forgotten by Mrs. Burkett, Thora's mother, and her family had heard nothing but praise for her from the old lady (who had mercifully gone back home, after confessing that she could not stand so many children 'running about the place!)

In her next communication, Merry went on to recap for our benefit, what Ben had told the Connaughts, once the excitement had died down, and he was able to talk seriously to them.

"I am not going to apologise for catching you unawares like this," he said, "for I'm sure that you understand why we wanted to keep your visitors a surprise. I know you would have preferred to have made preparations for their coming, but then, having seen how you can rise to the occasion in emergencies, as you did during the hurricane, I feel sure that you will cope, and, if necessary, Amy-Lee and I will help.

"Meredith is not a medical doctor, but has been taking excellent care of Tristan for some time now, and she is able to fill you in on all that is necessary for his future care and well-being. However, as I am sure that, more than any of us, she needs a good rest, I am going to ask you if you can possibly give her a room to herself, with perhaps a bell at Tristan's bedside, to call for assistance if he should need it. It has been a long day for all of us, but I don't know when last Merry had a proper night's sleep!"

He had just provided Thora with precisely the opportunity for which any mother would have been yearning.

"We can do better than that," she said, giving Merry a kiss. "I was a bit shy of intruding," she readily confessed, "but I'm sure I don't need to tell you that I am longing to get my boy to myself. If Meredith will tell us exactly what has to be done, Cliff and I will see to Tris until she is fully rested, and for as long as she likes, after that. We have a lot of catching up to do! Fortunately past experience had taught us always to have a few rooms ready for unexpected arrivals, so Tris and Merry can be taken to theirs right away, and I suggest that we put an extra bed in Tristan's, so that Cliff and I can take turns to watch over him. This is all like a dream! Please don't let me wake up and find that that is all it is!"

When Jasper had finished reading this email, he turned to me and said compassionately, "I don't believe that either of those parents could have slept a wink, and they wouldn't even have cared! Biddy, my dearest, just think of all that they and Tristan will have to say to one another. Imagine the catching up they will have to do...and imagine the joy and the relief when they learn how much he wanted to go home—to them! Now they can mourn his brother together, and that will lighten Tristan's heart, because a burden shared is never as heavy as one that has to be carried alone!...All I can think of now is that beautiful line, *And so He bringeth him to his desired haven!*' "

Merry said that they all had reason to be grateful for the chairlift that had been installed in the home, after Hurricane Katrina. This had been done at Amy-Lee's behest, because some of the children who had been brought to seek shelter in the mansion that had once been her family home, had not only been left without a roof over their heads. Of those who had been injured, some still had difficulty negotiating the impressive oak staircase with its curved, oak balustrade, and for Meredith to have had to toil up it that night, in order to get Tristan upstairs and into to bed, would have been more than she could have coped with.

Ash and Isaiah saw to that part of it, and presently, while Merry and Thora got Tris ready for the night, Amy-Lee went to the kitchen to fetch a snack for him. When he had eaten, his overwhelmed parents joined hands with the Ashtons and Meredith, and together they sang the very doxology that had once made Tristan shudder.

We did not hear from Meredith for three days after that, and it was Ash who telephoned to bring us up to date. Evidently, having been shown her room, she succeeded in locating her bathrobe, nightie and toothbrush, took a bath, dozing a few times in the process, then fell into bed, and did not wake until nearly noon next day. She was extremely apologetic, but Thora waved her apologies aside, and responded by taking her in her arms. Ash had conveyed to Tristan's mother the toll that the past months had taken on this small, courageous creature, not omitting a single detail of what it must have cost her to adjust to so many responsibilities; not least of them getting Tris from one place to another, along a challenging, and what must have seemed an endless, pilgrimage, to bring him at last to where he wanted to be.

How thankful her father and I were, to be told of how Tristan's parents treasured her! I could have told them that she was an adorable little person, but her father and I derived a great deal of comfort from an email sent us by my old friend Thora, who told us how charmed she and Cliff were with Merry, and how she was enjoying having a daughter to spoil. Meredith was encouraged to spend two days in bed. Her meals were brought to her, and it was all Thora could do to stop the curious young ones in the house, from peeping in on her when no one was looking. I chuckled as I pictured the little faces. How children love visitors in the home, provided they are nice visitors! Kids have this marvellous kind of sixth sense that enables them to sense the good and bad in people.

Another remark in Thora's email was beyond encouraging. I threw my hands up with delight and thanksgiving, when I read her account of how the burden of years of depression—which she now described as 'oppression'—had been lifted at what must have been precisely the same the time as Tristan's deliverance!

"My boy's eyes are smiling at last, Biddy," she wrote. "Do you remember how I used to sing to him when he was little? But, there was never any peace or joy to be discerned in the 'windows' of Tristan's soul, before!"

Tristan's quick adaptation to the transition was remarkable. He seemed to thrive under his parents' roof, and during the time Meredith stayed in bed, he was exceedingly solicitous. She was surprised that he should be concerned when he noticed that she kept rubbing her left shoulder, because, until then, she had not realized that he was gradually becoming more aware of the events of that fateful day.

"Do you mind if I check your arm, Meredith?" he asked diffidently, and seeing the look on her face, he reminded her, "I used to be doctor, if you remember!"

There were many other indications of his returning memory. When his parents had looked in on her together on that first afternoon, she had made a point of explaining to them—without mention of anything that might have troubled them unduly—how it had come about that Tristan had reverted to the language of his childhood; and she told them, too, of his extreme remorse at the sorrow he had caused them.

"Ash has already put us in the picture, dear," Thora said affectionately, and it was Clifford who put into words the measure of their gratitude, when they had been told, also, of their son's deliverance.

"That it should have been Bridget who was there with Benjamin Ashton," Father Clifford, observed, "is nothing short of Divine Intervention. God works in mysterious ways...She was there at his birth, and our Lord put her there again at his re-birth!"

Can you think of how overcome I was when Meredith relayed this conversation to me? God truly does work in marvellous ways! I was in awe by the time I reached the end of her letter.

"I had never thought of that," she wrote to her father and me, "until Father Clifford had the most incredible insight into the situation, and suddenly exclaimed with wonder in his voice: 'How astonishing! How far beyond all comprehension it is, that, having been re-born, Tristan has, in so many ways, become a child again! No wonder he speaks in the language of his childhood! But he is a grown man now, and I believe that, by the Grace of God, he will have all the best things about being that man, fully restored to him, in time. Already, today, I have heard him say a few words in English.'

" 'That's true!' I cried excitedly,' " Merry went on to relate. "Only then was I able to appreciate what Tris had said earlier. Not only did he remind me that he had been a physician, but he had unconsciously said that in English!"

"Isn't it a curious thing, too," Jasper remarked thoughtfully, "that the first words he was given to speak, were those of repentance! Do you recall, beloved, how distraught he was about Meredith? Sufficiently so, to emerge from a coma and immediately express regret? I have taken careful notice of the fact that he has not once experienced difficulty in speaking fluently, or finding the right words, when asking anyone for forgiveness?...Think of that day after the luncheon!"

I considered this for a minute or two, and told him that I agreed with everything he had said. Then I asked, "Jasper, dearest, do you think I should mention to Meredith that Jordan was in *Spoors-einde* for a week, but did not contact us? It was typical of Jordie that he would temporarily change places with Doctor Prinsloo, and take care of Doc Hugo's practice while that young man had to go to Pretoria, to see about his landed immigrant's visa for Canada, but I don't know whether to be hurt or not that I had to hear about that from Sally!"

"No!" said my husband, emphatically. "Trust me! The one who is hurting most is Jordan. Because he is not the kind of man who would readily get over someone he so clearly loves, I regard the very fact that he avoided coming here, as evidence of how acutely he is struggling! And please don't tell Merry. It won't do her any good to know that!"

The next communication came directly from our daughter. Meredith phoned just as I was getting out of bed one morning and, allowing for the time difference, she must have stayed up very late to be calling from where she was.

"Mother," came the sweet voice, apologetically "I have to ask you to get my father to do a very big favour for me. Would you please ask Dad to phone Jordie's office and find out where he is at the moment...?"

Needless to say I was taken aback. "Of course I'll do that, Merry-love, but why don't you ask him? I'll get him for you!— Or, better still, you must still have Jordan's number, so why don't you just phone his office, and find out for yourself?"

" I don't want to do either of those things, Mother. I did call once, hoping that it would not be Jordan's receptionist who answered, but it was—and I was too shy to speak so I rang off. She'd know my voice at once! For the same reason, I can't ask you to phone, and I am embarrassed to ask Daddy.

"If you or I were to call, and no one knew who we were, the first question we'd be asked is, 'Who shall I say is calling?' and neither of us would want to lie. But Dad can truthfully say,'Professor Hilliard' and no one would be any the wiser!— Besides they may think that he is a colleague and, Daddy would be connected without having to explain the reason for his call."

I was puzzled. "Sweetheart," I answered, "I'm sure that, if I explain to him, your father would do that for you, but why this sudden interest in Jordie's whereabouts? I thought that the two of you were studiously avoiding one another..."

"That's exactly why I must know where he is, Mother. The Ashton's have decided to remain here for Thanksgiving, and then go to *Bentleigh* for Christmas, because, I'm sure, that they are missing baby James and his parents....I have to go next-door tomorrow, to speak to Uncle Ash about Tristan's finances, and I certainly can't go over to *Beauclaire* if Jordan is there! All I need to know is whether he in the States or not!"

"Okay," I said. "I guess we can do that. We'll send you an email as soon as we have established anything."

But, after we had spoken to someone who answered the phone in Sandton, we hardly knew what to say to Meredith. "I'm sorry," Jasper was told, "Doctor Ashton is no longer with us. I can put you through to either Doctor Ian Mackenzie, or Doctor Theuns van Schalkwyk, if you like!"

Jasper then telephoned Reggie, who laughed and said, "I don't like that 'no longer with us' part, Prof. They make it sound as though he has departed this life! Jord's on six months' sabbatical while he sorts out his life. He's folded up his tent for a time, and I think he's gone to visit Matt Marais in Canada! He is not in the 'U.S. of A', that I do know!"

"And what about the house?"

"Well with Jordie not here, and Uncle Ash now having grandchildren in Nelspruit and the States, there would be no reason for him or Aunt Amy-Lee to want to stay in Bryanston. Even when Uncle Ash has business to attend to in Isando, he can stay at an hotel near the airport, or with the Marais family in Kempton Park, so, for the time being, there's no purpose in Jord's keeping his house open. It has been rented by a foreign embassy for one of its diplomats, and the servants will be retained. My mother and I will, however, continue to occupy the cottage and keep a watchful eye on the place.

"You know, Prof, one thing really has me worried, though. I can't understand why Jord would want to leave his clarinet with me. It's such a shame that he never plays it any more!"

But all we told Meredith was that Jordan was definitely not anywhere near her, in America!

Next morning she went to find Tristan, and was pleased to see that he was conscientiously using the parallel bars, installed as a gift from the Ashtons, and she tentatively sounded him out on the subject of paying a visit to *Beauclaire*.

"That gap in the hedge that Aunt Amy-Lee talks about, and through which you used to run to go next-door—is it wide enough to get a wheelchair through it?"

He stopped to wipe the perspiration out of his eyes. "It always used to be, but stuff grows so fast in this climate that it may have narrowed. Why do you ask?"

"I was thinking," she said, "if we want to put your fears to rest, finally, we should go that route to Beauclaire today. I need to speak to Uncle Ash, and it may give you pleasure to go back there again, after all this time. I'd like you to show me where James Ashton used to go and play his clarinet, long ago, and your father says that if we want to do that, we need to go before the heavy rainfall comes, because later, if the ground is muddy, it will be too hard for me to push you!"

"What you really mean is that you want to go to Jordie's favourite place, don't you?" he challenged her. "You need not be reluctant to own up, my dearest. Don't forget, I admitted long ago that I know how the two of you feel about one another, and I'm not resentful at all! I'm only grateful that you have been lent to me for as long as God sees fit to do so!

"I'm not letting you push my wheelchair any more, *mignon.* I have acquired a heavy pair of leather gloves, a gift from my dad, to protect my hands until the skin is no longer as sensitive as it is now, and most of the time you were out of commission, and with an escort of a few dozen merry little kids, all skipping along and urging me on, I practised going down the drive and around the house, where some of the terrain is quite uneven. This former doctor was also once a golf champion, never forget!"

"I shan't." She smiled and kissed him on the mouth. "Thank you for reminding me!"

"Hey!" he laughed delightedly. "I'm all sweaty! Give me a chance to be cleaned up, again with my dad's help, before you do that again, and then we'll be on our way!—You can sing to me like Platjie and Saartjie along the way—if you can still remember how to do that!"

***

Meredith and Tristan might have known that there was no way Ash was going to let them return the way they had come. "I think I feel rain in the air and, until I have checked the forecast, it is impossible to tell how heavy a downpour there will be," he said. "The rains seem to be a bit late this year, for which I am grateful, because we don't need any more flood damage in these parts. It presented quite a challenge on the last occasion, to bring all the kids from the shelter over to *Beauclaire* in time, but that was definitely the best solution, because it is situated on higher ground, and we all know what happened in New Orleans!"

He dropped them off after one of the happiest days Meredith had experienced for many months, despite the odd pang of sadness. To begin with, the moments she and Tristan spent in the clearing, amid the live oak, were almost hallowed to her. It was difficult for her to fight the emotion that threatened to overwhelm her, as she pictured Jordie there, playing his music while the young, plantation folk danced, and when she shared that with us later, her father and I were glad that we had not told her that he had gone away without taking the precious instrument with him!

They were treated to a variety of appetizing Cajun dishes at lunch, and then, while Amy-Lee took Tris to rest in the room he still regarded as his own, Merry was given the opportunity to discuss a number of troubling matters with Ash, and to seek his advice.

"Uncle Ash," she began, feeling free to unburden herself without preamble, "business affairs are beyond me! Financial planning is not one of my gifts. My father attended to such matters, and, in that regard I never thought beyond my research and passing my examinations. I had vague plans of establishing some sort of organization to help the Bushmen, but, because I also did not envisage ever having a life outside of the *Blouspruit* enclave, I gave no thought to how I might earn a living some day! My father pays for my cell phone, and he deposits money into my bank account as the balance diminishes, but clearly that has to stop now."

"Excuse me for asking, Merry, but has Tristan not supported you financially?"

"No, never," she admitted, "and that was probably my own fault. I realize that it will severely diminish your estimation of me, but, can you believe it...it never occurred to me, when I left home, that my father would not just automatically continue to support me? And, once Tristan began to treat me so badly, I would not have accepted a cent from him, even at gunpoint!"

Ash had noticed the way in which she kept clenching and unclenching her small fists, and he put his hand on her shoulder. "Go on, my dear," he said encouragingly. "I seem to think that I have told you before, that I have broad shoulders, and I don't mind it when pretty maidens in distress feel a need to cry on them!"

"Much as I would love to take advantage of that, I don't think that this is the time to indulge in tears or self-pity, Uncle Ash," she responded with a crooked smile. "I don't need to tell you that having to take leave of Jordie has left me almost numb, but I have to be practical. I think it has been one of the greatest disappointments of my life, that I could not continue to work with him in his clinic—but that, too, was impractical. I should have given some thought to earning a living. Most girls of my age do.

"Meanwhile, here I sit—an absolute idiot when it comes to money—and, even if I did understand, and knew how to manage Tristan's affairs for him until he is able to do so for himself, I can't, because I do not have his power-of-attorney!... There! At least that's something I have learnt!

"I see that, in addition to all you have already done for the two of us, you have generously provided Tris with the parallel bars he is now using, but that sort of thing has also got to stop! I don't know if, where, or how Tristan derives an income, and I don't know what I am supposed to do about the practice Doc Hugo left him. I don't know what to do about the share he may or may not have had in the Sandton practice, and I don't know how he will earn a living in future—but one thing I do know, and that is that I shall have to find some sort of employment! If you can come up with any ideas, Uncle Ash, I would greatly appreciate it!...You have made it clear that what you have done up to now, has been for Uncle Clifford and Aunt Thora, and that's fine....But you have already more than honoured that commitment, and we, Tristan and I, have to try and make our own way from now on!"

"Hmm," said Ash. "Will you give me a little while to think about that? Although few things would make me happier, I'm not going to offend you now by suggesting that I continue to help you out forever; but, what I can do, is to check on Tristan's affairs for you. For instance, there must be some income due to him from the practice, in lieu of rental for the house in *Spoors-einde*, and, if I can ascertain where my elusive, roving youngest is at this time, I'll find out about the Bryanston practice....Does Tris have a lawyer?"

"I don't know that, either," she confessed, "and I am not sure whether he is able to remember that yet, but you've given me something to think about, and I'm so grateful." She got up and impulsively gave Ash a hug! " How we all love you and Aunt Amy- Lee, dear Uncle Ash!"—but she restrained herself with difficulty from adding: "And how I love your son!"

Whereas the older children in Amy-Lee's shelter, were taken off to school by bus every morning, there was a pre-school in the mansion itself, for the little ones, who also spent a part of the day playing games outdoors, supervised by members of the staff. For this reason it was fortunate that the heavy rain held off until Thanksgiving, after which it poured steadily until well into the Christmas break.

Until then, leaving Tristan to spend time getting to know his parents all over again, Meredith had kept herself occupied by helping out in the kitchen when necessary, but she much preferred playing with the children, who would otherwise have become fractious as a result of the enforced stay indoors. Having for so long been responsible for Susan during her sister's early childhood, Merry had developed a talent for entertaining little people, and she soon had them playing all manner of games, ranging from musical chairs to 'K-I-N-G spells King!'

They sang nursery rhymes, and other well-loved children's songs, she taught them to sing 'Hold him down, you Zulu warrior!', and when she ran out of ideas, she would draw upon her father's innovations, borrowed from an earlier time. The small fry at that institution must have been the only kids in North America who spent their Christmas holidays, that year, participating in 'Underneath the Spreading Chestnut Tree', and even doing 'Hands-Knees-and-Boomps-a-Daisy!'—during which such squeals of delighted laughter emanated from that area, that very soon everyone in the house would be smiling, and often lured to go and join in the fun!

What the children liked best of all was for Meredith to tell them stories about the Kalahari, the animals and the Bushmen children. Some of the characters became firm favourites, and, before long she had a repertoire of tales. The more often she told them to her rapt audience who sat, cross-legged and chins in hands, on the floor, the more characters began to emerge; the most popular among them, a city lad called Fransie, who had a deformed leg due to malnutrition.

The children loved to hear about how he was brought by a kind young doctor, to live in the Kalahari sunshine with him—desert sun being particularly good for straightening crooked legs, of course!—and, spinning tales about Fransie, who was always nervous at the start of each new adventure, she soon had him talking !*Kabee*, and dancing with the *Saasi* children among the red dunes. But, in the beginning, and before his leg began to straighten, Fransie could not run as fast as they could, so they were forever rescuing him from lions and other predators, and killing scorpions before they could sting him. Her youthful audience also clamoured, again and again, to hear her clicking away, as she spoke in the supposed voices of the children, and often she had hardly come to the end of one tale, than there would be a chorus of "Tell that one again, Meredith!"... "Sing that song again!" or, "Do that Bushman dance again!"

She obligingly complied with all requests, with the confidence borne of many years of having actually experienced many of those adventures, herself, and, caught up in the story-telling one day, she was unaware that Ash and Amy-Lee, who had come to say goodbye before returning to *Bentleigh*, had been there all the time, listening to her.

The Ashtons were enchanted!

"Meredith, how can you doubt where your future lies?" Ash cried. " If you can write your stories down, just as you have told them to the children today"—he grinned broadly—"perhaps not making your supposedly mythical physician appear quite so familiar to those who know him well—you will never need to go looking for other employment! If, in addition, you can illustrate them as well you did those drawings for your thesis, I will undertake to show them to a publisher in New York, who will be delighted with them, I'm sure!...Send me one by email as soon as you have completed it!"

By now his business instincts were taking over. "I can even picture a CD, or a video, with you talking like that, and maybe featuring the Bushman children at *Blouspruit;* in their own environment!...My dearest girl, you've got it made!... You'll be killing two birds with one stone!...Making money, and donating some of the proceeds towards helping the people about whom you care so much!"

"I second that," Amy-Lee supported him enthusiastically. *"All of it!—Do it Merry! Start soon!"*

And now do you know, dear reader, where you have heard the name, 'Meredith Hilliard' before? Well that is also how a small, arid *dorp* in the far Northwest of the Southern Kalahari, came to be known as the home of one of the best-loved writers of children's books, in the world!

CHAPTER SEVENTEEN

Shortly before Easter, the following year, she received an enthusiastic response from the publisher to whom Ash had shown the first instalment of 'Fransie and the Saasi children', and this letter was swiftly followed by a request that she come to New York at her earliest convenience, to talk business. All her expenses, including airline tickets, and hotel expenses would be covered by the company.

"We look forward to meeting the author of these charming tales!" the letter read. "In addition to the fascinating information contained in them, and the insight into the characters, which you quite evidently possess, there is such a delightful, refreshing innocence and simplicity, in both the stories and the sketches you have submitted thus far, that we feel sure that they will appeal to children and adults alike.

"The directors, who have all read them, are of one mind. There is little on the market, for children today, other than violence and unearthly beings—which unfortunately seem to appeal to them most—but we are convinced that, once having read about the little people you describe with so much knowledge and affection, you will have difficulty in keeping up with the demand!

"When the time comes, and well before the books are released, we would like to arrange for a number of television interviews and other meetings with the media, to engender advance publicity. We think that it will be advantageous to introduce the writer of the stories—the story behind the story as it were—before the time, and Mr. Ashton has confirmed our supposition that only a person of equal charm and *simplicity would be able to write in this manner. Please advise us, as soon as possible, as to when you will find it convenient to meet with us!"*

Once again she was to experience the truth of the expression that it never rains but it pours. She had hardly digested that information than Isobel Ashton phoned, begging her to attend the baptism of little James Benjamin...

"Meredith," Izzie pleaded. "You must come! Please! James and I have discussed this at length, and we can think of no two people we would rather have as godparents to our little boy, than you and Jordie!"

I nearly had what I think the Americans would call a 'conniption fit'!

When she wrote and told us about these new developments, seeking our advice, I was almost as flabbergasted as she appeared to be. Our reasons for this differed considerably, however, and my husband tried to point this out to me.

"Jasper!" I exclaimed to her father with consternation, immediately disquieted by what we had read, "I think it's great that those people like her submissions so much—she gets that that talent from you, I have no doubt—but that little girl cannot be let loose in New York on her own!...New York! Of all places! She'll be eaten alive! You will have to stop her!"

"Dearest," he responded patiently, "she won't be 'let loose', by any means! And she won't be in any danger, I assure you! I know what you are thinking..... That her only experience of the world, so far, has been very limited. A stint in Johannesburg—always in the company of someone to watch over her—a trip to Nelspruit, where she was equally sheltered; a visit to *Bentleigh* where she was watched over very carefully by the Ashtons, and now a stay in Louisiana where she is positively cherished, have hardly made of her a 'woman of the world!'—But don't you think that, if she is so important to these publishers, they will see that she is equally well looked after?"

" That being 'always in the company of someone to watch over her', during the stint in Johannesburg, to which you refer, didn't do her much good, did it?" I retaliated, not the least bit satisfied! "It could not protect her from having her shoulder dislocated, could it, my love? And that despite the fact that the one who was looking after her, happened to be the person who possibly cares more for her than anyone else I know of... Jordan!"

"What happened to Meredith was an accident! It does not mean that she is necessarily at risk of the same thing happening to her in New York....Frankly, I don't think that what Merry is trying to convey to us, is apprehension at being in New York, per se. I surmise that it is the realization that she and Jordan will be thrown together again. Read the email again, dearest. Read it aloud to me and you'll see what I mean.

"Why would she tell us that her response to Isobel Ashton was that she would be honoured to be the baby's godmother, but only if this could be done by proxy, perhaps with Eugenie standing in for her? And I'm as sure as I'm alive, that, if she does go to New York, she will not let the Ashtons know that she is there!"

I did read the email again, and I gradually came around to Jasper's way of thinking—but right then neither we, nor Meredith, considered fitting Ash into the equation!

One of the first things Merry did after that, was to print out both emails and take them to Tristan. By this time, an extraordinary, comfortable relationship had sprung up between them, and she had no qualms about consulting him. He had become a trusted friend, and both knew that the one could be relied upon to want whatever was best for the other.

She thus had no compunction about candidly sharing with him her doubts about being in New York, and attending the Ashton infant's christening; admitting that both concerns were based on the possibility of seeing Jordan again. By the same token, Jordie might not attend the ceremony, either, if he knew that she was going to be there, and Tristan, who was older, and wanted nothing more than for her to be happy, first expressed his congratulations and excitement upon reading the glowing remarks about her stories, and then assured her that he trusted her unconditionally. She was thus at liberty to do whatever her heart desired.

This settled, she replied to Frederick Stein, the publisher, advising him that the dates he had suggested were acceptable, and that she would leave it to him to make the necessary arrangements. Immediately after that, she telephoned Isobel to confirm that she would be happy to be James Benjamin's godmother; again with the proviso that someone be found to stand in for her at the service, itself.

As I have already said, we were reckoning without Benjamin Ashton. Considering that he must have had a pretty close business association with Frederick Stein, it was not surprising that the publisher would lose no time in notifying him of Merry's decision, and the next phone call she had, came from Ash. It was immediately clear that he had regarded her reservations about being at the christening, in person, as being due to the fact that she did not want to leave Tristan, and he was positively jubilant at the news that she would be coming to New York.

"There's no way, you're staying in hotels, or travelling around the city in cabs, my child," he stated. "Consider

Bentleigh your second home, and Ferguson, the chauffeur will be at your command! I'm not going to leave your father and Biddy stewing about your safety all the time!

"The Nelspruit people, as well as Antoinette and her husband, will all be here for Easter, God willing, and just think of the glorious time we're all going to have! What better time for a baptism, hey? Praise the Lord! And everyone is so excited about your books!"

In years to come, Meredith would confess that no first experience of facing a television camera, or interview with a talk show host, had seemed as difficult as the prospect of seeing Jordan again. Her emotions had fluctuated between a desperate longing and nigh unbearable impatience for that to happen, and dread of betraying herself to everyone, including Jordie, himself. He arrived before Palm Sunday, from Canada, where he had been staying with Matt for several months, and, as she had requested that there be no further media interviews until after Easter Monday, they both spent their time studiously trying to avoid one another, and making sure that they were never left alone together.

She told me that when she and Jordie stood side-by-side at the service to make the necessary, solemn vows on behalf of their godchild, her knees were knocking to such an extent that she was afraid that, when the need arose, she might not have the strength to hold the baby securely. She said Jordan had never been quite as devastatingly handsome, or quite so dear to her as he was that day, all dressed up as he was, in honour of the occasion, and when their eyes happened to meet, she saw in his, the same pain that was almost suffocating her. The knowledge that his feelings had not changed should have been balm to her soul. Instead it simply made the impasse less easy to bear. They had not said a word to each other, except in the company of others; even then avoiding anything that might have been construed as a betrayal of Tristan, but she wondered how she would bear it when the time came for them to go their separate ways again. Just to be able to look at him was a delight she had never thought to have again.

More commitments followed after the holidays, and, on the day before Jordie was due to return to Canada, whether it happened by design or chance, Ferguson, the chauffeur, was obliged to take a day off. Ben and James had to be at the plant in New Jersey, and Jordan was left to drive her to a radio station, where he was able to listen in while he waited for her to conclude the interview. After that, they finally did talk—very seriously!

He parked the car a short distance from the gates of *Bentleigh*, to explain that it was because he had left it so late to make his travel arrangements, during this busy season, that he was still there. "I did not plan to stay so long, Merry," he told her. "I hope I have not caused you any uneasiness, and God knows, this has been a difficult time for me, too. I was not coming at all, until Isobel told me that you had not planned to be here, and, then I had to take what reservations I could get!"

"I'm sorry to have made things difficult for you, too, Jordie. I promise you that I was not even going to let any of you know that I was in the city at all, but your father found out and then I had no alternative but to stay at *Bentleigh*. You know how kind-hearted he is, and how persuasive he can be!...Now this is not a reproach, and I'm only asking as a point of interest.... Couldn't he have flown you from Toronto, himself?"

"No, he does not keep his plane in the States. Airspace is so congested, and he finds it aggravating to hover. He says that, despite the long waits at airports, he can at least read the newspaper while he waits, and he makes use of commercial services, even when he goes down to the Louisiana *Beauclaire*, where he keeps a car for local travel. It's different, when he's in South Africa.—By the way, how's Tris?"

"Fine, thanks. Making good progress, in every direction. He speaks quite fluently now—in both Creole and English, and gets on amazingly well with his parents."

"I'm glad to hear that. How does he treat you, Meredith?"

"Very well thank you. We have a good relationship. I find I can talk freely to him about anything, these days, without riling him up!"

"Do you...? Are you...?"

"No. Most certainly not!" She knew what he meant.

" I don't know whether that is good or bad, so I shan't press the point."

"And what have you been doing with yourself?" she asked him. "Any girlfriends?

Now it was his turn to say, "Of course not!" He looked surprised. "I spend a lot of time with Matt, when he's not working. He has a lovely family, and is a tremendous inspiration to me. He does not have much, by some standards, but is completely satisfied with his life. He cares very little for many things that other people might consider essential to their happiness, but nothing is too good for his wife and kids.

"During quiet times, when nobody else has been at home, or when I have gone for walks on my own, I have had time to meditate, and time to think, and I realize that I can never go back to the kind of life I led previously. I am going to make some drastic changes. I hope to continue practising medicine, but Johannesburg is not for me, any more.—That does not mean however, that I'll leave the people there holding the baby, in a manner of speaking. I'm thinking of selling Sandton practice, and will, for the time being, stay with Reg and Aunt Felicity, while I continue to work in the clinic, until my dad and I have found enough staff to keep it going without me!"

"What about the Bryanston house, Jordie? Will you hold onto that?"

"I probably shall. It's mine and it brings in a good rent, so I have no reason to sell it, but my reluctance to part with it is mostly because I don't want to disrupt Reg and his mother. I realize, too, that a time might come, when my people in South Africa might be glad to have the use of it as a family gathering place, once more. So I shall have to wait and see. And you, Merry? What are your plans?"

"I'm not really in a position to make any, am I? I'll be meeting with my publisher again, before I go back to Louisiana on the day after tomorrow, and I suppose I shall keep myself occupied for the rest of my life, telling stories!"

"Well," he said, with a deep sigh, "we shall probably never see one another again. I thought I would die when I saw you on television in Toronto, and I'm going to make very sure, in future, that the two of us are never again subjected to the torture we have had to endure this time. That is, if I am not presuming when I think that you might still have found our situation over the last week as agonizing and I did?"

And she could only nod.

He did not kiss her, but telling her how proud he was of her, he hugged her, and then took her back to the mansion. He left next day, and, seeing him go, this time, the only analogy that came to her was that of physical amputation—without an anaesthetic! This time she had a very strong feeling that she might never see him again!

She returned to Louisiana feeling that she had died another death. It was just as well if they never met again, she decided, because it had now been proved that, every time they did, it only became harder to part.

After consultation with Frederick Stein she came back to Louisiana, convinced that she honestly could not do any more sketches, or complete the ones she had already done, in watercolour, where she was. She was incapable of doing full justice to the people about whom she was writing, or recapturing the full splendour and the variation in the wondrous colours of the landscape, until she had been back to the Kalahari for a spell. When she explained this to the Connaughts, they understood, as only such people could understand, and, without hesitation, they urged her to go.

A month or so before she left, Thora, Clifford and Tris talked seriously to her. Tristan was the first to speak, and he kept eyes glued to floor, for the remainder of the conversation.

"Merry," he said, emotionally, "I have told my parents the whole truth about the two of us, and so I can say freely in their presence how much I valued your confiding in me when you came back from New York, and how you went out of your way to assure me that you and Jordan had not said or done anything that would hurt me. There was actually no need for you to have confessed that to me, because I have learned to know you so well that I would not at any time have expected less of you. If I have ever met anyone in my life, who is true to her word, it has to be you, my dearest....But now I'll let my father do the talking."

Father Clifford was quiet for a moment, as though he were praying, and then he began by telling her how touched they had been, when her first reaction to the good news from the publisher had been a remark about how she and Tristan would henceforth be assured of an income, and could thus become independent in the future.

"Meredith," he said, "I did not immediatelty react or thank you for your unselfishness, because for a moment you had robbed me of speech....You must be one of the most unselfish people I have ever come across, and I can only echo what my son said just now. You have no idea what a treasure you are to us, but now there is a rather sensitive issue that we have to discuss, and I'm not quite sure where to begin.

"While you were away, I was greatly blessed in that my son should have come to me, as his priest, rather than as his father, to make his Easter confession. His first ever, as he told me. I shall not be breaking any vows of confidentiality if I discuss some of what he confessed that night, because he has not only given me permission to do so, but has begged me to talk to you about it."

He cleared his throat and Thora squeezed his hand encouragingly. "My son tells me that..." he could hardly bring himself to say the words..."Well, I might as well begin by saying outright that my son tells me that he no longer wishes to be married!...Oh, dear, this is very difficult indeed! He tells me that he loves you deeply, but, with the long road to complete rehabilitation, ahead of him, and while he seeks to find direction, he would rather be free!"

Meredith was shocked! "I can understand that he would not want to be encumbered, Father Clifford!" she cried, "but I hope that I have never given him cause to think that I might be a burden on him, or he, on me...!"

"No, my dear," Tristan's father assured her. "There are other issues we need not go into right now, but my son also feels that he is being unfair to you! He is aware of how much Jordan Ashton means to you, and he also knows how much you love children, with whom it is very unlikely for the two of you to be blessed! Perhaps some day, but certainly not in the foreseeable future."

"Please, Merry," Tristan intervened. "Don't look like that! And please don't regard this as some great sacrifice on my part. I am not trying to make you feel bad about this! I have sought the Lord on this issue, and I want to remind you of what I said once.... That I knew you had been 'lent' to me! My father will tell you that I have made up my mind, and all I ask is that you listen to what he has to say. Please, I beg of you, do this for me. ... For us both, *mignon!*"

"I must state," Father Connaught went on, "that, as a priest, I would find it difficult to condone a divorce, but I am also a marriage officer, and have some knowledge of the laws governing this in the State of Louisiana, so, at Tristan's request, I have spent some time going through the current regulations for dissolution of marriage, to make sure that what I am about to tell you still pertains at this time.

"There are many valid and acceptable reasons for seeking a divorce. However, for some people, divorce carries a stigma, and they would rather their marriage be annulled. Others prefer an annulment because it may be easier to remarry in their church if they go through an annulment rather than a divorce. Within the Roman Catholic Church, for example, a couple may obtain a religious annulment after obtaining a civil divorce, so that one or both people may remarry, within the church or anywhere else, and have the second union recognized by the church.

"As a priest, albeit not of the Roman Catholic Church, I have to confess that this is what I would prefer for my son.... How does an annulment differ from a divorce? Well, like a divorce, an annulment is a court procedure that dissolves a marriage. But, unlike a divorce, an annulment treats the marriage as though it never happened. Grounds for annulment vary slightly from state to state. Generally, an annulment requires at least one of the reasons listed in the regulations, and I thank God that one of them no longer applies to Tristan! That is the one dealing with 'Concealment.'—For example, concealing an addiction to alcohol or drugs.

"One that can be applied in your case, is 'refusal or inability to consummate the marriage'. That, as stated in the regulations for this state, means ' refusal or inability of a spouse to have sexual intercourse with the other spouse....Then there is 'Misunderstanding'—for example if one person wanted children and the other did not—that would provide grounds for civil annulment."

By this time Clifford was also not looking at them directly. That he was acutely discomfited was obvious. "Since yours was a civil marriage, as Tristan has told me it was, I would personally have no difficulty—except for the sorrow this is causing Tristan's mother and me, at this moment—in assisting you to have yours annulled. This is what Tristan wants, and it leaves you free to go home to your family while you think about it, or give Tristan the word to go ahead with this immediately!"

Meredith was stunned to say the least. Her feelings were so mixed at that moment, that she could not have given him a firm answer, even if she had wanted to! Perhaps if she and Jordan had not parted for good, that would have made a difference. There might have been cause for jubilation. As it was, all she felt was the most incredible sorrow, and she could not look at Tristan for fear of what she might see in his face.

"Would you please excuse me now, Father Clifford and Aunt Thora? I think I need to be alone for a bit," was all she could say for the moment. But she did go over to where Tristan was sitting, and breathing hard as she stood beside his chair, she managed to say, "Oh, my dear Tris, I am so sorry!—Is this how it has to end? I do care very much about you, you know!" Then she kissed him on his forehead, and stumbled up the stairs to her bedroom.

When she said goodbye to Tristan, he asked, " Will you try to contact Jordan now?"

She shook her head. "No, I don't think so. I don't even know where he has gone, and he was quite definite about our not seeing each other again!"

"That's a shame!" Tristan said, and then, hugging her before she went through the departure gates at the airport, he whispered in her ear: "God be with you, sweetheart! I shall pray for you to be happy, wherever you go from here. Go now and do, with all your might 'whatsoever thy hand findeth to do!' I look forward to seeing your books in print."

"I'll send you the first one! Keep in touch, Tris. You have my email address and cell phone number."

"I'll do that," he responded, but she knew that she would never hear from him again...

***

Meredith, the little blighter, did not give us any warning of her coming. The first we knew of it was when Hennie Vercueil's taxi stopped in front of the house, and when both she and Sally got out of it, with Hennie, I realized that the three of them had been in cahoots. All the arrangements had been made over the phone, while Merry, having first ascertained whether or not Jordan was there, was getting over the jetlag in Reggie and Felicity's cottage.

What a commotion ensued! Susie and I crying, Jasper beaming with joy, and Mieta and Malgas scurrying to help Hennie carry in the luggage.

Now that she was home, we were all sworn to secrecy. Meredith was visibly worn out, and Jasper gave Susan strict instructions not to breathe a word to anyone that her sister was back home. For the next few days we left her to rest, but Susie was quick to notice whenever her sister surfaced, and of course, once those two got started, they could chatter worse than Magpies!

Oh, what music there was in the house once more! What laughter and story telling! Susan, back from her first semester at university, was completely beside herself at the mere thought of her sister's having become a 'TV Star', and said that she and her friends had stayed up until late to watch CNN. The South African media had not missed an opportunity, either, to report on the furore that had been created in the 'Big Apple' by a simple girl from the Kalahari.

A day or two later, while speaking to Sally on the phone, I was suddenly stricken with one of my incapacitating migraines, such as I had not suffered since I couldn't remember when. Well, at least not since the one I had conveniently developed when Tristan refused to take Merry to the cinema, and it was a blessing that Jasper and Meredith, who was now ready to face the world once more, were about to leave to go to *Spoorseinde*, in order to deposit her cheque from Frederick Stein and Company—Publishers.

I appealed to Meredith. "I'd really appreciate it if you could call in at Doc Hugo's consulting rooms, Merry, and ask the 'CP' if there's a record of what he usually gave me. And then, perhaps if the doctor will give you a prescription—because I can't remember whether or not Doc kept medicines like that in his little pharmacy—could you please pop in at the chemist's in *Spoors-einde*, and have Mike Wanneberg fill it while you go to the bank? I have only one tablet left, and I may need another before this headache passes.

"The 'CP'?" Merry frowned inquiringly.

Her father roared with mirth. "She means the 'Christmas Present!' The one I sent by helicopter to be Adriaan Prinsloo's earthly 'very present help in time of trouble'!...Sometimes also referred to by my wife as the 'CP'—the 'capable, adventurous, impervious-to-extreme-heat' lady. Margaret Gresham!"

Both Meredith and Jasper were most concerned, and would have changed their minds about going to the village, if I had not insisted that I could not manage without the tablets. "Please don't worry about me...I'll be fine in the meantime," I managed to assure them bravely. "I still have that one pill, which I'm going take right away. Then I'll just draw the curtains and go and lie down in a dark room, if Susan will listen for me, in case I need anything!"

I was, in fact, lying down, with a wet rag on my forehead, by the time they were ready, and Jasper bent down to kiss me, before they left. "My dearest," he said, still chuckling, "you are priceless! Here you are in agony and you can still make jokes!"...

Oh, boy! Did I feel dreadful then—for more than one reason!

As I heard the truck pass by my window, I asked God to forgive me, hung up the wet cloth to dry, and then went to the kitchen to make a batch of *soetkoekies*[17] for afternoon tea.

A few hours later, when the 'CP', although not yet having found my records, showed Meredith into the doctor's office, she, Merry—suddenly convulsed at the recollection of how I had referred to Margaret—had her head down, trying to suppress her mirth, and the first thing she noticed when she looked up, was a small pair of *velskoens* hanging on the wall behind the doctor. At the same time Jordie, who had been writing something, looked up, and they both gasped!

For a moment time stood still! They stared at one another wordlessly, as though in a state of suspended animation, and the spell was only broken when Margaret put her head around the door to say, apologetically, "I'm sorry, doctor, but I am unable to find a card for Mrs. Bridget Hilliard." She turned to Meredith, "And I apologize for keeping you waiting, Miss Hilliard. When last was your mother here to see the doctor?"

"It's alright, Margaret, thank you," Jordan said briskly. "Try looking among the 'W's' for Bridget Williams, and then, when you have found it, could you please make out a new one for her in the name of 'Hilliard'. Her address is now care of the '*Blouspruit*' mailbox at the post office.

"In the meantime, I can give her daughter some samples to go on with, because I know what Mrs. Hilliard takes for those headaches. I was probably the physician who prescribed them for her, in the first place!" And as she turned to go, he added: "By the way, Margaret, this is not Miss Hilliard. This is Mrs. Hilliard's married daughter, Mrs. Connaught!"

"Forgive me doctor," Merry said, with the corners of her mouth twitching. "You must be mistaken. I am 'Miss' Hilliard.—Miss Meredith Hilliard—and I am most certainly not married!"

The nurse looked bewildered, with good cause. "This is all very confusing!" she muttered, as she went out, and this was when Meredith began to laugh...

She sat down in the chair opposite Jordie, and laughed, almost hysterically, until he became concerned. "*Ach*, Jordie!" she shrieked. "How did we ever get ourselves into such a mess?"

The sun streaming into the room made a halo of his golden hair, and when she saw the concern in those blue eyes, she made an effort to control herself. "Oh, Jordie, your patients will be thinking that you have a mad woman in this room.... What must they be saying to each other?... But, oh dear, all I need to hear now is that *you're* married!...I'm not laughing because this is funny! I'm laughing...well, I don't really know why...! I guess I'm just hysterical!"

"And I'm almost speechless!" he exclaimed. "Can I get you anything? Water, maybe?...And no, I'm not married. That's all I can say, for now, except that I'd like to explore this mystery at greater length, but not here!"

It was a good thing that each of them had become familiar with what they referred to as their 'grasshopper minds' when they were together, for it did not seem the least bit strange or incongruous to him, that she should respond to this statement by asking, "Do you still have your clarinet?"

"I do," he said. "But I don't know when last I played it. I left it with Reg for a long time, and I only fetched it after I had bought the house and practice from Tristan, and was ready to come and live here, permanently. I have brought my piano, too, but how both will stand up to this climate remains to be seen!...And you? Do you still play?"

"My shoulder is quite better now, and I used to play for the kids in Louisiana, but mostly just simple tunes, to accompany them when they sang nursery rhymes and so on. Nothing serious. Somehow I just didn't have the heart...!"

"Why, Merry?"

"Why haven't you been playing your clarinet?"

"Touché!" he responded. "Perhaps I'll try again, some time!"

"You should perhaps ask my father how he has managed to maintain our piano in such good condition..."

"Maybe I'll do that. I'll come out and ask him, as soon as I have some time to myself. You know what it's like, here!"

"I do. I worked here, myself, for a little while, don't forget." She rose, thanked him for the samples and then said, "Well there's no hurry. My dad isn't going away, any time soon—and neither am I! Bring your clarinet when you come, because I just may have forgotten how to do justice to Gershwin and William Christopher Handy, and I could do with some help!"

There was wistfulness in her face as she reminisced. "I can still hear your father explaining to me one day, that Handy was not known as 'The Father of Blues', for nothing. The idea was to 'combine combine ragtime syncopation with a real melody in the spiritual tradition', he told me, and then demonstrated, and I still remember the absolute exhilaration I experienced in listening to him!"

Somehow the condition of Jordan's piano must have been more urgent than one would have thought. He came to consult Jasper that very same evening, and the clarinet sounded fine to me, but it was all rather restrained, and somehow not quite how I had expected this reunion to be. Merry put me on the spot by asking Jordie, in my presence, when Sally Vercueil had found out that he was back. Her observation that it must have been just about when I was afflicted with that headache, was mercifully left hanging in the air!

Next thing, they were talking about how Jordan should go about streamlining his office procedure, starting with the uploading of his patients' info into a computer, and Meredith, assuring him that she did not have to start on her next collection of stories immediately, offered to help. The problem was, that if she were to work on them, here, he would have no source of reference while the cards were with her—and for her to go from *Blouspruit* to *Spoors-einde* and back, each day, was out of the question—so, of course, it was unanimously agreed that the most sensible arrangement was for her to reside temporarily with Sally, and be within walking distance of what used to be Doc's place, until the task was done.

Jordan fetched her at the weekend, and, naturally, once she was installed in the Vercueil house, the evenings and times off could have been very boring for her, and quite lonely for the doctor, if she had not been available to keep him company whenever he had to take long drives into the country!

I still can't understand why they wasted so much time. It took him a good ten days to bring himself to stop the truck one moonlit evening, on the way home from the De Bruyn's place, turn off the ignition, and take her in his arms.

Once the kissing began, he could not refrain from telling her, over and over again, of the wonder of knowing that there was no longer anything to prevent them from doing so.

"Oh, my very dearest one," he murmured, "I still can't believe that I can hold you like this again, and not feel guilty about doing so! And this time I'm never going to let you go! Ever since you walked into my office and dropped the bombshell that you were free, I have been afraid to open my eyes each morning, dreading to find that it was only a dream!

"Even now, kissing you is unreal. Dreamlike! We have had such a history of meeting and having to be torn apart again...We have had such a history of loving from a distance, meeting, and separating each time, more hurt and bruised than before, that I was afraid to let myself believe that this time the dream could last...Say you'll marry me, my darling little Miss Muffet, or I shall expire...! Marry me, please, Meredith, and put me out of my misery, once and for all!"

She took his face in her hands, and gazed at him intently, in the moonlight, for quite a while, gently tracing every line of it with her soft fingertips, before she spoke. "My beloved," she said, "this is the face I have tried for so long to see, before closing my eyes to sleep, each night that I have had to be apart from you. How desperately I have had to commit it to memory in the past!

"How can I ever tell you how much I have longed to see this face, in reality, and, at each parting, trying not to feel pain at the knowledge that soon I might not see it any more!" She ran her fingers though his hair, and then drew his head down, towards her, and kissed him.

"Now that you really are here with me, at last, my darling, I shall cherish you for the rest of my life. As long as God spares you to me, and beyond!—How can you even ask!...*Of course* I shall marry you! I can't wait!"

***

It became obvious to Meredith that, if you had the blood of the Ashtons coursing through your veins, time meant nothing to you when there was good news to be told! Right there in the middle of the veld, standing in the sand, and oblivious of the fact that, if he wasn't wearing boots, he could have risked the possibility of treading on a scorpion or some other predator, Jordan stood talking on his cell phone, broadcasting jubilantly to every member of the family, the great news that Meredith had consented to marry him. Explanations of how and why this had become possible would be forthcoming later, he promised. Meredith had tried to remonstrate, reminding him of the time difference between where he was, and New York—but apparently, even the possibility that the Nelspruit people might be fast asleep—was no deterrent.

He was so ecstatic, Merry told me later, smiling fondly, that, at one stage he had shouted to the heavens: "Miss Muffet is going to marry me! Hallelujah!" Her laughing protestations that we might have gone to bed were to no avail. He simply entered the number and put the cell phone into her hand. "You tell them!" he said. And when Meredith heard her father's voice at the other end, and said to him, "Daddy, Jordie and I are engaged!" it no longer mattered whether she had got him out of bed, or not. She was not laughing any more. Like a typical woman, because she was so happy, she cried! Jasper assured her that he was up and had been working on his manuscript, and the next minute he was rushing down the passage to tell Susie and me the good news! And then, when Jasper said, "Jordan wants to speak to you and Susan, Biddy," Susie and I cried too.

My heart was so full of gratitude for all our blessings, that I could not sleep. None of us could. We three on the farm, gathered in the kitchen, and had tea around the table, speculating on where the wedding might take place, but not omitting to pray for the two who were so dear to us. This seemed a good time for me to print out and read to them an email I had received from Tristan, earlier that evening.

"*Dear Aunt Biddy,*

"*How incredibly much has happened in one, short year!*" he had written. "*It is almost impossible to believe how long it is since Uncle Hugo died.*

"*As the winter approaches in North America, I think of him so often, remembering how good he was to me, and I am so pleased to hear that the Spoors-Einde folks tend his grave so faithfully. That does not surprise me, however, because I am sure that there is no one there who does not owe him a debt of gratitude, for one reason or another.*

" *Christmas is still a long way off, I know, but when it does come, this year, I shall really be looking forward to it, for the first time in my life. It will mean something to me now. I am where I want to be, and where I believe I am supposed to be!*

"*So many things remind me of Meredith, though. On Thanksgiving Day, I shall be thinking of her, and of the turkey she was never given a chance to cook last year, and praying that she is well and happy, wherever she might be. When I think of how and where I was at this time last year, and the state I was in, it makes me even more grateful for the fact that I can be so contented with my lot.*

"*Uncle Ash is such a firm believer in the fact that there is no such thing as coincidence, and I firmly believe that Merry, bless her, was brought into my life to be an instrument of healing and salvation and, when you see her again, please tell her that I praise God for lending her to me, for long enough to carry out His purpose.*

"*My brother's death was an unspeakable tragedy for my parents, and I now feel as though I must fill his place as well as my own, to make up for what is past—but that is not meant to come across as shouldering a burden. I value the opportunity!*

"*What do you think of the fact that I am able to write an email to you? Isn't that a miracle in itself? Now I have discovered that I actually like children, and, as soon as I can move about with more agility, I want to devote myself to them, in the same way as Jamie Ashton did in Bethlehem. I have the opportunity to hone my skills here, in the 'Amy-Lee Ashton Centre', and then I hope to go and live in New Orleans, and become part of an organization that is working for the rehabilitation of the people there—especially the kids. So many of the people there are still suffering from the after-effects of the hurricane.*

"*Some of our kids, here in the centre, have been described as 'difficult', and, in view of my own experience, I cannot accept that it is only because they are intrinsically so. Bearing in mind, too, that in their case, it is very unlikely that some kind of demoniacal influence could be responsible for their behaviour, I began to think a great deal about all that Matt Marais had to say about 'post traumatic stress disorder', and based on my suspicions that what the children saw and experienced, and the losses they sustained during Hurricanes Katrina and Rita, had been responsible, I decided to try and draw them out.*

"Try to imagine, Aunt Biddy, what it must have been like for little ones, some as young as three years old, and barely able to express themselves in words! How very grateful I am that I can speak and understand Créole Lalouisiane! I have been so deeply touched and so delighted with every sign of improvement, no matter how slight, that I think I must now undertake specific studies in order to equip myself to go about this more knowledgeably and professionally.—Do you remember how cynically I used to tell you that I liked to know 'what made people tick'? I feel so ashamed now when I think of that!

"Anyhow, to make a long story shorter, I managed to contact Matt, by phoning the Ashton Facility near Toronto, and he has been most helpful—even to the extent of putting me in touch with people who can advise me. Although he was unable to be specific, he told me that Jordan was no longer in Johannesburg, but that, wherever he decides to settle, Jordie, plans to continue working with his, Matt's, Gauteng group, via the Net.

"While Merry was here, neither she nor I could get to church much, because I was still too greatly incapacitated, but now I am blessed to go with my parents and the children, to attend the services at the small church of which my father is the rector. I had never before appreciated his sermons, or my mother's ability to play the organ so well, but I make a point of remarking on both, every time we get home.

"Please give my best to Uncle Jasper, Susie, and whoever else is there with you, at this time. If Merry happens to be there, please be sure to beg her never to be unhappy about me. I am precisely where I believe God wants me to be, and every day brings a new and rewarding experience!

"With love and gratitude for all your kindness in the past,
"Tris."

I sat for some time, poring over this message, and then discussed it with Jasper and we came to the same conclusion, that it was really intended for Meredith, but that Tristan left it to our discretion whether to pass on his news to her, rather than for him to write to her directly. Did he know, we wondered, that she and Jordan would find one another again? And that being the case, did he want to set her mind at ease, without intruding into their relationship? Jasper and I decided to wait and think about this until we were sure about when to tell her that we had heard from him.

Meanwhile, my main concern about Meredith and Jordan starting off their lives as newly-weds, in *Spoors-einde*, was based entirely on Doc Hugo's history. Jordie had the same sense of responsibility and was equally selfless, and I agonized about how little time they would have to themselves, but not only was Jordan younger, he also belonged to a new generation, and, from the outset, he began to run the practice in accordance with modern-day standards. How often Doc would arrive home in the early hours, after having been out for most of the night, miles away from *Spoors-einde,* to receive a call, as soon as the telephone exchange opened, from someone who had tried to reach him urgently during the night, and have to go all the way back to a farm, half-way from where he had just been. Jordan's cell phone obviated that.

Once the premises had been upgraded, and with the advice and assistance of his father—who had built the premises on the *Beauclaire* citrus farm with his own hands—with Meredith and his mother, ever-ready to advise on refurbishing, and his patient files readily accessible on computers, he and

Merry, together, set up the lab where, equipped with another computer, for ready reference online, a microscope and other equipment, diagnoses could be made more quickly, rather than had been the procedure in the past, when it had been necessary to send all information to Upington for an opinion.

Never losing sight, for a minute, that Meredith had her own assignments, Jordan and his father saw to it that an extra room was added, comfortably furnished, and equipped according to her needs, for Merry to continue with her writing. And she, who had never 'defaced' a wall in her life, had a wonderful time painting murals depicting the desert and its animals, with all her small, human characters in the foreground, striking characteristic poses.

Jordan, who had great respect for the admirable Margaret Gresham, had been concerned that she would feel that she had been supplanted, but surprisingly she was both delighted and relieved when Jordan's parents arrived to help him work on the house, because she was then free to take up residence in the 'boarding house', close by, where she had nothing to do, other than tidying her room. The 'CP' was quite candid about the fact that she actually hated housekeeping, and, apart from that, the occasional spark had flown between herself and Katryntjie, Doc's faithful retainer. Fortunately Tryntjie took to Ash and Amy-Lee, at once, but that her real loyalty and admiration had long since been awarded to Merry, had been evident, ever since the kleinmiesies had first spoken to her in the ancient *Khoekhoegowap* language. Jordan and his parents loved to listen to the two of them chatting away in the kitchen whenever Merry was there. The Ashtons were impressed by the information—provided by their smitten son—that it was believed that, in this day and age, few could converse in it, and only about five to ten thousand people could even understand it.

Almost as though it would make their situation more real, Jordan had a desperate, quite touching yearning to see his ring on Meredith's finger, but, there was never an opportunity to take her down to Kimberley, where he particularly wanted to buy it, and he was more than thrilled when his mother presented him with the ring that had belonged to his father's revered grandmother, who had worn on it her wedding day, and which she, in turn, had given to Ash for Amy-Lee to wear, on hers. *Gran'mère* Beauclaire had been every bit as tiny as Meredith was, and not only was Merry enchanted with it, when Jordan slipped it onto her finger, but was quite overcome by the honour of wearing such a precious link to his family.

From the first moment Meredith had made her re-appearance in the office on a regular basis, 'that little Hilliard girl', as the regulars referred to her, was given a warm welcome. She was pretty enough to be a real tonic, they said, and, when she came in one day, wearing an engagement ring, speculation as to whom the lucky man might be, was instantly rife. It did not take them long to notice, however, that Doctor Jordan would sometimes hold onto her hand just a little too long, when she handed something to him, and she was seen far too often alone with him in his truck, they thought, for this to be condoned if she were engaged to some other fellow!

Jasper, who had installed the satellite dish at *Blouspruit*, was happy to do the same for Jordie, and soon, among other improvements, there were comfortable chairs and a small television set in the waiting room, and Jordan never seemed to mind that people, obviously blooming with health, sometimes came in to sit, in an air-conditioned room, just to watch. But few people are not thrilled to see a real-life romance played out before their eyes, and when their conjectures were confirmed, bashfully, but with evident pride by Jordie, himself, the consensus was that their 'nice little doctor' (all six-foot-four of him!) could not have made a better choice. So, taking everything into consideration, all was quiet on the home front!

There was much discussion about the wedding, itself. Jordan would have consented to its taking place on the ash heap, I'm sure, and in the middle of a sandstorm, if that was what Merry wanted, but there was never any doubt about October being the best time. After all, wasn't it Leipoldt's *'mooiste, mooiste, maand'*—the most beautiful month of the year? And where was it more beautiful than at *Beauclaire*, near Nelspruit, amid Benjamin Ashton's orange groves and surrounded by Bougainvilleas, Flame trees, Jacarandas and Poinsettias?

"I'd love it to be there!" Meredith said eagerly. "And what I would like, is to be taken in my wedding dress, in Uncle Ben's Jeep—this time by my bridegroom—to sit on the *kopjie* with him, when the sun goes down, and see the view from there with him, as I did that day with his father!"

"And what I would like best—" Jordan put in emphatically, "in fact, I insist upon it—is to dance with Meredith! If you have your old record player there, Dad, I would hope that you'd still have the vinyl recording of Al Martino singing, *'You'll never know just how much I love you!'* And I'm going sing it, very softly, in Meredith's ear!"

It was plain, after that, that Mrs. Nolte would have to be consulted, without delay, and, as was to be expected, she was able to cut through all problems like a hot knife through butter!

"That's simple!" she assured us. "If Jordie wants to dance, the wedding has got to be in the late afternoon, but not too late if Meredith still needs time to look at the view! If we're going to have dancing, we need to rent a floor, and I suggest that we also rent a large tent. It's not romantic to dance out in the open!... We'll have to arrange the flowers and the other decorations, and get the tables ready before we go off to the church, and that's another reason why the reception will have to be under cover.— No barbeque this time, Ash! It's got to be an elegant supper with a head table and the works!...How many years will it be before we can have another Ashton wedding, hey?"

"All you will have to see to now, is the church and the minister, and get the invitations out, so that we can know how many to expect. The hotels are always full in October, so bookings have to be made soon, and Meredith will have to decide on the colours for the flowers and the decorations!"

"Phew!" Ben exclaimed when he had rung off. "I'm exhausted, just listening to her, and yet that incredible woman managed to sort everything out in a matter of minutes!"

He repeated everything that Mrs. N had said, and then, asking Meredith about colours, instructed: "You don't have to decide now, my dear. Don't feel pressured in any way. Talk this over with your mother and sister, and Jordie's mother, if you like, and then let me know so that I can tell that wonderful, indefatigable person how to proceed!"

I don't think he would ever—not in million years—have thought that he would find a woman, let alone a daughter-in-law, who could make up her mind so quickly. Brides have a reputation for hysterics and they're entitled to prevaricate, but Meredith was able to tell him, then and there—without the slightest hesitation—what her preference was!

"Uncle Ash," she replied, "that day, when we were up on the *kopjie*, you pointed out a splash of mauve which, you told me, was made by your favourite tree in all the earth. You said that it was a Jacaranda, against which you could lean, with the rough bark next to your cheek, when you needed to call out and petition God.

"If Zhaynie and Isobel would consent to be my maids of honour, and Susie will be my bridesmaid, I would choose for them to wear dresses in the colour of that Jacaranda! It's been my favourite colour, ever since!"

Ben was bowled over! He rose and went over to Merry, bent down and kissed her on her forehead! Then he managed to say, "My girlie, I thought that your father and I had married two of the only perfect women in the world. How I praise God that my son has managed to find another!"

Who would ever have thought that a little girl from the Kalahari would marry a billionaire's son, and that people would come from many parts of the world to be present at her wedding? And who would ever have dreamt that the son of that billionaire would choose to live in *Spoors-einde*—of *all* places! We'd also forgotten that our tiny Doctor Hilliard was a celebrity in her own right, and that wedding pictures of her with her handsome bridegroom, would be splashed in newspapers around the world, to be seen even in New Orleans!

On the night before we left to go to Johannesburg to buy our outfits for the wedding, Meredith had a moment of sadness. I came across her, standing on the back stoep of *Blouspruit*, looking out across the veld, with a reflective look on her expressive little face, and I put my arms around her, to ask, "What's the matter, Merry-love?"

"I was just thinking of Tristan," she said. "I hope he's happy, too. None of what happened was his fault, Mother, and he's turned out to be a really good person. He deserves to be as happy as I am at this moment!"

And that was when I took her inside and gave her the email I had printed out for Jasper, and, when she had read it, she gave it back to me and said: "Thank you! Now I can go in peace!"

If Tristan's intention had been to give her his blessing, along with the gift of peace, he had succeeded.

What a wedding that was—with all the exuberant Ashtons there, in full force, to see their 'baby brother' marry the girl of his dreams! Saint Margaret's church was packed, and I still get a lump in my throat when I picture our beloved Meredith— surely the most beautiful bride there ever was!—looking adoringly at Jordie as she stood with him at the chancel steps; her retinue of attendants in their charming Jacaranda gowns behind her. Jordie, with James as his best man, looked as if he were going to burst with happiness, and Father Peter positively beamed at everyone. Amy-Lee looked gorgeous, our spouses magnificent, and I only hope I did my daughter proud.

Mrs. Nolte certainly did! *Beauclaire* was at its October best, and, with the perfume of orange blossom in the air, the reception was incredible! From the lobster mayonnaise, to the *koeksusters* and *Crème Brûlée*, the champagne cooled to just the right temperature, it couldn't have been more perfect, and I'll never forget Jordie's face when he took Meredith in his arms to dance with her. He seemed to have been transported to some celestial place, where only the two of them existed.

Just before sunset, James Ashton created a diversion which had us all rushing outside to see him drive up, horns blaring, in his father's Jeep—decorated with branches of Jacaranda and mauve balloons. He helped his new sister-in-law to climb up into it, bowed to his brother, and said, "Your carriage awaits, sir. You'd better get in there with her now, or one of us will!"

Of course I have no way of knowing what our two dear ones said to one another up there on the *kopjie*, and all we heard about it from them, was that the sunset and the view from there had been precisely what Meredith had wanted to share with Jordie, but they looked so happy when they returned, to be welcomed back by the glorious singing of *Beauclaire's* black people.

There was more dancing after that, but once Meredith had thrown the bouquet and the garter—caught by Reggie, if you please—and amid the usual laughter and handclapping, the bride and groom left, to go as far as Ash and Amy-Lee's cottage...the parents having arranged to spend the night in the big house, so that the children could be by themselves.

The moon was up in the deep, velvety, blue of the African sky, when Jordie's parents, and Jasper and I, went outside with them, to give them a last hug, before they drove off in the Jeep, under the Southern Cross, and we remained standing there, until they were hidden from sight by the Hibiscus hedge...

ENDNOTES

[1] *Dorp*: small town

[2] *Antoinette Verwey*: The stepdaughter of Father Peter Crawford, and the author of *'Dominic Verwey: The Samaritan of the Sahara.'*

[3] *Gauteng*: *The seSotho name given to an area comprising Pretoria, the Witwatersrand and the 'Vaal' Triangle, means 'Place of Gold', as a reference to the fact that the province has its economic and historic roots in the thriving gold industry sparked off by the discovery of gold in Johannesburg in 1886.*

Witwatersrand: An Afrikaans word meaning 'the ridge of white waters'. It spans the length of the gold-bearing 'Rand' or 'Reef', and is one of the largest industrial regions in the southern hemisphere, famous for being the source of 40% of the gold ever mined from the earth. South African currency, the 'Rand', takes it name from this.

Vaal: A muddy brown colour refers, in this instance, to the Vaal River, which is the boundary between what used to be known as the 'Transvaal', and the Orange Free State – now renamed just the 'Free State'.

The Free State: The granary of South Africa, with agriculture central to its economy, but also containing rich goldfields. A bean-shaped province which lies in the very centre of South Africa, with the Kingdom of Lesotho in the hollow of that 'bean'.

[4] *Muti: African word for medicine.*

[5] **_Braai_**: _Barbeque_

[6] **_Vetkoek:_** _Literally 'Fat cakes!'— But don't be put off by the name. A type of fluffy dumpling, deep-fried in oil. Often an emergency substitute for bread, and actually very good to eat._

[7] **_Tjorrie:_** _'Rust bucket'. A vehicle about to fall to pieces._

[8] **_Bakkie:_** _A small open truck,_

[9] **_Tokoloshe:_** _An evil spirit, or demon described by some as a small, black, hairy creature, and feared even by the most devout of Christians in many black tribes._

[10] **_Kaya:_** Hut, or, as in the case of Phineas's dwelling, a house.

[11]**Voortrekker Hoogte:** _Formerly 'Roberts Heights', the big military complex near Pretoria_

[12] **_Cleaning up Joubert Park_**

A well-planned crackdown conducted by a team of 400 Inner City Task Force members, 350 department of correctional service officers, department of home affairs officials, environmental health officers and about 300 police officers from the South African Police Service and the Johannesburg Metro Police Department in the vicinity of Joubert Park took place through the night of Thursday, 13 July, 2006, continuing into the early hours of Friday morning. Located near Park Station and the Noord Street taxi rank, this area has a high volume of pedestrians and vehicles where hundreds of illegal traders contribute to the filth. Crime levels are high and many of the high-rise buildings here, once offices, are in disrepair through being used as residential property. Smit Street in the north, Nugget Street on the east, Plein in the south and Wanderers Street in the west were cordoned off, and all the streets in between were targeted, while simultaneous roadblocks were set up on Louis Botha Avenue and on main roads leading to highways.

The police contingent and officers from the department of correctional services were on the lookout for drugs, weapons, escaped prisoners *and checking that prisoners on parole were not violating their parole rights.*

Places of entertainment that were operating without a licence were also closed down, and the department of home affairs were on hand to check the identities of people who were suspected to be in the country illegally. Once arrests had been made, the Inner City Task Team stepped in to hose down the streets and remove illegal structures and advertising.

From an article by Tammy O'Reilly, posted July 14, 2006

http://www.joburg.org.za/2006/july/jul14_joubertcleanup.stm

[13]:*When you know that you know, that you know: or The redemption of Benjamin Ashton, Dromedaris Books 2006*

[14]**Putu**: *very stiff cornmeal porridge*

[15]**Krummelpap:** - *Literally 'crumbly' porridge. Like **Putu** – but stiffer. Can be eaten for breakfast, with milk and sugar, but is equally popular with barbequed or stewed meat.*

[16] **Boot**: *In this case the trunk of the car.*

[17] *Soetkoekies: spiced, 'sugar cakes'.*